Swan Song Of My Era

UK Edition

Contemporary Fiction
Young Adult

Elsie Swain

Ukiyoto Publishing

MANHATTAN BOOK REVIEW

"The coming-of-age story of a bold and tenacious teen trying to figure out her true self and find her way. Spes' rough edges and pompous personality are balanced out by her intellect and vulnerability. Clever banter and emotional relationships dress this book up and set its reader up for some wonderful scenarios. Beautifully philosophical and entrancing."

- Kristi Elizabeth, Manhattan Book Review

About the Author

Elsie Swain is an author of contemporary and sci-fi fiction, including Swan Song of My Era and her upcoming sci-fi series: War of Evolution. Reigns of Utopia is the first book in the series and talks about a dystopia ruled by divides. When not writing, she can be found sketching or fashion designing.

You can chat with Elsie on Instagram at @elsie.iyle.

Dedication

To my Family,

For supporting and giving me the courage to take the risk that I had feared to take. For believing in me when I didn't believe in myself.

In the turmoil of my conflicting thoughts, lies my worst phase.

I am neither soaring nor admiring the walls of solitude.

Resisting the whirlwinds of the world that are manipulating my soul, I never expected to be torn by the jaws of betrayal.

How much time do I have before this trap tightens around the strings that web my life?

CONTENTS

"Creators of crowns lack the patience to wait for their ascend to the throne, enamoured by the prospect of making one for themselves."

Prologue

What are we remembered for?

What are we recognised for?

In an ideal world, we hope to be recognised for who we are. Just the person we are, to the people around us, to the people we care for. But we, humans, are greedy; we thrive in the pride of being recognised for our work.

The work, that we spend hours, days, and years, defining and harnessing our skills for. Skills that we were either fortunate to be gifted with or just fell in love with the passion, unapologetically.

But most of all, we are defined by our best work, our *swan song*.

The idiom 'Swan Song' arises from the folklore that narrates the most beautiful hymn of swans right before their death, rendering the stream of sounds they produce all their lives as subpar noises, in the line of creativity.

What happens when our '*swan song*' is sung way before our artistic flame is extinguished?

The best of our work, that renders our previous results subpar, just like the last breathtaking song of a swan before their death, that reduces their previous songs to mere meaningless noise.

But what happens when we reach the era of our best work before our lives have barely begun? The best work that marks an end to our creative drive.

What happens when our creative force burning inside us fades away when we are still falling in love with our passion yet have so much more to express… before we are even sure of who we are?

Who am I?

One glance at the waves of the asymmetric bob cut that I prided myself with chopping and styling to frame my bronze-toned skin, whose dark caramel brown colour was fading to reveal its original raven colour, was all it took to define me as a single word and to cage everything I am and limit me through one term.

She is just a *'girl.'*

I never had that moment of enlightenment where I suddenly knew exactly which category or term my feelings belonged to and never had I felt the need to do it either.

Maybe it was the years of recognising that I found it satisfying to possess the adamancy to neglect what was recommended by the standards that have been dedicated by the society, under the garb of *'attitude'*, which made it that much more significant over the years to enjoy my own pace of navigating my own identity.

At times, I fell short of the definitions thrown at me.

At times, I felt that I was much more than the definitions standardising me.

There are several times where we succumb to our worst moments and feel like *'nobodies'* when we fall prey to the caging opinions undermining us and the several dismissals of inconsideration towards our suffocating dilemma.

In the end, I only had two choices, decide my script or succumb to allowing my storyboard to be played according to the tunes of the opinions of other people determining my life.

People are variables.

People change. People love. People feel.

People betray, and people leave.

Through the sea of people, all that mattered was treasuring those people whose presence reminded me that we aren't just worth to be a '*somebody*'.

But, we are indeed worth to be 'us' defined by our own standards, outside the quantifying norms of the gender binary set by colonial construct.

And that recognition of the euphoria of feeling more like myself or rather that delusion hit me like a truck when I met '*Hope.*'

Hope Vale, four letters: consisting of their first name synchronising with the four letters of their last name.

It all started when I was reminded that the delusion already existed in my reality after I came across the person whose name embodied the meaning of my name.

I

*"Treasuring time and moments explicitly acts
as an illusion only to be embraced by
betrayal of an equal frequency."*

CHAPTER - I

"You gotta keep up, kiddo", all I could do while struggling to keep up with my mom's pace was groan in disdain at Ma's chide as she laughed heartily, jogging at the spot, waiting for me.

"Every time, every single time, I willingly let myself fall for your trick, to come along involuntarily... You know one of these days I might just not play along." I teased as I picked up my pace after catching my breath to continue our morning routine. It had been over two years since Ma made it a routine to jog along the sidesteps of Gombak river, ever since the changes in her shifts pushed her into daytime shifts from the usual night-time shifts, after going back to the hospital - except on Thursdays and Saturdays.

"Empty threats, my child, empty threats... You may act like a born-adult, but you can't deny that you act like gosling around me."

"Are you complaining Ma?" I asked, voice glinting with relaxed humour.

"I wouldn't trade it for the world. I know you like being in your own world." said Ma, with a slight smile that matched with mine as I checked the time for the number of hours I had to spare before school, as we crossed over the walkway bridge that spanned the river. "I couldn't be prouder of the fact that you have been independent since the time I can remember and can damn well survive on your own, so it's good to know that you still need me, and no, I won't trade that for anything in the world."

"Aww... You're going soft, but I'll always need you." I teased to ease the seriousness of my latter words, pursing my lips, as she tried to whack me behind my head while I slipped under her arm and quickened my pace. "Remember how people always used to call you a tigress when they tried to figure out our silent conversations."

"*Used to?*' You brat, you should be grateful that you have inherited the natural glare of mine." She laughed, rolling her lips at my words. "Hey, you are the one who insisted on preferring to have our daily talks, face-to-face because you distaste speaking over the phone." said Ma sharply, her voice holding no actual malice, she slowed down her pace as the indigo hues of the night disappeared to reveal the glowing pink and orange hues of the rising twilight Sun, floating around like spilt cocktails, permeating through the parched horizon, the sense of heat lost in the promising warmth basking our skin.

"Did I?"

Yet, I could consume nothing except the blank prints of the canvas stretching across my sight. "Still don't think it's beautiful?" She asked, looking at me, knowing I stayed indifferent, feeling nothing compared to her appreciation for the sheer beauty of nature.

I couldn't comprehend how she saw beauty through the rays casting its deceitful eyes upon the landscape, luring the viewer out with false promises of warmth and of light.

All it took was reminiscing a memory to be the catalyst in setting in motion similar recurring incidents to piece everything together.

I didn't know how to give up, but I also was the very same person who barely spared an ounce of effort into things that didn't catch my interest.

Perhaps, I may have never pursued art either, if I hadn't started exploring it, all by myself, a year after I had been enrolled into classes that every Asian kid growing up was undoubtedly familiar with.

The charm of growing up in an Asian Community was the fact that parents knew the demand for exceptional skills required to counter-balance the population, had to start young.

Encouraging their children into certain basic mandatory classes to discover the child's potential before they were capable of distinguishing their likes and dislikes beyond food and regular telecasted television shows.

Drawing classes were one of the 'discovering-child's-interest' classes that every Asian child must have taken up in their childhood, besides Piano or other instrumental classes or vocal classes, abacus classes, defensive judo/taekwondo classes, any form of dance classes, or lastly but not least likely, training beginner-classes in sports too - the *'Classic six zones of classes'*, starting from the time period of toddlerhood.

If I were to be enquired about my very first memory of art, it certainly wouldn't be pleasant, for I could distinctly remember being below sub-par in those classes before I quit within the span of a month. During all the times I quit anything in my life, I barely spent the span of over a fortnight or two before my tolerance highlighted that I truly was giving my nothing into them.

During all those times, Ma never questioned my decisions whenever I quit, even during the age it could easily be considered as slacking off or not giving a proper try. Despite that, she was always the first one to encourage even when I found my love in art, a year later on my own.

Perhaps, she was the first one to know that I discovered my tune in my passion in my own space, never proposing the idea of classes ever again unless I proposed the idea myself.

All I was sure of, was the fact that my first good memory in my passion began from Ma.

"I do - just not the sight though - I just appreciate the time of the moment with the person I spend it with regardless of the sight-" I said, as the both of us bathed in the sunlight in silence until I felt a comforting, familiar hand patting my shoulder, my mother's hand. "-but I appreciate this moment more because you are happier Ma."

"Think you will want to eat grilled prawns for dinner? Pax and Felicity insisted on having it for dinner today." asked Ma, hesitantly, knowing that I wasn't a big fan of sea-food.

"I might be too tired to have anything, after I wrap up my schedule for today."

"You can't pull the '*I am not hungry*' card. I am not letting you sacrifice your diet under my watch." She chastised firmly, not leaving any room for agreement, eyeing me as she caught on to my poor attempt of dismissing her proposal when I tried to squeeze my way out. "You need to stay healthy and full so that your brain has calories to burn, to motor through everything in your life. So, I am going to cook something else for you."

"No, no, no, I will eat the prawns. If there are any prawns in the world that I can bear to eat, then it has to be your cooking." I assured good-naturedly, knowing extremely well I couldn't squeeze my way out of this, nor could I let my mother work any harder than she already did. "Besides, it's Pax's favourite. With the way she is having her growth spurt, I fear that she might actually hit me and might not fear my threats anymore."

"Empty threats, I tell ya, empty threats." She taunted, rolling her eyes massively. "Your sister won't do that. All you three do is harmless bickering, and lemme remind you, I don't appreciate that noise."

"Well, maybe, you should tell that to Felicity, who throws a tantrum with eerie quietness." I said as we both started laughing while remembering the antics of the youngest, who dismissed any of our suggestions to prefer the complete silence, breaking it whenever the said occurrence took place in our home, insisting on some essential white noise.

Despite our annoyed expressions, she knew that she was doted on by all to be at her joyous state.

"Pax asked me if she could move in with your father until she completes the second year of her high school..." Ma sighed with a deadpan expression, the expressions of pain barely veiled under a tired smile, rubbing the ends of her palms against her chest.

For the past year, it may have started with Pax starting to act out and Ma letting it slide as an excuse for puberty.

Still, it was clear that it was so much more when she didn't just start arguing back strongly regarding every single thing Mom asked her to do, even for her own good, but also beginning to blame her blatantly and calling her selfish for the separation.

"Isn't Dad coming over this weekend after his trip to Singapore?"

"He is, but his weekly trips to Singapore are on break for a while for the next four months, you could say so."

"Then he will definitely be staying over with us... Does this mean Pax is going to move over after Dad's outstation trips become more frequent, once again?" I asked warily, as she nodded with a tight-lipped smile and arms falling in slack. "Ma-"

"We talked it out. You know Pax has always been closer to your Dad and will listen to him... right now. The highest priority is assuring Pax's mind space to allow her creative flow and her feelings to be in sync." Ma said, with a proud smile. Her calm expression not shifting by the slightest for the first time since this dawn, "Besides, it will be helpful for her to practice with the grand piano at your Dad's place."

At my silence, Ma looked over at me, waiting for a response with the situation of Pax wishing to stay alone during the nightfalls of the weekdays. Dad might be away for work for the entire year.

Reading her hopeful expression, I could tell Ma wasn't entirely on-board with the arrangement and wanted me to nudge Pax into changing her mind, "We barely have two years of an age gap between us. You grossly overestimate my influence on her. I don't think she is going to see my opinion regarding this as anything else but as mere interference." I scoffed wryly.

"Maybe, you don't have to choose your pick of words but rather-" as soon as I sensed the taut hesitation within her words, I picked up on what she was trying to say as my eyes widened in realisation before sighing in consideration.

"Fine, I will stay over with her when Dad is away, but I am pretty sure I am the significant reason behind this decision of hers-"

"We will take turns, between the three of us, to make it as least subtle as possible because she is going to know... but to heck with it, I am her mother, I am allowed to worry however I want." She announced, raising her hands in the finality of making up her mind.

I chuckled, knowing that Pax is going to realise in seconds that Ma found an apparent loophole through her constant request of asking Ma of respecting her space of not feeling *smothered* and still looking over her.

"Ma, you can't forget when I went through that rebellious phase where I retreated back regarding the smallest things, and I was a terrible pain in the ass." I winced in remembrance, not wanting to feel angry at the break of dawn. I was tired of the petulant routine of fighting with Pax that was becoming way too habitual for my liking and later feeling guilty for dismissing her feelings, for I knew we were always at each other's throats every chance we got, more so often behind Ma's back. " I mean… - granted, I did experience that way earlier than most people hitting their severe emotional rage during puberty."

"Over the smallest things like waking up early to get more hours before school, to get more time to sketch and study more."

"It's those very things that have made my dream closer to reality, got me the scholarship to study in a private arts high school, and there are only a few of those that exist around the world," I said sagely, not wanting to contemplate the fitting theme to even start the work for my final submission in the exhibition to mark the end of my schooling days.

"She told me regarding the *creative* statements you retreated back with for the past year, especially while dealing with certain people who had opinions about your Dad and my current situation for the past two years. Why did you never tell me?" She asked gingerly, waiting for an answer as I sighed with disdain.

"It's nothing. You know Pax likes to exaggerate things to get me in trouble when she is mad at me." I said austerely, with a forced smile. Fortunately, I couldn't help but sigh in relief, masked behind my heavy breathing, when she bought my dismissal and let it slide. There truly was nothing important to tell or make Ma worry about something that didn't matter. It was our family, so the pointless opinions of people who had no responsibility regarding the dynamics and togetherness of our family were nothing more than mere barks. "Trust me, Ma…if it were important, then I would definitely tell you…and Pax and I…we will talk it out."

I could still vividly remember Felicity and I trying to pull a clearly fuming Pax back onto a seat during the wedding reception of a distant relative the past year, whose relationship to my father's family would take a good time to break down and correlate. One of the many nosy nasally high-pitched *Aunties* behind us, tried to formulate her opinion regarding our parents' separation and the influence of their co-parenting on us, that occurred a year ago compared to the timeline of the incident.

It was clear that her attempts of whispering were rendering poorly to stay on the lower side on the scale of the decibel meter, as she scoffed while observing our parents.

Ma and Dad were acting friendly with each other and laughing while jovially bickering regarding their respective recommendations of which food would be the best to take a second handful of, in the buffet line, lost in their own world, as people kept flooding in and out of that distorted excuse of a line, like glowing moths among the whisperings.

-

"They are making a mockery out of the entire sacredness of marriage, look at them, do you even know the reason for their supposed separation?" The nasally pitch ripped demanding attention from all around her.

At this point, I could clearly feel Pax's seat morosely shift beside mine to turn around to give them a piece of her mind.

I felt her glare daggers at my head as I stared ahead at nothing while holding her upper arm in a vice grip to prevent her from turning around.

"What are you doing?" She asked hoarsely in a low snarl, trying to free her arm from my grip.

"Preventing you from giving them the very excuse to make those whispers a louder debacle in this boring place." said Felicity with a saturnine shrug, raising her eyebrows and laughing loudly as she wrapped her arm around Pax's shoulders to help me keep her in place, as she continued laughing at nothing to make it seem like we were lost in our own world.

"You are nine. What do you know?" whispered Pax rolling her lips and shifting her glare at Felicity, who merely stopped her boisterous attempt to laugh in a snap and stared back at her blankly.

"I wonder the same, yet I clearly foresee the obvious consequences of her potential temper unleashing, better than you." She said, rolling her eyes at Pax's familiar dismissal as we listened on to the conversation behind us, resume again.

"This is what happens when you go against your family's advice and marry a girl with no parents or family, and she is passing on her lack of sense of family and household to her kids." said the other almost in clear apprehension, her pitch clearly rivalling the previous in terms of irritation to the eardrums of the listener.

'*What does that have to do with anything and especially how we are brought up?*', at this point, I wasn't sure if I was holding Pax back or using Pax to hold myself back.

"You can't really blame the kids. That's how they were brought up. I pity them. I mean, look at them. One of them is wearing muddy green to a wedding." I smirked in triumph at the most minor things such as our clothing choices clearly bothering them, looking down at my olive jacket.

Winking back at Felicity, as she whispered, "Nice change of Olive, from your usual Grey collection", with a smile threatening to break, as mine broadened with the approval of my youngest sibling.

There was nothing like making a statement of the utter wastage of time of being here by wearing something as timeless as olive.

"Who are they to pity us? They are pitying us? When their *husbands' gluttonous bellies are getting refilled with cheap liquor* over the end of that stupid buffet line." Pax snapped almost in a low growl as Felicity and I started snickering while following Pax's line of vision frowning in disgust at the actual reality of her statement occurring at the end of the line.

"It's a shame, but they are really talented in fruitless dreams.-" said the former voice among the two gossiping, slurring her words before continuing "-the first one is doing something in that new private arts high school, but I guess she draws well, in fact, the middle one is enrolled there too, and she plays the piano."

"And the youngest one?" asked the latter curiously.

At this point, I really couldn't determine if her pointless nosiness was as equally intolerable as the noise of a screeching banshee or more.

"Oh, she is still in elementary school, but they are encouraging her interest to write and perform plays." Yep, her banshee like-tone never ceased to stop, before continuing, "If I were her mother, I would have set her straight at this age."

"True, they start young. It's better to discipline them early on to dream something worthwhile. Poor Victor."

"It's a phase where they slack of their studies. They will get over it when they get away from the shelter from the wretched woman and face the real world, it's not a wonder they are way too influenced by her…the first one is an arrogant idealist" It was amusing to not call her out for wincing at her own words in distaste. "-so it's not surprising that she acts like a colossal jerk when anyone hits the wrong nerves, which isn't a pretty sight 'cause she doesn't stop until she breaks the other's ego so pretty much knows to hit the right spots,-"

That unknowingly brought a smile to my face that didn't go unnoticed by Pax.

"Stop smiling. You look like an overgrown sinister kid." said Pax, almost in remorse, grinding her teeth in apprehension, when my smile just got wider.

"That's on Ma, and Spes just inherited Ma's naturally tighter collagens." said Felicity with a smirk, winking at me.

"How do you even know the meaning of 'collagens' at the age of nine?" asked Pax as Felicity rolled her eyes at the age card.

"There is something explicitly satisfying about people who observe you for just who you are." I said, winking back at my youngest sibling, whose set of milk teeth was still being replaced by her permanent ones, yet that didn't falter her smile in the slightest.

"-the middle one is the most normal one who acts her age and often entertains to be fooled to know her place but it's mostly due to her confusion and-"

"Confused?!"

As soon as the words were spoken, I felt Pax immediately stiffen, yet her arms and shoulders being held in grip by Felicity and me, loosened immediately. "-she doesn't hesitate to ruthlessly bite one's head off when triggered which is a trait shared by them all, but unlike her siblings, she actually cares about the morals as expected of the right society, that people advise her to, and doesn't dismiss them-"

"Who is this person, and how does she know us so accurately? I am amazed-" I immediately eyed Felicity to stop talking, who mouthed '*What?*'

Furrowing her eyebrows as I shifted my gaze back and forth swiftly from her to Pax, to express that it wasn't the right time. Pax was clearly upset by the words spoken regarding her character.

"-The last one likes to pull off the mask of being timid almost like she thrills in the joy of people underestimating her...-" there was no denying that she had precisely pin-pointed the major aspects of our personas well. "-so that none see her attacks coming when she is in the ringer, fortunately unlike the first two, she forgets and doesn't shut down people decisively, but she does share her oldest sister's trait of being way too calculative with her anger, so is almost equally merciless."

Granted, it's not like we were trying to conceal those aspects of ours we prided over, but something felt amiss as Pax petulantly stared down at her hands with a slack expression.

Almost like the words were a direct kick to her guts, I couldn't figure out the right words to address that or if it was right to say anything.

"Now I get what you were saying earlier." smiled Felicity cheekily, raising her hand behind Pax's back for a high five. I mouthed 'not now' sheepishly as I lightly tapped back her hand, nevertheless.

We were both startled when Pax stood up, immediately stumbling in imbalance. I held her back by clutching her hand before she could walk away.

"Look, I am not going to say anything to them or anyone to create any 'debacle' that you are vigilantly worried about, but just let me clear my mind."

"Not now, not like this." I said sternly.

"What is your deal? I told you-"

"I know. Even if you can barely stand me now, stay here, stay here with us, don't stay alone to your thoughts, not now…please just put up with us, now, at this moment." I said, not knowing if I was going to irritate her more by not respecting her boundaries or just being there for my sister when she was upset, as I hoped to convey.

No words were spoken further, as a small smile broke across my lower jaw, when Pax sat down between us bleakly, no longer putting up a fight, despite sighing heavily.

-

"Please do. You have to be there for each other... it's just that I know it's unfair for me to ask you to make the first move, but she is having a hard time...-"

"Ma, it's okay. We didn't exactly have a fight, it was more like her yelling at my face in a confused state, and she has been doing that a lot lately, and if I retort back every single time, she does that, then we would be in a damn war zone...and I just want a quieter place for us all." I wasn't a big fan of initiating conversations whenever things turned south between the both of us, especially if I didn't resort to yelling back at her to match every slight increase in the decibels. So, I let things slide whenever Pax started speaking again, wanting the formerly spoken words to be forgotten, and that had always been our gestures of truce. "I will speak to her after she drafts this week's composition for her Tchaikovsky trials...I mean, that is, if she doesn't speak to me first, before that," I added knowing that, offering assurance will eradicate at least the slightest traces of worry clearly reflecting through Ma's sunken coal orbs.

"We will figure it out, by living through each moment, by being there for each other. That's the only way we can adapt through the raging unpredictability of the future. We constantly antagonise over." Though I whined fondly over being dragged away from my embedded laziness, I did appreciate our wordless dedication to spend time with each other regularly.

I couldn't back but look back at the development over the past five years, where it was no longer just conversations between a mother and daughter duo, with the former mostly speaking to the latter as just an adult guiding a child and much less as their newly compared dynamic of our reliance as confidants, too.

"I guess I won't be waiting for Pax to head to school together." I scoffed tiredly, not knowing if I had ever lived through my life, without constantly contemplating the chain reactions to my actions in response to every possible circumstance I face. The only way that '*control*' offered me the stability in my life that I constantly craved for.

"She wants to have breakfast with her friends, at the cafeteria in your school." I caught up on the fact. She was trying to conclude the subject as she shifted back and forth on her heels, "Your plans after school? It's Tuesday, I think you might be heading there after school today?"

"I might, after reviewing my College Essay." I said heedlessly as she handed me the bottle wordlessly as we made our way back home.

"How is that coming along?"

"Still, the bane of my existence whenever I have to write anything with a limit." I sighed tiredly as Ma prompted another challenge to rush back home. "So, I am doomed for now."

***

I would be lying if I said if I didn't recognise the moment when I finally realised why I constantly skipped school since childhood…Sometimes, I skipped for days, and as I grew older, those days often turned into weeks.

At first, I mistook it to be my ignorance, to assume perhaps it was alright to do so because I caught up on the syllabus way earlier or barely understood the norm of struggle with the consequently written examinations, which did nothing to reprimand my ego, that just blinded the suffocation.

I didn't recognise that. It wasn't my ignorance, failing to pin-point all the times when I couldn't perceive or comprehend a single topic taught in class unless I made an effort to learn it on my own, perhaps later unless I did it earlier.

I did recognise that it wasn't because I was incapable of learning from my teachers in schools, because I did…I did whenever I forgot the existence of a crowd surrounding me.

I realised that the suffocation I felt for years was the environment of a crowd that I couldn't survive in.

It was a futile attempt, even if I tried to force myself to manipulate my mind into believing that I could concentrate in my own world, among my friends.

Or most importantly, the teachers who truly explored the subjects and theories beyond the standard requirements of tests, truly reinstalling the thirst for knowledge and the passion in their profession.

The promises of adulthood that guaranteed the pursuit of livelihood through their scopes of the field they were passionate about, was the future we sought, but the reality didn't hold that true for most.

In reality, they were only the rarest among the fortunate who could earn their livelihood by the survival of pursuing their passion.

By that time, I had realised the ugly truth. I couldn't back away from the fact that I truly couldn't thrive by barely holding on to my sanity and constantly feeling like my energy being drained in any situation that involved my involvement in a crowd.

The limitations and restrictions of following the set pace for everyone had always been the sole Satan to suffocate me, and I definitely couldn't learn to adapt my way through it, without questioning my worth consistently.

I wanted to have order in my tasks but not have them consumed into a routine, where I couldn't recognise my own pace or my creative freedom.

I remember recognising my ideals in only pursuing things that gave me a sense of purpose, from Ma's faith in me, and that made it so much harder to bring up the fact I was struggling...

I was barely surviving to finish my last year of high school without constantly feeling like my sanity was being submerged.

It was way too late to suggest an alternative method of schooling instead of just putting up with it.

How did she know when to push me into my commitment, and separate it from quitting and knowing something wasn't meant for me?

How does one know when to keep going against all odds or give up rightfully by recognising if the footing never belonged to our potential?

Was it luck?

Was it instincts?

Was it belief, if so, then in which one of the two: luck or instincts?

I had to think practically, I knew that neither our financial situation nor the harmony of the mental stability of our family could handle the hit of the rash choice if I decided to abandon the private arts high school in my last year.

Especially one guaranteed the future I had planned, none of my back-up plans could take the hit. We were a family of five, with the expenditure of finances that needed to reasonably fund Pax and Felicity's education right after me.

I knew that I would definitely be making the most impractical choice, to butcher one step that can possibly cause a domino effect and ruin my plans, especially when I had no back-up plans concrete enough to take that hit.

Despite all my reasonings to calm my frustration, I couldn't control the constant decline of energy I felt.

I felt drained, by merely thinking about the mandatory study-groups that I was forced to take up in my Foreign Language classes, especially AP Italian Language and Culture.

Needless to say, I didn't fancy being pushed into situations that required spending more time with a group of people, or rather blackmailed into situations where I didn't understand how getting influenced by someone else's pace would benefit me than irritate me.

-

"I don't know how it used to work earlier or in your previous schools, but I will not entertain your habit of constantly being absent at school. I don't even want to know how your parents allow you to do that." I knew that the new Vice-Chancellor, Tania Khalili, was more concerned about the PR and records than anything else and I was walking on thin ice by pushing it over the edge despite knowing that she clearly didn't like me. "But I can't put up with the paperwork that might put my school in jeopardy with your poor attendance record. So, I recommend you to join the study groups if you still want your own exhibition to be considered for the application of the University of your choice."

"But Ma'am, I can't-"

"The recommendation was just a polite way of ordering you to take it up, and not particularly ask your opinion if you can and can't..." She leered, pressing her lips with a slight frown. "Be grateful that I am trying to help you, instead of assuring that you don't get a recommendation letter from any of my faculty here, or do you want me to assure that as well and make things easier for us both?"

"No, Ma'am."

"Good, because I am certain you don't want me to speak to your Parents and tell them how your pride has gotten over your head, and you have absolutely no manners after winning the Hugo Boss Award." I couldn't even look away from my shoes, as I focused my glare on them instead of looking up. Knowing that I would make things worse, and the impending consequences weren't a mere threat because she clearly knew what I was most afraid of. "I am sure, you wouldn't want me to call them and inform them how you are refusing my clear advice for you and destroying your own path?"

"No, Ma'am" I said, sternly with a fake smile, trying not to grit my teeth while trying to calm my temper.

"It would be a shame if you actually didn't worry about the fear of ever burdening your Parents. Isn't that what you stated in your interviews?" At this point, I didn't know if my temper was clouding my cochlea into morphing the condescending tone of the voice, or if it was capturing it right. "You are most afraid of the guilt of ever burdening your Parents even unintentionally? Am I right, Miss Zrey?"

"Yes, that's right." I said, gingerly twisting my mouth... finally looking at her wide forehead synchronising with her raccoon-like eyes being covered by the frameless rectangular glasses perched up atop the relatively larger nose, with her hair held in a gigantic bun. "I will try my best to attend the study groups."

"Not just try, you must. If you were actually stating the truth, then you would have spared your parents the trouble of chasing a more secure future." It took everything in me to hope that my expressions weren't stricken, as her head snapped up, staring at me pointedly and shaking her head with a half-smile. "Every year, someone is awarded that acclaim, but in the end...you will end up being a burden to your Parents by the time you are forty, so try to work up to more connections by fixing that attitude of yours, instead of being so difficult."

-

I knew that I wasn't just imagining the condescending tone in her voice.

She knew my desire of seeking another solo exhibition this year, that she wouldn't easily sign off on, making it difficult for me to grab my shot in pursuing a degree in Fashion.

I was well aware of getting a place in Fine Arts, as my last back-up plan but so did she.

But nothing explained her blatant disregard for our interests.

It wasn't much of a surprise that she was brought in specifically to get PR for the school, and barely cared about the pursuits.

Despite being one of the elite private arts high schools, Wau Bulan Arts High School was highly in demand with an acceptance rate of only 4.5%.

It was still new, having been established only 5 years ago and the board wasn't looking for recruiting the best, but rather prey on recruiting more people, that the previous Vice-Chancellor wouldn't have recruited.

They wanted to recruit them by taking advantage of their desire in their dreams.

They wanted to exploit the price of securing their place with money, which constantly hung over their heads as a reminder of the gigantic doubt that can engulf the youth: '*Am I choosing the right path?*'

What if the right path of mine is concreted differently than the dream I seek?

Do I really have to buy my risk?

Will the belief in myself be enough to secure my dream? -

"They should have gone for a Tudor arch or a segmental arch for the pillars." The significantly mini-version of Aquarium KLCC, set near the Gombak river, '*Aquaria Imaginaire*' which initially started as a present of a Parents' love for their child's love for Corals, ended up being a sense of joy and wonder for millions across the country and around the globe.

To me, it was my space of recharging myself while recognising the quietness in me.

Feeling my existence around life, unlike the gigantic loneliness that engulfed my entire existence reminding me that I wouldn't matter among billions of people around me.

Billions that came before me and that will come after me, if I let go of my purpose and hold on to the fear of the hurdles of my reality, instead.

And at this moment, I couldn't believe the *audacity* of the voice interrupting my train of thoughts, drifting my focus from the manatees inside the Poseidon chamber section of the Aquaria.

"Are you talking to me?" I asked with an incredulous snort, throwing my head back, and sighing in disdain.

"Not particularly. I like expressing the fascination of all my thoughts that spark my interest, out loud, that's just who I am." said the voice, the beatific joy in her tone never wavering even by the slightest. "I know that most people tend to get embarrassed when they accidentally speak their thoughts out loud, but I don't... I mean, why would I? When I speak about the thoughts that drive my sense of will in my life."

My eyebrows shot up immediately, as I listened to the voice, the voice that I chose to ignore a while ago, without giving it a chance.

"You absolutely should." I answered, shifting on my feet with a small smile as I watched a manatee feeding on the seaweed.

The motion of its biting in stark contrast to its barely-satisfiable hunger shaping its rather rested comfortable volume like a glutinous bear who had its fill of salmons and was seconds away from hibernating, as the rest floated by with no regards for the competition of the continuing depletion of the current fodder.

Was it their usual serene kinetic muscle memory that swallowed up its sense of security of the periodical replenishment of its fodder by its care-taker?

Does the cut-throat viciousness of humans ever seep inside them?

Or was their survival instincts in the danger of competition of fodder activated when the source of its nutrition was completely stripped?

It certainly had to be the former, given their ideology to be harmonious, unlike humans who were wired with a desperation to panic...

It wasn't just an opinion but rather a fact that Manatees are harmonious, they are peaceful.

And so was the Contralto voice of this person, whose face I had yet to spare a glance, to match it with their voice, but there were least likely chances of meeting them ever again, so there was no point in placing a face or name to their voice.

It was best to just live in the moment.

I smiled at my recognition of the voice range mostly due to the several nights spent, hours speaking with Pax of imagining the world around her in notes and tones, when we were thirteen and eleven, respectively.

Though those days seemed like nothing but a distant memory now.

Given how we could barely stand to be around each other in the same room without snapping at each other if it surpassed over a quarter of an hour, those memories significantly influenced my perspective of life, even more now.

I missed those nights…

"Changed your mind?"

"Regarding?"

"I could have sworn, you are certainly one of those people who doesn't like being disturbed in their space, so why are you letting me do that, or more specifically what exactly did I say, that changed your mind?" I chuckled at her observation. Maybe, it might end up being a conversation I wouldn't just remember, but possibly cherish too…

"Does it matter?" I asked with a smirk, not shifting my gaze from massive glass separating the aquatic world from ours. The luminosity descending through the chambers of the manatees, sleepily in ease as their movement, almost like moving in lazy strokes of a paintbrush filling in the first layers of the base of a painting on a lonelier canvas.

"Hey, now that's not fair, even if you knew that I might not have cared about your opinion earlier,-" She protested, chuckling with slight accusation. "-then I would definitely care now because of the reverse psychology gambling the seed of curiosity that you have tossed."

"Ah, so you are familiar with that?" I asked. Oh, I was definitely going to remember this conversation, one that I truly did want to remember, compared to the numerous ones I would pay a fortune for, to forget.

"When it comes to gambling the chances of sparking curiosity into the other's mind? I would definitely own a Casino." The said voice, chuckled proudly. "I would be the queen of that casino!"

"I don't know about that yet, but I am certain that your '*thought-out-loud*' arches would go great along with ionic pillars, and perfectly fit along with, what I assume Poseidon's throne room must have looked like in Atlantis." I said, shrugging my shoulders lightly as if I hadn't spent months with my friend, Grace Elamin, talking about the possible accuracy of the architecture fitting the imaginary throne room in the lost city of Atlantis: the child who had truly transformed her love for corals into incorporating them into her creations and designs of Jewelleries.

"You are warming up to me."

Although the only light across the pathway was the illumination mostly from the lights inside the aquatic chambers, darker than the lights blinding enough to strain one's corneas yet brighter than the lurching luminescence of lost hallways. I could still feel the surprised glee beaming from the person beside me, the silhouette giving away her frame to be roughly as high as mine, while trying to lean sideways to watch my expressions mostly hidden by my cap and turtleneck pulled over my entire lower jaw. " Uh huh, no, no, no smiling, my arrogance might drop your mood instantly, so it's better to stay neutral."

"Aww… you are actually nice."

"It's called being civil!" I scoffed before snickering.

"It's just a pleasant surprise and usually my *'thought-out-loud'* words don't get continued around people that aren't my people."

"Yeah, I am familiar with that, but then again, you have to account for the fact that 93% of the time, you are most likely to end up interacting with imbecile insolents."

"93%?!"

"You would be surprised that I am actually underwhelming the percentile." I laughed, finding myself smiling back at her strangely adorning whimsical laughter.

"But they have done a brilliant job in mimicking the throne room, especially the broken head of Poseidon, the long stairway of steps and the seven iconic pillars, to describe the archway of the entrance,-" She said fondly, an unmistakable grace wrapping around the syllables of every word she spoke, "-The seven doric pillars designed here,...they mold perfectly with the corbel arches."

Although all students in the visual arts department, did have knowledge on basic architecture, some of us did find it easy to venture in exploring it.

I wasn't sure if there were coincidental chances of her being enrolled in Wau Bulan Arts High School, already or she was a tourist visiting the country or someone who frequented visiting here and lived in the neighbourhood, but the only guaranteed assuring was the fact that she was truly passionate regarding what she spoke about.

"Yeah, so do the arcade arches or pseudo-three-centred arches. But for ionic pillars, the perfect fit would be the-"

"Classic Roman arches" we said in unison.

"I like how the manatees' tunnel is designed with the authentic destroyed design of the lost city of Atlantis," She said sheepishly almost as if she were admitting it out-loud first time without being chided

"Understandable."

Not many people relished in the beauty and variations of the corals used in each section to normalise the habitat of each specimen, especially the pale, bleached coloured appearance that had probably calloused like weathering rocks. "To mimic the mythical mer-people and sea-creature, and there is something about the type of corals in this one, that just makes it more realistic…"

"Stony Corals." I remarked. Yet the questionable hymn in her tone, surprisingly made me want to explain more instead of being irritated that I usually would have around a stranger. "I meant, the type of corals in here, they are stony corals."

"Really?!" The surprise in her voice made me want to question her sincerity, not wanting to bask in the delusion that this was a genuine conversation and not just a small talk, unless it wasn't a delusion.

"You seem questionably fascinated for something so simple." I scoffed with a tsk, but it did nothing to waver the joy in her tone.

"I am going to dodge the '*questionable*' condescending tone of yours despite not knowing me, you have not spared me the benefit of formality-" She chastised cordially. "...but yes, indeed I am remarkably fascinated, because there is always beauty in simplicity. We just take it for granted to encapture it, so how can I not be fascinated by this?"

"It would be a more challenging feat, not to be."

"Exactly!" She agreed, without hesitation. I found myself being amazed by her calling me out for the first time, feeling better than she wasn't exaggerating her interest but was just being true to her wonder. "And the fact, that you know and take solace in the details of this place tells me that you are equally fascinated as well, and just want to protect your memories with them..."

"So, that justifies my condescending tone?"

"It's not that easy to define yes or no to someone's reason behind their actions." She prompted quietly, voice firm. "All I do know is that I understand being protective of all that are precious to me."

"You are something else." I answered, laughing heartily.

"So are you, but something tells me you know more about these details not merely out of seeking facts but more out of their significant value to you." My eyes widened at the sheer observance of this person, of not only truly listening to each word spoken but truly understanding every bit of it. "And that makes me wanna continue this conversation even more."

"I am sorry-" I said, looking down to play with my fingers. "-regarding my tone earlier."

"It's alright, but I am gonna hold against you until you answer me this." Even if I didn't turn around to confirm the smirk on her face, I could practically sense the smirk in her tone.

"You weren't kidding when you said you were the queen." I chuckled, pushing my tongue against the inside of my cheeks. "Impressive, your majesty."

"Why? Thank you very much."

"Go ahead"

"Huh? Go where?" She quipped with a teasing glint. I sighed tiredly, feeling tangible in the relevance of the potential question, for that had been withheld throughout the entire conversation.

"Your question, go ahead..." I confirmed with clarification. "Ask me..."

"Oh that?" she asked, with a delayed chuckle. "Nah nah nah, I am not going to ask it right away and give you a pass to let you walk away in an instant, especially when I am enjoying this conversation."

"I feel like I am being held hostage." I teased, raising my left wrist, to look at the dial of my watch engulfing the upper half of its circumference.

"Noooo... consider it more like a duty to your *queen*."

"So, we are considering this as a permanent terminology, now?" I asked, half-amused and half-curious.

"Took it too far?" She asked, sheepishly.

"With that terminology?" I purposely delayed my words as I heard the nervous gritted chewing sounds in the air. "Never." I answered, sharply.

"Is it too far-fetched to believe and ask what art or particularly architecture means to you?"

"Is that your question?" I asked, monotonously trying to conceal the satisfaction behind my response to that question.

"No, but I have been dying to ask this ever since we spoke about the pillars... and I don't think I can ask anything else before knowing this."

"I wouldn't mind answering that if you answer your question as well." I said, raising the corners of my eyebrows in sync with shrugging my shoulders.

"You will not back away when I do ask you the question that I am holding over you as a bait, right?"

"You have my word." I agreed, knowing that it didn't matter if we ever crossed paths again or not, but I wouldn't certainly back away to answer the question if the circumstances aligned.

"For the record, it wasn't a big deal... I mean, I hope you know that it's completely okay... and I am just teasing you-"

"I get it-" I repeated my words with a softer and a firmer tone, emphasising that I was well aware of the jovial tone, yet it would never decline the seriousness of my words. "-I'm more particularly invested in symbolism art involving portraits of humans but if I had to summarise my connection to art...then I would define my life as a canvas portrayed by the colours that capture our moments, to paint the storyboard of our life, by the chances we take in our lives."

"Wow, you really have a way with your words, now I am not certain if I wanna tell you, my answer."

"You do know that would be unfair, right?"

"It's more like I have always asked myself what defines an artist, what makes me an artist, or if I can even call myself an artist?-" She prompted, sagely. I nodded along, with the familiarity of those doubts, questioning my reasons often. "-At first, I thought it was the quantity of classes I took and the hours I spent in them, so I always felt guilty whenever I missed or skipped classes …but the answer has always existed right in front of me ever since I fell in love with art. All my doubts had their sense of reasoning since the beginning…"

"What was the reasoning that had always extinguished those doubts." I asked, clearing my throat, as the silence enveloping us continued for several moments to classify it as hesitation?

"It's boring…"

"Is it true to yourself?"

"W-what?" The shock in her stutter almost made me want to turn towards her to reassure the aura of her natural confidence, as if it always been a programmed habit.

"The reasoning,…as long as it is true to yourself, that's all that matters." I answered, slowly realising that I paid no heed to the time, despite having checked my watch earlier, indicating my usual time to head back home for dinner. "We often confuse the terminology of '*boring*' with granted solace of stability, that only seems 'boring' because you are used to its certainty,… but it doesn't lessen the magic of the exquisite happiness of that solace, any less."

"Okay, people must absolutely tell you often that you are really good with your words…I am sure of this…" At this point, I wouldn't need a fluttering second, to recognise that chuckle anywhere.

"Tell me your reason…" I asked, repeating my words once again, after the chuckle died down, my gaze downcast.

"You are very persistent."

"So are you."

Most people definitely found it stubborn.

Heck even I did…

It was always easier to believe in the aggressive aspects of myself, than the rather better aspects, before people threw that in my face by being blind to remember the person I am or the reasoning behind my actions.

"Art is my expression, it's my voice in this world." Among all her waves of laughters until now, this one had to be the most content. "It's the truest voice of my thoughts."

"Then you have the makings of an authentic creator as well as must be one hell of an artist."

"But you haven't even seen a single fragment of my artworks or even know the form of art-"

"You have the drive." I said, interrupting her mid-sentence, knowing extremely well, why my words must have lacked the authenticity than its intention without the elaboration of my reason. "The definition of '*what*' and '*how*' of an artist doesn't have any concrete purpose until you know the '*why*'… and yours is one of the most compassionate, I have ever heard. So, I mean every single word I just said, because of these instincts."

"What's your '*why*'?"

"Well, it wouldn't be fair for me to play against the Queen in her Casino, without having the right cards up my sleeves, either." I gave a small shrug, a smile still playing on my lips…

"Ooooo… smart choice!" She teased back, as I finally felt my phone vibrate, chuckling at my Mom's antics through her text message as a reminder to head back home - '*Running away from Prawns? I am gonna spare you fifteen more minutes for being late for dinner, but you are going to love it today!*'

"I have to head back home now." I announced, waving my home sideways, before sending back a quick reply - '*You know I love your cooking, Ma. I will be back in a few.*'

"Yeah…yeah, of course…Bye-" I felt them humming in thought, trying to remember my name to complete the courtesy of ending the conversation. "Wow I never asked your name…All this while I have been speaking to you and I have never asked for your name and that's absurdly rude-"

"No, it wasn't. I never asked for your name either." I said, interjecting the statement, softly

"That's right! You didn't!" The voice wavered, laughing a little breathlessly, as I merely inclined my head. "Wait, you aren't escaping the questions, because you gave me your word and I am hoping to believe that you are a person who upholds your words."

"You place faith in people, way too easily."

"So, is it because you believe in fate, for us to meet again-" She scoffed, trying to stop her laughter.

Based on one conversation?

"No, I don't…" I said, sternly before turning around and taking slow strides backward.

I believe in now -

I believe in me and I also believe in my instincts, and my instincts tell me that -

Despite being equally surprised that we are complete strangers, neither one of us made an effort to even spare or initiate eye-contact.

Yet, we were completely ourselves during this conversation,…

"It's Hope. I am Hope Vale." called out the fading voice, as my strides took me farther away from the fading silhouette of the figure. "Won't you tell me yours?"

"Coincidentally, my name means the same as yours."

***

CHAPTER - II

Time became liquid, unknown, as I mindlessly found my hands under running water… my sight failing to fool my subconscious that was drowning in the delusion of the memory. I couldn't walk away from the scraped nails bruised against the friction of the concrete.

No matter, how hard I tried to unsee the smudged grease, like tarnished globes of cotton flowers rained down by remnants of burnt ashes that just ignited nothing but suffocating fury of the inevitable that had befallen, smeared across my hands that just didn't exist no matter how much I prolonged wasting water, washing over my hands aimlessly.

"You are doing it, again." said Pax, staring at me pointedly before reaching over my shoulders to turn the tap off over the sink.

She refused to budge, staring me down and waiting for an answer to be uttered over the years, to justify an explanation to her doubts that had been numbed over the years from the initial questions.

Unlike me, both my siblings had significantly acquired the taller genes of our father and a softer gaze that was unfamiliarly distinguishable especially when compared to mine that had ended up being a blueprint to that of Ma's resting piercing gaze.

Although all three of us had the same bloated almond-shaped eyes and bronze skin with warm undertones, inheriting Ma's Cambodian descent, only Pax had ended up with a slightly wider expansion of nose and higher arch of eyebrows due to our mixed genes of both Cambodian and Malaysian descents.

While I had ended up being the one with a distinctly deeper pronounced valley of the cupid's bow among my siblings to accommodate the ratio of the height of the lips that lied on the higher end.

"The warm water helps to soothe the ligaments around the metacarpals of my right hand." I said, monotonously dodging the obvious implication, we both knew she was emphasising. "My hand hurts... I was up all night trying to design a few of my rather shapely ideas."

I had always been at being quiet when I needed to be...perhaps I always would be...

"Suit yourself. It's not like you are going to change your mind, if you haven't wavered for years." said Pax, tying her hair onto a loose bun and grabbing the toast from the breakfast Ma had laid out before leaving for her shift rather earlier today, immediately after our morning run. "You are unbelievably stubborn."

Unlike my sisters who preferred keeping their hair long, I liked chopping my hair on to the shorter end like Ma. Using the kitchen scissors to cut down the ends of the length extending beyond the jugular of my throat.

I still remember acting sheepishly when I got caught for cutting my own hair, as Ma shrugged, her face unreadable while explaining it was impossible to pass through the span of over 6 months without the length of my hair changing by the slightest. I was not prepared for her proposal, to style her hair, henceforth instead of giving me a warning.

"It's called Consistency." I teased, raising my eyebrows, knowing extremely well that it was merely going to irritate her further.

Felicity looked between the both of us trying to make sense of our conversation while pouring over more milk into her unfinished bowl of cereal, before passing over the carton over to me when I took my seat beside her.

"I wish there was a way of calling out some people on their claims of support, besides the reason of '*oh it's just my intuition*'." piped Felicity, catching onto Pax rolling her eyes and glaring her eyes, and preventing a possible routine of our usual fitting disagreements.

"You are just overthinking it" said Pax, dismissing her immediately, as she raised her hand to signal me to pass over the milk placed near my side of the table.

"See what I mean?" said Felicity, sighing in defeat, playing with the last spoonfuls of her breakfast.

"What's the situation here?" I asked, encouraging her to elaborate.

"Argh, there is this possibility that my next play might take place in Istana Budaya-" It was huge for Felicity, to have the play, that she had been involved in especially with the screenplay writing besides being part of the cast, to be featured in the theatres of Istana Budaya: A dream that was one of the wonders she sought to accomplish among the bucket list of her vision through this field. "-and there are limited tickets this time, so I don't know how not to give away those tickets to some people who I know _won't_ sit through the whole thing or even actually watch it."

"You are just slaying it, aren't you?" I grinned widely, ruffling her hair, as my youngest sibling smiled with barely controllable glee.

"But they showed up, right?" asked Pax, incredulously. I just looked at her, puzzled, at the focus on this irrelevant part of the question, _why on earth was she worried for others over her own sister?_

I tsked, unable to comprehend why there was even a need for justification demanded here? When it came down to the dreams of our own sister and the incompetent feelings of strangers, I didn't see the point of the consideration of the pointless latter choice or why it should even be considered as a choice.

"I mean, y-yeah." answered Felicity, with a deadpanned tone. "I gave them the tickets, so they showed up but technically, they had to pay for their own rides-"

"If they showed up, then they support you, and that's all that matters," said Pax, ignoring as I scowled. "You are just throwing a fit if you nitpick them not watching the whole thing or remembering any of it, they showed up when they had time. Why does your intuition feel like they don't support you?"

"I mean, it's not that. It constantly feels like they could be doing anything better than watch my play and I should owe them for watching my work,-"

Felicity sighed in disdain, placing her hands over her face. At this point, I wanted to advise Felicity to shred these people out of her life, as soon as she possibly could. "-and even when I joked about it to test the waters like Spes would, they didn't deny it-"

Before I could beam with pride at my sister's wise survival instincts of peeling out the facades, Pax interrupted her saying the very words, I dreaded to hear.

"You do owe them."

"What? No, she doesn't!" I scoffed, trying to figure the placement of the overgrown replacement for Pax's head.

"Yes, she does!"

"Felicity, never confuse support with the compromise of respecting your work born out of your dreams, especially if they make you feel like you owe them their time for supporting you." I said firmly, as Pax batted her hands over Felicity's ears to make her stop humming in affirmation.

"I do like the sound of that, much more than yours, Pax." Felicity said bluntly, elbowing Pax, lightly to stop.

"They should at least try to authentically listen and understand your plays, 'cause each of them is a part of who you are." I was tired of fighting with Pax over our stark opposite principles over this, but I am not going to permit her to pass on her accessible sacrifice of the worth of self-respect over the feelings of anyone, onto Felicity.

"You can't place your ridiculously high-levels of expectations on everyone." Pax chided, narrowing her eyes at me.

My gaze refused to shift by the slightest as they zeroed on Pax, as I addressed Felicity. "I mean, yeah it's alright to slide across works that are accomplished out of duty, as we all have different domains, but never compromise the support on your dreams."

I could get where Pax came from, because she had a big heart unlike me, but I could never understand her lack of protectiveness of her pride over her dreams and values, when it came to people's feelings.

"*Compromise*? Don't you think you are being a little cynical with your words, even for someone like you-" Pax's lips thinned, expression turning pale and stony as I cut her off merely out of pettiness, pretending as if I hadn't heard her at all.

"So, your intuition is never wrong is signalling out any form of negligence or disrespect to something valuable to you." I said, grinning smugly, "Trust your intuitions. Don't dismiss them."

What she considered as kindness was something criminally unfathomable to my ideals.

Because I couldn't stand people who disrespected my dreams and values by the slightest. Their feelings were of little significance to me, henceforth.

"At this rate, you won't have anyone to support if you nitpick-"

"She doesn't need the *so-called* support of people who have the slightest respect for her dreams-" There was no turning back from the screaming fit, we both were clearly in, undeniably agitated. "-and make her feel like she owes them for making time to be there for her to support her dreams."

"Why are you making a big deal about this?" She asked, shaking her head in disbelief. My eyes widened at the audacity of her question. "Maybe they didn't realise she asked them as a joke so they might have just nodded along, at least they aren't mocking her dreams. Isn't that good enough?"

I pinched the bridge of my nose, chanting that she was my sister as a remainder while trying to calm my nerves to not utter anything unnecessarily hurtful, that I would undoubtedly regret later. '*Pax is my sister. She is my sister...*'

"That's the standard you are setting for the value of her dreams?" I sighed in disbelief, at the lowest standards of self-pride, being set in these expectations.

"Yeah, people have a lot of things going on so what's the issue if they don't watch her plays '*genuinely*'." She slammed her finished plate against the table, raising the corners of her eyebrows to challenge me when I didn't flinch by the slightest and stared at her with a bored gaze. "They congratulate you, don't they?-" She asked, shifting her gaze towards Felicity.

"Yes, but-"

"People are always *busy* with their own schedules to fulfill, and lives to live. There isn't anything astonishingly new about that." I felt momentarily guilty for interrupting Felicity, knowing how much I hated when that occurred to me, yet I just couldn't tolerate Pax seeking to tell Felicity to compromise for the sake of others at the expense of anything involving her dreams. "So, genuine support for other's dreams should be that much more authentic than mere words that feel thrown. Besides, that's mere courtesy born through time spent together."

"And *'you'* of all people, know how to distinguish when the words are genuine and when they are just being thrown?" asked Pax chuckling in mockery.

"Well yeah." I chided with a smug smirk, watching Pax gritting her teeth. "I wouldn't call myself supportive if I wish people *'Congratulations'* on their achievements and celebration of recurrences or occasions, that's defined as being nice or more specifically courteous…manners."

"Yeah, that helps me more. How do you separate them?…" asked Felicity, shaking my forearm slightly, to shift my gaze from Pax towards her. "I mean, I write plays. I know how well people can put up an act…."

"I can't believe that, this is being encouraged…" said Pax, raising her hands in disbelief and sighing in disdain.

"How do you do it?" asked Felicity, her eyes beaming with intrigue.

"You don't actually believe that she must actually have some sort of plan-" I don't see how Dad took one look at Pax and had decided that she looked 'peaceful' and decided to name her after it.

"I do, actually." I answered, merely swirling the last gulp of oat milk through my glass, as Pax eyed me to stop talking already.

"Finally, something helpful! Tell me!" said Felicity, hurriedly swallowing up the last mouthfuls of her cereal, and scraping the sides of the bowl to clean it up for better.

I chuckled at her excitement, as she placed over her bowl in the sink and took one last look at the wall clock to check if her bus would be arriving anytime soon, before shaking my shoulders vigorously to get me to speak sooner.

"Well, it's kinda simple, you can just test the waters by throwing in words that don't exactly render away the complete value of your dreams but still pushes enough to undermine your potential in your dreams." I had faced my own stream of facades who wanted to take the easy way out between putting up a front of being 'nice' to be classified as supportive. "The key is not pushing beyond that or else you just come across questioning the esteem of your dream and no gamble is worth that."

I detested conflicts and felt my energy drain immediately whenever I knew there was no way out of it, when I had to set things straight despite the hours of internal-groaning. I was well-aware of the evident defensive comebacks that would merely enrage me even further.

"My god-"

"How does it work?" asked Felicity, confusion flashing behind her eyes, interrupting Pax before she could finish her words. "You have done this before, haven't you?"

"Yes, I have." I said, nodding. "Yes I do, always."

"You trick people into believing that they are not supportive and make them feel bad-" Pax would never know that, the reason I pulled this trick instead of calling them out on their so-called insincere claims of *'support'*, because I didn't want to be constantly heartless to other people, was because of her.

But I couldn't compromise on my standards of support either.

"Remember that if people are actually supportive of you then they will fight against you even when you remotely doubt your dream." I admitted, tightly.

"I like the standards of that…" said Felicity, humming in affirmation.

"They will fight against those doubts to remind you of your faith in your dreams. If they don't, they will just laugh it off or ignore your statement by merely changing the subject…-" I scoffed, sighing tiredly.

When I had been nominated for the Hugo Boss Award, several people who couldn't even spare me the time to show up for the exhibition.

Or even give me the time of their day, to just review the ideas I wanted to bounce off with them and just check their approval of the shaping concepts, in the name of respecting them as artists as well as trust in the call of friendship.

Somewhere along with my instincts, I was furious with myself for giving them the importance, to allow them to dismiss the value of my works. Or even getting fooled by the compromise Pax constantly told me to seek with people who were *'nice'* to me.

"I wish there was a presence of a swarm of fireflies conveniently trailing above them to shut them up when they laugh it off." Felicity said gingerly, as I shook my head chuckling and admitting that I had hoped for that too, but the luck wasn't always in our favour.

Pax stiffened further, stabbing the fork against her empty bowl. I threw my arm over a startled Felicity who was clearly taken aback at the screeching sound. Pax dropped the fork in agitation, as I looked over at her with an unamused expression taunting her that she was wasting her anger by stabbing mere utensils, by jutting her chin forward and squinting her eyes.

"Nothing is worth the slightest crush on your dreams." I said, narrowing my eyes to retaliate against Pax's never-ending glare. "Especially not due to the dismissals of people offering false or ignorant pretences of support."

'Nice' according to her ideologies was nothing more than 'civil' to me, so we both knew it was not going to last for long, before I snapped back at those very same people singing to be 'Proud of me' out of nowhere, when I did manage to actually win the award.

How on earth are you proud of me, despite not knowing anything about the journey of my working process?

"Whoa! Is there no actual end to this? Do you two even hear me?" yelled Pax, to gain our attention.

"Give me your own scenario to understand this better." said Felicity, not being fazed by the slightest.

Although, she barely feared either of us on the account of being older than her, she knew how to get on our nerves to get back at us whenever we dismissed her words.

"I may or may not throw around that I am an amateur when it comes to my skills in art-"

"That's ridiculous!" I groaned in disapproval, scrunching my nose to drain out the loudness of their combined yelling in protest, even Pax who was seconds away from kicking the both of us out of our home, looked like she wanted to knock sense into my head with Felicity.

I raised my hands in defence, as a means of requesting them to calm down and lemme finish my statement, by hearing me out.

"-I mean, I know the judgemental opinion that can spring across when I tell people I took no prior training or classes for drawing before applying here or even the blank answer while completing my application regarding my previous training."

"Please don't tell me that you actually believe that nuisance?" Felicity immediately began to stand

"I don't believe that, because I accomplish my art justifying in sync to my imagination" I said quickly, offering a gentle smile, to get her to sit down.

"With your level of stubbornness..." Felicity looked relieved "You can't blame me for actually believing that you would beat yourself over the most unpredictable aspects in the world."

I shrugged my shoulders, knowing her words weren't completely untrue.

"I don't like wasting my breath on speaking about my dreams when they don't acknowledge its importance..." I said without preamble, expression hardening reminiscing the times I had several inner-conflicts over stopping myself from being reactive towards people dismissing them with a false sense of courteous words. "So, whenever I sense way too many compliments from a single source, I often do this to test the authenticity of their words."

Silence enveloped us for several moments, each waiting for either one of us to react, before Felicity's eyes grew wider with remembrance, coincidentally in sync with the blaring horn of her bus, that must have arrived in front of our home.

"That's right, you do say that often" She smirked, checking the closed zips of her backpack for one last time and rushing out through the front door, as we aimlessly followed her to ensure that she didn't fall on her back, in her haste and wave her goodbye before she left for her school. "Man, you are golden!"

"Sometimes, you just have to bring on the game of your facade to find the leak in the facades of others." I said, winking swiftly, as she got in the bus to sit beside someone who wasted time in asking her about the answer key about the practice sets of their upcoming UPSR Exam in November.

"Thanks! You are the best!" She yelled through the window, with a broad smile splitting her lips, as the school bus geared up to leave the lane.

"Anytime sis." I waved my hand in a motion to ask her to not lean so close to the window.

"Anytime to strengthen our survival skills."

"That's my kinda language!" Once the sight of the bus was no longer in front of our sight, we headed back into our dining room, in our slippers, with just 30 more minutes to go before we had to head for our school.

"Just because you are cynical and have major trust issues-" Pax quipped, as she placed all the finished plates of food, in the sink, while handing me over the carton of milk to be placed inside the door of the refrigerator. "-You should at least have the audacity to not pass on your desperate need to mistrust everyone as '*survival skills*' to our baby sister."

"I don't trust people. I just have the arrogance to admit it unlike holding on to the false pretences of that belief, like you." I said, slamming the door of the refrigerator harder than necessary.

I hated that she could see me as nothing beyond being cynical for prioritising my feelings.

It's not like I was blind to the jabbering questions Pax received, to get an explanation for my rudeness especially due to my staggering reactions shifting from 'mood swings' to being congratulated for winning the Hugo Boss Award.

"Of course, it's always like you to choose your ambition towards your dreams over people."

"I don't chase anything that I can't control. I don't ever wanna chase people in my life 'cause I never wanna control them, so I don't..." I dropped the knot of the tie I was trying to tie over my collar, unable to let go of the fact she chose to say this, despite knowing that I was never selfish to her. "I am clingy to my people, but I hardly ever get that instinct from anyone in my life. But when I do, you can be damn assured that I trust the damn consistency in their chase, especially their dreams."

It was a low blow for her, for she knew the stark difference and standards between the ways I chose to deal and behave with other people and my own people.

"Yeah, if people evolve from their *facades* and not change due to fickleness according to *your* standards." Pax scoffed, her expression sour.

"Every human is capable of maintaining their facade, I just don't whine over pretending to not have one…" I said carefully, choosing my words with difficulty so that they didn't come across as completely bitter "So it's not just the weightage of the words I hold accountable but rather the consistency of their sincerity.

"No, you just happen to be unforgiving to hypocritical facades, which only *you* seem to recognise." Unlike me, Pax didn't hold back laughing bitterly at my face.

"The only way you can recognise the facade of hypocrisy from sincerity is to catch on to the way one treats their people." I stated brokenly, starting to get used to the unpredictability in my usual quiet atmosphere that I was used to, during my visits here. "We treat people the way we wish to be treated." I added with finality.

"Not everyone lives life as cut and dry as you do!" I winced at her words, immediately, holding up my hands at once as she stepped forward to apologise. "I didn't mean to-"

"Hypocrites lack the responsibility to tenaciously bear the weightage of the consistency between both." I couldn't help the heaviness in my tone, as I tried to even my breaths. "Among these variables, that sincerity is rare and I will only start acting humane when I recognise that within someone, or else I would relish behind the norms of my facade."

"Given your facade that is seconds away from being termed as a feral wilderness creature, are you calling yourself a hypocrite, while expecting people to be supportive of you?" I knew the moment I called out Pax on being hurt over compromising herself for maintaining the fragile bonds with those so-called friends of her, who didn't hesitate to sobbingly blame her, if she dared to point out their actions affecting her feelings...

We all feared the prospect of being alone but was it worth holding on to people, who unintentionally thrived on the guilt of compromising because they feared being accountable to their actions?

We, humans, are defined by limits, so why should we wait until the limit of tolerance is surpassed? It shouldn't have to be about settling for tolerance, but rather acceptance.

Was it so absurd to not spare the time of the day to people, the moment they start treating us like our worth can be nothing more than being tolerated by them?

Why do we have to shape our acceptance according to them and take ourselves for granted?

"If you ever knew me at all-" I smirked, before raising my eyebrows and scrunching my nose and staring at her flatly. "-then you would know how much I blindly prioritise supporting the people who truly support me and have often fallen prey to the separation between authenticity and facade of support."

"Is that all that matters to you?" She asked, unfazed. I scoffed, amazed that her despondence towards me was due to the separation, and as long as she blamed me, she was going to view me for my worst.

"No, but it's the starting ground."

"With your impossible standards of expectations to earn your trust, you are going to end up alone." Her condescending tone vibrated clearly through the running water of the tap, as she cleaned the bowls, before passing me the towel to dry them.

"I am good at being alone and I would rather be alone than compromise myself and my fears out of the notion of the fear of loneliness.-" I was really not looking forward to a repetition of this, especially on this day just before my interview that Mrs. Khalili had repeatedly warned me about and simultaneously raved about it being highly mandatory for boosting my works in the industry as well as the reputation of the school. I was already agitated from having been forced to attend the study groups. I didn't want to make things worse for myself and get on her worse side than I already had been. "-'cause to me… compromising myself for the sake of other people and not recognising myself is scarier and I would not dare to live in that regret."

"Not everyone operates on a motive."

"If they don't, then you can be damn sure that they are either lying or just don't have a drive, in their life." I said, hanging the towel over the handle of the counter over the sink, and adjusting my tie.

"You always have to seize the last say in every argument, don't you?" She asked, flinging the remnant water droplets sticking off the washing gloves quite furiously, with a purpose of flinging them at me.

"I mean, if you compare this in the analogy of *'eat or be eaten'* policy, living as a human among other humans is a battle of facades." I smirked in mockery, before snatching the gloves from her hands and hanging them near the towel.

"Of course, everything according to you has to be a cut-throat battle."

"Look, I can't change my preference of putting up a facade to get a guarantee on my intuitions." I said, glaring back at her, as she stood in front of the Aqua-Purifier refusing to budge by an inch to let me fill our bottles with water. "At least I don't ever put up a pretence in believing the dreams of people if they trust me enough to listen, so I am not gonna apologise for catching on to the facade of people doing so...-"

"Yeah, you just happen to live your life in a constant inflexible war zone." Pax spat, sighing defeatedly.

"It's not like I am giving them a hard time." I shrugged simply. "I am just being tactical about sparing myself from the frequent hard times. It's a shield for my generally sensitive feelings."

"That's certainly not living life cut and dry." Pax scoffed, the diminutive sounding definitively sarcastic with how forcefully she said it.

"I would rather play with their facade and value my dreams by not wasting my breath and speaking about it with them." I gave her a pointed look, challenging her to say the words she had almost felt sorry for, saying them earlier. I was awfully proud of living my life that '*cut and dry*'. "I understand the value of my dreams so I am never going to sabotage the value of anyone else's dreams with my words or lack of words."

"So, your solution is to fool people when you need to confirm your pessimistic intuitions?" She asked, stepping out of my way.

I sighed in defeat, throwing my head back in tiredness.

"Yeah, because people absolutely love voicing out the truth when they are just stringing along." I chided in mockery, before gritting my teeth in irritation. "I pull off my facade for my benefit because most of the time, I am way too unapologetic to hide who I am even if it doesn't fit your standards of civility."

"You don't have to be so rude to everyone without knowing them. You could actually start glaring them coldly after getting to know them and not liking them reasonably and actually be nice instead of the other around." said Pax, softly as I froze immediately hearing her words.

I couldn't help but burst out in laughter at the irony of my own sister speaking the very words, I had grown to hate.

Words uttered by the people who didn't hesitate to completely ignore the reasoning of my opinions having absolutely no respect and ignorantly failing to understand me beyond their judgement as they advised me on how to '*act properly*'...

I just never expected Pax to get to the point of finally treating like she was tolerating the likes of me, like them.

"Who are you kidding?" I asked, as she looked at me bewildered that I was laughing at this moment. "You think anyone is going to fend for you when you truly need someone if you keep up your facade of biting down your worth to just appease the ego of others?"

I knew that I had taken a step too far by taking a jab at her choice of people, whose jealousy was painfully visible when they dismissed her achievements and whined about their shortcomings, making her consult them during her own celebrations of victory. "If you wish to appease anyone's ego, why not appeal yours?"

Unlike me, Pax had sought the support of her friends during the possible process of separation of our Parents.

Although she never spoke about it, I had seen and known the clear dismissal of her pain, by her friends merely asking her to '*Calm down and relax, as Parents had disagreements all the time in every family*', before changing the topic.

We both had the possible fears of abandonment when the process of separation began, not knowing that the outcome would gradually turn out to be positive, without the loss of anyone's presence in our lives and never facing the tough decision of having to choose sides.

Yet, it had impacted the both of us largely, unlike Felicity. The latter had always been the type to significantly handle the situation as it came by and never analyse it beforehand, where it made me more vigilant on being unforgivable to compromise my morals or feelings for the sake of others.

At the same time, Pax left no boundaries guarded to compromise for the sake of avoiding abandonment.

"Why on earth are you so proud of being so egoistic?" She asked, rolling her eyes and giving me a flat look.

"Because the other option is being apologetic of my actions, being apologetic of who I am, and I would rather stay nauseous definitively than go down that road." I grumbled, offering a one-shouldered shrug.

"You will have no one by your side if you keep that up."

"I already have all the people I need, and I sure as hell am not compromising myself to hold on to people who don't understand me." My eyes narrowed spitefully, as I snapped back in an almost-snarl. Silence hanging up between us like a curse, loud and pent-up anger.

"You expect people to understand your hailing egoism?" After a long moment, she finally scoffed back at me, her expression dark. Despite everything, I couldn't help but remember the silhouette in the aquarium, who went by the name of 'Hope', and chuckled to myself as soon as I heard the word 'hail'.

"This is a whole new level of arrogance even for you and that's saying something!"

"The only person I expect to keep up with my expectations is myself. Why on earth should I project my expectations on anybody else?" I took in a sharp breath, as I felt my mouth settle into a dangerously thin line. "I don't want people to understand anything, but I would acknowledge them understanding me for who I am, as I am."

"That scenario you gave away to Felicity, you pull that with your personality too, don't you? It's not just your dreams." We both knew it wasn't a question but rather an acknowledged fact, the tensed guarantee of it, seeping like a formidable solvent between us. "You play that gamble by playing with words that people say behind your back for your negative evil facade. Spawn of Satan." Before settling onto a sly expression, my eyes immediately darkened that made Pax ground her teeth, definitively.

"Hey, you do you, and if my facades protect me from getting swayed and hurt by the parading pretence of other facades, then I am going to laze on the throne of Satan after claiming it as my own…" I sneered, feeling my smirk tilt to the side, as her eyebrows knit in shock at my response. "-And for the record, my 'negative evil facade' isn't a facade, it's a part of my true persona."

"You are unbelievable!"

***

Conceptualising my thoughts into art had been the easiest fitting way to succumb to the train of thoughts barging through my limited mind-space.

Since the beginning, I had strayed my interest in capturing my works through the kaleidoscope of the perspectives of the conflicting array of emotions that humans had a presumed notion of running away from.

Growing up in a South-East Asian developing country, we learn as girls that in ways both subtle and obvious, our value as females is largely determined by our physical parameters.

The mass production and value of skin-whitening products looming over the society's standardised expected perception of the definition of beauty, over generations will continue to sting and hinder the acceptance of the positive reflection of the worth of healthy skin and the liberty of proudly breathing in our natural shade of skin. Just like the sting of transparent moon jelly-fishes, whose appearance reminded me of nothing but the obsessed idolisation of the privileged white colour over any other shade of skin tone.

Subconsciously, that had ended up being the driving theme to inspire the works of my very own first leading exhibition: *Stigma Of Colours*, that wouldn't have had the slim chances to come into existence before my last year of high school if it hadn't been for the blinding faith of our Art History teacher, Alodie Bronywyn.

Her distinctively tall frame and wild hair shaping her dynamic intimidating aura fell short compared to her gigantic passion of radiating wisdom through the expanse of knowledge as well as addressing the invisible or partially erased realism of the difficult truths of the world to all her students.

I wouldn't have had a collection to be featured exclusively in the National Art Gallery or even be nominated for the Hugo Boss Award, if it weren't for her guidance along every step.

It was the reassurance she offered as a guarantee the scopes of my imagination and skills were never determined by anything but efforts, even when everyone else was more concerned about my creative force running out of its fuel and luck, because I had managed to snag the award on my very first try.

And that would always make me seek her approval the most in this domain as well as her respect for the person I shape out to be.

Unfortunately, she was no longer in charge of taking care of segregating the interviews that mandatorily shaped the marketing of our further works over the random array of interviews that could care much less about our work but more about our age and gender, instead.

I would be lying if I wasn't nervous about appeasing the interviewer that the Vice-Chancellor had repeatedly warned me about, rather than the interview itself.

This interview was going to be printed in the notorious '*Savoire Faire*', and the mention of any rising new artist on this magazine across all fields was the ultimate ticket to be recognised by the best Curators and Designers in the industry.

So, I understood the weight of the opportunity being secured for me, to seize the better reality of the next stages of my career as well as Ms. Khalili's demanding warnings to not dare to mess up this interview, no matter what the questions might be.

I didn't know what to expect as I walked into the Filming equipment room set-up in the basement of the eastern wing opposite to the open Arena, after my AP English Literature class, to have a woman probably in her early-thirties with a slender build and pristine flowing raven hair, who had to be the interviewer given her poise of repeatedly clearing her throat to check her pitch, flashing me a fake smile before her expression turned blank once again…

I couldn't dwell on her emotions and let it guide my anxiousness… *It was just another interview and I just needed to get over with it to get the funding for my exhibition.*

So, I merely fixed the mic-piece over my tie before sitting across her, after forcibly nodding off to dismiss the so-called *'kind suggestion'* of the Audio Set-Up in-charge of the interviewer who recommended me to fix my slightly overcrowding front incisors, to look *better.*

A side glance was thrown in from the Vice-Chancellor standing across the room behind the camera to remind me that any move to botch up this interview and the people involved on behalf of the magazine team, would have severe consequences.

"Shall we get started?" She asked for confirmation, one last time, waving her recorder before switching it on as I nodded my head.

I wasn't surprised to hear the condescending tone indicating that the reason I might have snagged the Hugo Boss Award might have been beginner's luck during my introduction.

During all my interviews, my age was thrown into the factor of luck, as a laughing tone to challenge the unexpected win and the undertone whether I could surpass not letting it get over my head.

As if my age was directly bound to my inexperienced unawareness of reality heightening the pride confining my future.

"If there is any artist you would love to collaborate with, who would it be?"

There were several times we were so moved and inspired by a person's journey and the devotion towards their work that we can't help but seek out to get a chance to experience their work ethics and process, up close.

Most often, they tend to be people so out of our personal radar revolving in the luminance of fame, dead or alive, for we dream to have a similar resonance of success in our canvas, the same way they found theirs through all the hurdles that must have obstructed their reality.

We tend to be so wrapped up in the inspiration of the end outcome that we forget to admire dreamers walking alongside our path. "René Fares." I said, with a small smile.

"Interesting." She said, quirking the ends of her eyebrows, dramatically, "So, among all artists dead and alive, you would rather work with an upcoming artist who is *just making a name* in the industry by being the youngest recipient of another honourable award, like you, than established artists?"

What kind of angle was she trying to head in?

I don't care if I get called out for biting back my sour expression since the start, but something about her plastic smile just didn't sit right with me.

"It's impossible not to be amazed by the revolutionary feminism she portrays through her pop art." It didn't sit well with me, the way she chastised Fares' works by the quantity of prestigious acclaims in her possession. "Her sense of individualism in every work of hers, encouraging the sense of femininity in all to balance the masculine sides of every walking human to nullify the societal demands and expectations associated with both, always stood out."

"You seem to have no animosity for a person who might have more advantages than you in terms of resources?"

Whether it was the portrayal of the appreciation of family time of cooking together to depict the growing normality of the served breakfast on our tables by our mothers, being taken for granted over time.

Her paintings always signified the value of understanding the need for evolving and not just growing.

It was clearly reflected in never wanting to compromise for mediocrity, that could be lost in the magic of her works, even *before* she won the Vincent Award for her last work, that beautifully addressed that the sense of harmony isn't indebted to women.

From our very first encounter, she never spared the time of her day to people who couldn't perceive her through her works, and only had negative pointless opinions after failing to snag an opportunity to work along with her, for boosting their own agenda. "I am certain that neither of us ever gave the impression that ever was any."

"Would you consider her as a friendly foe who motivates you to do better?"

"I would find it challenging to wanna collaborate with a rival, and even if I did, I already attempt that with every single work of mine."

"You have collaborated with your rivals before?"

"Yeah, considering the fact that the only person I have always challenged to be my rival is my previous self." Even if I wasn't right earlier, I could sense a falter of her true expressions through that plastered unwavering smile, as if she was clearly disappointed with my answer. "That's the best perspective of finding oneself in the world of creativity, and that's the notion that motivates me and seeking the larger picture of who I am, through my works." I said, finally relishing in the slight comfort of hopefully directing the interview into my works, for I wasn't completely sure of the concise concept of my future works for the next exhibition, yet...

Probably why this interview couldn't have arrived at a worse timing.

I hated being unsure of things, but I couldn't find a way out of the loop of helplessness, navigating from my background of Fine Arts into Fashion Designing.

At times, I find it laughable why my adamance couldn't have gripped its tentacles around something that had to establish my style in this domain, instead of having to hear the same words along the lines of- *'But why do you wish to not venture further into something, that you are good at?'*, every time I tried to showcase the sketches or speak about wanting to explore more into my dream of creating my own line.

I knew my words would continue getting unheard, after the unopened file of sketches were shoved aside, while being questioned over my words regarding the incorporation of symbolism into my next paintings.

But I had always been the type to be greedy to constantly seek more until it met my expectations.

I could never forget the prolonged timeline of the dissatisfaction I had to bite down, whenever my enthusiasm to explain my concepts were dismissed by most.

Until I was nominated for the Hugo Boss Award, and that just made me want to seize the farther clouds of my dreams even if they seem difficult to be anywhere near my horizon, now... because over time, the wind will bring them closer to me if I stay rooted with resilience instead of taking the easier way out and getting swayed away by the wind.

"In your earlier interviews, it has even mentioned that you have two younger siblings, one of whom is known for being the second Asian winner in the Young Pianist Category of *'Ibiza International Piano Competition'*, but unlike you, she does have her father's last name, how has that impacted your lifestyle?" It was like someone had shoved an icicle down my spine and asked me to smile through that, as I stared at the Vice-Chancellor demanding an explanation, who just nodded her head to direct me to play along with questions.

How dare they?

"I don't ever remember mentioning any of that in any of my previous interviews..." I had to force myself to narrow my eyes at the reflection of the sheeted windows behind the interviewer, instead of glaring at her. I was well aware of their tactics of throwing in the play of *collecting information* by researching previous interviews. Her expression darkened immediately, when I gave her no room for excuse, almost challenging as if she had no intentions of ending the directive of this subject. "Not because I have forgotten, but because I am very sure you wouldn't know that unless you looked through my personal records-"

"Would you say your Parents' Separation finally gave you that tragic artistic euphoria to snag the Hugo Boss Award, and be the youngest awardee to win it?" She asked, looking unfazed and cocking her head to the side, a small smile tugging at the edges of her mouth.

"So, I need to have a tragic backstory for you to make sense of my inspiration behind my arts?" I scoffed, practically glowering at her.

At this point, I was surprised I had managed to stay seated, without storming off or doing something worse like shoving the mic piece down the interviewer's throat.

"Everyone likes a good inspirational story, it helps advertising your portfolio too, and in turn, your career-" Her eyes were hard, glinting with mirth as she stared on, even as it seemed like she physically tried to make her posture less aggressive.

Either way, she failed miserably.

"Not if you wish to make a mockery out of my family, deciding to make your undermining opinions by snooping through my personal records." I felt way too many emotions all at once, to the point where it felt like it was overloading my system, most evidently wrath.

I should have taken the time to notice the pattern of the stories of the artists printed on their magazine. *But,* I had stayed ignorant, to not let the thrill of the opportunity cloud my judgement or head down the dark ends of doubt.

"Well, your Dean was clever enough to give a story that would interest readers, and there is no point clinging on to the pride or being ashamed of what happened between your Paren-"

"Kindly shut up before you finish that statement." There was clear silence echoing around the room, signalling that I had indeed crossed the line to keep my tolerance at bay. My eyes refused to flicker towards the mentioned person, who had the nerve to look proud as if she indeed had created a masterpiece by orchestrating the perfect play to make the story *interesting.* "I don't appreciate *you* making orthodox opinions of the circumstances of my family or use a *story* that clearly isn't mine or yours to sell." My words rang against my eardrums, dangerous and decisive.

Ashamed?

Who gave either of them the right to interfere or even have an opinion about my Parents' decisions?

I nearly tore off the fabric of my tie while pulling off the mic piece, ignoring the prolific apologies of Ms. Khalili towards the entire team, while glaring at me from the ends of her eyes, drawing her fingers across her throat in a threat to emphasise seizing up my vocal cords voluntarily just to shut up. She pointed sharply to get back to take a seat on the chair across from the interviewer.

"I apologise if you are offended-" said the interviewer standing up on her feet, and ignoring the noise around us.

She knew that her condescending words would make me halt in my tracks to march out of here, while simultaneously worsening the situation for me, evidently aware that it would make the Vice-Chancellor's anger rise and hurt her pride if I rebuked the apologies of the person, she was trying to make amends with, profusely.

"I don't need that when you find the need to use the necessity of *'if'* in your half-hearted apology."

"You clearly have some nerve to have no manners while speaking to people older than you." Her expression morphing from sly to agitated very evidently, her eyes turning steely, as if to drive a point home.

"I would clearly disagree, given how disrespectful you have been to my people and my works, that matter the most to me." The irony of her words was so jarring to hear that I couldn't help but tsk in a challenging undertone.

"You want to be smart with me?" She scoffed, asking it so matter-of-factly that she must have thought she had misheard me for a moment. "Then get this through that arrogant mannerless head of yours. Every decision of a Parent affects their child's, so their story is your story, especially one as big as their separation-"

There was nothing else to call it really - a complete and utter disaster.

I felt something sickly rise in my guts, choking out air and reminding me of the sheer audacity of this woman to continue giving her condescending opinions about the people I cared for.

"Those circumstances impacted them as decisions made separately between *individuals* and them together as a *couple*." I hated owing any explanation to people who couldn't wrap their conscience to back off instead of spewing trash. I hated having to defend the right in a world that couldn't move past its cocoon of biased judgements of always defining one by their misery, regardless of the chaos interrupting their happiness or not. "They haven't made any decisions or differences that have changed and impacted their roles as our Parents, so even according to your analogy, there is no story to tell." I dug my fingers into my thighs and glared at her face.

"How long do you think people will remember your works?-" She looked surprised, and pulled back regarding my expressions carefully. It seemed as though she was having an internal conflict to continue this any further. "-Or your credentials in this field, to provide you a steady income throughout your life, without a *wow* factor in your portfolio and admit it or not, people thrive in selling sob stories. You can use one if you let go of your pride and let me run that."

She didn't even have any ounce of respect for my works or the pursuit of the choice of my career much less as a person.

I couldn't help but chuckle helplessly at the realisation, that she was one of those people who worked merely because she loved only the income aspect of her work.

She was least interested about the topics or the choices of the people, she was perhaps forced to write about...or maybe because this profession might have been the closest thing to her actual dream.

I could care any less about the pairs of eyes concerned about my sanity, looking at me as if I had finally lost my mind due to my *unkempt* manners and anger management, since the second I started laughing at this utter pointlessness of this so-called *Interview.*

"Please officially declare that I have cancelled this interview by not showing up at all due to my arrogance that *you* must have been familiarised with, by *now*...- but if you print a single word about my family-"

Of all the people I had to put up with during these interviews that didn't just affect me, they had to send an ignorant hard-headed *adult* who had already been chastising this profession - *given the boredom of mockery swimming through her eyes and the snide scoff at my unintentional or intentional rebuking of the direction, she sought head with her questions, to put up with this and the hassle of making a drama worth capturing the readers like controversial gossip* - even before she was probably shoved, by her seniors, into taking it.

To interview people and write about the domain, she could care any less about.

"I sincerely apologise and I assure you that I won't, but lemme ask you regarding something that you have actually stated in your previous interviews. Like you said - *Youth is an era defined by passion*, I am offering to make a story that can actually earn a consistent living as long as the marketing survives." She pressed with a condescending smile.

Could she sound any more disingenuous?

Why on earth was I still talking by entertaining this woman?

"I clearly missed the memo"

"The entire world runs on money, buying out passion, for a chance of it to survive its reality." She declared with finality, almost amused, "Do you think people around you and before you lacked passion? *No*, they all ignited in them, to pick a living that earns a livelihood by growing up and becoming an adult."

"With all due respect, you don't even know me, why do you think my dream is limited to my passion? Why are you so certain that the livelihood I seek won't be built out of my passion?" I demanded cholericly, snapping at the anger sparking, eyes flashing like a dagger flying through the air.

In several instances, it's common to hear that *'success can be lonely'* but that's because we fail to remember that it's truly *'struggle'* that's lonely, and the unpredictability of its outcome or its timeline resonates that loneliness.

Struggle isn't worth being a story until the outcome results in success.

Most often we use those stories to motivate ourselves during our struggle.

It's not saddening or disappointing to acknowledge the fact no one is truly invested in listening to the person we are, during our worst moments of struggle because they truly can't, and neither can I for someone else's struggle...

Neither can understand the burden either has had to shoulder during every step of the struggle.

No matter how much we try to empathise to offer words of comfort, we will always fall short and that's not a shortcoming on either party.

It's just humane.

We are all chasing our own desired outcomes through incarnating our dreams into reality.

So, it's humane to never completely empathise with the struggle of another human's, no matter how much we care for them, because we don't have the accountability or the capacity to absorb their emotions and contain the emotions coinciding the struggles of theirs as well as ours.

If we do, we either end up blaming them for no fault of theirs for confiding or losing our drive for failing to recognise the boundaries we needed for ourselves, instead of getting swayed from the entitlement of '*selfishness*' that is immorally crowned with '*loneliness*.'

"I am advising you as an adult, to grow up and stop day-dreaming before you end up in regrets, without having any reasonable back-up plan to fall into-" She said, scornfully.

"What defines you as an *adult*?" I asked nearly snarling, cutting her off mid-sentence once again.

We always received biased reviews throughout our life, whether they were *mannerism* compliments or undermining critics, in both subtle and obvious ways respectively.

With the former, we become familiarised with hearing three common types of statements.

Type A form of Compliment: '*You are so talented for achieving this at such a young age!*'

What it actually meant to me: Ah! The age factor, that doesn't care or even wish to take the time to fully comprehend my work, to perceive what it truly is.

Type B form of Compliment: '*You must have worked so hard for this!*'

This one was clearly tricky, but it was always used by people who don't/no longer have a concrete existence of their presence in your life to anything valuable in our lives and could care any less to be bothered by it.

The '*must*' in the statement was a clear giveaway that they were just guessing and was just another kind of mannerism reaction that lacks authenticity. How on earth would they know? They weren't there while I worked on this to assume the parameters of my effort.

Yet the most infuriating form of mannerism statement that combined both was Type C form of Compliment: *'I am so proud of you'*

Why? In what way were they involved or concerned regarding the process of my journey to have the nerve to claim to be proud of the outcome?

These nefarious wrenches never had the accountability to be bothered by the worth of our dreams or the journey to get there but had the thick-skinned shameless to pretend to know everything.

Although it shouldn't bother them that they were perhaps just being happy being our well-wishers, their words just echoed in the emptiness in comparison to people who stuck by our side through thick and thin.

I felt like throwing up at their audacity of spewing those words and reducing the value of that statement coming from people who stayed all along.

"W-what? What does that- Are you blind? I am over thirty-"

"Besides your age, what makes you an adult?" There was no denying I was dealing with a critic, who was the hell-bent version of Type A mannerism who was eyeing me with a very clear warning in her eyes: *watch yourself*. I couldn't help but tenaciously pester this subject further, with slight smugness in my tone, with the realisation that her eyes shone with agitation that she had no clear answer to my question, behind her look of distaste towards my adamance. "The fact that you earn? I do that too, through my commission work, not as regularly as you, so besides that what makes you an adult?" It wasn't petulant or snide. Just…bitter.

"I am responsible enough to not pursue day-dreams that *waste* my time-" She snarled, tightening her fist around her pen.

"Good for you." I smirked, scoffing.

There was only a handful who got into the art department, and a fewer handful who stayed unwaveringly without the doubt of not having back-up of exploration plunging and sidelining their first choice, opting to perhaps reconsider it later in their lives.

But has *'later'* ever even been guaranteed anything further than an excuse to not face the uncertainty of *'now'*?

The moment she snapped with her expression set in cold blithe, I knew that she felt outraged more-over my brass tenacity of standing my ground than my dream. "My age is defined by my experiences that guarantee me the wisdom to know what's best."

"So am I." I said, flatly. "I am responsible for my decisions and my dreams. So, what gives you the right to determine if I am going to regret when I haven't been satisfied with giving my best yet?"

At this point, my anger was merely masking the demanding curiosity of a hurt child who couldn't understand the confinements of the prejudices of reality over perspectives that just destroyed on the account of no concrete reasons other than the preference of opting out of a fixed dream predetermined for all.

A reality that reacted with filling the child the promises of the dreams of one *fixed domain*, since the minute they take their first steps on this planet.

A reality that was puzzled by the pursuit of the domain of creative intellect over their *fixed* idolisation of the *domain* of analytical intellect.

Most often, even if the child starts showcasing early signs of harbouring a dominant creative side, it's often side-lined as a hobby. All the colouring books a growing child receives are never given in the promises of anything else beyond engaging them in a hobby, to occupy time and calm their bubbling energy.

"I am warning you of the future-"

"Seems more like you are predicting the end of my story when it isn't yours to tell, especially when I have barely begun." I shrugged, resisting the urge to roll my eyes. "Because no matter what, the future is unpredictable, and I don't want to let that fear constrict my dream to find my excuse of giving up." The hardest part was…her tone was no longer out of spiteful defensiveness, but rather ignorantly frustrated as if she wished she could knock my mind to show me a *better* path. "How can I regret something that I haven't given in my best yet?"I asked, quirking an eyebrow in challenge

The Proclaim of most adults talking about their child possessing the ability to *draw well*, is to signify the implication of bragging the pursuit of that *talent* as nothing more than -what they perceive as- a *hobby*, and much less as a consideration to even dream of their child's future as an artist.

How can they…when the reality is busy confining in setting the parameters of marks and grades surrounding the scopes of analytical intellect to determine the domain of a child's future?

A child's only *concrete* future worth valuing in that reality.

It takes a lot of faith and courage for Parents to believe their child over the reality. To encourage them to prioritise their dominant creative intellect over the norms of analytical intellect preached in School Life.

"There is no denying that you are talented, but you aren't going to end up far with that naive stubbornness" she sighed airily, confused what aspect of her words was unacceptable for me to grasp. "That's just plain foolishness."

There were several things I wanted to say or rather scream but I knew that would be nothing more than a continued waste of breath and time - *Stop defining the expanse of my future with the predicaments of reality for me. You have no rights to undermine my dreams or my potential. You don't know me so have the audacity to not determine the possibilities of my dreams surviving in reality.* - leaving several words left unsaid.

We both live in the same reality, I would rather be lost in chasing my dreams than be bitter about not chasing mine and chastising others for chasing theirs 'cause of the lingering regret of succumbing to fears, due to their lack of will and courage.

"I would rather be foolish than fear all the possible hurdles I need to overcome to make my dream my reality." I said firmly, sharper than I intended.

"You-"

There was something bubbling in my guts. And it was no longer. Injustice. Maybe that's what it was. "I appreciate your wisdom, but I would like to see the end of my story by actually trying to get to the end of it." I demanded, grinning like a madman. "Because I am incapable of consulting myself to let go of my dream due to all the possible hardships and fears as adapting to a logical reality when all I would be doing is merely covering my regret."

"If you don't start learning manners you will get gobbled up in seconds" The woman's eyes casted over me as if I were dirt. "With that arrogance you are not going to head anywhere"

"You see-" I tilted my head, expression hardening. "-the thrill that keeps me going is my so-called arrogance and faith in myself to not want to suit the likes and mannerisms of mindless sheep like you." I said firmly, quirking an eyebrow as the woman glared at me with her lower opening in slack. "Unlike you I don't need a herd to guide me, and as far gobbling goes, the sheep don't prey on the wolf. It's always the other way around."

"With that kind of attitude, how are you going to provide time for your family when your dreams are still unstable?" She demanded, accusingly, the remaining people around us stayed frozen in their spots as if they didn't exist in the room and feared to disrupt the air of tension by the smallest attempts of interruptions.

"My family would continue supporting me as they are now, as I continue to pursue them."

"I meant your future family. You are a growing young woman." She chided with mockery, her eyes narrowing. "Surely, you must understand prioritising your time to maintain the balance of a family over your ongoing dreams."

"Actually, I don't. Where is my current family going to disappear in the *future*?" I pressed firmly, raising my eyebrows, as she rolled her eyes primly in apprehension as I twisted her words. My blood, feeling heavy in my veins.

"Is it because you haven't thought about it yet?" I flinched, as she asked more to herself, nodding sagely.

"No, it's because I've. I already have a support system that understands the priority of my own space and the vision for my dreams." I snapped, my voice stiffened with memory. "I don't see the necessity of failing to provide time for more people who may or may not be consistent in my life, sincerely. I don't wish to pursue anything half-heartedly and that includes providing time for people who understand me."

"Is it because you are young, your mother hasn't spoken to you about the priority of family over your ambition?"

"No, it's because my mother has never shied away from discussing the inevitable reality and respecting my opinions and decisions to handle it, which prevents any sort of fickleness in my decisions." I said, firmly as I felt my blood roaring in my ears, though it ran cold. "So, both my parents have heard and respected my decision to prioritise my ambition over any potential new people shifting through my life.-" Anger, injustice, and pain coursed through my chest, as I glared at her. "-For the support system I already possess, I would prioritise wanting to live their lives as individuals too instead of constantly living their lives as Parents of three children."

"So, your Parents are encouraging your priority of chasing your ambition over family life?" She scoffed with a quiet laugh. "Even when you are a *growing young lady*? I suppose it's your mother's fault...you can't be blamed." My vision blurred as my expression paled at her words. "I mean, why go through the drama of a divorce when you have *three* grown children?"

"My answers aren't going to change by the slightest, no matter how many times you insist on repeating that question or emphasising that I am a '*growing young lady*'. I am well aware of my age and gender too." How dare she question my Parents for supporting me, for who I was, completely? "However, I fail to share your shocked sentiments over those *two* factors with respect to my answer-" How dare she feign ignorance of interfering and insulting the way they have raised me? "-or the fact that you have single-handedly avoided every possible question regarding my works besides defining them as futile day-dreams or temporary pursuits catalysed by passion."

"I am trying to help you and my job here is to marketise your works and your image, by using a story that people actually read-" she explained, as I turned away from all of them, having had enough of their *so-called* opinions ringing through my eardrums for today. "Where are you going?"

"I don't know you well enough to owe you my last word." I slammed the door behind me, face burning with every emotion that tried to crawl out of my skin.

***

Glancing at Mey, who was trying to offer an alternative after being one of the many to know about the '*utter disaster that befell on the reputation of the upbringing of the school, when I walked out of the interview.*' I don't think I had time to wrap my head around the aftermath of losing out on my solo exhibition, that the Vice-Chancellor didn't hesitate to rip out as soon as the interviewer's team was out of her hair.

"Maybe we could use the pictorial cover for our orchestra piece. It would be unique instead of using photography?" Mey quipped sympathetically. I merely nodded back at her, understanding her gesture to nullify the bickering whispers around the class snickering about my arrogance being a warpath with no boundaries of destruction.

Mey was perhaps the closest classmate with whom I had a consistent dynamic with.

Knowing Mey was looking at a person who was just endearingly passionate and naively honest to the way she lived her life or belted jarringly different vocal ranges of songs, with effortless ease.

It was almost jarringly easy how we confided things with each other - whether it was the agony of getting stuck with the wrong team from time-to-time where none of the team members shared the same level of dedication to the project or even family - that we wouldn't normally voice out to others yet were clueless regarding the random small things about each other.

In a way, Meymona was the only one in this school I had spoken to, who had the closest idea regarding the new dynamics of my family ever since the separation.

We didn't speak often yet were always knowingly around each other's vicinity when we had to speak regarding things only the other would understand… but the very thing that began the dynamic and never changed was our support for either's dreams and understanding of the struggle of the hassles that came along the path.

Getting lost in the forsake of new adventures instead of appreciating the stability of people, who never let us compromise ourselves, by ever feeling guilty for being ungrateful by recognising the emptiness of the lack of accountability in their words as well as their presence. "At least, until you find a new team that hasn't submitted their request for their proposal of getting their own exhibitions."

"During this time, it would be easier to just find someone submitting their proposal for toasting loaves of bread in the exhibition rather than finding a team that hasn't submitted their proposal yet." I said, trying to ease the situation, as Mey tried to smile with sympathy when the last bell rang to signal the end of school for the day.

'Great, just what I needed to calm my mind, swarming through crowds with hordes of people rushing through like bees overdosed on an amuse bouchée of spiked honey.'

"Is there any way you could speak to her again and get her to reconsider?" asked Mey, patiently trying to maintain her pace with mine as I scoffed in return at the slightest chances of the possibility of her suggestion. "It wasn't your fault, that the interviewer crossed a line, and you have every right to protect your choices…"

"All I can do right now is worry about damage control, especially Quinsy." I sighed defeatedly.

"The junior prefect of the Photography section?"

Gods, I really admired that kid's loyalty to work with me, when she could have easily opted for her own Photography exhibition.

Her wide eyes gleaming with naive kindness were just deceiving to hide the sheer force of nature captured in her works. Although we may have initially connected over our Cambodian roots, it had to be the obsolete unapologetic loudness of our voices around each other that sealed the bond over the years. "Usually, Grace or Theus wouldn't have hesitated to take the lead in this situation, but with both of them gone, there is no one to take the lead-"

Rather than having the time to yell back at the person who stormed away after tumbling across their step and colliding their shoulder against me, all I could focus on was the eccentric book fallen across the ground, swiftly changing its pages.

It seemed more like an over-filled diary as I hastily picked it up moments before it got stamped over by rushing feet.

"Spes! Are you alright?" I barely got to hear the ringing chants of Mey beside me, as I looked around for a frantic face searching for their diary among the sea of chaos.

Within mere glances of the rustling pages continuing to turn due to the flowing wind, it wasn't a game-changer to be intrigued by the numerous sketches of eyes coloured by the testing shadow palettes pointing to the scribbled notes of capturing the tone of various genus of flowers.

I closed the note-book, immediately after picking up, feeling oddly ashamed to look through the pages of something that seemed to be craved with several memories, dusting across the cover sparingly irritated by the fact that the owner of this property had been so careless.

"Yeah, I am good." I confirmed, readjusting the straps of my bag as I glared at the book in my hand. Following my line of vision, Mey prompted gingerly. "This seems way too used, not to be personal."

"Well, they shouldn't have been so careless about dropping it in crowds." I snapped unintentionally, debating whether I should just throw it away on the ground or make the unwilling route of dumping it in the lost-and-found room to ease my consciousness.

"Do you know who it belongs to?" asked Mey, peeking over my shoulder, to get a look at the initials slashed rather elegantly at the bottom corner of the cover. "HP? Do you perhaps know anyone by those initials ?"

"I am just going to drop in this lost-and-found room." I said, with a forced smile. This is the last thing I wanted to deal with.

"But it seems way too personal, to just leave it there." said Mey, hesitantly as if she was conflicted while thinking of a better solution. "We know that, with the number of things locked up in that room, this diary will just get sucked up into a black-hole."

"I can't deal with this right now. This isn't mine, so this is the least of my concerns." I scoffed, merely shoving the diary into my bag. "I will probably keep it with me until I decide what to do with it…or rather hope for pathetically miraculous luck for the owner of this book to cross paths with me - whoever this negligent HP person might be."

"It's definitely a better alternative than letting it get lost forever in that clucked-up room."

***

II

"The constellations of greed prey on every desire, swaying the inevitable hope of the fading luminosity."

CHAPTER - III

More than I ever realised, Art has started becoming an anchor to remind me that I wasn't an inhumane empty shell incapable of feeling anything at ease but constantly reacting whenever there was a leak in everything I tried to bottle.

At first, it merely seemed like a chase to practice as often as I could, until I chased the endless lines of correcting the lines until they felt perfect. A perfection that I could seek purely from my own standards and find contentment through it.

What began with dabbling in hundreds of sketches depicting styles and tales of Roman and Indian Mythology shifted towards finding their roots and home in the renaissance, specifically rococo, woven through symbolism techniques.

I don't know why my hands found their script to always draw humans, determined to capture the look of one's gaze holding all they felt in their irises, following the eyes of the beholder, no matter the angle approached to look at the piece.

That's when it sunk why I was lying to myself to believe that - Physical parameters always seemed like the parameters of ratio that I always sought to capture into my art and nothing beyond that. What my mind had consciously failed to depict, my hands had subconsciously sketched their way to earnestly pour out the unspoken words swimming through one's eyes in every piece I finished painting, … - several unspoken words that I have always held to myself.

Sometimes, it was way too habitual to wonder if the talons of hypocrisy had sunk way too deep to blur the division between my raw thoughts from what I truly wanted to believe.

Everyone was influenced by the physical parameters that defined the appearance tuning up the significance of their sight.

Was I any different?

Or did I not wish to admit that I wasn't any different?

Yet, all I could feel by the perception of attraction, merely through those parameters, were: *Maybe I could incorporate these facial ratios onto the muse of my next concept… Will they weave along with the concept I already have in my mind, or do I need to wait until I think of a fitting one?*

Wasn't that much worse?

It was so easy to confuse that perhaps I could never like another being outside my canvases.

Still, I found myself liking people for their values and ideals and dreams shaping the person they are, and only then the physical parameters developed into the acknowledgement of physical appearance beyond just the scale of parameters and liked them as a part of the person they are… the details separating them became more magnified, primarily through something that shone right at my face visually: clothing style, and I couldn't help but relish in the thrill of the challenge of how fashion stood as a simple yet impact statement to bring out the aura of the person adorning the creation.

Each pattern, each fabric, each cut bringing out the shift in the aura of the confidence by volumes.

An extension of their personality, radiating its volume and depth in an eternal ebb-and-flow, mimicking the theatrical style of the asymmetry and illusion of rococo being permeable with stronger regal palettes than the usual pastel colours of my preferred art style.

I really didn't mind fixing my roots in fine arts, yet I didn't want any easy way out from the pull of inspiration I felt through fashion designing. Perhaps, it may be easier just to accept the many offers of pursuing my major in Fine Arts in any major art school in Europe that came after the win, and pursue fashion designing '*later*', if that '*later*' ever came.

But I didn't want to succumb to the false pretence of that 'later' that was nothing more than an excuse of never actually delving into the rarely undertaken risk of throwing away the stability built over the years.

Even if I considered the possibility of joining any other team at the last minute due to lack of options, I wouldn't have the creative space to expand on my concepts but feel constricted to respect to work according to the one in-charge, or worse, create incompetent work.

I needed someone from the Fine-Arts department, who had a similar style of concepts, to push past my personal hesitance of being irritated of having to meet and deal with a new person, and easily focus on working through the exhibition together by just being blindingly grateful on lucking out on the sync of the frequency of having a similar style to arrive to the same concept, avoiding the painful waste of time roping in the draw of clashing ideas, leading nowhere.

So far, I was drawing blanks on finding anyone - or rather remembering anyone, that magically fit that category.

Then again, that was solely due to my lack of acknowledgement towards everything around me, unless it involved people, I directly invested time with.

Why on earth couldn't they just keep the minimum number of people required in a team for a solo exhibition centralising on a particular concept, to be three to four instead of five, this year?

Through all racing thoughts across my mind, I needed to indulge myself in a steady pace of events to find an alternative carefully and effectively.

I couldn't help but feel better reading Ma's text after finishing my assignments and revising my AP notes for the day, and unexpectedly smiling at the words that provided the assurance from letting my mind swim through my biggest concern after losing out on the solo exhibition.

'Spes, you need to stop worrying about money. That's what we are here for. You just need to be concerned about concentrating on your work and the lifestyle around it. Starlight, just focus on yourself. You can rely on us. You are not alone.'

As an unconscious smile broke through my lips, slipping outside my room, I made my way into the living room to check up on my sisters and perhaps, have an early dinner together, knowing that Ma's rounds won't be getting over anytime soon today.

Maybe food could provide the aphrodisiac distraction to get into my zone on getting back the inspiration to draw the rough idea sketched on my practice sheets on to the canvas.

I chuckled, remembering the times Ma merely sighed in irritation, getting tired of correcting people pronouncing my name as 'Space' and breaking down the phonics of 'EZ' instead of 'ace' in my name while explaining the meaning of my name from its Latin origin. So, she resorted to calling me her 'starlight' to get back at people who had the ignorance to laugh in mockery, despite mispronouncing my name as '*Space*'.

Deep inside, I knew that better than anyone else. Yet, the guilt of burdening kept overwhelming me as I thought about the aftermath of that sentence. My parents will never be able to get a break to live as individuals but constantly as parents providing for their children, and there were three of us.

'I never asked for your help, Spes. Winning this art exhibition doesn't matter to me as it does to you. Maybe you need this because of your parents' separation… But I don't.'

Perhaps I was really incapable of care, for someone I trusted to resort to this method and blame me, in order to stop me.

'They hate me, Spes. Because you keep winning and I hoped that our team would withdraw from the art competition just for this year.'

Why? Why go that far to be liked by people who clearly wanted to sabotage us, who clearly had an advantage through nepotism?

Nepotism that blindly favoured skills, yet I was blamed for refusing to back down.

'Don't think you are being ungrateful to your parents by not having any sense of humility?

Won't they be hurt if they found out that all their hard-work is ending up inside your pride to presume to be better than anyone else?'

Of all times, I really didn't know why these words started ringing through my ears again.

As much as I wished that the words of the world couldn't have swayed my reality, it physically ripped me to admit that it had.

What had I ever done even to showcase that I had let pride in over my head if I struggled even to accept the fulfilment of my goals and constantly feel empty inside, even when people kept telling me that *'they were proud of me?'* Why did my quietness come across as a lack of humility? Why did my refusal to accept their opinions come across as arrogance?

'We are just trying to help you, and to do that, we need to get to the root of your outbursts of violence.'

Outbursts of violence? *Help me?*

'You need to tell us the truth…'

I did, I always did…all this time, that's what I have been trying to do, yet you have already made up your mind that the lack of my bawling tear-streaked face as the other person made it impossible to accept my truth.

'If you continue being like this, then you are going to end up alone.'

Well, you are already taking care of that by drilling that inside my head, aren't you?

'You need to take responsibility for your actions…'

Yet, I am suffering from being forced down to take the responsibilities for something I haven't done.

'You are a kid. You don't have the right to act like a teacher to go around telling your classmate what not to do when they are sick and hit them when they win against you. Even as teachers, we would never do that to children, because that's humanity.'

You haven't only framed me as a bully but as someone who is just inhumane.

'Don't you have any respect for your elders?! Do you really take them for granted too?'

The only reason I have been bearing through months of this, besides the fear of causing an inconvenience to my parents, is that I am trying to be respectful.

'I have never expected this from a child like her. What should we do with her?'

Maybe it was time I got out of here and grew up sooner to get into an Arts specialised School because adults were always biased.

'If we don't fix this when she is a child and stop these counselling sessions denying our responsibility as teachers, then the consequences of this will manifest into something very dire when she grows up.'

Perhaps what I felt for the betrayal of the so-called friendship wasn't anger towards him but anger towards me. Anger towards my circumstances. Anger towards these so-called adults for believing his twisted story.

But most of all, hopelessness for him having to resort adding glue to my drink and excusing the risk to fatality because of my stubbornness to give up, in order to get those teachers' kids to win.

'She doesn't feel sorry for hurting her own friend to the point where he is physically scared to breathe the same air as her.'

Tell me something new. I felt my nails dig further into my fists as I wanted to scream out the hypocrisy of the validation of my words being crushed because I was a kid.

Yet, the whole ordeal began over the fever-induced delusional words of another '*kid*'. Who gave them the right to decide the standards of '*right*'?

Right, because they were '*adults*'? A child's words were nothing more than a fleeting breeze compared to their judgement.

All I did was scream back at the guy who had shoved her violently and laughed at her while mocking her for being a *'weak hindrance'* for showing up to school in *'this'* state.

The one single thing Ma had requested, when Pax and I had asked her, egging on about the ways how we could help with the baby - all she had asked for was to - help her by staying our best and learning to deal with our own problems, independently.

This was my problem, and I am going to keep my word by not letting it create a chain reaction to bother anyone else than it already had.

'Does this happen often, where you tend to black-out the memories after your out-burst? Do you remember anything?'

Out-burst? It was your *kid's* so-called friends who threw their plates at me, when I am just counting the seconds of stepping away from this hellhole so that you don't get another excuse to exploit my fear of troubling my parents if I don't show up to face this every day.

Trust me, I counted the days of tolerating their nuisance, silently and bruising my hands to avoid being hit on my face instead and explain injuries that I can't possibly hide by just pulling on my sleeves.

Fifty-two days.

Fifty-two long days, before I threw back that wretched steel plate at them in your so-called luncheon hallways. *Fifty-two long days,* until the biting agony of being tired of the wincing pain, every time I tried to use my hands to write and draw, it got impossible to keep at bay. Ma has already started noticing the pain-relief cream running out within less than a month in our first-aid kit.

Adulthood. I am never going to let myself wait to grow up to be like them.

I don't need to be an adult like them to grow up.

I don't want to be an adult to ever dare to take anyone's life, words, and feelings for granted as they have.

I don't want to be an adult to possess the capacity to exploit anyone's feelings, like them.

I am going to be more than the chaos around me.

No, I want to stop remembering and suffocating myself from the same cycle of wondering how I was replaced into the guy in her memories. One hundred forty-six days of these interrogations, yet all it took to be asked to move past this immediately was just her saying, '*I am really sorry, I was confused, it was an accident. It was a mistake, but if you were ever my friend you would understand why I needed them on my side or else they would have started to make things harder for me.*'

There was nothing she could have done about it otherwise.

There was nothing anyone could do about it.

I hated apologies.

I hated confusion.

I hated accidents, I hated that '*sorry*', but most of all, I couldn't escape the loophole of wondering was it my interference that caused them to even lead to the delusion?

Did I cross boundaries and disrespect them by selfishly being intolerant of what I felt was wrong?

Although I had no right to determine the extent of what caused someone their pain, was it wrong to wonder that there had to be something more to lead that extent of fear? I don't even know why these memories are reliving in my mind, like a pathetic fly-swatting around street food. *Was it because Felicity's UPSR exams were arriving soon, that I couldn't help but think about my time during the same period?*

But how the hell did I end up from the hallways of that wretched hellhole, to choking on the ground of that damn concrete entrance of the clinic, within mere seconds instead of years. *Whose brilliant idea was it to create a concrete pavement at the entrance?*

Crowds. I hated crowds.

I hated when people didn't listen to me, yet I was the one struggling to keep my consciousness awake from scraping down my throat as if it would miraculously remove the glue mixed in that wretched energy drink.

I can't even breathe evenly through this wretched suffocation-

Jerking myself awake and blinking my eyes open, I pressed the ends of my palms over my closed eyes, forcefully wondering when the heck I had fallen asleep on the couch.

This is why I hated sleeping. Unwanted memories, blending together in a messy cauldron, having no business creeping back into my mind.

"Since when have I been asleep?" I snapped, my voice hoarse, looking around my surroundings to find Pax and Felicity, both sprawled across the carpeted floor raising their feet on the coffee table while leaning their backs at the end of the couch, consumed in one of their endless banters which often involved comparing theories on the lyrics of the soundtrack harmonising an ongoing scene of the movie, that they were watching on TV.

"Thankfully, four hours. The longest you have slept in the last three weeks." I stiffened immediately at the warning tone that was way too calculative for Pax as she lowered the volume of the movie playing in the background. She clearly wasn't in the mood to drop this almost as equally as I didn't wish to spare a second to indulge in this, any further.

"I told you to wake me up at seven." I sighed tiredly, staring at the hands of the wall clock struck at half-past-seven. "I don't like wasting my time over something so useless."

"I would rather be useless than lose my sanity by refusing to sleep." Pax scoffed, as Felicity laughed nervously, trying to ease the tension, as I sat upright immediately, shoving myself from the couch, and glaring back at Pax.

"This is my individualistic opinion." I snapped, throat catching. "Respect it or just shut up and keep your rationalisation to yourself. Don't patronise me."

"Why are you acting like you are committing a sin by sleeping?-" She asked firmly, not giving me any excuse to insist that she was merely exaggerating her words. "-And stop giving me the bullshit that you were revolted to let yourself sleep because of losing out on time. You were flinching in your sleep."

I winced, expression twisting like I was about to fight back, feeling my breathing grow heavier each second. *Why the hell was she so persistent today? I have to focus on getting all my drive in completing the commission, today.*

"Why the hell were you watching me sleep in the first place?" I scoffed, a little frantic, that not only were these wretched incidents messing with my head all over again but causing a reaction that could evidently be picked up by someone else. I did the only thing I could to agitate Pax enough, to not press this further. Argue back with irrelevant comebacks. "This is why I prefer to relax in my room instead of resting here for a while."

"Sorry to break it to you, but you won't exactly move mountains by functioning during the time you claimed to have lost by sleeping," said Pax, quietly. Yet it was the gentle tone that set me off, when she placed her hand on my knee as a comfort stance, to coax further.

With our constant fights after the separation, we rarely expressed our concerns for each other, vocally and whenever we did, it only occurred over things that scared us the most about the other.

Over the years, the cognitive paradox of the ruthless cycle of constantly chasing away my fear of never doing enough as time flies by, made me seek the notion in the belief that - *'I have to live my life, busily to have a purpose in my life'* yet I knew I never wished to ever acknowledge that I could ever be *busy* in my life.

Knowing that the moment I constantly felt 'busy' in my life, I would always find an excuse to continue things that matter to me, for granted, instead of trying my best to devote my time to them. Ever since the interviewer mentioned her snide remark about *'never wasting her time in foolish daydreams.'*

I couldn't help but feel the desperate need to claw my way towards wrapping myself in the former aspect of my conflict, to never let my dreams manifesting onto my reality, lose their ground merely due to the turns of time.

"I am barely doing anything productive to move a rock, by functioning during the minimal hours I actually do something." I swallowed thickly, staring at the Pax's hand on my knee. People around the world faced more challenging problems, problems that conquered through, and here I am, letting myself be pathetically affected *by mere dents along the road.* I stared intently as I took in slow, deep breaths at the audacity of what my mind was trying to do- *I was trying to whine over nothing.*

"You were repeating - *'I am sick of this. I didn't do it. I don't need to bawl my eyes out in my defence to be sorry for something I haven't done.'* - in your sleep, like a broken record." Pax pressed gingerly, trying to read my expression, as my head hung low between my knees. She knew way too much, *way too much to be worried about this as if they were worth to be considered as an inconvenience.* "People usually call that a nightmare."

"It was nothing. I have never had dreams during my sleep." I said, dull but firm, eyes darker as they lifted to stare at Pax. I couldn't blame anyone but myself for worrying Pax about this, all over again. *An unnecessary burden on her shoulders. I hate this.*

"Recollecting a past memory-"

"Exactly, it wasn't a dream, much less a nightmare. It's nothing!" For a person who wanted to end this conversation, I was doing a poor job of biting down the glaring snarl in my tone. Why couldn't I just say that I had to head to the Convenience store sooner today? It was time for my shift already, and it wouldn't hurt to help the other part-time employees in re-stalking the shelves. Well, mostly *Jove.*

"Yeah, I am crazy for not believing someone, when they insist that *'it's nothing'* especially after they wake up looking like someone has electrocuted them in their sleep." Pax noted, following behind my trail, as I merely headed back to our room, to just pull out the charger of my phone from the socket.

"My mind must have unconsciously wandered off recollecting memories. So, it's nothing." I sighed, leaning on the doors of the wardrobe, wondering why Pax had decided to place the grand piano in her room, and just sleep in my room, instead.

"You weren't choking in your sleep, but rather talking in your sleep, so I am pretty sure I know what that was about," said Pax, tactful and brisk.

"Has anyone ever told you that it's still creepy to watch someone sleep, even if it's your own family?" I sighed heavily, rubbing at my eyes. *I really needed to absorb rather happy emotions to distract myself from my own wandering mind.* "There is actually something called boundaries-"

"I don't care! With what you went through-"

"Don't. Not now." I snapped sharply, breathing harshly, every other breath seeming to stick in my throat. All attempts of trying to manipulate my mind into distracting myself, flying out the window.

"Will you ever talk about it? It's been two years. I am rather glad that you were talking in your sleep, because unlike everyone else, I know, what went down with respect to that, but-" she said in a rush, as if she has been preparing to drown me with this, after staying quiet for all those days.

"There is nothing to talk about." I whispered, hurriedly, trying to even out my breaths. "Like you said, It happened years ago. I don't remember it."

"Why the hell did I have to pick you up from the clinic that day?"

"I am *sorry* for the inconvenience-"

"You, stubborn prick! You think I actually believe that you were just sitting outside the clinic that day because you felt dizzy over fever?" I couldn't even focus my gaze at her, to warn her that I had enough for the day, as my fists clenched at my sides, holding back from spewing several things that she wanted to know. Answer to all her questions, that just wouldn't change anything. "I have seen you pretend that you don't have a fever for days when you fall sick until someone catches on that you are unwell, through your denials?" She snarled, hissing quietly as I stared at her darkly. "You don't actually believe that I actually bought your excuse, that the missed call from the school infirmary was because you are sick."

"Are you implying that you don't think catching a fever isn't a concrete reason for the infirmary to call the family or that you were annoyed-" I scoffed, feeling uneasy trying to dismiss me who was genuinely worried about me instead of reacting to her as if she was actually patronising me?

Someone who would genuinely understand me, instead of rationalising her own opinions.

Yet, I couldn't.

"You don't think I haven't started noticing your tick of refilling water bottles in repetition just to throw it in the sink, coming back again, this morning?" She asked carefully, as I winced immediately, forgetting that even if anyone had those habits, Pax hounded behind them like a wolf, catching on at the slightest cracks.

"It's always better to ensure that they are thoroughly cleaned."

"Ma washes them. It can't get any cleaner when she cleans them. She is a certified Oncology nurse-"

"I don't need you to remind me of our mother's profession." There was no point talking about it now.

She was worried to the point that she was merely going to pity me and direct her despondence due to the separation by shifting the blame from me to someone else.

I can't control that, at least when it's directed at me, I could.

"Then don't make you remind you that I am very much aware of the fact that the reason you are avoiding your sleep again, is because the last time you slept, you woke up choking-"

"Get off my face, before I say something regrettable for the both of us. You have crossed way too many boundaries." I said flatly. I glared at her as she challenged me to back out of the conversation if I wanted to end this, knowing extremely well how it agitated me to leave any conversation unfinished, considering it to be disrespectful.

Sometimes, I really don't understand the rigidity of the adamance over my own principles of respect.

"Spes, if this is about today's interview, then you have to know that-"

Why on earth was she going back and forth, being angry at being careful with her words?

"No, it's not. Don't worry, I will handle it. I know that this is unfair to you, and I shouldn't have snapped at you when you are just concerned for me." Despite the blurred shifting of her tones irritating me at this state, I knew that she wouldn't be concerned if she didn't care, and the least I could do was to not bite her head off. "But I don't want to apologise for that now, when my mind is in haywire. Not like this.-"

"Have you considered that you won't be living with us, from next year, what happens then?" She asked, almost solemnly. "You can't exactly drown this issue with hypnotic sleeping tablets. We all know what happened the last time you were prescribed-"

"Why are you being so insistent on talking about incidents from the past, as if I wasn't there to experience them?" I hissed in a whisper, in retaliation at the resurfacing of the issues that we avoided speaking about, completely.

"If this happens again, you are running out of time to hide. This is my last straw." She said with a tight-lipped smile and clasping her hands over her head. "I think I have been quite patient and '*respectful*' even by your so-called standards."

"What do you want from me? Gossip like middle-school girls about something that can't change?" I spat, warning her that I was at my end of tolerating this. "What good will talking about it bring to any of us?" I demanded quietly through gritted teeth.

"Isn't that what you do, yourself… when you feel someone around you is troubled?" She demanded dolefully, with a wide stance. "Why is it so hard for you to let someone around you do the same for you?"

Because it feels like whining and insulting their time and effort over nothing.

"Because *their* problems are worth being acknowledged as problems that have truly troubled them for a while, while I am troubled over nothing!" I hissed bitterly, trying to keep my voice down watching over Felicity's eyes still glued to the TV. "That's just selfish! Is it going to change anything?"

"I am not breaking down the necessity of that all over again. I can't physically stand your imprudent arrogance any longer." She pressed her lips together, as if trying to tame down something welling in her chest. "So, consider it my last warning, if I catch you in this state, once again, I am going to start talking."

I jerked my head towards her immediately, knowing that she wasn't kidding by the slightest.

Yet, I couldn't scoff at the notion, she had gotten to the point over the years, to finally hold this over my head.

"Are you threatening me now? What do you intend to do?" I taunted with a smirk and playing with my sleeves, watching her flinch at the slightest *ting* from my phone which most likely had to be a text from Jove, just checking on my whereabouts before our shift. As soon as she caught my gaze zeroing down on her hands shaking badly, she shoved them behind her back. *This clearly wasn't easy for her either.* "Exploit by broadcasting the moments when I was utterly useless and couldn't handle ordinary issues that aren't even *worth* being considered as issues?"

"*Exploit?* All that anger, how long are you going to hate yourself in the fear of someone criticising you, if you actually consider being kind to be yourself?" She breathed sullenly, moving back towards the opposite wall of our room, needing to take a seat on her bed, angled towards me.

"Be kind to myself? What am I supposed to be? A self-absorbed fairy godmother? You don't get to undermine how I live my life." I stared at her as if we were falling in a plane together, and she was somehow promising me to get us out, alive.

"Not undermining it,… the way you suffocate yourself I morally can't, I am just stating the facts." I froze immediately, as she asked almost brokenly, something in her expression breaking down. It wasn't a hiss. Not a bitter spat or a growl, that was usual in our fights. Just a quiet, torn whisper - as if she were begging to know the answer to a legitimate question. "You should like that better than anyone, right? Given how frantically you constantly push yourself to be wrapped in your ambition."

The distraction I desperately needed all day, to escape the possibility of being consumed by the overwhelming doubts concurring due to the downfall of my initial plan, after completing my notes and pending assignments for the day, came in the form of a call from Jove passing her first screening to be a news anchor.

Yet, I couldn't even have the mind-space to be completely happy for Jove to finally seize the goal that she had been persistently working for.

The opportunity I had been waiting for her to get.

The opportunity that she deserved to get, for ages.

As I glanced down at my sister, hands shaking where they clenched each other so tightly, her skin paling around them.

I was used to being calculative of every word I spoke, every consequent action of ensuring that no one invaded my personal space other than the people who already existed in my life, clutching on to the finer threads of ensuring that I never took them for granted, by sparing my time for anyone new in my life, even more so since the *misfortune damned circumstance* that coincidentally occurred before our parents told us about their decision regarding their separation.

Yet my friendship with Jove, was the most unplanned course of events in my life.

I never realised the elapsing of the moments fleeting by, of establishing a bond with someone who had to work twice as harder to break through the prejudices of people not seeing past pitying her wheelchair, to demand the worth she clearly radiated through her work ethics as an aspiring reporter and the person she was - since the first time we met when I was trying to flee away from the reporters after the first display of my *'Stigma Of Colours'* works in the Kuala Lumpur City Gallery.

Wanting to take a breath from the suffocation of the repeating questions that were merely interested over my age or just sheer luck of getting this far. Needless to say, it was the only interview I had ever given, that didn't end up with distasteful memories.

I never knew friendship existed without the forcible acceptance of the repeated unfortunate coincidence, that the other party was always busy whenever I needed them, until I met Jove. The best way to describe our friendship was merely - *relaxed*.

It wasn't *easy*, it was *relaxed*.

Since the very beginning of our dynamic, one of the very things we had always lost in the past and were sick of compromising was - *Clarity*.

Clarity that we couldn't ask for, by merely biting down the disappointment of holding on to memories that no longer existed in the present variability of the person from our past, whom we no longer recognised - just to prevent chaos.

The pointless compromise of time that could never be spared for us in reciprocation. Those were the times where I truly questioned my decision to connect optimism with an unnecessary compromise of my feelings.

Yet, the person calling me was someone I least expected to call. It was at times like this, the irony of me loving to mock the miraculous movie-coincidences came back to hit me like a boomerang.

"I hope this hello makes you recognise, who I am, Zrey." The said voice, chuckled almost challengingly in the aftermath that would befall if I didn't recognise that banter.

"Fares?" I asked, almost baffled to have the person who had a knack for sparing me from the impending boredom after refusing to '*brag*' for the sake of *representing* the school as well as the country, constantly advised by the teacher accompanying me, during my brief tour in Europe. *I wish Mrs. Bronywyn had accompanied me instead.*

Yet, all I could do was flee away from the teacher accompanying, the moment she started to jab me to confidently speak up about my *credentials,* by either trying to climb up and down the ramps of the continuous concrete ribs or sticking to the concavity of the limestone walls.

To prove that there was a reason my works were being displayed in Europe, with the possibility of my next solo exhibition at the Guggenheim Museum, if I won among the other nominees. *Why do my credentials need to matter, when all that should matter was my art connecting with the viewer?*

"Glad to know that you are still occupied in your own world rather than indulging in the massive chaos around you." said René, teasing with a dramatic sigh as I scoffed at the start of one of our usual banters, that wasn't limited to her teasing my Italian despite my fluency, as a native speaker herself.

It wouldn't be an exaggeration to claim that the highlight of visiting the art galleries displaying my work was coincidentally running into the nominee of the Vincent award, René Fares, whispering her own set of profanities behind the structural pillars uplifting the glass dome reflecting the star-lit midnight sky, while trying hard to sway away from the questions concerned more about her father's business expansion than her works.

"What are the sudden pleasantries for?"

"I guess you aren't aware of the fact that I actually decided to follow in my father's footsteps and ended up here at your school." said René, laughing nervously as I stood baffled trying to process her words.

Considering that ambition ran in René's blood wasn't a far-fetched cry, her dream to follow her father's footsteps to build her own empire from ground zero always got misinterpreted by those very reporters as René wanting to take over her Parents' industrial empire from her older brother or foolishness to not use her advantage to use her *social* and *financial* status, to kickstart her vision to rebranding Asia as the next 'Fashion Empire', being *stubbornly ungrateful* of her dismissing roots.

Never bothering to see the fire within her that blindly admired the origin story of her parents starting from their ground zero to build their vision and desiring to repeat history through her own passion.

"Hold on, you are actually in Malaysia, enrolled at Wau Bulan Arts High School?" I repeated, laughing at the irony of the events occurring today.

"Let's say, there has been a mishap in my plans of securing the solo exhibition that guarantees my ticket into Parsons, especially its School of Fashion." One of the reasons, we developed a quick comfortable bickering bond, besides the similarity of our concept styles, was our shared interest in shifting from our roots of fine arts onto Fashion Designing. If I had to provide a comparison analogy, it was like my shared frequency of similar mindset with Jove was equivalent to the bandwidths of the similarity of concept themes with René. "The interviewer that you walked out on, earlier this noon?"

"So, you are actually here?" I asked again, still trying to wrap my head around the girl revisiting her Asian roots for the first time, despite having never set her foot outside Europe since her birth.

It was almost easy to mistake René as a European with her tanned complexion possessing massively low concentration of melanin, with thin lips and the dark roots of the fading dark blonde hair peeking through, if it weren't for the partial epicanthic folds of her eyes.

"While you take your time accepting that. You would be quite pleased to know that I am actually satisfied with your loyalty, that you mentioned my name in reference to the artist you wish to collaborate with, too." said René, as Pax gave a questioning glare to ask if I wasn't speaking with Jove.

"Lemme guess, you were interviewed by the same interviewer, in exchange for the guarantee of your solo exhibition on designing your own collection, despite being in the Fine Arts department." I said, slowly putting the pieces together, while shaking my head towards Pax to signal a 'No' in response to her look, as she whispered back an 'I-will-inform-Jove-that-you-might-be-late-for-your-shift', before walking out of the room, immediately. Not waiting to look behind for a response. I wasn't even sure I could have articulated any words in response, either.

"Damn, that interviewer seemed to be in a rush to publish my interview,-" She laughed, before scoffing in disbelief "-as if she could use that to get back at me, for challenging her to write about a field that she refuses to appreciate genuinely."

"Please, she doesn't know who she is dealing with." I chuckled back at the boisterous laughter at the other end of the call, struggling to repeat 'Yes' in between her laughs.

"My parents are pretty amused with my catch-phrase of '*I don't want you to expect to be the best, I expect you to work at your best because I don't see the benefit of me, compromising to your mediocrity…*' displayed as the headline of that article. To look past my *image* portrayed in her article." said René, as I rolled my eyes in fondness, remembering the exact words uttered by her behind the principles of her retaliation of never liking to work in a group unless they didn't settle with their *mediocrity*, while proposing to collaborate with me once we got into Parsons. "My luck ran out while negotiating with the Vice-chancellor, who seemed to be in tears when she ripped off the grant for my solo exhibition, because it seemed like the safer option for her to get back at me."

"Why the hell have they phrased your concepts into just a subsidiary business expansion of your father's investments into trying his hand into the fashion industry and *tossing you* to take the lead over it because of *your interest* in art?" I snarled, scrolling the article on my phone before switching the phone on speaker mode. "The *audacity*-"

"Do you remember the most common trope we came up with, as the rough foundation for our first collaboration when we get accepted into Parsons?" She asked, as I scoffed reading further through the article that designed to frame René's image as nothing but 'using her silver spoon for good, to *explore her options* before she decided to settle for taking over the portion of her Parents' business not handled by her older brother. '*People wanted to know my background after I had seized the Vincent award and am the youngest one in history to do so…*' I couldn't help but scoff onto a smug grin, to read how the interviewer wanted to desperately snub René's reality check and refusal to put up with her marketing image, as nothing but eluding it as mere *arrogance*, instead. '*Next time you wish to speak about the financial records of my family, contact his secretary, don't seek me out. I don't like being fooled.'*

So, this is the *so-called image* she built for René?

One of the rough concepts we ended up developing during the exhibition of René's works being displayed along before my collection, in Berlin, was to base our designs on 'Feminine Ambition.'

It was common hypocrisy of viewers compelled into wanting to know the backstory of male antagonists and justify romanticising them, yet surprisingly finding the same ambition in female antagonists: *bitchy.*

We could create a collection that defines the link of the transparency and radiance of one's persona, once they adorn our collection.

Our vision would be rooted to draw out the volume of the shoulders to sync with accentuating the waist with a preferred peplum arc, in creating the depth of an eternal ebb-and-flow, that would authentically scream the elegant strength of their feminism and individuality.

That's the brand we could hope to create.

"Do you think we could fast-forward our timings on that collaboration, and start that collection from now?" René asked again, straying me back from my wandering thoughts. "I have found a loophole, to take control of our disturbingly similar situation, and get back at it."

Then it clicked in an instant to me that, although both of us were sacked from having our own solo individual solo exhibitions, we were never denied from having the joint exhibition in fact that was the only option we had and were possibly dreading to be stuck with bending our concepts with restricted creative freedom, according to the team we would have to join, in order to even graduate.

Only the students from fine-arts majors could lead the exhibition, so it fit perfectly, to have the easiest solution served on a platter.

"I am down without any second thoughts, but I need to confirm with Quinsy-"

"Yeah, I knew your noble pride might cause hindrances to agree with this deal, without checking with your team. Fortunately, I only had to convince one to get her on board, after reviewing her works." I chuckled good-naturedly at her actions, knowing that it was something René would do by default as I whined about contradicting the coining of *'noble pride'* as nothing but *basic manners*. "She is on board, so we need to look for one team-mate, because she told me your friend pursuing Modelling is still on board to model the outfits for the exhibition, despite shifting her major to Ballet."

"You really took care of everything, to get a head start against the hindrance she threw our way."

"Can't wait to slay this by joining forces, Zrey."

***

"I am not down for *branding* my credentials as my identity, among people who follow the same line of

craft like me. That's what my artworks are for."
scoffed René, throwing a half-bitten breadstick across
the three-seated rounded table at the farthest corner
of the arena, usually used by teams to plan their
exhibition after class hours, to emphasise her dislike
for the staleness of the food. Quinsy mutely glared
back at her when the food fell near her most-prized
selection of the camera. "I never created them with
the intention of grabbing credentials, I don't even
think it's possible to '*create*' anything with those
intentions. So, I am not going to change my identity
represented through my art shift into being vocalised
solely by my credentials."

Over the last few weeks since the extension of the
deadline of finalising teams, I had developed an odd
attachment to the diary filled with the pages separated
by the thin plastic sheets, to prevent the smudging of
the - what must definitively be the artist's preferred
medium of choice: *dry pastels* - scribbled notes and
designs of the palettes besides the drawings of the
flowers, between the pages.

I didn't believe in the existence of natural skills that
could pre-exist without the craze of practicing to
refine the finer details of the sketches, as much as
possible.

There were days where the inspiration of the muse
might not be strong enough to create a concrete
concept that could be painted well enough for a
commission, yet it was a developing habit that could
have been instilled into my mind through Ma's
influence: to prioritise *consistency*.

To motivate myself to continue working on an
unfinished painting, even if it may have been based

on a sloppy, rough sketch developed from the fragment of partial concept. For they helped me to piece together a wholesome concept, to start a new painting that could pass to be sold. Giving me a rather jubilant sense of accomplishment.

"I agree, how does the vibe sync if they are more interested in working with my credentials than working with my style?" I said, voice sombre enough that Quinsy looked at me, almost in worry.

I waved her off in reassurance, raising the diary to merely signal my thoughts being lost in looking through the diary. She huffed in relief before rolling her eyes fondly to retaliate my constant defence of being attached to the diary, merely because of my growing interest in the medium of *dry pastels.*

Although it wasn't a lie, I felt way too attached to voice out my actual reason for feeling an unexplainable drive to create more.

The brief loom of being in art blocks in a randomised wavelength of frequency, disappearing within seconds as I thought about the sincerity of the owner of the diary, reflecting through her portrayal of the flower symbolism used to mimic the colours highlighted to portray the emotions varying according to the eye shape, with side-lined notes of the occasion, or the variety of the oils to be mixed with the dry shadow palettes and bronzers varying according to the texture of the skin as well as the prevailing weather.

The outline of every page stalked up the details, like layered concrete hardening over-built, and the finished foundation base of the shades written like, the artist wanted to enchant the way they had found themselves through the gradient among the tones.

I couldn't help but get lost in the greed of wanting to remain embedded in that craze to weave my concepts meticulously and paint them well enough to provide justice to the picture swimming through my imaginations.

"Oh gods! Now there are two of them." Quinsy groaned with mockery, pressing the heels of her palms against her temple before flipping through the portfolios of all the people that had turned up immediately after the change in our recruitments' notice.

It was surprisingly disturbing to see an alarmingly high number of people, who had abandoned their teams, to join ours, merely due to the branding of our combined credentials, Quinsy had put up.

Yet, I could empathise with Quinsy's worry of us running out of time, to find the last fitting team-mate despite joining René in turning down the few handful portfolios we had initially received, based on the Concepts' criteria that we had set up in our previous notice.

Despite our initial complaining against Quinsy's idea of using our credentials to go through more portfolios as quickly as possible.

It was hard not to finally accept that her rational reasoning overshadowed our stubbornness by several folds, "I can't even disagree with this, Without the right synergy between similar concepts as a single comprehensive picture, it would just end up in creating two different entities."

"Unfortunately, we grew up in a society, where credentials are required to define a person's work ethics and skills, in the quickest way possible." I said, monotonously as René elbowed Quinsy's sides to ask if the cafeteria sold any other beverage than the tetra-packs of coconut drinks, that I always bought. "You can't exactly ask them to prove all those accumulated knowledge and experience all over again, most effectively during the interview."

"But our line of work is *literally* the definition of *a picture speaks a thousand words*." said René, throwing her hands in the air dramatically as Quinsy glared back at the slight movement of the table shifting her camera and parting her hair to throw it up onto a loose updo. "I don't get the reason for getting influenced by credentials in our domain, especially while looking through the prospect of creating a work, together."

For hours, since Quinsy updated the notice, both René and I were trying to decide which one of us should be thrown in the ringer, for using only one of our credentials along with Quinsy's credentials, on our final permanent notice.

So, that we could take down at least one of our credentials since the flow of portfolios due to the temporary notice containing the credentials of all three of us.

We couldn't switch back to our very first notice either as rules mentioned on the notice for recruitment can't be repeated if the team isn't formed or disbanded earlier than the first deadline of the submission of the final selection.

"Coin toss?" René asked smugly, knowing extremely well by now that neither of us would back down logically, and ended up merely prolonging our stay among the buzzing noise of several other unconfirmed groups sprawled around the open arena lit by the blazing late noon's rays sprawled through an overcooked yolky sun, until we got our own space after finalising our team.

"That's what I was thinking." I smirked, before eyeing Quinsy to miraculously pick her side, as the latter rolled her eyes and glared at both of us to emphasise her position as the unbiased referee before asking us to pick 'Heads' or Tails'. "The loser has to pin their credentials as branding for recruitments as well as deal with the selection with Quinsy."

"Hold on, you sly prick." René started chuckling with disbelief as her eyes widened dramatically, when I merely shrugged my shoulders in response. "That wasn't decided, and you know it, you can't just toss another proposal along, that's unfair." Neither of us accounting for the fact that the one who would end up suffering the most would be Quinsy who had gotten on to a routine of merely sighing '*I didn't sign up for this*'.

Whenever she ran out of concrete words to feel the need to explain our behaviour to the recruits who questioned our pride immediately after we turned them down based on their lack of interest in bothering to care if their artistic style matched with ours.

Sometimes she acted as a buffer, as either of us explained our rigid work ethics, agitated by their fickleness to question why we were taking this so seriously beforehand.

And sometimes…she yelled back louder than both René and I combined, with her chin appearing pointer than usual as it jutted outwards as she promulgated about how we had always been unforgiving towards our attachment to our works even before we started considering 'art' as a career.

That may have been an *exaggeration*. Yet, there was no denying we were highly sensitive towards the slightest intrusions or interferences of any kind towards the very world of art of our own, that provided our very sense of drive and belonging to be the closest thing to define us.

It was infuriating to watch people act like this was a secondary choice, as they had already made up their minds that they would have to be forced to walk back into more '*stereotypical stable-based careers defined by the standards of the society*'.

It wasn't a subtle reaction to watch them get enraged with our desire to protect our dreams.

But was it fair to claim that the carelessness to not hold to this dream as strongly as they would have wanted to, without the constant jeering of a *doomed outcome?*

Especially when our current reality sets up all odds to design it to be hard not to get influenced by the round undermining of most adults around us who didn't snatch a breath to remind us that our efforts would be futile.

"So is letting the random possibilities of luck decide the circumstances, so we are way past *fair* now."

"Fine I will throw in another one." said René, winking cheekily as if she was up to no good to get even. "The winner deals with tolerating with all the number of bizarre people who claim ownership over that diary." Despite her early teasing regarding the lack of much incorporation of flowers with blazing significance in my recent works and calling me out my obsessive nature to keep my hands clean and fretting over the slightest stains of paints or graphite remains, to ever be interested in dry pastels, her question still stumped me: *'What happens when you meet the owner of the diary, when they come to claim it? Knowing you, you definitely could care less much about the person to ever let your judgement be clouded to let anyone in your personal space despite your severe attachment to the artist's works.'*

As my attachment to the diary grew, to the point where I spent my breaks during my shifts in the convenience store searching up the meanings of more flowers with Jove - especially the rare ones drawn in the diary when there weren't any customers walking onto the store. I felt more guilty not finding the owner faster to return their diary back to them.

Yet, I was getting nowhere.

Finding no one in the Arts Department with the initial 'HP', so I had to resort to the last option of contemplating to put up another notice along with the Recruitments notice, mentioning the lost diary of a person, interested in make-up, with the initials HP.

'I don't know but I am certain that I am going to try my best to make an effort to convince that person to be on our team, if

they aren't already part of a finalised team. The style of this make-up artist and the eccentric yet natural look she plays with, would not only complete our collection yet bring out an elevation that we would regret passing out on.'

And all René did after cornering me with this question, during our smug silent celebration of the Vice-Chancellor's distraught expressions peeking through her poor attempts of remaining nonchalant while signing on the submission of our joint project, was smile softly at my answer and say, *'I couldn't agree more.'*

"WHAT?!" The shock resonating to the high decibel rise in my voice, turned several heads around in the direction of our table before I snapped my head momentarily towards their direction to glare in irritation.

The eyes staring at us a while ago, merely shifted their gaze elsewhere as they pretended to go back to ignoring us, as I shifted my guess back to René to hope that she was kidding.

"Oh yeah, I am attaching the notification for the proclaiming of a lost diary along with the recruitment's notice." René said, signalling Quinsy that she was picking tails before looking straight to give me a look that *'It was about time'*, more specifically the timing I had asked to choose to put up my notice, only when it was time to take on that last resort, I would certainly hesitate to take myself. "If I am going down, you are going down too. Have the first taste of teamwork when I am in your team."

***

Looking back to this moment, I wasn't sure if I would change the impractical coincidence that I never expected to happen off-screen.

Even back then, the sharp timber-coloured orbs shone with something so unexplainable to me, that I couldn't help but feel confused, trying to pinpoint them.

The softened gaze stood in sync with the finesse of her make-up, that almost appeared natural except her eyes, until she stood closer.

Yet, they contrasted the stature of her shoulders, which radiated the eased stance for her freshly dyed chestnut hair, reaching the back of her neck.

Since the moment she spoke, perhaps I had already recognised the voice but didn't wish to admit that the face I refused to place with the voice in the Aquaria, was standing in front of me claiming to be the owner of the diary.

It was way too gigantic of a baffling coincidence to be crossing paths with her again.

Man, if it were Pax who had absolute pitch, she would have confirmed right away with a guarantee.

I merely stared at her monotonously as she stated her stance for owning the diary, and knowing the contents of the book while ignoring the whispers of Quinsy who seemed to know *her* by face: '*It makes sense she is the unique make-up artist who made that catchy speech about choosing this form of art, to eradicate the presence of whitening products, hindering the acceptance of true beauty*', as René and Quinsy got back to our usual table at the arena after finally getting René the first cup of instant coffee from the cafeteria, that didn't spew out within her first sip. '*I have heard several people constantly talk about her like an experiment, because of her vitiligo.*'

I couldn't comprehend why people who had no business going through the trouble of seeking something personal waste their efforts to claim ownership over something that wasn't theirs to belong with.

Yet just like René had predicted, there would be several bizarre people who wanted to own the diary and look through it, because it must contain something important enough to be put up on notice than being neglected away somewhere forgotten.

As days passed by, they became better at probably overhearing the term 'flower symbolism' while either René or Quinsy teased me about the diary.

To use that proclaim to know about the contents of the diary to claim it.

I couldn't help but get irritated by *her* being the seventh person to mention 'flower symbolism' as the contents of the diary, to prove that the diary was hers.

Great, another person who wouldn't know anything further about the diary, besides the term she must have overheard from us just like the rest before her.

"Why haven't you just used the ideas, if you like them?" Yet her voice held no stutter as she threw a question at me, instead. Her eyes held a fond amusement blending with confusion reflecting through the fleeting heads of René and Quinsy shifting between both of us, like meerkats. "-And I think if it didn't catch your eye, you would have thrown that diary a long time ago instead of going through the trouble of returning this to the owner?"

Was this her play at reverse psychology?

"I doubt you are in the position to be the one asking the questions here." I snapped darkly, trying to figure out her play. "If this truly belongs to you -...you wouldn't want to risk irritating me to throw this away."

"You would have done that already if you intended to and wouldn't have paid that much effort to assure giving it to the right person instead of flinging it back at the first person lying to claim it or merely throwing it away in trash." She said, demanding carefully as if she knew what type of person I was. Yet it was that damned soft glint flashing across her irises, that infuriated me, more than anything else. "So, humour me."

"Do you take me for a clown to entertain you now?" I smirked, raising my eyebrows, eyeing her to quit her act. I couldn't even figure out if it even was an act.

"No, I am just really surprised to not pick up an ulterior motive, yet."

"You seem to have rushed to that, pretty blindly."

"Not blindly, I still can't decide if you have not used them because you think they aren't worth being considered good enough to be incorporated into a concept-" her voice remaining calm, as she pushed back the long strands of hair, falling on her face. "-or have some sort of unexplainable noble pride."

"You are welcome to think whatever you want." I said apathetically, after figuring out this person wasn't in a rush to get back their diary unlike others, and yet I still couldn't find out her reason for investing her time to voluntarily speak with a stranger. "I think I have been courteous enough to tolerate this conversation with a stranger without any relevant purpose for far too long. Pardon me, but I can't indulge in your hypotheses any longer."

"You seem pretty attached to that diary with random ideas using something basic as symbolism in colours and flowers for inspiration." She asked carefully, her eyes finally zeroing in onto the diary laid on the table in front of her, my hands still clutching on to the spine of the diary, tightly. As if, it was a stern habit like her tightly fastened tie, bearing the emblem of the school.

The moment she uttered those words, I couldn't think straight to even consider the *audacity* of this person to give her *mediocre* opinions.

"*Random*? Who the hell do you think you are to undermine - every single idea, so completely concrete incorporated into these concepts." I snarled, standing up to meet her gaze who seemed momentarily taken aback for a split second, before smiling sincerely. *Why on earth was she smiling at this situation?* Were my eyes losing their sight, was I mistaking the authenticity of that smile? Yet it felt wrong to even question that, as their hands remained crossed behind their back as she shifted lightly on her heels. "I don't care what barks you might have caught on to know about the vague description of the notes on this diary. But you don't get to speak another word about the sincerity roped in these notes to achieve the revolutionary vision of the bigger picture, this person wishes to achieve. Get-"

"Here. That diary is invaluable to me..." She said, stolidly cutting me off mid-way. I lost my voice getting ready to yell at her for interrupting me. I couldn't tear my eyes away from the rectangular strip of paper, she handed me carefully. The drawing of bluebell sketched regally on the paper, immediately gave away the signature of the drawing style using those familiar waxed dry pastels - that she indeed is HP. "For caring enough to not hand over my diary to just anyone or carelessly throwing it away in the trash."

It wasn't the drawing or even the recognition that she indeed was the artist who owned the diary, but rather the symbolism of the flower drawn.

Bluebells represented several feelings - loyalty, constancy, humility, and gratitude. Most significantly *Gratitude*.

"What the hell is going on?" I didn't know why I acted in reflex to snatch the paper from René and Quinsy's peeping eyes, trying to figure what on earth was on that paper to elicit such a reaction.

"Bluebells...It's you." I said, repeating my words, as if I were trying to reconfirm that it was quite classic of her to use flowers as a language.

"I can't decide if I should have opted this when I won the coin toss or bought popcorn instead of this damn instant coffee, to enjoy this properly." René smirked, her eyes widening dramatically in amusement, tilting her head sideways to get a better look at Hope's expressions, as the latter took back her diary.

"Hope Vale Fadel." She said introducing herself, her voice remaining sombre, giving small smiles to René and Quinsy before addressing me. *Hope Vale*, it was there all along used as a signature scrawled at the right corner of every page in a style that was significantly classic to her style: *Blue iris covered by a sheer veil* - Blue irises symbolising faith or Hope, to represent her first name and the veil used as a homophone for *Vale*. "I had an ulterior motive besides taking back my diary."

"You did, didn't you?" asked René, enjoying this way too much for anyone's logical comprehension "Tell me more?"

"Can I join your team?" Despite René being the one asking the question, I couldn't help but raise my eyebrows in bewilderment as Hope looked at me instead, as if I had asked the question instead. "If my diary can be considered as a preview into my concepts' portfolio?" Although René noticed this immediately, she seemed more entertained than offended, that she usually would have. *Why is she adding on to my confusion about this entire situation?*

"I thought you would never ask-" Before René could extend her hand towards Hope, to finalise our team, I pulled her by her elbow, dragging her back as she struggled, stumbling in her steps.

"What do you think you are doing?" I hissed, quietly trying to look back at Quinsy scratching the back of her neck awkwardly, trying to initiate small talks with Hope, as her expression fell trying to read our mouths. "I think you are taking your amusement in this way too-"

"We both know, I never settle for anything unless they are the best." René's expression swiftly became stiff, but her eyes became even brighter than before. "We had seriously considered really wanting to work with this person, if she ever crossed paths to claim back her diary."

"I know but-"

"She has walked right into our doorsteps. This opportunity is like a movie miracle. Besides your flustered state from her cryptic flowery note, that you certainly seem to have understood, do you have any objections working with her?" René asked firmly, as if it were paramount that I understand that she would regret being feeble about this, not letting me speak as I tried to deny the clear rising warmth of my cheeks, since Hope spoke about her habit of writing her initials as HP, using the ends of the curves of those letters to write *o* and *e*, respectively, and handing me the drawing. "We need a make-up artist to elevate our concepts to the top. You have said it yourself, 'her sense of individuality stands out well, yet blends well with our style as the chromes of the shadow palettes in her notes.'

"I am NOT flustered!…" My voice rose up immediately, to the point where Hope and Quinsy took a step towards us, worried. René smirked jubilantly, as I sighed, before waving at them with a forced smile to assure that they had nothing to worry about. "- No, I don't." I confirmed, knowing that there really was nothing to reconsider about when things were working for the best.

"There you go, was that so hard to admit?" René smiled smugly. I chuckled back at René, before walking back along with her, to agree with Hope's proposal that we would have raised nevertheless and welcome her to our team.

***

CHAPTER - IV

I wanted to say something, yet I knew that the anger I felt due to the unfairness of the situation was just a minuscule of the pain Jove must be feeling after the ignorance of the thirteenth network channel to offer false hope.

Despite, adapting to shift her dream from a field reporter to a news anchor, after her accident, to be practical to the excuses she would face to be turned down from her former dream, the interviewers never saw past the wheelchair and found it so carelessly easy to throw the scores of the past screening tests set before the final interview.

The last thing I wanted to do was say things that were merely dismissals disguised as ambiguous promises just to lighten the situation, to a person who didn't tolerate an ounce of the pretence of time fixing the future of reality or repeat things that she didn't already know.

In the current circumstances, it would come across as nothing but disrespecting her as if she hadn't considered the possibility of it, herself.

Why on earth did they care about a wheelchair, when she was applying for a desk anchor?

I had hoped that the call back to meet after the final screening of the last interview was the final call through to recruit her, especially after informing someone that they had scored the highest among all the applicants. I thought back to the sheer joy Jove finally relished in, after we celebrated to the end of the routine of sending resumes to as many 'Open Recruitments' as possible.

Even if it was the start of the rising pedestal of what she was capable of, I still wanted us to celebrate with our usual habit of buying each other the foods we would never get sick of- canned lychees and peanut pancakes or just commonly known as *Apam balik* in our native.

After that call from René, I had lost the right timing to grab the turnover pancakes filled with chocolate, which were Jove's favourites, and was slightly peeved to get the peanut butter ones available in the restaurant, only a couple of blocks away from Jove's Convenience store.

"I don't like the silence, Spes." I could see the near-imperceptible wince in Jove's eyebrows from the corners mirroring the monotone sharpness in her tone. Practically a violent flinch for the collected and reserved older.

Most often, I had developed a habit of walking a step behind, whenever Jove manoeuvred the wheels on her own, pushing the rims of the rear wheels, and grab onto the handles attached to the upper rear to push, just in case her hands got tired, as a signal.

Almost never, did Jove like the help of unwanted pushing unless she felt lost not having the will to do anything to cope with her situation, especially when we had to cross a rather steeper path on our way from the bus-stop to the Jove's family Convenience store, where she helped out by working as the cashier during my shift.

The breeze ruffling past us, feeling nothing but just like a cold reminder of the restless passage of sand through an hourglass, as we passed from neighbourhood and trees into more concrete surroundings and streetlights lighting up like the ends of gigantic fireflies, the final rays of the setting Sun flicking across the horizon, like throwing flakes of metal into flame and watching it spark.

Picking on the tone, Jove was merely holding back from venting as if she had a lot to say and just didn't know where to start.

Anger was the emotion that I was most familiar with, so over the past two years, it was no surprise we often got each other to talk regarding any hindrances we faced, by venting along with each other.

"I know, I don't either, but I don't think my vocabulary is rich enough to share my opinions regarding those orthodox aged-reptiles denying the desk-anchor to a person, who was the best fit for the position." I asked, voice heavy, level and flat as I stared back at the passerby walking past us eyeing the wheelchair with a heavy gaze. "I can't comprehend the meaning of *Open-recruitment* if they were going to let their pathetic biased-judgements get in the way."

"Exactly! Yeah, I can't *stand*, but I had applied for the position of a desk-anchor. The person *you* chose to hire isn't going to be doing much standing either." She muttered, huffing with something close to amusement, rolling her eyes. "The job literally demands their rears attached to a chair!"

"The fact that they were clearly aware of informing you of your scores and wanted to call you to turn you down to offer the position you clearly deserved, to someone who scored lower than you, is the very thing that infuriates me the most." My blood felt icy, realising the times we had to adapt to the resilience of forced acceptance of having to bite down from speaking back against the stereotypes that constantly fell across our path. Knowing the risks of jeopardising our dreams increased by folds if we choose to act on the anger, against adults who clearly baited us with the handling of the opportunity of our dreams. "They are so ignorant that they can't even realise that '*respectful call*' was barely cloaking their pitying excuses."

Despite knowing that several disguised opportunities were nothing more than baits, hope easily succumbed onto desperation to force ourselves to be silent among the yells. Apathetic among the anger. Still as a statue among the shoves. To keep going, and not letting them the satisfaction of robbing our will.

"Who the hell are they to *pity* me?"

"It's nothing but the manifestation of them pitying themselves to ease the guilt of their conscience, for pointless orthodox biasness." I muttered bitterly.

"One of them actually told me that *I had way too much potential to be stuck in a wheelchair.*"

"I never thought there could be anything more ignorant than the excuse they gave you during your interview in December - '*You are way too pretty to be in a wheelchair.*'"

"I really can't understand how my potential as a news anchor has anything to do with my wheelchair or how it figuratively *reduces* my potential." She asked, turning back her head, her eyes lost on the path that we had passed by, as her hand stilled searing against as I pushed the handle. "I get that for a rookie, I might have obstructed the confined paths through the cut-throat stampede while securing the finer details of the incidents first, among field-reporters of other channels." She made a helpless gesture with her other hand clutched tightly on her heels until her knuckles paled, as I pressed back on the hand atop mine, turning my palm upwards. "I adapted my dream according to my circumstances, but they are basically asking me to chop off my wings entirely."

"We are never going to let that happen. The more they hinder, the stronger you fight." I declared, feeling inadequate with just the comforting gesture of a reassuring hold or pat, that Jove preferred. "If anyone can conquer this, then it's gotta be you."

Stability was one of the rarer things in life that I sought, to fight against the unpredictable future. Most often, it was quite common to have people get tired by my mindset to blurt out - *I must live my life easier, to be so inflexible towards everything in my life.*

I can't comprehend living my life in a way where I constantly gave up whatever I wanted to seize, without any attempts, merely because of the inevitable hardships that it brought along. I just have to keep trying until I feel at my best trying to accomplish it.

Was I being shallow minded at lacking empathy towards people who gave up trying or never attempted to try enough to get what they want, guided by all the possible hardships it sprung forth?

Weren't they scared of the notion of giving up, too?

It was more futile to waste my breath explaining myself merely to accommodate to their standards. It was convenient to either keep my principles to myself or throw a clear line if they tried to force their fickleness to be adapted through the disguise of *easy-going*.

Yet, Jove had always been raw when it came to balancing between being practical and striving for the best through consistency, so we frequently liked to relish in the joy of meeting each other to finally get the chance to live through: treating people through the principle of '*reflection*'.

Even in our worse states of unintentional hostility around each other, we had several hours of conversation to be jarringly familiar with each other's boundaries to grasp on to the clarity that lightened up even the rather difficult topics, to always be the calming ground for the other and never getting enraged reflexively due to the atmosphere, knowing the frustration was never directed towards each other.

We never felt cautious enough to hide our words mid-away and even if we did, the other one caught on to the hesitation immediately.

So, it didn't come as a surprise as Jove serenely spoke about her ceaseless growth that pulls her through every possible outcome that would befall before she reached her success, she dreamed for each of her goals - *Isn't it important to just try?*

To keep trying at our own pace, without ever worrying about the limitations of being good or bad at the progression of our attempts?

Aren't we at our best while centering the only belief that should matter to us, towards ourselves: Believing in ourselves?

"I am tired of the constant rejections. I knew that, this wouldn't come easy-" Each word fell like rocks splashing in the water, rings of ripples running into each other, crossing paths, cutting each other off, creating a chaotic symphony that made our ears ring. I wanted to assure that it was humane for the batteries of our ambition to get tired from time to time and felt slightly glad that Jove was speaking her mind instead of pretending to hide her true feelings, yet I felt angry at the reality for setting its loophole on a person who had always been so authentic. "-...I was prepared for this rigorous lane, so I don't know why it's still getting to me."

As soon as Jove's hands reached over to grasp the rears of the wheels of the wheelchair, my hands immediately left the handles, knowing that it was her way of indicating that we had crossed over the uphill portion of the path.

Jove chuckled with a broken laugh, as I stepped towards her left, when she chided me fondly to walk beside her and not behind her, preferring to be outside of the sidewalk.

"Because you should have already gotten that position by now, and you were robbed away from it merely out of complete injustice." I ground out, still trying to even out my breaths to prevent gritting my teeth leeringly, at the sheer brutality of the prolonging loophole of hurdles set by the prejudices of the interviewers.

We had met each other at our lowest points of trust towards the outer world, yet the bitterness towards the anger we had towards the past, never clashed.... For neither of us ever fumbled with the need to even rush through the security of the trust of the bond, letting time plays its role in assuring the genuineness of our words and actions.

"I feel tired of wondering when it won't be snatched away once again, especially when I come close to finally having my dream." Jove sighed playing with the ends of her long wavy hair impassively as if it were paramount that I understood that she was merely taking her moment to recharge her battery of sedulous ambition, that we were both familiar with.

"Do you remember when we created that mail during that time when the slow progression of physical therapies got to me..." I nodded my head in acknowledgement.

"Of course, how could I forget the amount of times I had assure you that this is okay." I chuckled as she shook her head, scoffing at my dramatics.

Remembering the times, Jove refused my first attempts to accompany her to attend the sessions that could change the only aspect that the interviewers constantly looked down upon. Until Jove made it her priority to have the aspect they looked down upon, be a part of her identity. "I didn't wish to try, because I knew the plausibility of the outcomes ending up like this were much higher, but I found it easier to fight the lower plausibility when you came up with the proposal of creating a new email for me for sending in my resume and applications using that mail." Her expression was distantly slack as she pinched the long bridge of her nose. "So that you would monitor and act as a filter only to the mails that have accepted me for the second screening."

"That system worked well, didn't it? I am not going to ever admit defeat to the hurdles of the harsh reality and am going to keep trying until I get what I want." I huffed with slight joy.

"Absolutely, I might have gotten more furious actually going all through the mails, even the ones that turned me down, without-" Knowing Jove, it wasn't much of a gander to interrupt her before she dared to sell herself short in the name of gratitude, as if she wouldn't have done the same by herself, sooner or later.

"No matter how much we are prepared, sometimes the negative outcomes of our attempts make us doubt-" I said, carefully. Despite everything, I didn't want to lie. I couldn't even sugarcoat my words to save my own forsaken life, if I ever tried to. "-whether we should keep going with the plausibility that this might occur several times more."

"One of the first values we shared was directing all our ambition towards our dreams." Jove chuckled, her smile growing as I beamed with pride at the notion of the shared prospect between us. "And the thing that surprises me to this date is - you have that ambition for supporting the dreams of other people, even if they are someone you care for. We both know that's hard to come by."

It's true that we can get good at being alone, and find out happiness through that but is there ever a limit to happiness?

Why not take that limit for a possibility, when things get better when we have someone to share with?

Yet, the bitter reality was that jealousy tended to bind from people whom we least expected to rise from, and what starts as negligence towards the shared happiness ends up developing into something more vicious as sabotaging the very same happiness, without hesitance.

"There should be no limits to our dreams, even our attempts to seize them." It was quite habitual for me to vocalise things that I ceaselessly believed in, especially around Jove, without any care worrying about how my words may sound… for I knew my words weren't wasted in the flow of noise in air but rather resonated along. Perhaps, we all ended up questioning the purpose of our lives at several points in our lives, yet we all ended up being most protective of that very purpose, once we became certain of them. The more protective we became, the more ambitious we became to fight the doubts that were unyieldingly humane to question our choice and efforts, from time to time. "During our doubts through our rough times, it's natural to influence each other with that reminder. *Safety Net*, remember?"

Life is short, and if we could help it, wasn't it better to prioritise our time to our dreams?

With all the unpredictable hindrances that were bound to come by, wasn't it better to stay by those who never succumbed to excuses of undermining that very purpose?

Didn't we owe it to our dream to not abandon them to remain stagnant in our imagination? Didn't that account for negligence as well?

"You are my guardian angel."

"No, I am the righteous spawn of Satan." I grinned widely, winking cheekily. Jove snickered at my antics, the atmosphere that odd mixture of heavy-light. "I am gonna direct this anger to send your resume to more channels."

"I don't like the sound of that."

"What? It's better than directing my anger by marching off to give my opinions to certain *reprehensible* people." I assured her, as Jove stopped again to look at me like I was crazy.

"I wouldn't be against that and you know very well that,-" she muttered, as I winked at her for swinging along with my neglected direction of irateness. "That's not what I meant."

"If I knew, I would put more effort into the dramatics of faking to be surprised!" I scoffed. "Instead of actually being clueless."

"You are going to do that while sacrificing your sleep, won't you?" Jove rolled her eyes, pointing the sharper end of her heels as I raised my hands in mock-surrender. "Nope, I won't let you."

"What?! NO! You know I am only going to do it when I am free!" I defended, when Jove zeroed her eyes further, the higher arches of her eyebrows squinting towards the rather higher bridge of her nose, not taking me for my words.

"Exactly! You describe sleep as '*boring*' and that's just your way of calling it as free time and not important in any accords." Jove noted, the normalcy not quite forced. cracked a smile, but the base heaviness didn't wear away.

"Fine, I will send it during my shift in the store, during the times there are no customers. I will use those breaks well." I sighed, voice rising in urgency at Jove's unamused glare.

"With you, you will find some way to not stop for a second during an activity that you promised me to give you so that you could use to relax."

"You have known me long enough to know that you can't change my mind." I shrugged, as I walked behind Jove, opening the lock of the doors of the store and snatching canned lychees from the aisle to toss back at me.

"So, we are just going to ignore that you have been dodging my question since you picked me up at the bus-stop?" Jove asked, smacking my arm when I rushed to put the can on my tab, as she pressed further about the absent look when she asked me about my day.

I really didn't know how to answer that or rather sum it up accurately, besides coming up with the closest answer - "Quite unpredictable…"

Yet, the weighing impact that reared its variable claws of consequences along with its challenges didn't sprout from the Chancellor's strike to pull out the fundings for our exhibition.

I had considered it as one of the worst consequences we could face in retaliation, only as a last resort... Not wanting to dwell in the troubles of an '*if*' that demanded more dejected worries than the drive to just focus on the only thing we were supposed to care about - creation.

"Without that PR, the interview that *You* significantly threw-" All I could hope for in that very moment is - if the decision to keep this between me and René didn't cause a counter-reaction that caused more harm to the team. "-that could have gotten you the budget for the scale of the exhibition you both are demanding. My hands are tied."

"How is that possible? Earlier there was *enough* budget to fund both of our exhibitions separately-" René snapped, seething and cracking.

"Lemme phrase it this way, everything comes at a price and *this* is the cost of your pride." As she scoffed, completely disregarding us, I knew this wasn't a matter of getting back at us or even the excuse of the *budget* as she claimed. This was her way of putting us down for not following her words, mindlessly, much less put her in a position where she had to end up apologising to someone, that was meant to boost her rep. "I am your teacher and it's about time someone taught you manners and made you face the consequences, when you don't follow them."

"So, you are willing to jeopardise our careers to prove your point?" I demanded, as if it would make any difference

"Precisely, you need to learn to have a good character, first." It was a firm conclusion, that spoke of the full volumes of bindings that we were in, once again.

What you can't see past as our pride, is actually protectiveness of humility and devotion to our creativity, and we aren't going to sacrifice that when things get hard for us.

Despite the bait, she threw at René to push her limits and face how much worse it could get for us if René decided to use her own funds.

I was glad that René grumbled in annoyance yet agreed to try seeking our only chance of approaching every single curator and established artist or fund-raiser invested in art, possible to get the funds we needed.

It was the only way, where she wouldn't find another excuse to obstruct us.

We had to get approval from the source, the very same source that funded the exhibitions for the school.

Except we had to be prepared for the obvious declines that will come along our way, for the sheer doubts of approaching them without the middle messenger - the school.

Getting a head start on the list of the curators and fund-raisers, we could attend to get our fundings, from Mrs. Bronywyn after our Art History class ended up being a good neutraliser for the hindrances materialised upon us. Her encouraging support to gain an upper hand against *people who dared undermine the spectrum of art-* was a perfect boost for self-esteem.

Borrowing the Thoth tarot decks painted by Lady Frieda, from Mrs. Bronywyn helped to have an easier access of reference for chiselling on to the natural leather of the obi belts.

Among the four of us, Hope was the only one fluently knowledgeable of the graphic vitality of the symbolism cemented on to the arts portrayed through the Major Arcana cards of the deck, most specifically the final card - *the World.*

I really couldn't understand this person, who didn't mind getting lost in conversations of the insight into the optimistic view of the future, to explore the unknown and look inside ourselves through the esoteric dimensions of the divinatory arts celebrated in the designs accentuated in the peculiarity of the Tarots of Marseille and its cardinal virtues.

Most specifically that of *Fortitude* and *Prudence.* Over the past three weeks, it had become a habit to just throw over the belt over my shirt, and work on excavating and sculpting the leather to obtain a 3D impression, whenever and wherever it was convenient.

Yet, the most unpredictable moment I had to live through was realising the accuracy of Quinsy's words - *You two are quite similar in several ways. Have you realised that the only person she isn't severely uptight around among the three of us, is you?*

Despite my strong denial, to ceaselessly believe that it was merely due to the lingering gratitude for holding to her missing diary. Even if I couldn't comprehend the reason behind it, I got peeved whenever she thanked me for keeping her diary, from time to time...

She had absolutely no reason to thank me.

I wasn't certain about Quinsy's words, for all I cared about was that Hope was fitting in well with the team and didn't feel out of place, to speak her mind and work in her comfort zone.

It had almost become habitual to hide a triumphant smile when Hope defended my favoured beverage choice against René and Quinsy's teasings, as I merely stood behind with a smug smirk making faces at their betrayed looks, to egg them further.

"Okay preferences, priorities set or open to change?" Hope asked, after choosing the coconut drink to prove her point against René and Quinsy's snickering.

"Priorities set", I said, merely using the straw to pierce the tetra-pack, before leaning back to throw it inside the trash can behind me. Merely raising my eyebrows, to ask her choice regarding the same.

"Priorities may change." Hope said, still laughing quietly, almost demurely. "You go ahead..."

"I am pretty much an unsupervised *infant* at this, I don't think it's the best idea to let me decide." I shrugged, rechecking her proposal to work on the final step of waxing the belt to colour it after I finish chiselling in the artisanal effects of the guided layout on it.

"Chicken." Hope chuckled, shaking her head good-naturedly before assuring that she wouldn't have proposed something that she couldn't handle.

"Very mature." I chided, before rolling my eyes fondly as Hope sighed dramatically.

"Alright, the most treasured value you seek to maintain in any relationship?"

"Respect." I nodded, before angling back my hand to throw the tetra-pack in the trash-can and getting back to chiselling the belt as Hope got back to sketching on her sheet, using the familiar dry pastels.

René sent me a side look, asking if I was in the same state as her, trying to dodge Quinsy's glare that did not buy our made-up answers regarding Vice-Chancellor having nothing important to say to us.

"Love." A weak smile flitted over her lower jaw, as I forced my tongue to unglue itself from the roof of my mouth, not quite surprised with her choice. *Hope was quite jarringly optimistic when it came to people.* "Wait respect?"

"Yeah, basic foundation." I said, offering my hand to throw away the finished drink in her hand. "I don't think there can be any complete truth on your positive feelings regarding any person if you take them for granted."

Hope's jaw tightened immediately, something in her eyes shifting. I realised the impact of my words, a second later, yet I had nothing to offer to shift my words.

How could I?

When I didn't believe otherwise?

"Spes, maybe you can convince her to stop working in the studio and stop cutting down on our time together." It was the way one of them said it, that irked me, while waiting for Hope to pack up and pass the invite along to me.

I merely glanced back at Hope, waiting for her response. But she smiled sheepishly despite her fists tightening near her sides.

"Why on earth should I or anyone convince her to stop doing something that gives her joy?" I asked, narrowing my eyes as their laughings died down to awkward chuckles.

"It's just a joke. But as her friends who have known her longer, we are just worried." One of them defended condescendingly as if I had slapped her instead.

"I never knew demotivating someone was a method of showcasing concern." I scoffed.

"We just don't want her wasting her efforts in vain, especially in a place that is prejudiced to someone with her kind of looks." They continued as if Hope was standing right in front of them. "We are just being protective and practical."

Her kind of looks?!

Before one of them could take a seat near Hope packing her pastels, I kicked the leg of the red-cushioned chair, watching it tumble over. I stared at them with a deadpanned look, challenging them to pick up the chair, as I threw my legs over the upturned chair.

"If you know it's hard for me, then you could just cheer me about it instead of making me feel worse about it." Hope teased, laughing forcibly.

"We just miss you. We are just worried you are spending less time with us only to work in a judgemental, stressful environment." If they seemed taken aback by her words, they made a poor attempt of concealing it by joining in the laughter. Just as poorly as my attempt to bite back my smile at Hope's words.

"Don't worry, I can handle myself."

It was quite bothersome, yet I had no place to say so. Hope was unexplainably forgiving to the neglected ignorance of several familiar faces around her.

People that made no attempts to right their ways of blatantly undermining her fierce desire to speak about the poisonous treachery of platoons of businesses pushing on the agenda of the *'preferred beauty standards'* through their *whitening* products.

That nobility of hers, felt like watching her being shouldered with an unnecessary weightage, when she forced herself to smile back, at their jeering routine of jokes that reduced her vision of using that motive to create her own line, as an *overreaction* to dealing with the prejudice she faced because of her skin tones.

I made no attempts of hiding my sour expression whenever they came near our space of working.

Neither did I hesitate fist-bumping René, with a satisfied smirk as they begrudgingly asked Hope if I struggled in tolerating their guts. *Well, they were finally right about something.*

People always confuse equality over colour being the morality and judgment of seeking the notion of the statement: '*Colour shouldn't matter*' especially by the people who were privileged by colour that had been favoured by the orthodox beauty standards of the society for ages.

So, it's important to speak out and destroy that notion, to remind people that '*Colour does matter*', and every colour should be acknowledged and accepted as well as the years of their fight and struggle to reach their self-love and self-appreciation in their skin, worth and the world around us, that had been disregarded and tarnished by our society for several eras.

"You know, you make it really hard to disagree with the logic behind your values." Hope finally said, humming with affirmation and nodding with finality, as I furrowed my eyebrows to wonder when I had ever bothered convincing people, much less be good at it. She merely shook her head gently, as if she were stunned. "Okay, choice of your lack in compromise- Productivity or Routine?"

"Productivity."

"Me too!" Hope laughed airly, so ecstatically, that I couldn't help but drop the cutter on the belt, before pressing the heels of my palms against the side of my temple and chuckling along with her. "Hey, it's the first time we didn't pick opposite teams."

"Alright, your first red flag on a value you can't compromise?" I asked quickly, as René and Quinsy paused from photographing the final selection of fabrics for our brand, shaking my hands sharply to assure that we weren't laughing out of misguided clownery. "Honesty or Consideration?"

"That's a tough one…" Hope admitted, before murmuring her answer, choosing between the two choices. "Consideration."

I couldn't help but stare. I paused, Hope's smile fading at my sudden stillness.

"Yeah, although I would prefer both in balance aiding each other." I hesitated, wondering if this was way too out of the blue, yet I found myself admitting the same, pleasantly startled by finding myself wanting the same. "If I had to choose then it would be… Consideration, too."

"Rationalise or Understand?"

"Understand."

"Really?" Hope asked, even more, confused than she had ever been.

I raised my eyebrows at her, merely resonating the confusion back at her surprised stance that I failed to share before she swiftly started rambling off a string of apologies that she wasn't presuming anything based on the supposed *image* she had overheard.

Her eyes glued to the tips of her shoes as she tried to explain the intention of her question was more out of genuine curiosity while trying to scold herself for making things uncomfortable.

I felt slightly guilty for trying to hold back my laughter at her state. She was clearly embarrassed already and letting her continue would probably only make it worse.

"It's just that merely rationalising is like undermining the feelings of a person, and their worth unintentionally." I said, cutting her off before she continued explaining herself when she had nothing to apologise for. "It's their life, their experience. I don't have the right to rationalise my opinions over what they have lived through." I knew that I had to choose my words carefully, as I offered a small smile while twiddling my fingers together.

"Exactly! Spare me the rationality, to dictate logic over *my* life as if I am incapable of it." Hope beamed energetically. Maybe she was the type of person who had an infectious laughter. I couldn't help but chuckle fondly, as the edges of her eyes crinkled. "I hate that, they don't pause to consider the rarity of people living through similar experiences yet not winding up with the exact same thoughts and feelings. It impacts differently, but they don't pause to consider the-"

I found it amusing that it didn't seem to fade, even when she seemed slightly dejected with herself much like a child in a dilemma while choosing their favourite ice-cream flavour, as she struggled to find the right words.

"-Difference in Individuality." I offered, angling my head down towards my feet much like Hope's was, earlier, and shifting the belt to a different angle, to chisel the remaining portion, after drawing the next guided layout on top. Before I could pick up my pencil, Hope snapped her fingers in agreement.

"Fancy words, but perfectly fitting." She teased, before picking up her brush to even the shadings.

"That's not *fancy*!" I scoffed, rolling my eyes at her as she waved her hands in disagreement.

"Understanding requires patience while rationalising my opinions over someone else is like jumping to conclusions" Hope said, dusting her hands on her hands as she tried to get a better look at the progress of her work. "-...More along the lines of a dismissal." Even if I wanted to inquire further about the weight of her latter words mirroring her defeated look, I knew that I had no right to ask without possibly crossing boundaries.

I had to bite down from asking anything that was directed by an unexplained glower towards those who had dismissed her.

I barely knew her, why on earth am I bothered about what might have happened?

Maybe, it was my general hatred towards insufferable ignorants.

"As if it's an equation instead of an actual living human's experience and their feelings." I gritted my teeth even further, as she nodded her head with a surprised sigh as if I had said something that made sense that she wasn't used to hearing.

I fail to understand why those undeserving reprehensible reptiles couldn't see past their self-absorbed opinions to jump onto rationalising over someone else's feelings as if they were the ones to live through it.

"Alright, now you are a *supervised* infant." Hope asked, clearly to change the tone of the atmosphere. As she puffed out cheeks and forced a smile to drive away from the silence. I didn't even try to press any further, on the sudden change in her expressions. "So, try."

"They are equally helpless." I said with a pointed look, as I switched to a softer pencil, and looked over to the tarots, to recheck the design of the gothic thrones drawn on the background, for reference. "Supervised or unsupervised, hence the term: infant-"

"Stop yapping and ask the damn question." My eyes widened at her remark, as she hit my shoulder to hurry up with the question.

Her eyebrows had the finely detailed slit across them, for today. A detail that I hadn't noticed before.

Or vocalise my appreciation for the lethal finesse of the sequined finer crystals placed over the slit, yet.

When I did, I couldn't help but flash a betrayed look for getting hit over my shoulder, once again as Hope rushed through her repeating her words to remind me to ask the question.

"Sequins or Stripes?"

"Probably Sequins." She quipped, brows drawn down, before quietly asking me to state my preference between the two.

"Stripes"

"Pastel or Jewel Palette?"

"That's a tough one, I like both but if I had to choose, I would go with Jewel." I paused, contemplating between the two for a while.

"Really? I would be biased to incline towards Pastels."

"Talk to a stranger you may never cross paths with again or talk to a friend in collapsing ambiguous terms?"

"The stranger is going to listen to me, right?" The moment she pressed further, I sighed with disdain, for not thinking through the random question that I had thrown.

"It's a stranger, I can't provide credibility for their reactions." I shrugged, not comprehending how the specifics mattered until I looked over at Hope who was contemplating this, quite seriously. "But yeah, let's say that they nod along out of civility regardless of the fact if they are truly listening or not." I added cautiously, despite not understanding the plausibility of needing the specifics of a choice that wasn't going to be chosen. I couldn't have been any more wrong.

"Still, my answer would still be the same: talk to a stranger." Hope decided, as I stopped working completely to check if she had sprouted another head. "In fact, one of my best memories is from conversing with a stranger in the local aquaria behind the Gombak river. Collapsing terms is pretty much worse than an enemy." It seemed as if she read my disbelief radiating, as she closed her sketch-pad in amusement to take her time to break down her perspective somehow knowing that I needed more time to wrap my head around it.

"I don't know whether to be surprised or concerned that you didn't walk away much less talk with this stranger who might as well have been lurking." I teased, doing the only thing I could do to press further when I actually respected to consider the other's perspective.

Looking back, maybe I really wanted to pull all the cords in my mind to not believe in the possibility of that coincidental encounter.

"No, it's not like that. Actually, I interrupted this person accidentally." Hope said with the most bored expression of disbelief.

"So, you were the lurker in this scenario?" I asked her with a cheeky smile to egg her further.

"Would you stop saying that?" Hope complained, trying to hold back her laughter, as she tried to kick me under the table. "No one was lurking. In fact, neither of us got a chance to look at each other."

"Why? Were you roped into an intricate game of hide-and-seek?" I pressed further, pursuing my lips onto an exaggerated downward slant as Hope looked around with an unamused expression, for the nearest object that she could use to throw at me. "Okay okay, I will stop teasing, go ahead." I chuckled, raising my hands in mock surrender, as her gaze locked onto the cover of Quinsy's new camera strap.

Yeah, I was definitely gonna get hit by Quinsy again, if she knew that something that protected her most treasured possession was used as a weapon.

"No, it was quite dark. But it wasn't that-"

"I don't know Hope, this pretty much borderlines into the weirdness of lurking…" I don't know why I was being silly enough to dilly-dally the flow of a conversation by constant teasing without any concrete purpose.

"I am going to beat you up with the cans of one of those canned lychees you eat if you don't shut up."

Hope said with a side smirk, as I pushed my chair back to howl in laughter to not disturb the progress on the chiselling, as I heard René tell Quinsy to capture the hyena-impression that was impossibly rare to ever occur again, ignoring my profanities thrown at her in retaliation as she walked over to confirm with the next fabric pattern they had finalised with the concept. "I mean I don't know how to explain it,…it was just that easy, and coincidentally they knew a lot about art and about that place…"

"Was it the Tour Guide?" I asked half-heartedly after we confirmed the pattern while René patted my shoulders good-naturedly and headed back towards noting down the details with Quinsy.

"Maybe? I just know that we were both in our bubbles of safe havens at this place and yet could exist harmoniously."

"How many times have you crossed paths with this lurking tour guide?"

"Once, around the end of last month." Hope rolled her eyes sarcastically, as I refused to correct my description regarding the person, she had crossed paths with, in the aquaria.

Like I said, it could be nothing but a coincidence.

"Last month?" I asked, repeating the words while choking on my own saliva.

Mere Coincidence!

"I guess I can't completely abide by my choice 'cause I would do anything to cross paths with them again."

"*Anything* is a pretty huge territory, Hope." I chided jokingly, as Hope flipped through her pad, to finish her sketch.

"I know that I can't explain it right, but that kind of rare special is sorta unexplainable." Hope muttered with an unexplainable expression, and it most definitively had to be the most confusing words I had ever come across. "Hey, you never told me what choice you would pick?"

"Neither." I scoffed cringing my face in dismay, as Hope burst out in laughter, slapping her leg in an attempt to catch her breath. "I would rather bet on hell freezing over."

"You lose! You know you kinda dug your own grave on this one." I looked over at her in concern before whipping back my extended hand in shock, as she pumped her fists in the air, with victory for the twelfth time in a row.

"I know." I shook my head up and down looking over at an excited Hope who was jumping like an excited puppy. "Alright, so are going to tab this wish too and use a grant now?"

"Tab." Hope confirmed, with a rise in her voice. "I am not going to play my cards that early."

"You are something else." I admitted with a tiny smile.

Perhaps in retrospective, I knew that I was directing my anger at the faces, towards Hope.

Why was I bothered that they had no right over to interfere to proclaim my evidently distasteful yet brutally honest opinions regarding their undeserving habitual jokes to mock Hope as if it's nuisance to hear about someone talking about their passion and looking at their life through that prospective? I had to remind myself:

You barely know her or her dynamic with them.

It's not my place to bother to understand her compassion towards people who chose to reduce Hope's excitement to use her first pay from working over a month at the make-up studio, to buy essential oils onto just working at an oil mine.

I failed to see the amusement in those apparent jokes.

"Sure, what is it?" I asked, as Hope coughed like she was ready to start a presentation as she stepped forward. She waited anxiously, while I rechecked packing all my belongings onto my bag and merely keeping my AP Statistics Practice Questionnaire book outside, to get some questions done while waiting for Pax before we could head-down home, together. I only had two more days before the commencement of my last AP exam. "I can stay after-hours to speak through whatever you have in mind for the symbolism you wanna play using our finalised concept."

"No no, it's not important…"

"It is important." I insisted, assuring that every single detail about bouncing rough thoughts to build every concrete concept that would bring us closer to framing the title of the main agenda, besides just winging on to *'The Unscripted Storyboard'*, for now.

"That's not what I meant, it's not regarding the exhibition. I was wondering if you had time to hang out-"

"Sorry, I can't make time for that, today." I declined immediately. I didn't hold back my resentment, when they tried to reassure Hope with blithe that they would extend their courtesy and get used to my grumpiness over time just like they *tolerate* Hope's quirks.

Neither did I hold back my smugness at their chagrined scowl at my words directed at them.

I was truly trying my best to frame my words as kindly as I possibly could, and I most certainly did a great job at that if I could say so myself: '*Being kind and being civil are two different perspectives. Don't offer false hope to them if you can't be accountable to your own tolerance of patience or the hard times of their resistance against accepting you, instantly. Not everything revolves around pleasing your timing.*'

"Oh, that's alright-"

"So lemme know about the choices of your colour palettes based on the concepts we have narrowed down to…" I forced a smile at her, trying not to glare back at the offending looks of the faces behind her. I barely knew her, there was absolutely no reason to be bothered by this, by investing more time with her than required. "And if you find one that fits the best and we will improve the concept further around that." I wasn't going to push my limits by holding back my words by getting attached.

***

It was after two whole weeks, when Hope proposed the same ordeal once again right before the mid-year break at the end of May, after René and I tried to sneak in another toss between the two of us, to split yet another ordeal.

At the current rate, of the continuous streak of rejects we had received in managing to secure the funds of the final screening of our exhibition, we ended up satisfied up with the bargain each of us got stuck with.

It wasn't much of a shocker when they instantly switched from being vibrantly enthusiastic to being less than thrilled to fund for an exhibition held on school grounds, outside the payments to the school trust fund. Neither were their derisive looks that spilled to ask *as if we were outlaws smuggling something notoriously illegal* when we explained our proposal.

René merely shrugged nonchalantly as if she hadn't wanted to handle presenting the proposals to get the funds from the fund-raisers and curators, -*who thankfully happened to be*- present in the Galas she had to attend with her family, nevertheless. While I sighed with relief, that we didn't have a repeat in the excuse of choosing the outcomes among the best of three, to handle meeting curators and artists in their studios.

Sometimes, I wonder why René and I couldn't just stick to choosing what we wanted from the start instead of teasing others to be stuck with a choice we didn't wanna end up with. Quinsy had a self-declared *stolid* explanation for it - *'You two are obnoxiously stubborn to tease each other like normal 18-year olds, so you handle it by pretending to be 80-year olds.'*

"Sure, if it's important I will certainly make time for it." Even if I knew where it might head, I was hoping that it had to do something more about the market research on helping her set the look for the denim-inspired Victorian street jackets, we were still tweaking.

Things had gotten back to the usual, since the last time, she had asked the very same question. When Hope pretended that the incident hadn't occurred between us, I jumped at the chance to merely go along with it.

"Oh no no, it's nothing like that." Hope's voice was small and inscrutably bleak, but it was enough to silence the space around me. "It's to just hang out if you have time." She added hurriedly, fingers twisting.

"No as in *'it's not important'*? Or no as in *'there is no particular reason for your proposal'*?"

"You need a particular reason to relax and hang-" I grit my teeth since the moment I could recognise the hurt in Hope's tone. She sounded like a wounded puppy and I couldn't even bring my eyes up to look at her when I cut her off mid-sentence.

"Yes, I do."

"You don't like to converse without a purpose?" She demanded lowly. My eyes shot up at her expressions drawn into an almost quiet dour. Perhaps it was at this moment, I felt more at ease at seeing Hope not trying to swallow down her true feelings behind the facade to be unapologetically forgiving towards everyone over her own feelings. "Do you plan every single breath of your life?"

"No, I hate small talks and I would like to prevent that as much as possible." I snapped clicking my tongue in mockery, not bothering with any courtesy I had been holding onto for the past weeks. "I don't know you well enough to engage in a conversation with you without a purpose or topic to drive it outside these premises, so the only plausible conclusion would be tolerating unnecessary awkward small talks to fill the space."

"Have you wondered that you wouldn't actually get to know a person, without sparing a chance to speak to them?" Hope pressed, with a crestfallen expression. I really wanted to end this conversation before I asked things, that merely crawled up as nothing but interference as if I had learnt nothing from my past.

"This is exactly what I hate tolerating."

"Because it's absolutely bonkers for a person to even consider the possibility that we could be friends-" Hope finally asked bitterly- voice more serious than I had ever heard it. "-and get to know each other when we have a similar frequency mindset while working through the concept and click well while working together?"

I knew that everyone had a different perspective of living through their choices, at different wavelengths. Different things held meaning for them. Different things were important. Yet, I didn't know why I was being so reactive to this.

"Why are you so hell-bent on wanting to be anywhere near my vicinity when we are not working, especially when I have been nothing but a jerk to you?" I asked firmly. I didn't know why I was pushing my limits to throw away her consideration for others over herself.

I hated every single minute of it being taken for granted and I was trying everything to distance myself away from to stop getting bothered by it, yet she was being frustratingly persistent to let it go.

The more I saw the repeated instances of the feigned ignorance of those so-called friends dismissing the real turmoils of insults Hope often faced under a regular basis for her looks or her personal choices, under the disguise of jokes, the more I annoyed I got.

I was barely holding back and stopping myself from barging through someone else's boundaries and interfering disrespectfully.

There was a stark difference between someone burying their inner-self to stand up for themselves and jarringly sliding things forcibly on the account of familiarity out of consideration due to their hearts of gold.

I had seen Hope charmingly set people onto their rightful places if they barked their pointless opinions advising her on how to live *her life*.

I had enjoyed those moments way too smugly with unexplainable pride, to recognise when her forgiving nature was being sacrificed over her own self.

"Your tone seems to say otherwise. I am not trying to crowd you. I just assumed from our conversations during lunch that we clicked, and I know it's just in my head, but the only reason-" Hope snapped pointedly, slowly. Her gaze was sharper than ever. "I have tried to ask again pushing past the way you basically spit down on my proposals, is because I didn't want to regret that I hadn't tried hard enough."

"Why?" I demanded "Why are you even trying?"

"Trust me your warm-and-cold personality kicks me enough." I stared at her with eyes that held that same pain I couldn't spare her but dyed a rainbow of every other emotion that tormented me.

"That's why I am sparing your time-" I snapped blithely. "-from wasting your efforts being around my vicinity further than work related to the exhibition."

"Sparing me? What do you think you are-"

"Definitely not someone worth knowing personally." I said, obtusely.

"Shouldn't I get to decide that-"

"Do you actually buy their excuses?" I asked, grimacing immediately with fists curling tightly around the spine of my Art history book, for letting the words slip by.

"W-What?" Hope asked clearly startled and blinked furtively, giving away that she was well aware of the identities of the people I was referring to.

"I get the part of forgiving and perhaps forgetting to get closure to move past it." I said, hesitantly. "But *you* - You go *beyond* to actually do everything to ease their guilt, at the cost of sacrificing *your* own feelings even when they take your compassion for granted!"

"People make mistakes, and there must be pain hidden behind their facades-" Hope said, almost desperately as her shoulders slumped down even further than the last second.

"I am not trying to vilify them…but their flippant negligence isn't something that needs to be sympathised on the account of their pain." I sighed in annoyance, pinching the bridge of my nose to breathe evenly. "It becomes nothing but a sob story if they use it as an excuse to hurt someone repeatedly with their ignorance."

"Because I know what it feels like to not have anyone by your side when you are at your worst and just need the solace of someone-" It was the first time I had seen Hope snap without holding back her raw self, her shoulders rose as if to violently shove back the anger that tried to rise.

"Nothing is worth sacrificing yourself to the point, where you are constantly taken for granted." I said passively, cutting her off mid-sentence, once again. "You don't use your vulnerability as an excuse to dismiss others."

"So, you want me to get even, and stoop down to their level?" Hope actually snorted, chuckling in mockery with a slack expression. "Be vengeful because they don't respect my dreams, and get back at them by mocking theirs?"

"No, but you don't deserve the mockery of your dreams, any more than constantly tolerating this ignorance disguised as jokes, no matter who they might be." I said, thickly.

As soon as Hope's expression into something less defensive, I looked away doing nothing at the growing distance that was bound to concentrate due to my stupid ego that was earnestly brewing pointlessly out of fear that I couldn't recognise.

"Congratulations…You were right all along. *We* don't know each other well enough for you to decide how I should invest my efforts." As Hope sighed quietly glowering and drawing her arms closer to herself, I knew that I was stone-walling someone under the failed attempts of convincing myself that *People come and People go.* "If I can do anything to just be there for someone without judging them… to give them a chance- a space to trust to be honest outside their facade- their pain, then I am going to try. No matter who they might be. Everybody deserves that. It's humanity."

Anything I could say or rather phrase my words accordingly to ensure that I was bothered to be tempted to make the same mistake of interfering ever again.

"No that's not humanity, that's a sacrifice." I said, mercilessly ignoring the unsettling sickening feelings seeping in my guts, as her head weighed low dolefully with finality. This was just too different. "Because you are willingly throwing away the plausibility of the very first person who *deserves* that - *yourself.*"

There were *several* words I wanted to say. Several *more.* Yet I couldn't decide if it had been right to hold them back or worse:

—*Even if you feel like you don't owe them your compassion, yet choose to do so, you owe yourself that very compassion instead of taking yourself for granted.*

Everything associated with humans is limited, someone is bound to end up taken for granted.

And in this case- it's you,Hope.

I am not denying the plausibility of often blurring the lines of modesty and selling ourselves short, more frequently than we would like to admit. But *'this'-*

I don't want to be bothered by the fact that I have never seen anyone take this notion to a new height.

Even hours later, I was distracted throughout my attempts to begin my negative space assignment, sitting in front of a canvas with black paint dripping from my brush. I was too distracted to be creative and I began placing semi-random strokes, trying to figure out what shape I wanted to go for.

As much as I would like to believe that it's my unceasing adamance to finish working on any piece, I start. It's nothing more than just a fancy make-believe.

I can't disagree with the fact that the only reason, I don't actually tear down the canvases mid-way during my frequent panics of fretting over ruining my paintings might actually because of Ma. Her constant threats to disown me and whacking me behind my head if I ever followed through my distressed thoughts.

That woman would be practically dozing off near me while I am working on my paintings, yet she doesn't hesitate to glare daggers at me whenever I consider if the progress has ruined the painting.

"So, I am supposed to ignore that the person who lets their skin -that is- sensitive enough to tear with the repeated use of varnish to clean clay and paint on their hands, due to their hatred of oil-" I knew Pax was up to no good, as she placed the blanket over Ma who had dozed off on my bed. I could practically feel the tease in her voice, as I held the brush idly waiting for her next words. "-is suddenly applying hand cream and finally getting rid of their habit of making their hands pruny under running water?"

I immediately shoved the hand cream among my paint-tubes, sighing heavily remembering the words of the person who had given it to me.

-

"Spes, do you know about grapefruit essential oil?" I felt the lead of the pencil scratch against the canvas- a dark streak of pencil streaking its way through the pristine sketch, as I nodded my head slowly in response to Hope's question.

"I do." I said, informing her that my mere knowledge regarding the subject was because of her. "It's one of the essential oils you wish to buy with your first pay from the make-up studio."

In a way, we were lucky that they hadn't cut down our access to use the materials needed for presenting our exhibition, yet the absence of René and Quinsy was certainly felt during their trip to capture photos in the vice of symbolism from daily life, portraying the concept of the brand of the outfits.

"I got my first pay…"

"Seriously, why on earth aren't we celebrating this?" I made no attempts to hide my excitement, almost bouncing on the balls of my feet, as Hope's eyes practically sparkled with near amusement and delight.

"It's not a big deal-"

"Yeah, I am neither letting you finish that sentence and nor are you going to stop letting me buy the laksa you like."

"Alright, I will accept it." Hope smiled warmly, as I stood up immediately looking at her in bewilderment as she made no attempts to get her favourite food. "Only, if you accept something else."

"Please tell me, you actually did buy the essential oils that you had been wanting to get your hands on for ages." I made a negative noise in the back of my throat and didn't even warrant a full glare, merely narrowing my eyes.

"I did." She said with the barest kick up of her lips.

"Good." I smiled gently, before pressing further. "Which one was it? German Chamomile oil?"

"For someone who distastes the clever usage of coconut oil to wash off the clay after pottery, you do remember them well." Hope chuckled innocently, as I stopped shading in the shadows, staring at her cluelessly.

"I dislike using it because the greasiness bothers me-" I said flatly before raising an eyebrow to question her puzzled reaction. "-but what does that have to do with remembering your words?"

"People don't remember things that are important to them yet spoken by others." Hope said, as if she was faced with a puzzle "You can't blame me for being surprised that you bother to remember things unimportant to you."

"Not bother, but rather cherish it." I clarified, feeling oddly amused and delighted at her eyes genuinely sparkling with innocent glee. "They are important to you because they are elements of your dream, I understand the value of that because the elements of my dream mean the same to me."

"They are certain aspects of life with respect to everything, unbiasedly and this is yours." Hope said, as if this was just dawning on her.

"Precisely." I agreed with a small smile.

"I will take you up on that bowl of laksa, if you use this-"

"Hope, you had been looking forward to buy-"

"I did... Grapefruit essential oil. I used it to make this hand cream along with my collection of plumerias." Hope smiled gently, taking a breath of fresh air. I nodded remembering the excitement in her voice when she spoke about reminiscing the times of collecting her favourite scented flowers, so it made no sense as she opened my fist clutching the top end of my canvas, to place something in my open palm. "This won't be greasy and you mentioned preferring the citrusy smell, so this should help the tick of using this instead of running them over water when you seem massively worried about something…"

I wondered what astronomical odds had aligned for someone to be so utterly unbelievable. And confusing.

I didn't have the coherency to say a single word to comprehend that a person would go to such lengths to accommodate my ridiculous sabotaging habits much less even notice them.

"I don't know what to say…this-"

"I know that I could be wrong, and this gesture could come across as possibly rude-"

"You aren't." I confirmed, placing my hands over the fumbling hands, explaining in panic.

"-rather than my intentions of assuring that this is my way of being there for you instead of rudely breaking your boundaries and asking you to speak about things that you may not want to…Even if they might be things that trouble you."

I didn't know what else to say to provide the right assurance to subdue that panic, so I said the only thing that mattered to weigh the gesture I couldn't repay.

"Thank you." I nodded, with a small smile "Seriously, I can't thank you enough for this."

"You can, by using it whenever you possibly can. Just promise me that"

-

"Yes, you are."

"That's not fair!" Pax called out. "I gotta know details about the source that managed to do this."

"It's a promise, that's all you get to know." I argued back, waving a flippant hand.

"To the source?" asked Pax with a cheeky grin on her face that wiped away immediately when I made no attempts to speak past that point.

Abandonment isn't always equivalent to negligence by disappearance.

Most often, negligence morphs in the form of unintentional actions of taking people for granted, and no matter how much we try to prevent it we end up hurting at least one person or more through our negligence.

What matters is we learn not to defend our actions to change the narrative of the person who was hurt by our negligence but accept it if we truly care for them and be better to them.

In my hatred of getting bothered by that negligence towards a person I barely knew, hadn't I ended up doing the same? How much longer was I going to hide behind the convenience of using the excuse of the time-period of familiarity with a person?

I shouldn't care…

People were capable of holding on to their facades for years…I knew that better than anyone else. Why was I thrown off-guard, now?

Most of all, I hate the damned downplays of this wretched time providing no guarantee over the masquerade of facades…

I really loathe this Unpredictability.

III

"Wallowing in the guilt over the hues of regret to succumb into the abyss of the gambling blame"

CHAPTER - V

"So, when will you be back next?" Destiny asked, raising her soft arched eyebrows with a somber expression. If '*Legally Blonde*' ever got remade in its Asian version, the protagonist would manifest in the calculative form of Destiny Eve Beck.

"Awww you miss me already…" Grace answered back chuckling good-naturedly, shrugging her shoulders without giving a clear answer. "I thought you would never admit that."

"When did we ever deny that?" I asked, clicking my tongue amusedly as Grace chuckled taking pride that we were indeed enjoying her decision to change the usual location of our meets, from the Aquaria to her winning pool.

Was I glad to avoid the very place that had provided me silence for years, because it suddenly reminded me of nothing but the person I had pushed away on the excuse of time?

Perhaps Yes.

"I am glad that at least one of us skipped town instead of roped into the interrogation routine that hits us, every week." Destiny merely rolled her lips with a small smile, when Grace placed her hand over her shoulder as a gesture of comfort "I swear I can't make a single move without being reminded of all the possible ways my future is going to be '*slowed down*'."

Destiny was one of the top students of Modelling and advertising, being only one of the youngest Asian models to be one of the top favourites of the designers, to walk on several runaways for Givenchy and Moschino.

So, it didn't come as a surprise that the Vice-Chancellor didn't handle it well when Destiny wanted to rediscover herself by changing her major to Ballet, in her last year. To embrace her natural grace, that brought out the natural poise as a model.

"If we are talking about the old gang, then it's actually two of us." Grace reminded, before picking up another one of Destiny's macarons. With her recent cooking spree venturing onto Italian bakery, it was absolutely a beatific blessing for all. "Theus was the first one to take up his offer to fly off to Australia."

Despite the joint exhibition, each of us wanted to illustrate our colour to symbolise our own identity, so it was a step closer to the dreams, to get early acceptance onto the foundation year of the course, that was reflected through our works.

Several offers especially from the Universities and Art Schools of our dreams for each of us, and yet most of us chose different paths to move at our own pace.

"Technically, he was the only one who got that offer." I said, with a small smile leaning back on my elbows, pushing the silverware holding the remaining crumbles of the macarons, away from the edge of the pool.

Grace took over enhancing the originality of the Jewellery Collection that her Uncle had launched for the past decade, by incorporating the corals' crafting, herself - barely having time to finish her last year to opt for anything besides homeschooling. Choosing to take the GED test instead, just like Theus.

 What had started out as a fascination while waiting in airports, walking up to the salesperson and trying on various watches on display especially the ones with larger dials just highlighting the analog style.

Manifested on to the notion of creating her own design instead of never being satisfied with existing jewellery on display and always wanting to tweak them... and now, here she was...

'Establishing the vision of my preferences into my creation. Every moment and every iteration has the magic to shape the expression of our creation,... and mine is yet to behold its true form.'

I could still remember our first encounter and I couldn't help but smile reminiscing the passage of time over the past six years, some things hadn't changed- and that included the unvarying ebullient personality of the tall jewellery creator, whose angora-cat like features stood in contrast to the large puppy-like traits that magnetically drew everyone towards her.

Being the same person who hadn't hesitated to give my company while still giving me the silence I needed, through the chaos of the crowds around us, even during the early days.

"I mean he was the only one among us invested in architectural design." Grace mused lightly, with a tired smile on her lips, as she poked my shoulder jovially. "But you got plenty of offers to get a jump-start in Italy, too."

While Theus didn't hesitate to have any second thoughts, to get a head start on the strategy of the planned steps to his dream and take up the offer to finish his final year of high school in the foundational year of his dream college, instead. Sometimes it was hard to tell if the guy who had a strong resemblance to a rather pale raw Sienna-toned James McAvoy with deep-set onyx eyes and freckles preferred having unrivalled patience or an exemplary sense of humour.

Yet the very core of Theus Brumoy that remained undeviated was his love for French history and his own heritage, and that reflected irrefutably through the interfusion of medieval French architecture and modern Asian architecture in all the blueprints of his designs that had become a classic when it came to him.

"In Fine-arts, not fashion-design." Destiny couldn't help but kick up her lips in bemusement, as she reminded Grace good-naturedly. "Besides, it was that very investment in medieval French architecture of both you and Theus that actually jump-started us syncing well in working together professionally."

"Yeah" I said, nodding at Destiny.

Destiny was silent for a moment "I missed the old gang."

"All we are missing is just dragging Theus' head from Australia." I chuckled, feeling the left side of my mouth quirk up in amusement.

It was as if I could practically hear Theus teasing *'Spes, sometimes I can't decide if you are an angel hiding under the disguise of a spawn of Satan or vice versa.'*

"If my sources are right, you are actually enjoying the company of your new team…" Grace teased cheekily, fluffing her hair and spreading her arms as I rolled my eyes at her remark.

"What sources?" I asked, squinting my eyes and tilting my head back.

"Good team results in good outcomes, and so far-" Destiny muttered, chin resting on her fist, expression relaxed. "-I am loving the style of outfits exclusively designed for me, for the final screening."

"A-And it's not that new, just one new team member." I pressed, shrugging my left shoulder in order to divert the topic. "Quinsy was there…the last time, too."

"I am so glad that for the last-minute decision that Theus made to mandate a photographer onto our team." Hope broke in expectantly, giving me a 'You-are-going-to-owe-me-for-this-later' look, as I closed my eyes and nodded wordlessly releasing the breath that I had been holding in.

"Technically, didn't you stumble across Quinsy's works before asking her to join the team?" Grace offered firmly, as she waved her hand over my face and checked if my attention had wavered off to being lost in my own thoughts.

"Not stumble." I reminded, wrapping my fingers around Grace's wrist, waving over my shut eyelids, and placing it on the concrete beside the owner. "I had been following her works for quite some time."

"You should know by now, that her spontaneous decisions aren't random but pretty calculative as well."

Destiny clarified with a small smirk, reflecting the smug grin stretching across mine as Grace swatted my arms, laughing loudly. "They might seem spontaneous, but they might have been brewing in there for a definitive period of time."

"How is she holding up with the new team?"

"It's pretty smooth-sailing besides picking up on the unnecessary hurdles due to the aftermaths of screwing up my interview." I hummed, gingerly.

Destiny winced immediately, expression tightening. "*She* is pretty set on using the excuse of '*molding our character*' every time we decide for ourselves-" Crossing her arms firmly as she glared darkly, talking about the methods of the newly appointed Vice-Chancellor. "-that upsets the statistics of her reputation of running this place."

"We have always had people like her pretty much go haywire, i-if-" I sighed, voice catching at the end of my words as I felt my jaws tighten. " -if we strayed out of their upper strands but none that retaliated to jeopardise our decision in such a major way."

"The hilarious part is the fact that they want to direct our life…" Destiny stressed bitterly, that linger tension unambiguously resonating in her voice. "They leave no chances to mock our work, without having a single clue about the work-life balance."

"Ohhh the most familiar one has to be '*Do you have many thoughts? Are you troubled by them?*'" Grace reminisced with a sour laugh, dipping her feet in the water of the pool.

"I fell for that stupid bait, all the time." Destiny said, sighing numbly.

"We all did." I said, grimacing lowly.

Was it just me or did the dusk setting upon us, looked like the desserts of evenings, like damson plums, a perfectly round bite out of the horizon?

Damn, Ma was right, maybe there was a certain beauty in the nature she had always proclaimed.

Maybe I could portray that reflecting through the celestial glasses reflecting through the eyes of the unfinished portrait of the Khmer dancer in her traditional wear. Huh, maybe that could enhance the pastel monochromes of the background-

'Spes, you have a way of portraying pastel colours that has 'grace' to be embedded 'forever', like the red of the salvia blending artfully with the lightest of purples, like the petals playing a game of hide and seek.'

'Hope-'

" 'Cause then it leads down the road of *'You must have a lot of time in your hands if you can spend time to just sit and think around.'* " Grace broke the silence, thankfully pulling me away from my wandering thoughts.

"Oh yeah, absolutely because it's impossible to actually have emotions-" Destiny snorted, taking another long drink of her beverage. "-or any thoughts sprouting from our brains besides constantly working as algorithm-driven machines."

"Don't we have enough of those morons whining and sighing every two seconds?" I snapped, as Grace gently pushed the untouched plate of tropical fruits towards me.

"God forbid if I wish to spare myself from being sucked into that purposeless routine, where I can't recognise why I am even functioning?" Destiny hummed in affirmation, before scoffing in disdain.

"I wish none of us had beaten ourselves struggling to breathe…" Grace groaned tiredly, nose scrunching tiredly. "Constantly feeling like we were never working hard enough to have our dreams close to being our reality, at least once in our lives."

"I think it's kinda poetic that in a world that constantly lives through endless comparison like scorecards,-" I said, voice a little too even for my own familiarity with it. "-we chose to live our lives by allowing ourselves to our own narrative defined by our individualistic stream of thoughts, like our own scripts."

Grace's lips ticked up higher as something brightened in her eyes. "Are you sure, it's just not your words that are poetic?"

"Shut Up, that was a good line and very true." Destiny warned harmlessly before grinning.

"I know!" Grace shrugged, eyebrows lifting. "But I am allowed to tease and lighten the atmosphere."

"We are three 18-year olds, munching on tropical fruits while lazing near the swimming pool in fall?" Destiny asked, huffing a brief laugh and leaning back on the concrete. "How much lighter can it get?"

"Hey! My swimming pool, my rules!" Grace excused, a small laugh leaving her lips.

"Meh, fair enough." I hummed, as Grace pouted in disbelief before muttering "Ganging up with two against one isn't a fair play."

Destiny threw her a look that was exasperatedly amused. "Oh please, you are lucky I haven't pushed you into the water."

I couldn't help the quiet laugh that escaped.

"T-that's- actually true- please don't." Grace conceded, bowing her head. "I just finished styling my hair, three hours ago."

"We will see about that."

***

"Since when have you been interested in fairy tales cosplay?" Pax looked torn between utterly disgusted by me or rather baffled by me as if I had finally managed to sprout another head. "You do know that you aren't coming along to buy a piano, right?"

Oh, this was going to be fun!

"It was either this-" I pressed, giving Pax a carefully calculated look of being unimpressed at her exasperated sigh. "-or the denim obi-belt that I had created last week, which you literally shoved back into my wardrobe."

"Why are you dressed like a *-what's that-* a fancy military coat with a long-wound shoe-lace replacing buttons?" Pax scoffed weakly. In a very peculiar habit, it was her way of assuring that the piece was finally taking its shape, compared to my constant hazed state of just throwing over the unfinished garment so I could use all the time I could get to the garment, sewn up by hand.

"No, you ignorant peasant." I huffed, rolling my eyes, vaguely amused. It was one of my attempts to give a distant perception of an asian feel to the core of western elements. To easternise the jacket, by switching the reversal play in the inspiration of the westernisation of the *'Cheongsam dress'*, that had occurred over eras. "It's a Victorian street jacket that I have peaked a little."

"Is the collar clip necessary?"

"Just get going." I sighed grudgingly. I was not getting rid of the new collar-clip Dad got me, from his last trip. "I don't get paid enough for this."

"I don't pay you anything-" Pax gasped, glaring sagely as I pulled over the beanie she was wearing, over her eyes. "-and you are the one coming along!"

"Yeah, you almost left without your bass cleft sheets." I reminded quietly, nudging my leg with hers as she twisted her hands nervously, after taking over the missing sheets that I handed over. "You got this." I offered.

Even when it seemed like her nerves clawed over her excitement like a hyena hunting its prey, she didn't let it halt reviewing her notes, earnestly. Taking over as the tutor piano accompaniment symphonies to the new students at her mentor's concert hall, half-heartedly by the slightest.

"Even if I don't say this enough, you do know that I really appreciate you coming along for my first class, right?" Pax murmured, muted but entirely genuine, before pulling away the sewing pins attached to my jacket. *Guess some things truly don't change after all.* I could really get used to this consistency. "Don't hold this over me."

"Yeah, that's not happening." I chided harmlessly, as Pax elbowed me to not forget to get the right brand of the microfibre polishing cloth for her piano, from the shopping mall adjacent to the concert hall, as she completed teaching her first class.

***

If there were words that spoke of tomorrow, the relentless current and the upcoming to the same point as churning oceans, then they would have to be the words of Brene Brown: *'Vulnerability is the birthplace of innovation, creativity and change'.*

We grow up being subjected to a society that promulgated the notion of associating vulnerability with weakness and adorn our facade for survival to shield ourselves against betrayal and suffering.

They found it unfathomable to sacrifice one's individuality as collateral damage as long as we manifested our vulnerability as a dead carcass to be shoved in the graveyard.

More than ever, it was always the ones who adorned the happiest facades most frequently in the existence of their timeline, who ended up trying the hardest.

I didn't like investing time willingly to be around the vicinity of people, whose true vulnerable side seemed way too veiled. I hated having that distance I maintained from them being barged in without the steady clearance of that fogged veil.

But most of all, why on earth were inscrutable coincidences happening way too often in my reality, now?

I hate this unpredictability...

Of course.

Out of all the places, the make-up studio Hope worked in, had to be in this shopping mall...

Yet the audacity of the words of this stout, curly-haired customer who seemed to be in her late-30s inside that studio, seemed to get on my nerves, more than any other self-absorbed orthodox individual that I had come across.

"I can't believe you expect my make-up to be done by someone who can't even use make-up to cover up looking like a zebra instead of a human." I really couldn't comprehend what concoction this woman was yammering.

Seriously, why wasn't she getting her eyes checked instead?

"I assure you." Hope confirmed monotonously, as she carefully washed in the basin once again to retaliate against the woman's scorn. "I was hired with similar standards of qualifications as anyone else."

"They have dropped their standards to hire someone like you." I really wish Hope could shove some of that cleanser she was using to cleanse that woman's face, onto her mouth, to *cleanse* the outrage spilling from her mouth. "Don't you know how to use basic foundation to cover up patches?"

The orthodox standards of beauty have been nothing but a hoax.

Creating the confinements of narrowing mind-space that refuses to behold the truest form of one's magnetic form in its definitive individuality of colour, beyond the romanticised idolisation of the diluted concentration of melanin.

Yet, many perish under the fittings of those confinements without getting a chance to cherish the light of their parameters or torment others who never cared for those confinements.

"I am wearing a natural make-up look-" Hope said, sagely with a forced smile. "-and have clear skin so I avoid going for a look that doesn't suit me." It was vehement moments like these, when Hope chopped down outright nuisance with crafty class, that honestly made my day. So did the fugitive grimace adorning the foam-covered face of the customer.

"Is there any that would, especially with *your* condition?"

It was times like these when I truly wondered if I could ever get used to Hope's astronomical magnitudes of patience.

"I think a dewy look would suit you, and just pull it through like a foundation magnet." Hope suggested flatly. "I will mattify the T-zone to suit with a brighter lip. So, that it doesn't look like it's just layered on top in the noon."

"You are right, I do have good skin." Despite her constant glowering, the broad-shouldered woman couldn't help but nod gingerly in veneration.

"For your eyes, I am not going to add a lot of structure, to add a dimension that doesn't exist." Hope continued explaining, one side of her mouth quirked up politely.

"Doesn't exist?!-" The woman interjected with an exasperated gasp, turning around in her chair in a jerk.

"Yes, it would appear fake." Hope added crisply as she glanced at the reflection of the woman slowly, before turning the chair around. "So, it would be better to use just two eye shadow colours, and just add a little black at the base of your lash line to draw out that dimension."

"Maybe you really do know the basics of what you are hired for." The latter shrugged, huffing lightly feigning in leer. It took me the combined quizzical look of one of the make-up artists in the studio to usher me in and another blaring remainder from Pax to get that *damn* microfibre polishing cloth already, to realise that my feet were frozen outside the studio, inscrutably.

"-And clean up by going underneath with the eyeliner to give a gentle smokey eye." As Hope's voice faded onto the background, I couldn't help but check how much time I might have wasted standing in front of a place, without any concrete purpose. "I will finish to shape out the face with the highlighter."

I just needed some air. A little space to clear my head, even if I wasn't really sure what was fogging it.

By the time I had finished getting that polishing cloth for Pax and taking a quick detour to even get the time to get few other things as well, I wasn't the only one puzzled by the sudden stampede drawing towards a screeching outrage, like wasps rushing onto their nest before the onset of a natural calamity.

Even before I could stray away from the concentrated crowd, it didn't take much time to recognise that disgruntled outcry.

"You expect me to pay up for the work of someone like you?" It was that same burly woman hissing in outrage, as she refused to pay after getting her make-up done.

"If you are genuinely satisfied with my work-" Hope replied passively, trying to get the lady to calm down as she pulled in a larger spectacle, every passing second with her shriek. "-please refrain from letting it cloud with your personal opinions regarding my looks." Her expression was nothing but cordial as she inclined her head.

"Is this how you treat customers here? I am not leaving anywhere until I speak to the one who has made the error of hiring you." She jeered, rolling her eyes. I really don't get why those who seem to be in-charge wait to appear in the spotlight, until things are at their complete worst. It's like they had their personal cue to arrive during the peak note of a banshee's shrill if they adorned a darker shade of the same half-vest, unlike the other employees. "Can't believe the utter garbage of this place of hiring anyone to mess with people's faces-"

Turns out, the lanky in-charge with a prominent birthmark on her cupid's bow was named Nor, at least according to her name tag. "Ma'am, I am sorry for the trouble caused. Let's head outside to solve this before the commotion disturbs other customers?" Nor asked, hands stiff by her side as if she had zoned out the entire commotion until this moment as she asked Hope to break down the situation to her.

"You are kicking me out after making me look like this?" The curly-haired woman gagged, the sound of chairs scratching against the tiles.

"We will compensate for the troubles, Ma'am." Nor inclined her head deeply, before throwing more chagrined words towards Hope. "Did the make-up artist not confirm the look she intended to go for, after cleansing?"

"I did-" Before Hope could interject the truth, Nor barked an order, crossing arms over her chest.

Wow, that's an additional brand new individual making my blood boil, within the span of mere hours.

"Head outside. I think you have caused enough trouble for today." Nor sneered angrily, speaking out her words through gritted teeth, by turning her head towards Hope to the slightest. "Lemme handle this alone and sort this mess."

"It's not about that! You should be lucky that I don't sue this place for letting someone like her touch my face." The woman spat bitterly as she jabbed her finger against Nor's name-tag repeatedly, causing the latter to stumble back in her step. "I don't even know if the patches on her hands aren't contagious to get on my skin-"

"I assure you Ma'am that-"

"What are you still doing here?" Nor demanded darkly, trying to maintain face as the authority when Hope marched out of the studio before Nor could finish her words. "Get out, before I actually don't waste me in reconsidering to keep you here instead of firing you at the spot."

At this moment, I could care less about my last conversation with Hope besides assuring that she wasn't alone with her thoughts.

Yet, I didn't want to barge into her space until I cooled down myself.

The customer continued her rant, as Nor flushed red clearly riled up. "But I let her do it because I have been a regular here for years."

"We appreciate that, Ma'am. We will leave no stones unturned that you are satisfied with your experience here." The spectacle that had drawn in, fizzled out though Nor continued to fume. "I will immediately request another one of our employees to create a new look-"

Yet it made no sense why that lady was looking at me, trying to place a name as if she recognised me.

Had I already crossed paths with this woman to the point she beamed unrelentingly in recognition, and had passed on the chance to give her a piece of my mind?

Why on earth would I make such an error?

"Thank god, you are here." I tried to keep my expression impassive with a forced smile as she pulled my arm to drag me inside the studio. "I am guessing your mother has finally handed you the reigns overlooking over this branch."

"Your mother has been quite enthusiastically speaking about your take-over." Nor broke in, blinking rapidly as I tried to make sense of the stunned grating of the woman clinging on to my arm.

Was I the type of person who took the advantage of adapting the situation according to me, due to a mistaken identity?

Yes indeed.

"Please stop hiring mutts like them. Is this a PR stunt?" I could practically feel my ears bleed, as she continued to narrate her pointless opinions. "Did you have her clinically tested? You have a lot to learn from your mother-" My blood ran cold, hoping my lips weren't curled in a snarl, at the word - *'mutt'*.

"Are you satisfied with your look?" I asked as calmly as I could with my jaws tightened.

"W-What?"

"Earlier you didn't deny that when the previous make-up artist confirmed with the look she was going for, after cleansing." I tilted my head, having picked up on Nor's words on things that were expected here. "So, are you satisfied with your finished look?" I repeated, as tonelessly as I possibly could.

"I will be fixing that right way." Nor prompted anxiously, trying to summon another employee, sorting through the brushes while attending to another customer. "I have already informed Farah to head over here after she is done with her customer."

"That's not necessary, it's not so bad…I don't want to trouble 'efficient' workers." She croaked furtively, voice small, as Nor played around with asking how to ask the lady for payment. "It's not so bad, I am letting it slide because I have been a regular here for years-"

"So, would you like to pay via card or cash?" I asked immediately after I caught on to Nor muttering to herself about cutting down on the newbie's salary if she didn't get the payment and keeping the money to herself to put up with this trouble.

I truly hope she pays by card.

"Oh yes yes, I am sorry… I am sure you have to check over the other customers." As the rapacious woman fumbled through her purse, dropping her card onto the floor through her shaky hands. "It's your first official day to work-" \Before Nor could help her to pick up the credit card from the floor, she knocked over the remaining sticky preservative inside the can of my canned lychees, placed at the edge of the make-up table.

Wow! All this time, I had been struggling to throw this can because I couldn't find a trash can.

Fate does have its magical ways of clearing out inconveniences.

Despite everything, I couldn't help but feel slightly sorry for her as she handed over the credit card to Nor, as the sticky sweetener cascaded over her hair like lava flowing after the eruption of a dormant volcano

"Oh shit, lemme get some tissue papers-" Nor gasped, after swiftly swiping the card and handing it back to her. She rushed over to get more tissues when

I ran out of tissues to hand over, from the packet placed near the array of shadow palettes.

"Ohh no it's my fault. I was going to get this make-up washed up anyways." She quipped with a crestfallen look when the tissues kept falling apart rather than help soak up the candied liquid. While half the customers just ignored the commotion by closing their eyes and the remaining stared along sympathetically. "This will be like an egg-yolk treatment."

"It smells sweet, more like honey treatment..." Nor clarified trying to pacify the commotion, as the woman just handed her sticky torn tissues and rushed out. "That's good, too...Ma'am."

"It's actually just preserved sweetened water." I declared with a shrug before throwing the can onto the trash inside the studio and walking out as Nor continued staring at the pile of tissues she was holding, in startled disgust.

Rain? Seriously?

I wish I could nag Pax about picking this day to get that *damn* polishing cloth, but if it weren't for her obsession with checking on the weather news after school, I really wouldn't have ended up being grateful for dragging along her umbrella.

Perhaps, also be petty and get back at her a little.

By the time, I had finally found Hope outside the concrete pavements near the exit. She was aimlessly letting herself be drenched under the pouring rain, leaning her elbows on the railing.

"Why… are you sometimes nice… and sometimes not?" She asked, without even flicking that it might have been a stranger as we stood under the glaucous umbrella. Her voice, the kind of hoarse that only came when something was breaking her heart.

"I am never nice to anyone who barges into my personal space." I winced slightly. I had been so convinced that I had been nothing but a colossal jerk to maintain my distance from any mistaken attachment due to negligence of time, that I hadn't realised my actions had ended up being something I utterly loathe - *flippant*. "I just need time to get used to their presence, but that doesn't mean I am going to walk away."

"Do you think I need your sympathy now, because you suddenly feel sorry for me, now?" Hope asked, voice as sharp as ice-shards.

"Not sorry, definitely not sorry…but I am not going anywhere." I said, clutching the handle of the umbrella even tighter and tilting it towards her. "I will give you some space, but I am not going anywhere."

"Why don't you think that anyone else needs their personal space?-" Hope asked, brows furrowed and rolling her lips tightly "-is it because they really wanted to spend time with you after you shot them down-" She stared at me startled like a baby chick staring at their very first mealworm, waiting for me to explain the bottle I was handing over.

"You mentioned preferring to drink cold water, especially when you start feeling dizzy-" I muttered as a matter of fact to break the silence. "-that tends to occur when you have to bottle up the words you can't express, when you are upset."

"What?-"

"I paid for it from the refrigerator near the vending machine outside your make-up studio." I assured quickly before she waved her hands to interject what she really meant.

"How did you know about that?"

"The preferences questions that you often initiate after lunch." I recalled, raising my eyebrows in bewilderment to ask why she was surprised about something that she had spoken, herself. "This was one of the things you had mentioned, while talking about appreciating the simplicity in life, through surprising experiences."

"How do you remember-"

"Do you... want me to stay with you?" I offered carefully when Hope hadn't moved. "Just until you settle-"

"No," Hope said, snapping back into actual awareness as she stared at me. "No, you don't have to, it's fine, I-"

"It's not the matter of 'have', as long as I am not overstepping your personal space." I repeated, firmly as Hope nodded quietly and finally took the bottle that I had offered. "I am not going anywhere."

"I'm sorry," she finally managed, staring at her feet, not lifting her head. "I'm sorry I snapped at you... I shouldn't have yelled like that, I just... I've just been having a shitty week, usually their words don't get to me, but today...I just don't know why I let it get to me, today."

"Don't you dare apologise." I pressed firmly. "You shouldn't have to get used to that trash, and even if you have gotten used to it to not waste your breath fighting with someone who isn't worth your time."

"It's not like I have a choice here." Her expression was apathetic - but like a riptide current, languid bleak still rippling beneath her calm eyes. "I already know that, yet I am just whining like a child throwing a tantrum over spilled milk." Her jaw was so tight enough to break that I almost felt my eyes were playing tricks, as if she were made of stone for how stiffly she stood.

"It's alright to just pause and take a breath as you move past her pointless bark and continue envisioning your dream." I called, heart clenching unexplainably as she took a step closer.

Hope laughed almost bitterly. But she shook her head. "Why didn't you defend my accusations by merely justifying your actions of getting back at that lady, to get her to pay the money after I left ?" She asked, glancing up at my tight expression, not expecting her to have witnessed the stunt I had pulled after I thought she had walked away.

"What?" I winced feeling my throat burn, my left fist clenching up around the bags, immediately. "I don't know what-"

"Please don't feign with that clueless act. I saw everything." She said, much quieter against the mist that looked like a deranged ghost attempting the *Thriller* choreography, her voice hoarse.

Interference.

I had taken yet another stupid and selfish gamble, that hadn't hesitated to barge in disrespecting another person's boundaries.

After all these years, I had learnt nothing.

"I am sorry." I muttered abjectly. "That's the only thing I could think of, instead of throwing the candied water left in my lychee can, at her face-"

Hope looked surprised by my words, eyebrows raising, but then it softened into something neutral. "Why are you apologising for standing up for me?"

"I didn't know if I had the place to interfere."

"I really don't get you." Hope huffed quietly. "You do things like *these*, and then look like you want to hide it instead of taking credit for it." She breathed weakly, sighing tiredly in confusion. "On top of that, you are worried if you had somehow interfered. Yet, you bite my head off if I wish to spend more time with you. I really don't get you."

I made a face before sighing in disdain "I don't think anyone would understand the wiring of my action, so it's easier to just say that I am a hyper-sensitive person" I defended before returning to serious.

"Indulge me. You owe that to me." Hope balked for a moment as I kicked at the ground and sighed heavily.

"I have a tendency to not take words for granted, whether they are words I say or hear." I muttered reflectively, an odd sense of calm tiredness washing over me. "So, I end up having a hard time living with people. Most of whom prefer an easy-going perspective of living, away from that rigidity."

"Good, which means you will understand when I say this - I don't like playing games, neither do I like being played." Hope bit out, one hand wrapping around my fist clutching the umbrella tightly to keep it from twisting further. "Unfortunately, you are doing exactly that through your actions, don't push me away if you are going to treat me like this."

"Like what?" I swallowed, frowning in bewilderment at her not snapping at me, instead.

"Just me, just as I am."

-

Maybe later that night, as I stared at the painting of a single flower stalk in a vase etched across the canvas, Pax found another way to snatch my phone and coax a million questions about the painting.

"Felicity is going to hunt this person down if she finds out she is being replaced as your favourite person." Pax smirked smugly, before Felicity barged into our room due to the commotion. "Since when do *you* collect essential oils?"

I really should have asked Ma to stop Pax from using her merit to get that *damn* grand piano in her room, and now I am stuck with rooming with her, all over again.

"It's not for me. It's a gift-" I sighed, crossing my arms. "-and no one is getting replaced."

Felicity joined in feigning offence, placing a hand on her chest "Who am I hunting now?"

"I would never change the order." I assured Felicity calmly. "You are still my second favourite person in existence."

Pax wasn't even trying to hide a burst of rather more reserved laughter behind a hand as she taunted Felicity.

"That's it." Felicity threatened, as I pressed the heels of palms against the sides of my temple, to ask Pax to give my phone back already. "I am going to throw whoever is your first favourite as fodder for sharks."

"Come on, Felicity...you can't blame me for this." I said calmly, throwing a side glare towards Pax who made no attempts to hand over my phone. "You weren't the first to come along-" I added coyly, staring at Pax.

Pax stopped prancing around looking back at me frozen, waiting for me to give a name, already.

Felicity interjected, hitting my shoulder before I could finish my words "Who is this insolent imbecile?"

"-My favourite person has always been Ma." I admitted honestly, with a shrug as Felicity froze over her previous words.

"Pompous jerk." Pax muttered, rolling her eyes when she realised I had intentionally prolonged the time to give a name. "It's ironic how she is specific with her insults as you, I think I should enlighten Ma about this."

"That's unfair!" Felicity called, trying to hold Pax chuckling like a maniac and yelling to summon Ma to our room. "I thought she was going to name a stranger or someone else!"

The only way I could get them to back off was to let them gang up on each other instead of ganging up on me.

I chuckled watching them trying to play like two sea-monsters thrashing around - hell bent on cackling, as I finally snatched back my phone from Pax.

The only reason I was able to recognise those flowers was because I had seen them so many times.

Geranium. *Stupidity.*

Cymbidium. *Friendship.*

I couldn't help but smile re-reading the message sent over the painting still fresh with paint on the canvas. -

'I hope you consider this as the last warning for your stupidity to not assume boundaries on your own ~ '

***

"Guys, I am not in my senior year unlike you three." Quinsy said, flopping onto the seat next to me as she disclosed the rough pre-shots, she had finalised until now. "So, I can create some solid shots of you guys working on your pieces as well as the final screening of Destiny modelling the finished outfits as well."

"I mean our finalised works would be based around the same concept." René shook her head slowly, pointing to our obvious lack of progress in scoring the funds as well as coming up with the symbolism for a strong concrete umbrella concept to tie up all our works. "Spes, don't worry we will bring our A-game in the canvases of our main paintings, we have time to incorporate the concept of the brand of our outfits in them as well."

"It's not about that, it's about giving our best and even if we don't like it... We owe it to ourselves to bring out the similar style and level of artistry from our previous works." I explained firmly, not understanding why both of them were giving up already. "Quinsy, you have the capacity to play with lights in your shots unlike anyone else, but you need the right imagery to boost up the live canvas in front of you."

"I think it's best we skip on incorporating pop-art along with the screening of the outfits." René sighed tiredly, letting the table scrambled with unfinished sewn garments, take more of her weight, as Quinsy nodded along wryly. "We don't have a concept for that. The current run down of our painting based on the concept we have set for the outfits still fits our deadline, adequately."

"That sounds like you have already made up your mind." Hope said, matter-of-factly.

"We can't get upset about what we already have... By trying to force elements to mend according to an established concept or create a new concept completely and try to fit whatever we already have according to that." René said with finality, rubbing at her tired eyes and accidentally taking a large sip of the instant coffee before wincing in disdain. "It's not worth the risk."

"But compromising due to a half-hearted fear is even riskier-" I said, something unlocking in my jaw, at the half-heartedness of the situation.

"We are drawing blanks. You two are sort of the residents in incorporating symbolism in pop art phenomenons among us." Quinsy couldn't help but kick up her lips abjectly towards René and I, as if she had already made up her mind. "If you guys haven't come up with anything-"

"Maybe, they are right." René stressed, leaning back against her chair. "Maybe we did use up all that drive that inspired our muse in our last works."

"No, we aren't giving up like this-" I rolled my lips, staring off to the side to nullify my growing frustration

"Yeah, we could push time and try-" Hope interjected firmly, breaking the tense atmosphere concentrating around us.

"Look buddy, I am all down for that '*try till the end*' crap, but we have got nothing to try on." René mused, with an apologetic forced smile on her lips, as her expression pulled down rapidly. "We can't beat ourselves over it again today when we have got nothing now, we can't force ourselves to do that today- any ideas we do come up with will be absolutely disastrous."

"I mean she is right... The best works always sprout from random epiphanies concentrated over time." Quinsy broke in, as she continued rubbing at her face for a few minutes. "I think we just need to wait for that moment. - Until then, I think it's best to call it a day."

"Sorry Spes, I am sure we might come up with something later to compensate for this." René said, expression pulled down with hooded eyes, as she slowly started packing up. "Don't worry." She added, humming to end the conversation as Quinsy followed suit.

Maybe I really need to rethink my schedule.

Maybe I could find the right space of mind to conjure up the right epiphany that we had been hitting amiss, after wrapping up the entrance test for getting into Politecnico Milano.

I really needed my back-up plan to be as secure as my first.

I couldn't afford anymore slip-ups.

"You aren't leaving, now?" I muttered, chin resting on my fist, when I noticed Hope hadn't moved by the slightest.

"No, not yet…" Hope whispered, almost to herself, like she hadn't meant to say it loud. "I wanted to ask you something."

"Yeah." I nodded in confirmation, straightening up in my seat. "Go ahead."

"Even if you believe that speaking about it, might evoke nothing about unintentional comparison-" Hope said carefully, expression pinching in concern as she rolled up the blueprints of the graphic layouts used for the cut-outs chiselled on the leather. "-to inspirations similar to the same concept you ended up using the last time-"

"Not my words." I laughed, humourlessly. "Those are René's words." I reminded with a queasy expression as I pulled the threads of the discarded fabric, aimlessly. "But yeah, that notion does often scare me, too. I am guessing, you wanted to ask me about the 'Stigma of Colours'?"

"Indulge me?" Hope asked quietly, with a small smile.

"I don't know where to start." I said stiffly, hating the way my voice came out tighter than I had intended to. "What to do you wanna know?"

"Why the lion-mane jelly-fish?" She asked, gently "I mean I know that you synced the floating lanterns that mimicked the shape of the hood of the jellyfish to move with the sounds of the Lub-dubs of a beating heart with the movements of a jellyfish." She continued, as I chuckled with a half-smile when her eyes beamed bright and honest like it had been ages since someone had such a pure view of their lives. "And there were the corroding wind-chimes to mimic the corals, in Quinsy's photoshoots-"

"Yeah, I remember covering it just over a day, just a stroll through the city." I explained, finding myself relishing in reminiscing the memories of the past, as Hope kept staring with an unexplainable smile, her eyes earnest and warm and comforting... "We took random shots of swift movements of street artists working on their arts, in the streets of Jalan Raja.-"

I couldn't remember if Quinsy played with the lights or movement of the camera, to get those shots but they perfectly looked like the tentacles of jellyfish.

Some shots captured were the wobbling steps while walking along the edge of a bridge alongside a river.

Some were just the scenes of the front load washing machine in the laundry rooms to portray the movement of revolving sting-rays and seaweeds rustled by the school of fishes.

Meanwhile, some shots captured the making of an artificial bonsai tree using luminous synthetic bristles to mimic corals under the sea.

"You find your muse in finding your chosen stillness within the constant movement of the racing time, kinda like finding the roots through that unexpected bubble that provides belonging." Hope murmured and clicked her fingers as if she had finally hit the gold mine. "To live in the moment, that magnifies your envision to view the bigger picture."

"Yeah…you are absolutely right." I nodded, with a small chuckle.

"That gives me an idea, come with me." Hope pressed standing up in a jerk and scrambling up to pack both her things as well as mine, speaking more to herself as I stared at her, cluelessly. "One question, should we travel by cycles or feet?"

"Huh?"

"Spes, we are going to get ripped by the taxi fares, if we travel by taxi…" Hope said, matter-of-factly, as if her words were self-explanatory. "That's the most basic one-on-one tip of living in this city for ages."

Where on earth was this heading?

"Travel? Hope, I don't do crowds. I mean it-" I warned, firmly as Hope continued dragging outside the school premises through the whispering ends of the stampede after the dismissal signalling the end of schooling hours for the day.

"Trust me, it's market research for finding my muse as well." Hope continued, her excitement not wavering by the slightest.

***

CHAPTER - VI

"I think I'm dying."

"You're not dying-" Hope laughed, rolling her eyes as I fanned my mouth with my hands. "I can't believe you have never had Laksa."

"I have!" I prompted, glaring at Hope who was gleeful in amusement, as the street vendor looked over from her stall towards our table, in sympathy clearly knowing that I was struggling. "Especially ones that were edible!" I breathed heavily, forcing an okay sign with my hands to indicate that I had had enough experience for the day, as she asked if we were full and wanted a second handful in strong Malay.

"Yeah, but not the classic one! I know that you must have had only the Ipoh style laksa cause your Mom grew up there." Hope offered, trying to stop her laughter with an apologetic smile. "But you are missing out if you haven't had the laksa cooked in Penang style."

"I can't feel my tongue!" I burst, looking at Hope desperately. "Why does it hurt so bad? What did they put in this?"

"Flavour, this is a legend among the best of street foods around the world." Hope said as she ate another bite, laughing perhaps a bit cruelly. "It's not that spicy, just add some pineapples to it."

I was fondly betrayed, taking a bite and snatching the container of cendol closer to myself. "These are mine," I declared. "Since everything else you ordered is poisoned."

"It's not poison, you big baby, I don't know how you have been missing out on this for your entire life, Spes." Hope laughed, throwing a wooden fork at me. "It's good stuff- and it's cheap, too. You wanted the experience, didn't you?"

"It's a bad experience," I muttered, taking a long sip of my coconut drink to chase away the spice. "You're trying to kill me. I actually agreed step out of my laziness to paint together, and you're trying to kill me-"

Hope seemed comfortable as she laughed. I wanted to be scared by how comfortable I felt with Hope, but I was too high on genuine laughter and good food. Hope seemed happy and content as she poked fun at me, as I responded like a child being teased, that would embarrassingly come to realise later and bash my head over.

I didn't hesitate even by the slightest, when Hope offered to finish my laksa bowl, pushing over the bowl viciously, as our own laughter veiled over us like a Wednesday morning, on the cusp of possibility, against the buzzing crowd.

That's when the reality of Jove's words dawned on me - *'Over time I have realised that the only thing that prevents us from being corroded away with time, is recognising our own individuality by living in the moment.'*

I could never comprehend the value of *'living in the moment'* until the casting promises of the chopsticks swirling in a laksa bowl mimicking the hands of a clock against the soup resembling molten dawns, dawned the unexplainable epiphany of *'living in the moment against racing time.'*

Even throughout the growing magnitudes of the bristling crowds, every single person looming near the stalls was lost in their own worlds without the chase of cunning time ravening behind us.

"Flowers... are like notes left behind."

"Like a game, but more." I nodded with a small smile, as we headed into the store for the market research that Hope had initially proposed.

"I am sorry if I am rambling about this-" She called gingerly, shaking her head.

"It's not rambling if it's relevant to us." I interjected immediately, staring at her in confusion at the sudden unexplainable apology sprouting out of nowhere.

"So, you don't think flowers are cheesy?" Hope mumbled, head dropping low.

"No, they're elegant."

"When I do create my own line, would you end up inclining for skin-care products or colour-cosmetics products?" She asked, in a monotone, even though her eyes continued to flicker around, voice dropping once more to a mumble "Just based on your personal preference?

"I might be biased towards the former."

Overtime, it was almost like rolling down a hill during spring, when Pax dared me that I wouldn't. That free-fall and innocence that bubbled up in laughter when you couldn't believe you were actually doing something, to recognise the eras Hope liked to inspire her looks from, based on her mood.

Art was the thing I had let myself be selfish for. Even today, watching the golden safety-pins hanging as loops through her ear piercings matching with the Arabic eyeliner shape fleeting off to be drawn onto paying homage to the pins holding iconic Versace dress worn by Elizabeth Hurley while maintaining its golden sequined ambience portraying along with her pale chestnut irises to centre the head of the pin.

It was like reminiscing a nuance that I had failed to recognise all my life, during the clouding time we spent speaking about the looks, every time I managed to accurately place the inspiration reflecting the tone she had decided to embrace for the day.

Did I have a boisterous sense of pride in my perfect record of placing right with the inspired looks?

Yes Indeed.

Even if I was used to getting lost for ages revolving in conversations inside this domain with René, Grace, or Destiny. I couldn't recognise the shift, that was unmistakably different while doing the same with Hope.

"Fine, but you might have to test out both, when I finally release my line." She chuckled, almost uncontrollably, her mood lifting back to its earlier barely uncontrollable glee.

"Hmmm… you drive a hard bargain." I chided harmlessly, pretending to think.

"Stop teasing me."

"I certainly will test out both." I admitted honestly, raising my hands in mock surrender as she tried to glare, playing with her fingers nervously.

"I am going to hold you on to that." She called out, before asking the saleswoman to direct us towards the updated collection of the lip tints from my favourite cosmetic brand. "Deal?"

"Deal"

"When it comes to lip products, the shape of applicators plays a major role." Hope explained as she picked up a coral tint to etch the colour across the back of her hand, with a spark in her eyes.

It wasn't ...a spark like that caught things on fire.

It was a spark, like a fuse running along to an explosive that lit up her entire world into colouring the moment they recognised their dream, the moment they began chasing it as the purpose of their life, the moment they envisioned their future around it...

"So, you have a lot of ground on basing the shape based on the texture..." I nodded slowly trying to see if the rest in the array were separated by the number or name of the colour. "Like this one is a bit bent to enhance the colour's depth."

Hope blinked a bit harder than usual, expression clearing into something lighter with a small grin. "I don't get to do this a lot, so I am going to nag your ears off, today."

"You are something else." I laughed, head falling back as I shook it, assuring that she could take her time.

***

"If this was an individual setting for your collaboration-" As soon as I noticed the apologetic smile, I couldn't help but nod knowingly, how this was going to head. This was like going through the rewind of this moment for the forty-seventh try. "-I would be approaching you with the funds to actually start this instead, but-"

"But this isn't just about the funds, it's about the never-ending hassle of dealing with the administration of a larger entity-" I sighed tiredly. This was the last established gallery curator in town, on my list to convince investing in our final showcase. Now we were finally down to investors visiting the country for their pop-up art gigs being displayed in the gallery, during fixed weeks. "-that has cut off our funds."

"You seem quite prepared for this." The curator stated curiously, a delicate eyebrow raised. "Almost as if you were expecting this, yet geared for something that I can't predict..."

"I know that you must hear this quite often, and it's quite true everyone is driven by the purpose of fulfilling their dream." I smiled quietly. "But I also know that the hurdles of reality against it, aren't something to be feared."

"If not feared, then ignored?"

"No, that chaos leads to negligence of abandoning the very purpose." I responded, the idle portfolio sheets in my hand, waiting to be put back in my bag.

"So, what must be done against these hurdles?" She hummed, intrigued more to herself as she walked me out with a lost gaze, glancing at the gigantic letters hanging over the entrance to her gallery - 'HUDA STUDIOS'.

I eyed her, as if trying to see if she was buying time, but even if she was, I had to gamble the chance of indulging her.

Looking back then, I couldn't tell why she was prolonging this, despite having made half her mind about her decision.

"You were right, it was the perfect decision to use the remaining denim from the Victorian street jacket-" I broke in calmly, after adjusting the tea-rose knit jumper over Destiny's shoulders and handing over the denim corset-belt."-to make the corset belt." But René was way too calm, too stoic to elicit a response.

René grimaced in a whisper leaning back on the rough-cast concrete of one of the structural pillars holding up the skyline of the arena, as Destiny called over to recheck if she had picked up the right shade of platform doc marten boots. "We are down to the thirty-second rejection down our list."

I knew that it wouldn't do any good correcting the number to forty-seven. I didn't have a concrete answer to that.

"Perhaps, it's perfectly wise to truly take a break from this until you rejuvenate your drive to get back at this." I said, earnestly as René pressed the sides of her temple trying to put up a forced smile.

"Now can you lose the poise of a model?" René definitely turned heads, even Quinsy who walked over to recheck if the angles of the props and lighting she had set beside the separating walls of the yard - were right. "I just want to check the vibe of the design on a random customer."

With the onset of the scorching summer, the reflection of the sunlight wasn't tormenting enough to damage the corneas, as they bounced against the accurate matchings of the golden vertical distances of the open Arena mimicking to serve an ode to the southern part of the Shah-Mosque, complimenting the lightings set by the props.

Who knew when we could set another date, to have the arena for ourselves after school hours?

"Okay…by *'Perhaps'*, I mean *'Undoubtedly'*." I whispered flatly, tugging René's elbow slightly in warning.

Destiny prompted, voice level and calm, despite her eyebrows drawing in confusion. "That's rather impossible for me…"

"Why so? *'Cause I said 'random customer'*?" René asked, eyes wide and staring puzzled. "Okay just lemme rephrase that with a *fancy customer*, instead-"

"No, asking me to lose the poise of a model is like…" Destiny explained, voice a bit stiffer than before. "Asking you to not visualise your observations as an artist."

René praised graciously shrugging her shoulders, shifting her mood in seconds. "Fair analogy…actually that was a really good one."

After the first testing of the outfits, it was significantly clear that, now more than ever that along with signature style, and fabric texture, and pattern, we could amplify the intangible individuality of the brand by having a signature colour as well.

"Rouge?"

"No, that just stands out completely instead of a perfect synergy of making both the person stand out along with the colour." René muttered, eyes widening with a stolid expression, shifting her jaw by the slightest movement, as she crisply placed the outfits worn for the demo run, back on the hangers. "It only suits a few and on the opposite ends of the concentration of the melanoma factor, and for the rest along the scale…it just doesn't sync."

"Yeah, let's head for something that's a lot more subtle." Quinsy hummed in affirmation, cleaning the lenses of her camera with practised ease.

"How about lavender?" Hope asked with barely veiled radiance, looking over with a small smile that I returned without any second thoughts. It was still an amazement how she swiftly changed every single look, that pulled out the right amplification to every single outfit we had designed for Destiny to try on for the demo run. "It symbolises the strength of feminism and elegance…"

"I like it, let's along with the palette down that colour." Quinsy muttered, chin resting on her fist, blinking. Most of our chrome preference in the fabrics we used - were split into Pastel and Jewel palettes. "Until we hit the once that's the perfect blend of the power of masculinity and femininity. Just a bolder shade."

I felt like a kid.

One who didn't understand how the real world worked and was still wading through a sea of douchebags to find my person or rather my reality.

Waiting for the perfect manifestation of my dream into reality.

I had convinced myself that perfection didn't exist outside my canvased world of art. That was just real life.

For every excuse I have not to pursue my dream due to the pursuits of time, I wanted to make every second count to pursue mine.

There is a difference between discipline and routines, and routines confine creativity. We can't exactly pursue our dreams if we don't live our lives.

Was I truly living mine?

I don't think I am capable of living life happily, but I want to live my life as it matters, say every word, act upon every action that matter to me-

"Flowers were so delicate... but so resilient, under the right care. Just like us." Hope carefully twisted a daisy around until it was in the right spot, smiling quietly at it as she stroked the petals gently. More than ever, Destiny had truly picked up the gleaming stalk of daisy, as a token of gratitude after her first meeting with Hope, for doing her make-up. "They remind me of the colours of pastels. We could use that."

It was barely a whisper muttered in air, so barely audible that it rivalled the falling rustle of the first wine-red pigmented leaf in fall.

I couldn't help but think back to the time I had found Hope looking more lost than anyone else, waiting outside the gates of the flattened exterior glass-building with a cantilevered roof, housing the examination hall.

-

The last person I had expected to meet after completing my admission test for Politecnico Milano, was anyone - much less, Hope.

"Hope?"

"You are the only one I know who doesn't rush to proclaim that my vision is nothing-" Hope said quietly, eyes hardening, so unlike her stoicism from before. "-but a foolish dream." I swallowed the urge to interject immediately, before carefully nudging her elbow to sit down on the pavement barricading the mallows. Hope shook her head slowly, eyeshot of someone who had slept none. Her voice was hollow. "I am tired of trying to put up with people whose twisted sense of satisfaction is derived from the numerous ways to make me quit."

My mouth tasted like copper as I sat. "Who are they?"

"At this point, I am tired of sliding past the mockery in their eyes or their superficial words." Hope bit out sharply. "Having no regard for their opinions that affect the opinions even at my work."

I felt my fingers tightening in my fists, realising that the so-called jeering opinions of those faces at school had reached as far as to Hope's make-up studio, to affect her working atmosphere even further.

This wasn't what was supposed to happen.

This…this was ignorance sprouting its head from their combined fickleness and envy, crossing its limits beyond insufferable tolerance.

"You can't tell me that you can't look at someone's eyes and know whether they're a good person or not-" I pressed, expression pleading. "-You could search the faces of the people of this school and know exactly which ones are going to torment or ignore you. You can't tell me that's superficial-"

"People can act, and I know you recognise it better than anyone else." Hope snapped, expression stormy. I really couldn't tell if I wanted to ever know the cause behind Hope being this defeated and never act upon it.

Ever since I met her, it troubled me to watch all the times' people took her consideration for granted, and now that she was considering the stop to pull back from indulging them…I couldn't help but feel helpless.

Despite the friction I wished she had against that aspect… I didn't want her to lose who she was on any accords.

For the very first time, I was a little afraid to see the emotion reflecting across her irises.

Defeat.

"That's certainly true, people around here do nothing but play the part of what's most beneficial to them." I agreed, with a soft smile amazed that she observed and trusted my intuitions instead of automatically associating them with cold rudeness. "But all I care about at this moment is the person right in front of me. Are you acting?" I asked quietly, looking at her eyes so brilliantly curious. Innocent.

I wanted to remind her once again, that I was merely reprioritising my importance

I was here because this was as equally important to me, but it seemed like she was going deafen those words murmuring "You shouldn't be here…I ruined it… that conversation seemed really important." to herself over and over again like a broken chant.

I really hated that Hope immediately recognised the curator I had met outside the examination hall, from our visit to the exhibition of metalworking for the inspiration of our next muse.

Yet, it gave me a little relief to know she had no idea what the conversation was about before I spotted her standing at the entrance of the building, looking utterly lost. I wasn't ready to break down the whole complicated situation involving the funds or the repeat of yet another rejection.

Despite my lack of belonging to my home country, I couldn't help but admire the foundation behind Hope's inspiration towards her dream of creating her own cosmetics brand. - '*I want to target my own heritage, to bring out the natural shade of the comfort of our own skin in a long-lasting effect.*'

Besides celebrating the traditional holidays, more often than not, my family barely travelled around the country to recognise the individuality of its origins.

I felt more connection in knowing more about my Cambodian heritage from Quinsy, rather than my own step on to the Khmer land, during Ma's second trip to her homeland.

Quinsy's photography always followed the play in movement over lights, when it came to the shots of her own heritage.

It was that very reminder that had drawn me to at least try in getting a chance in recruiting her onto our team.

Regardless of my bare minimum attributes in the possession of my Khmer ethnicity, Quinsy never let any moment slip by, to share the naive excitement in my fascination to appreciate every little aspect or new discovery of trying to connect with it.

Even throughout my pretence of hesitating at first, I got used to looking forward to absorbing the symbolism through my trips around the city with Hope, to rediscover the muse sourcing behind our works.

Her lips thinned, and she shifted her weight slightly. "No," she said quietly. "No, I never try to act."

I made a vague gesture with my hand as if to say, "See my point?" My expression softened slightly. "Focus on me for now... for my selfish sake." I insisted, knowing that the only way I could speak to her, past her guilt-clouded mind which wanted to push me away every moment I tried to interject that conversation had already reached its end.

It's not that I had anything against people who put up an act, because I did understand they have their own reasons and reactions to do so - for I certainly can't lie not putting up facades during several circumstances especially while trying my best to deal with such people.

But I always knew I was going to end up feeling drained if I ever got invested in the imbalance of finding a bond with my natural self in contrast to one of their facades.

Investment leads to expectations and expectations from someone's life are demandingly messed up on so many levels that the outcome leads to nothing but disappointment.

I know it should be easy just acting civil with their facades during the fleeting moments of interaction, but that's not easy for me not when I can't respect their choice or the situation that they must have faced to adorn that facade as their identity.

So the best I can do is be earnestly apathetic to them and I can't help if that comes across as rude.

It's undeniable to admit that it must not be easy for them to adorn their facades, but Nobody said it was going to be easy embracing our true selves.

There has to be at least one mutual understanding of each other's values to wanna invest further time with another, and this is mine.

"Of all the people we have intuitions about during our first impressions regarding them." Hope chuckled bitterly to break the silence, expression tight and controlled. "I wasn't expecting to be wrong about yours…"

I stared at Hope as if she had just slapped me, taken aback by her words.

"What is that supposed to mean?"

"It's nothing, I was just expecting you to be *'different'*..." Hope pressed firmly, expression twisting with eyes that were hurting. "I just had a different image of you from my interpretation of your concepts portrayed in your works."

I really couldn't comprehend what was happening. Hope looked like she was drowning, struggling for air, for something to hold onto, something-

"I am still stuck in the vagueness of the question rather catching on to what you actually might be implying." I prompted in bewilderment, more like punctuation to thought than a capital at the beginning of another sentence.

"I don't know if it's your expression, but it's very difficult to read whether you are pretending to ignore my vitiligo-" Hope said, not looking up, voice weak. "-as if you are appalled by it or want to stay ignorant to it by pitying me as if I am like everyone else?"

"What? NO!...It's not that at all! Why would I be *'appalled'*-"

"Then what is it? I am asking you point-blank, right now." Hope opened her eyes, looking up with knives in her irises...

"I know that it might sound ignorant to say that I honestly don't acknowledge physical parameters of anything around me unless I develop an attachment to them or know that I can never invest an attachment with them." I chewed my lips, needing something to stop the racing of my blood. "I am still in the thresholds of the former with you."

Silence rang, long enough to suffocate the atmosphere even further.

"Spes, we have been around each other long enough to know that you aren't blind to the glares following me or deaf towards the constant jeerings around me." Hope didn't look away, firm and resolute as a mountain against a rainstorm, deceptively voice even.

"I don't pity you or am appalled by you in any accords… I wish you would have spared more credit than that, but I also didn't ask anything because I was respecting boundaries." I said, slowly, letting my thoughts come through coherently. I waited for several heartbeats before crossing my arms. "I just didn't think you owed me or anyone any explanation about how you look…"

"I don't…but I also don't like to beat around the bush." Hope hummed stiffly, voice shaking only a little. "The reality is a lot harsher than your perception to let me grant that gigantic credibility to everyone when most can't see past their shallow judgements."

"That's why, you do wish to ask me something because of your belief in its credibility." I prompted, watching the way Hope's eyes flickered, silent admission passing over her irises. Her mouth opened, but nothing came out, brows furrowing, as if confused as to why she wasn't actually saying anything.

"The entire world is defined by mapping the first value of a person or anything around them by its appearance… you are an artist." Hope said, voice firm and strong and icy. "You can't claim that you don't capture the aspects that are worth portraying based on your liking towards their appearance."

Well, what had I done to warrant the benefit of doubt?

"Would you believe what I have to say about my perspective from my artistic point-of-view?" I questioned, taking a hesitant step forward.

"Truthfully?" Hope sighed in disdain, flicking back to the fire that wasn't fuelled by anger but fuelled by frustration and exhaustion. "Right now, I don't think I have the emotional capacity to believe that completely."

"Then would you wish to hear what I have to say regardless of the fact whether you choose to believe it-" I didn't want to allow myself the ease of breaking contact, forcing myself to maintain eye contact. I asked carefully, shaking my head heavily. "-if I do end up earning your trust to give me that chance?

"What do you have to say?" Hope asked, clenching her jaw, eyes glassy with a sharp gaze, voice coming out like a broken disc.

"Besides the days, I have gotten to know you...it has always felt like an unfamiliar reflex to admire the sheer confidence you carry yourself with and your tenacity to fulfil your dream in a world that chews it up in both subtle and obvious ways." I admitted, the words tumbling out without any second thoughts. "It doesn't stray further away from my perception regarding you from my artistic vision... that you are still just '*magnetically incredible*'."

I had never been good at...talking.

At voicing the changes, I had felt in my chest but after everything, I didn't dare feel any hesitation over something so...so simple.

I looked down sharply, neck aching at the swift movement, as my eyes landed on the hands sandwiching mine and clutching around it, tightly. I blinked in confusion, waiting for an explanation.

"You call that *not being good* with your words?" Hope's expression shifted, something more surprised as if that was the last thing, she expected me to say.

"I don't know, I have always struggled a lot with that." I shook my head, nose curling up in disdain.

"I find that hard to believe." Hope murmured resolutely. "You can't build up boundaries on your own in the name of what you think might or might not disrespect me…"

"I know…but I was given a choice of feeling guilty over crossing boundaries or holding back…" I sighed helplessly. "I would choose the latter."

"Why? It just delays the inevitable of prolonging their excuses."

"I don't regret slamming the door towards people who break the values that I expect from a bond, over time…" I sighed, eyes scanning Hope's face as I grasped the hand atop mine, gingerly. "But I have hated feeling guilty when they perceived my actions and honesty towards things, I feared hurting them, as nothing but being nosy or nagging."

"Well, people have a knack for being ungrateful in retaliation for being defensive of their inferiority." Hope broke in firmly, pulling away enough that I could see her eyes - shattered and open, like a broken window. "I am tired of being the one feeling guilty instead. How did you get past such people?"

"When I tried to respect the very boundaries, they reprimanded me for, they claimed to feel like that I no longer cared." I said heavily, feeling my gut twist sharply.

"But it's you." Hope said, something almost like confidence blending into her posture, straightening only slightly, giving extra pressure to her hands grasping mine. "It doesn't take rocket science to determine you have always been the type to be all or nothing, and I have only known you for a few months."

The exhaustion. The apprehension. The disbelief.

The warmth.

I felt my jaw tighten, everything in me telling me that Hope wasn't completely right.

"I tried to find a middle ground through that by extending the time limit to the span of the bond-" I half-smiled tiredly, voicing out the aspects titled over the years. "-before I crossed boundaries to help without disrespecting them - unless they state it earlier themselves, on their own accords."

"But, you are the most guarded person I have ever met." Hope said firmly, something dancing deep in her eyes behind the apprehension. "I don't think I have met anyone who values the aspect of '*respect*' more than you or anyone with a lower tolerance of bullshit compared to you...I can't ever imagine you ever daring to be '*nosy*'.

"Humans are *complicated*." I chuckled, weak and barely held together.

"That we are." Hope mumbled softly, head tilting.

"All I know is that I can never be right regarding the boundaries I set in order to respect the other person." I felt my body stiffen and freeze as soon as I realised my lips had upturned in a quiet smile, as I felt Hope's head resting atop my shoulder. "Because it differs from person to person, and circumstance to circumstance."

"What happens when you miss to recognise that difference?" Hope questioned with a small, exasperated sigh. "By misplacing your trust?"

I shrugged helplessly. "I am going to make mistakes, but I can try to learn and improve by getting to know them better." Glancing at Hope for only a moment, wondering the reason behind her sudden actions. "By being clearly vocal with them regarding it...perhaps if they stay consistent."

"I don't want people to ever get to know the real '*you*'."

"What?" I asked, frowning.

There was another prolonging silence enveloping us, and I kept waiting for Hope to say something or explain her words further, but there was only the silence pounding at my ears enough to hurt.

God, I used to almost wish for Hope to say something, just so the two of us could clarify these very *'puzzling'* statements.

But now, I only got a strange look reflecting across Hope's eyes, that I could never quite place in an emotional category.

I blinked as I looked fully at Hope again, my shoulders squaring.

And Hope was still hard to read.

I could see her face still unwavering with an unexplainable smile, but I never knew what the expressions meant.

 I never knew what they were trying to convey-

"I fear that most people who have ever gotten to know the real *'you'* have unexpectedly used you for your maturity and compassion-" Hope said, smiling softly in contrast to her tone taking on a sudden air of severity. "-only during their moments of vulnerability and volatility…"

"Vulnerability encourages vulnerability." I said, nodding.

"But what if they can't own up to bear that same maturity that disrupts their fickle child-like nature that is ages away from that maturity…-" Hope asked, voice falling down once more. "-and end up taking it for granted to abandon it during their happiness.

"I am quite used to hearing that *I am too serious for my own good-*" I said petulantly, feeling my voice stiffen with memory "-but I like that stability regardless of the fact whether they perceive it as a burden or not."

"You don't deserve that." Hope sighed in disappointed frustration, hoping that maybe that would be adequate for an explanation, when the manifestation was the farthest from reality. "You need a guardian for your wise old soul."

"Guardian? Really?" I frowned, my confusion deepening with every passing second. "Who on earth is going to put up with my grumpiness for that long?"

"Oh please!" Hope laughed, not quite bitter, but nothing humorous. "I am not denying that you do indeed put up that grumpy act really well to hide your invaluable warm and kind side, and I know that side."

"I think you should have this." I played with my fingers after handing over the very object, the curator had handed over at the end of the conversation.

"Is this what you were working on, in the metal-working workshop?" Hope asked quietly "But I didn't get you anything." I simply couldn't help but send a pointed glare at the sheer absurdity of that statement.

"Yeah, I wanted to personalise the iconic Versace safety pin."

"With an Aquarius hieroglyphic." Hope smiled while pinning it on to her collar and adjusting the ribbons of her soft-knot bow-tie, clueless to the quiet snarl that was needed to be hinted on to the couple staring in our direction scornfully, to either walk away or find a valid purpose in being invested in their own business.

"Well, Irises seemed a little tough to try, during my first try." I chuckled, fluffing the hairs at the back of my neck.

"Maybe my Nonna might finally beam with glee that someone cared enough to remember my birth flower." Hope grinned with a lost gaze, that seemed confusing enough to be almost surprisingly bitter, that I couldn't read. "To even attempt to incorporate them into something that's just mine."

I could still remember the sheer joy she had reigning in her tone as she reminisced her first love of flower symbolism was due to the irises gifted by her Nonna on her birthdays, who wished for nothing but to spend more time with her grand-daughter celebrating the older's appreciation for practising Hanzi.

The very first thing she had treasured since her arrival to Penang. It didn't come as a surprise that the ancient Meroitic hieroglyphs of Chinese characters had drawn her in, especially when she still cherished practising the writings of Mi'kmaq hieroglyphs, passing on the interest to her grand-daughter.

"I don't like... needing people," I murmured, my tongue felt heavy as I watched her, like waiting for something to break. "Needing things." I swallowed, as my voice felt heavy while I tried to take even breaths between my words. "Because anything can get taken away. That's what I've learned, Hope. Anything can be taken away. And if you lose something that you need... what the hell are you supposed to do?" I admitted in a breath, feeling like a boulder was slowly being lifted off of my chest.

I was losing my voice to it, the syllables weakening as I paused, taking a moment to breathe, more level.

If things and people were disposable, then it meant nothing when we lost them-

"It's different for the others. I- It's different, and I can't explain it, but the thought..." Hope's eyes were as open as I could ever remember seeing, genuine and hooded and gentle, as she stared at the strays of mallows around us. "So, I am going to guard that side, timelessly."

The silence between us was gentler, not so suffocating to make either of us burst out a need to fill it, when it dawned on me that the colour of *mauve* piercing through the *mallows* reflected what they meant, quite jarringly -

They were the *guardians* of the house, they belonged to.

For a stark, shining moment, all the doubts faded.

I still couldn't imagine the magnitude of all the monumental odds that had oriented for someone like Hope to continue existing, around someone like me.

-

"I would want our signature colour to be mauve." I smiled absently, so hard until I felt the sides of my mouth hurt watching Hope mouthing *'Mallows'* before her grin got even wider - *'Guardian'*.

"Huh…mauve does give me the vibes of royalty-" Quinsy clicked her fingers in excitement, pausing her lost haze in editing the photos from the photoshoot shot earlier, today "-compared to the solid boldness of rogue."

"It's subtle, yet demandingly regal." Hope murmured, with a warm, nostalgic smile, not wavering by the slightest.

"Fitting for the concept." René swallowed, biting the inside of her cheek. "You own it once you adorn it." She added nodding slowly with a single incline of her head.

***

Art appreciation class was a boring class, despite my investment in the subject.

It dragged by with minimal hassle because it was nothing more than a TA clicking next on Powerpoint slides with the dull scratching of pens against the paper.

But the concave walls of the buildings of the Fine Arts Department in the Northern Wing of the school, made it convenient to never be disturbed while keeping to myself at the back of this class.

Sketching was a more hands-on class usually occurring after Arts' History, and I wanted to grind my teeth to stumps as the chatter never seemed to stop, making me frequently pause so my tight grip didn't destroy the angles that I had been measuring so meticulously.

I wasn't even sure that the other people in the class were *working*.

It was only a couple of days into our classes since the last break that Mrs. Bronywyn paused by my desk, while she made her rounds.

"Excellent shadowing, Spes." She complimented, as she did with most people who bothered to make an effort. "However, if you are having trouble concentrating, you may work with headphones in, so long as you can hear any instructions I give." She smirked knowingly.

I stared at her in shock, as she smiled kindly before moving on.

I usually kept my volume down, but it was enough that I could drown out the constant yammering around me.

Today was no different- my head going in and my mind focusing on making the fireflies atop Seri Sauna bridge, like fireworks lighting the night sky.

Like finishing salt across the dense crumb of the forest floor with a twist of the lemony moon, as accurate as my memories from the firefly hunting, Hope had dragged me into, to pay up for one of our many, many bets that I had lost against her. Paying no heed to my confusion for her need of celebration of wrapping up an entrance test.

Ma always said I had steady hands.

That they were an artist's hands- even as I would draw the same figures repeatedly across my bedroom wall as a child, much too focused on my movements, even if the picture still turned out like nothing.

One mistake I had made upon coming here: I assumed people would simply ignore me and go about their day.

I switched to a softer pencil, placing it against the light reflecting against the side profile of the portrait, leaning against the railings of the bridge, I had drawn-

I felt something bump into my back.

I felt the lead of the pencil scratch against the thick paper- a dark streak of pencil streaking its way through the pristine sketch.

I was wrong.

Because even if the numerous faces got offended by ignorance, it didn't stop them from ratting out undermining cruel degrading opinions about several unfamiliar names, to me. I still couldn't get where I had failed to give the impression that I could be any less festive to be made aware of their opinions.

I stared in horror for a moment, whipping around and ripping my headphones out-

A boy (whose face seemed familiar over years yet I still couldn't place a name) quickly stepped away from me, looking like he was biting back a smile as he stared in overly exaggerated horror. "Oh, no, I am *sorry*, I didn't mean to-"

" RAY! "

I couldn't help but flinch at Mrs. Bronywyn's voice shrieking across the classroom even if it wasn't directed towards me, her eyes livid. "Detention!"

Ray's expression dropped in true horror. "*What?* That's bull-"

"Argue with me, and we will make it a trip to the Vice-Chancellor's office!" She said mercilessly. "You are done for today- leave, for disrupting class. See me later for details about your detention."

"You can't-"

"NOW."

Ray cursed beneath his breath, stomping to his bag and tearing it away from the ground, storming from the classroom and slamming the door hard enough to knock a painting from the wall.

Mrs. Bronywyn was suddenly standing at the edge of my table, clicking her tongue regretfully. "I am sorry about that, Spes. I doubt you will have time to fix it today, but if you have free time, tomorrow, you may come in to finish and correct it."

I stared at her, mouth agape as I tried to remember and recheck my schedule for tomorrow.

I had my shift at Jove's convenience store right after classes, so my only chance was during lunch, so I nodded in confirmation. "I have a break right during lunch."

Mrs. Bronywyn nodded quietly, looking genuinely apologetic for the chaos occurring out of her control. "That will be fine. If I am in a meeting with someone, just come in and sit quietly, alright?"

I nodded, thanking her graciously. She was under no obligation to give me time to fix it before the due date, and I thanked my stars that I would be allowed to.

I could not take any hit to my grade, especially in this class.

When Mrs. Bronywyn left me to begin fixing the dark streak, I took a quick glance across the classroom.

Most of the people were still staring at me - either with shock or hiding laughter behind their hands.

However, for the first time since I could remember, Hope was staring back from the seat, from the front end of the class.

Since when did Hope and I share the same class timings?

She stared at me silently. Lips pressed together and eyes dark with something that almost looked sorry.

I returned to my work, shoving my headphones back in, not letting the stress have a chance to get to me. I am used to working on a deadline, and I could do it again.

Class ended without me finishing my corrections, but I had managed to make sure every dark part had been erased carefully and had begun redrawing the tarnished portion.

I was glad to be the first one to leave, shoving my things away and putting my sketch back on the rack it would wait on. I left the classroom without a glance back until I stopped in my tracks nearing Hope waiting in the hallways.

Turns out, Hope had the same schedule for the past two years.

Hope merely laughed at my shock as we sat under the shade of a single Belian tree in the middle of the courtyard running parallel to the main path leading to the library.

The courtyard was never very full- with most people preferring to stay inside, safe from the sun and the weather. A few students were scattered beneath umbrellas (at the picnic tables that I always avoided) chatting cordially or laughing obnoxiously loud.

But it was always better than the cafeteria, where some rambunctious face was bound to splatter their lunch against the floor, food getting everywhere, where some moron would take up the neurotic challenge to punch through a damn watermelon during the end of summer lunch picnic (which had not been a picnic - there were wedding tents and tile flooring brought out for Christ's sake)

"I don't know why it's coming as a surprise to you that you tend to zone out everything around you, when you are sketching or studying." Hope burst out laughing, shockingly loud as I returned an unimpressed look. "You pretty much only acknowledge the people revolving in your own world."

"I can't believe myself-"

"You were always the only one to give me spare supplies, even when you didn't know me." Hope merely grinned, playing with the chopped grass on the ground. "Granted, it was my pathetic attempts to start a conversation with you. You never looked or asked me once, while assuring to give me the newer art supplies."

"Seriously?-"

"You do know that I live around the convenience store you work at, right?" Hope questioned genuinely, as I stared at her in disbelief, feeling my lower jaw go slack. The more I heard, the more I couldn't help but wonder why she hadn't approached sooner to seek her diary, from the notices Quinsy had put up.

"You are kidding, right?"

"No, I am not." Hope admitted quietly with an apologetic smile. "Even through minimal tasks, you were always lost seemed in your own world. In fact, you always recommended the best options for the new selection of beverages."

"Wow, Pax was right, I *am* pompous." I groaned in dismay, covering my face with my hands.

"Come on, that's not true." Hope chuckled before hitting my shoulder lightly. "I had fun staring at the shocked faces of people staring at me even more than usual as if I actually have the snout of a zebra."

"I am sorry for my ignorance-"

"Don't be. It's special." Hope interjected sternly. "I don't think you realise why it's rare to have someone that treats the people they care for, as if the world revolves only around them." Hope offered a wrapped coconut pound rice cake, before continuing obtusely as I shook my head with a polite decline reminding her that she barely had anything of the very sweet, that happened to be her favourite. "It would be *weird* if you did that without taking your time to know someone."

Before I could even take the chance to object again, she merely shoved the rice cake inside my mouth and trying to stop her laughter behind her hand, as I stared at the empty wrapper in my hand and covering my mouth with my hands while trying my best to not spit while chewing the whole thing in one go.

"You are really nice," I said, staring at the little paper wrapper. "Like… obscenely nice. Are you sure they don't have a statue of you built somewhere around here?"

"Why? Are you gonna build me one if they don't?" Hope huffed a laugh, before startling herself and wincing immediately.

"What?" I couldn't help but snicker as her face flushed red in response to her own words.

"I-I am sorry. I don't handle compliments well." Hope went quickly, looking like she had been waiting to get this out for a while. "It's your fault!"

"My fault?" I asked in sheer amusement, rubbing my cheek, absently.

"You give out compliments as if you are talking about *'the Earth revolving around the Sun'*!" She tsked, before huffing in disdain and trying to glare at me.

"Well, I am stating the facts." I assured good-naturedly, before raising my hands in mock-defeat. "I can't even sugarcoat my words, to save my own forsaken life."

"In my defence, you started it!"

"Your defence? Why would you even need a defence in this case." I laughed weakly at her frantic state, dropping my head to rest against my knees. "I appreciate the gesture."

"But why?" Hope looked genuinely surprised as I stared back at her in disbelief. "You do it quite often, like a habit for everyone around you."

"Are you sure, you are not mistaking me for someone else?"

"Oh, trust me." Hope's smile brightened, unexplainably vibrant as if she was proud to know the secrets to something that no one else did. "You are something else."

I think my father once told me that- Personal space was like salt, it's important and even if I am a person

who prefers salty food, I wouldn't exactly crave sea
water like embracing complete solidarity.

I think I developed a pathological need of seeking
comfort from anything constant that reminded me I
did have something good inside me besides my anger.

'Good'- that wasn't defined by my skills but rather just
by the person I am.

So, I ended up fighting against every single thread of
the source that feels like a threat against the comfort
building inside me, and I am so tired of it...

Everytime I started convincing myself it's okay to
stop, my trust starts being rattled in the most
unexpected way possible. I think all I was doing was
constantly reacting instead of responding...

It's easier to feel anger than anything else because I
don't feel anything if that gets robbed, and I can
handle that... I can handle the familiarity of that.

I was tired of fighting.

I was tired of fakeness.

I was tired of thinking and worrying.

I was tired of everything.

I thought I was testing the waters from the safety of
the shallows, but somehow, I had missed the riptide
coming through and pulling me out to sea.

I hadn't realised how far the shore had gotten.

Had let myself think- just a little further and then I'll
turn back, just a little further, just a little-

And I was foolish enough to think I was strong enough a swimmer to go against the current.

Thought I could fight my way back to solid ground. I had just been tiring myself out. Fighting a losing battle.

I had been fooling myself.

I actually liked my working shift at the convenience store, and it was easy work - restocking the convenience store shelves, greeting customers, ringing up items…

Most people who came in just wanted to get in and out, which was good, and most weren't obnoxiously rude, so I was grateful for it. Usually, I had plenty of time during my shift to study for any tests I had coming up.

It was a good deal.

But during certain occasions, there were certain ignorants who associated regression of the brain with the sight of wheelchairs, preferring to stand in the line that is longer than get their billing done sooner, by someone who practically owned the store.

Most times, I bit down from expressing my opinions to their clear lack of respect merely checking with Jove as she handled the situation.

Then we would spend our time, eating stupid sweets and possibly increasing our chances of getting diabetes - she laughed as we took our time venting out profanities against nuisances, held back earlier in the name of customer service.

Although today, all the monumental hurdles our reality withered away against the will of Jove's dream. No prejudices.

No denials.

No delusions.

Just fairness of skills being recognised for the deserving potential, for the fitting position.

A fair chance.

"So, it's temporary for the next six months, until you see me permanently at 7 PM." Jove smiled vibrantly, tapping her pen against the table near the cashier, as I closed my Advanced Geometry workbook, resting my chin against the heel of my palm, smiling in equal resonance.

There were hardly any breaks between our AP results being declared and CLEP exams beginning soon within the next two months.

"Well, you do know the right person to choose power-suits with, right?" I teased sombrely, twirling my pen between my fingers.

"I don't know but if a certain *Zrey* doesn't accompany me, we are going to exchange words." Jove simply grabbed a strawberry cake from the counter with a gentle smile, before winking.

"She is on board." I huffed in half-amusement, as she opened the packet to have the cake.

"I feel like finally recognising the strength in me, that was constantly ripped away from my grasp." Jove said earnestly, like she didn't know how else to articulate it.

"Jove, you have always been invincible-"

"Spes, only you choose to view it like that, regardless of any ups and downs-" Jove shrugged simply, expression sobering slightly, though still keeping that brightness.

"Jove, what defines your strength is your unwavering love for your dream, no matter which day it might be." I said firmly, placing my hand on her shoulder and giving it a small squeeze for reassurance "You constantly functioned on an accelerating gear of continuing to fight against any injustice and prejudice that overshadowed your efforts."

"I hope it continues to stay this way."

Then, it finally dawned on me, what this was truly about.

This was never about doubts, but hesitance towards the News Broadcasting Channel deciding to, perhaps, reconsider their decision.

Hesitance towards the possibility of the call-back from the CMNC (Central Malaysian News Company) Network was just another false hope waiting to be ripped away, yet once again when this was the closest, she had ever gotten to her dream.

Hesitance towards the notion of if her zeal might falter, if this chance turned out to be mockery.

"Your shield wasn't built over a day." I assured quietly. "You are the one who has gotten you all the way through everything to your present. To this moment."

"You are right." Jove sighed in relief, grinning widely with her eyes practically sparkling. "I am one hell of a fighter. I am going to be one hell of a journalist."

"You got this-" I winked, bouncing on the balls of my feet, when I heard the shop bell tinkle in sync with the ring of my phone.

Hope stood just inside - smiling at both Jove and me, nodding in greeting, walking down the beverages aisle.

"Good evening, welcome-" Jove smiled in return, as I excused myself to take Felicity's call.

I stopped myself, feeling my brain short-circuit.

The last time I had heard Felicity be this frantic, was when she woke up to Pax and I screaming at each other at the latest update of the court-hearing for custody, getting prolonged due to our Grandparents' intervening with their lawyer.

***

Perhaps I know when the nightmares began three years ago. They are why I stopped sleeping in the first place.

No, I never told people what the nightmares were about.

Not even Pax.

Not even Ma.

I barely told one therapist after everything, but then I locked all those stupid images my brain gave me away and never let them see the light of day again.

They still haunted me. They were like a smudge on the edge of the glass.

Clearly, my stubbornness just elevated the catastrophically *wrong fit* for my first and only try. There was no time for any trials and errors, for now.

If you searched for them, if you knew they were there, you could remember what they were. Otherwise, you would never have even noticed something was off, something was wrong in that little corner.

What good would bringing up these nightmares do?

Just stop thinking.

Things could go so much smoother if I just stopped thinking.

I was so tired, and my brain was so sluggish from everything that had been happening, and I just wanted to let it all go.

The same fear of negligence of getting on someone's nerves far enough that they didn't stop to break my hands or struggling to breathe to the point where no matter how long I tried to scrape out the glue that no-longer existed along the linings of my throat - just closed it up.

Where I would leave my dreams unfinished or cause damage to the point that I would finally would not be able to prevent the ugly truth that I wasn't to blame for the final straw to not do anything to prevent the separation.

Maybe I was sparing myself the excuse of believing that I was trying my best to respect their choices, to never attempt to join Pax in preventing it.

There wasn't a single night where I slept that I didn't wake up reaching for the steel tongue-scraper. I would think that I was choking, that I had ended up drinking the mixture all over again, that there was someone bound to try it again…but there never was.

Maybe if I hadn't ended up discovering about the separation before our parents broke it out to us, then perhaps they wouldn't have felt the need to come close enough to discover the scrapped throat while I spoke or my clear lack of sleep, to assure that I would support them after their respective explanations.

When I refused to speak for months to the therapist owing my Ma a favour for taking care of her mother during her final days, he merely suggested I just take some sleeping pills.

Which was great.

Because now I got a full eight hours of night terrors, unable to wake up from them. It was worse than not sleeping or the nightmares alone. I was exhausted, I was… I just took them anyway. And I just suffered through waking up feeling like I had been shot in the chest.

At least I was sleeping.

Sort of.

I wasn't really sleeping. I was just unconscious.

I took them every night. Maybe my body had gotten too used to them, but even three or four pills didn't let me sleep for anything more than a couple of hours long.

I was too afraid to take more or stronger ones, so I stopped, and I just… didn't sleep again.

I was tired of being forced inside these nightmares.

But it was… definitely affecting my concentration, and I couldn't let that affect my schedule, to find the excuse to practise less or come up with subpar concepts.

I was twitchy, going over great lengths to stop drinking water for days, or throwing away food.

My nerves were shot.

The nightmares actually did lessen, with time, as I moved on from the *incident*. I didn't relive it every time I closed my eyes. But I guess I had gotten used to not sleeping. I hated myself for being stuck in the loop-hole of my self-imposed insomnia.

It felt like everyday my body was trying to shut down, but it never slept.

But when I started delaying my commissions and started being negligent to my own family, barely maintaining my attention when they confided in me. I couldn't even be there for Pax, when our Parents finally broke the news to us…

I decided I didn't care about nightmares or consequences, I just wanted to actually sleep, to get my act in order.

I remembered walking to my bathroom cabinet, the little bottle I had been too afraid to go back to.

I woke up in the hospital with my stomach pumped, and a doctor scolding me about taking so many, how I should have known better...

Despite my attempts of forgetting it, I could never manipulate my mind to forget it completely.

My only distraction while recovering was the fragments of memories of conversing with the person named *Fadel,* admitted in the next room, through the writings across network-deprived, nearly broken tablets - that could barely function as anything but writing pad or a calculator, being one of the only objects mandated to be allowed inside the individual wards - displayed through the narrow slab of glass in-built within the concrete wall separating us, barely reaching my eyes.

-

> **Fadel:** *'How many days since you have been here?'*
>
> **- 'Just five. I will be leaving on Tuesday.'**

All I knew, all I saw was cerulean-blue dyed hair framing eyes that were clouded over-like a diamond that someone had thrown away and let collect dust, never bothering to clean it.

Not apathy.

Not flippancy.

The rest of the face was covered by a mask from the tip of the nose, despite the impact of humidity, clearly visibly through the sweat running across the forehead.

Even if I couldn't help but nearly quip about it in my thoughts, it wasn't my place to blatantly ask about it, given the obvious surroundings we were confined to.

Fadel: '*So am I. Well, it would be nice to have a conversation outside this 4x15 inch glass dimension.*'

I couldn't help but laugh as soon as I read the message etched across the screen.

I needed a distraction.

Something calm away from the chaos entailing because of my helplessness of being trapped in here, instead of staying beside Ma.

I knew that Dad would immediately stop the chiding of his Parents towards Ma, as they found some way to blame her. Ma and Dad always kept us away from his parents ever chiding against our Ma to us, visiting them only when it was necessary for family weddings.

They never missed an opportunity to express their distaste about Ma being an adopted child, who lost her foster Parents before she could complete the final year of her Nursing School.

- '**That's alarmingly accurate**.'

For the first time, Ma and Dad were genuinely *talking* to each other, since years.

That's when I had realised, when people fight, there is still a glaringly large choice to salvage.

When they start being indifferent to each other - they have already given up.

Fadel: *'Can you blame me? I was bored. The flowers are already wilting in my room and I need a distraction from feeling helpless to do anything to prevent that.'*

Flowers?

- **'The stillness is eating my brain alive.'**

Fadel: *'Tell me about it. I can feel the hands of the giant clock in my room animatedly speaking to me as if I am stuck in the musical - "Beauty and the Beast".'*

- **'There are times where I feel that perhaps I needed this stillness to gain perspective, but-'**

Fadel: *'Being used to the thrill of finding purpose and chasing that against the racing of time is hard to shake off.'*

- **'Time is limited.'**

Fadel: *'Yeah, so is our life. Yet it's neither of those that are scary but rather the prospect of regret that always torments us.'*

- **'In a way, our dreams define our life, the moments with the people we love and ourselves defines our time.'**

I typed things in for a long time, as the eyebrows on the other side of the glass creased together in a frown.

Knocking on the glass, to demand what I was doing.

Fadel: *'It's the fear of regret of chasing the wrong one in both aspects, that overwhelms us.'*

> **- 'Perhaps that's the very notion that holds us back from self-reflecting and we can't help but beat ourselves if it ends up happening again, even when we know that's humane.'**

Fadel: *'Why are you here?'*

My tongue felt like lead. As if I could still taste bitter guilt in the back of my throat.

> **- 'We aren't third graders swapping secrets at a sleepover.'**

Fadel: *'In all fairness, we still don't know the actuality of that from both sides, and I am fine keeping it that way. Maybe that would preserve the authenticity of this.'*

I felt my tongue suddenly unstuck from the roof of my mouth, as I sighed in disdain.

So, I chose the adequate word that was fitting enough to sum up everything. The cause of the incident as well as my reaction to it.

> **- 'Carelessness.'**

Fadel: '*What's your opinion on norms instilled around you since the time you are born?*'

I stared at the eyes that stayed unwaveringly still, the expression reflecting across the orbs slightly stricken.

It wasn't a question I could take my time to think about or hide from it like I was being followed by a hunting dog on a scent.

> **- 'It's not an opinion but a fact, that I am going to continue finding myself outside those quantifying norms and shouldn't let those limitations define me.'**

Fadel: '*Even it comes at the cost of disappointing those around you?*'

> **- 'Did it cost you the cost of disappointing yourself?'**

The air around me had started feeling denser. As if someone had taken a fan and started waving away the smog, clouding my vision.

The words were so vague yet held so much weightage that I didn't want to say anything negative as if I were slipping or sliding down a slope or anything positive that didn't guarantee any accountability - toxic positivity.

Fadel: '*No, I feel free. 'Felt' free.*'

> **- 'Then that's all that should matter the most.'**

Fadel: '*Then why does it still feel so suffocating? It's my life. My time. My worth. I just want the space to lemme breathe in the choices of my decisions.*'

> **- 'It's your life. To hell with their standards. You needn't acknowledge nor bother with them.'**

Fadel: '*I can't just rip them off my life, even when they refuse to accept me completely.*'

Despite our conversations for the past four days, I felt my fingers curl into my fists, wondering who might have made this person who was so jarringly authentic - feel unacceptable.

What rights did they have?

Her expression stayed unreadable, a little shaken, as I tried to wonder what was continuing to spawn in relation to it.

> **- 'They aren't going to live your life, You are. So, the only standards worth acknowledging are your own.'**

This was the purest form of communication I had had in ages.

Not yelling.

Not waiting for one side to say the wrong thing.

There was no purpose in saying all of this other than passing along hopes of understanding.

Fadel: *'I really want to cherish it at my own pace. To refuel my zeal and determination, without their interference.'*

> - 'Perhaps it's projected guilt from sensing their disappointment and their choice of prioritising those norms.'

Fadel: *'Do you propose to have a way to control that?'*

> - 'No, I don't. Because all you can do is wait for them to come around... and that wait would always be burdensome.'

Fadel: *'What would you prioritise?'*

> - 'I would prioritise myself.'

I wanted to say something more.

Felt like I needed to say something as the eyes staring back at me looked like they had swallowed sour milk.

But what on earth could I possibly say that wouldn't be dismissive under these circumstances?

Fadel: *'But aren't we being selfish according to the expected ideals ongoing for ages? Which one is right?'*

> - 'Expected ideals?'

Fadel: *'One ideal expects us to live with the possibility of slowly losing ourselves for others even if it's for the people we love while the other ideal expects us to live with the possibility of being alone?'*

I felt her eyes flicker over mine, like an animal trying to find the best way around a threat - the long strands of their hair framing her face mimicking the fur standing on end.

> - '**Maybe none of these ideals can survive because I am not certain if these ideals can abide within the changes existing in the different individualities of people.**'

Fadel: '*Why?*'

The ideal balance of our existence is the value of cherishing the worth of '*us*', and it's true people around us advising or rather shoving our heads into the significance of making all our decisions based on the priority of how those decisions affect the '*us*' - our family, our friends and all our dear ones and sacrifice accordingly.

They are not wrong, it's the ultimate harmony we seek to maintain.

But it's not right to make those sacrifices a mandatory deed.

It's *noble,* but not mandatory.

It shouldn't be taken for granted in the name of it being mandatory.

'Cause women all around the world are expected to make this choice.

It's not much of a choice but undermining their empathy and rights as always, 'cause once again it's an expectation sought from them for withholding their household, that's when the value of *'us'* is already being uprooted by hypocrisy.

> - 'Because I think appreciating that difference is the only ideal that should be immortalised.'

Fadel: *'What if it ends up being too tiresome for the morals already instilled in us?'*

It was clear that whatever this was, it had coloured a manifestation, debilitating and raw, that I wouldn't dare to rush through.

> - 'We need to wholeheartedly prioritise the worth of *'me'*, to understand the harmony of having the choice of sacrificing that *'me'* shouldn't exist if there actually is an *'us'*, because the moment that happens there is no *'us'*, there is no *'You and I'*, there is just *'You'*.'

Fadel: *'Do you think your difference helps you decide what's right and wrong for you?'*

It was like a punch to my sternum, choking my lungs.

Even through the vagueness, the words demanded something heavy.

Hard. Concrete.

> - 'It helps me learn and evolve, helps me find me.'

Fadel: '*When do you think we reach the end of the certainty of knowing who we are?*

It wasn't a question.

It wasn't a demand.

It was alarmingly calm but vibrating beneath the surface, like the beginning thrums of an earthquake...

- '**I am still figuring that out**.'

Fadel: '*Let's just say that the double marginalisation of an aspect of something that was always visible along with the discovery of an aspect that is a part of me, isn't being handled enthusiastically by the people around me.*'

-

"...I don't know where Pax is. She just stormed out after Ma left for her shift. She is not picking up her call." I could hear Felicity choking up frantically through the phone as she tried to explain the circumstances. "The fight between them was *pretty* bad, like worse than fights between you guys.-"

"Felicity, please tell me you are at home." I asked poignantly, praying that Felicity wasn't looking for Pax late at night.

"Yes, yes I-I am, but I didn't know what to do-"

"That's good. That's very good." I sighed in relief, feeling the growing weight settling in my chest disappear staring at the amber lighting of the street light pole I was leaning against, as I tried to think coherently as Felicity keep chanting '*I want to help but I don't know what to do. I should have stopped them.*' "Felicity, listen to me… I need your help. Let's handle this together."

"Yes, I will do anything." She pressed desperately.

"Make sure to get updates from Ma as soon as she reaches the hospital." I said, pinching the bridge of my nose and hoping that my voice was steady as possible, the last thing I wanted was to influence Felicity's worry by detecting mine. There was a huge chance that Ma must have driven to work soon after, in a sour mood and I needed one of us to check on her while I tracked Pax. "I will find Pax. Don't hesitate to call me for anything, but please stay at home, no matter what."

"Pax isn't picking up her call-"

"It's okay, I think I might know where she might be." I assured desperately, as a reassurance meant more for myself. "We will come home soon."

***

IV

"The depths of empathy rope in the warmth of security that coaxes the fragile heart at bay."

CHAPTER - VII

Perhaps this had been long overdue. Yet, a part of me had hoped we could mend this without the truth leading Pax to any guilt-ridden realisations…

———

"Words fail, and I think it's amazing that you forgive several things easily 'cause you are so hell-bent on holding people accountable on their words 'cause you know that words fail." Pax burst angrily, glaring at me as she pushed me by my shoulders in my attempt to hug her while trying to convince her that our grandparents wanted Ma to lose custody completely. "It's not fair that you determine the worth of a person based on their words 'cause you know it's the simplest yet the most difficult aspect a person can carelessly take for granted."

We could still hear Dad asking- nearly yelling at his parents to go back and withdraw their lawyer from their case, in the hallways of the Hospital, as I closed the door to my room. They weren't sparing any chance to use Pax's statement against Ma, being unfit for custody.

I knew that Pax refused to believe that nothing would change, refused to believe that Dad won't leave us. The shock prevented her to pay heed even when we were approached by the same lawyer individually, to explain the circumstances and the procedure to wrap this up quickly where the natural custody would be given to Ma.

Unless neither of us said anything that would open the can of worms to brew this onto a complicated case of a custody battle.

Joint custody was quite foreign to exist around in our communities, so our parents had always agreed to wrap this up in the quietest way possible, where they both knew that they didn't require any papers to know that each of them had equal custody of their children.

"Can we have this conversation later?" I hissed harshly, eyeing Felicity who was fast asleep, as I refused to address Pax's questions about today's hearing for one of us had to take care of Felicity.

Especially when our grandparents were trying to sway Pax's vulnerability of wanting to make our parents reverse the divorce, which had already been finalised.

"Why? Because you get to hide and decide who gets to know the information that could affect people besides *yourself*?" Pax scoffed

"What-"

"It's not fair that you are right not to trust people on the basis of their words,-" Pax spat, eyes flashing. "-'cause most people who easily go back on their words carelessly always find it easy to betray."

"Who betrayed you?! Tell me about it right now-" I questioned, mouth tasting worse than the hospital porridge could ever. I couldn't decide if it was unceremoniously bland and ridiculously hot. "-and I will worry about apologising about not respecting your boundaries later, after I destroy the inferiority complex of that bastard."

I was well aware of Pax's friends being aware of the separation and telling her to find people that would delay the court's hearing, just to shut her up.

"How are you even so certain that they might have an inferiority complex?" Pax snapped, her voice icy.

" 'Cause people who betray other people, feel empty inside themselves 'cause of their inferiority complex." I huffed, running a hand through my hair, stomach and chest and mind churning and whirling sickeningly. Pax couldn't understand. " 'Cause they are always looking for others to fill their void, so they find it easy to use people when they need them and walk away without realising any of it."

"See, this is why you make us feel like the ones who can't even comprehend empathy." Pax snarled, looking up to glare at me.

It was a surprise that Felicity hadn't woken up earlier.

"I-what?"

"Shut up!" Pax yelled darkly, voice tingling towards exasperated. "Will you just shut up and admit that you are pissed at me for throwing away a piece about you, when we both know you hate talking about yourself."

Our grandparents being here during this time, gave them another reason to blame Ma for my situation as well as remind me to study *real and serious subjects* and stop wasting time.

"This isn't about me-" I said firmly, aching fists clenching, sitting by the edge of my bed and trying to nudge Felicity to go back to sleep as she looked at Pax in alarm. I gave her a forced small smile as she tiredly asked me to check, if things were alright. Because subconsciously or not, I saw Felicity's face relax- the tiniest, smallest, most minuscule bit- at the attempts of my smile. "-and that's what angers me about you in this situation that you don't get it that, this isn't about me!"

"Then what?" She demanded, rubbing the sides of her temple with the heels of her palms. " 'Cause mom looks hella guilty and even apologised to me and even Dad-"

I knew that Pax felt betrayed when I refused to help her along with this plan, just to force our parents to be together.

For days, I had truly considered this because unlike her I had known about their decision longer than she had.

For days, I feared that this truly meant our family was falling apart.

I understood why she had been equally shocked by their decision for we had never watched our parents fight, but the decisions they took on their own started taking a toll.

Our grandparents just happened to be the right people interfering to delay the court's hearing to declare our mother unfit for custody, against our Parents' decision. Even today, the events ended up in nothing but unnecessarily delay and complicate the process.

"THAT'S WHAT PISSES ME OFF, THAT RIGHT THERE!" I couldn't help but snarl, with a growing displeasure twisting in my mouth, hearing both Ma and Dad feel constantly guilty for taking a decision as independent individuals, for once. "You don't get it! I hate that they feel guilty about this when they were dragged into something that they weren't supposed to be a part of!"

While it was understandable why Dad chose never to say the negative bumps of managing the financial assets of the clients in his company and merely keep the impacts of it to himself, by filtering what he spoke to only ever bring up the positive outcomes.

He never wanted us to worry, but over years Ma started developing a habit of speaking to him on a need-to-know basis, giving up her stance to demand clarity through thick and thin.

They barely acknowledged each other during dinner, centering the attention on us, to spend time with us after work, with Pax leaning more towards Dad jamming classics with him, while I spent hours talking about our days and wild concepts with Ma.

It was clear that they must have been initially scared about their decision as well.

"They are our Parents." Pax scoffed, humming stiffly. "They will always get dragged into everything involving us, they did that when they decided to drag us into their mess."

Looking back, I could remember the times there was a sudden shift where Ma didn't just whole-heartedly cheer Pax in her recitals or accompany her to all her classes like she had been doing since the beginning, but spent hours genuinely trying to listen Pax speak about her composing process.

While Dad didn't just tease me about waiting to redecorate the interiors of our home by replacing my old works hanging in the room with the newer ones, suddenly making more time to rope me in while introducing me to his favourite classics in movies or songs or food.

The only times we spent together so coherently that it was impossible to recognise the growing apathy between Ma and Dad, was when we ganged up to spoil Felicity, who was barely in her early stages of schooling.

"THEY DID NOT!" I spat, feeling my teeth starting to grind. "They always prioritised us! Even now they are still prioritising us-"

"Yeah, you made sure of that, didn't you?"

All my efforts to keep Pax unaware of today's hearing, would go in vain, once our grandparents started using reverse psychology to blame her instead, if things didn't work in their favour or if Dad avoided them with determination because of their interference.

Not hesitating to throw it at her face that they wouldn't be here, if she hadn't called them for help.

I couldn't let them hurt Pax, especially not when all she was doing was trying to prevent the recent change of events.

But at this point, that was starting to be a growing challenge, every passing second.

"What is that supposed to mean?" I asked, quietly, hopping up from the bed and taking a step towards Pax.

"It's ironic despite all your talk about insisting on respecting boundaries-" She snorted bitterly, as my stomach sank further. "-the secrets you kept to yourself might have been the unspoken words that would have saved our family."

"*Saved our family?* Why does our family need saving?" I demanded, voice breaking at the end as I stormed forward a couple of steps.

"Don't you hear what people say?! That we are making a mockery out of a family by having our parents separated but still planning to co-parent?" Pax asked, blinking with more streaks cascading down her cheeks, as she threw the tissue box- that I offered- towards the corner of the room. "Nothing has *changed?* Why did you encourage Ma to go ahead with the separation? You should have stopped her, if it weren't for you then we would be a *normal* family!"

"No, I don't hear them, 'cause *those people* don't know us, *those people* don't matter to me and neither does their opinion of our family." I shook my head, nose curling in self-disgust "I don't know what's the definition of *normal* you are seeking but we are a family. We are always there for each other and that's all that matters."

"Yeah, why would you care?" Pax scoffed, rolling her eyes, more tears falling as she blinked to clear them. "You are so emotionally stunted, so far as to drive our own father away, by creating this mess and branding us a laughing stock around everybody."

"What did *you* just say?"

"I can't imagine the level of hypocrisy fitting into your head,-" She whispered staring at the ground, voice hoarse. "-that you drive a wedge between everyone around you 'cause of your pride and ego."

"Tell me something new." I couldn't blink, at this point, I was surprised that I hadn't physically thrown up, yet. "If you have nothing important to say then I am getting late for-"

"Are you even capable of letting go of self-respect or ego in the name of love?" She asked, voice thick with tears. "Actually, are you even capable of love?"

"I never sought to rationalise their situation, it's not even my place to do so." I said, heavily, losing the strength in my feet to stand any longer and just slump down to the floor. "Rather than jumping on to rationalising based on my assumptions, I just wanted to understand."

"They aren't being rational about this." She sighed tiredly. I could see her eyes- shattered and open, like a broken window-

The fear.

The apprehension.

The disbelief.

"That's not your place to determine." I pressed, trying my best to reason. "Neither is it, mine or yours or Felicity's and especially not our grandparents' who are outside."

"They are making a big mistake!"

"So? It's their feelings, their space, their decision…" I begged, more as a desperate excuse to see the things, she was choosing to be oblivious to. "Why is it a mistake to act upon it?"

They were happy around the presence of each other, since the longest time, I had ever watched them be.

More than anyone else I hated *change*, but this was a *change* that was miraculously precious.

This was a change that felt truer than the existing past that we were used to.

"Why are you so unfazed about this?!" Pax spat, her jaw tightening, something dancing deep in her eyes behind the apprehension. "They are letting their emotions cloud their judgement and aren't thinking straight."

"I think you should stop undermining their feelings, much less see it as an inhumane hindrance influencing their capacity to think clearly." I swallowed, sighing tiredly. My voice almost failing. "They have every right to process their feelings, rather than bottle it up in the name of logical judgement."

"Do you want this to happen?" Pax asked, voice quick as a blade unsheathing.

"That's not on me! I am not passing my judgement on their feelings and decisions as a couple! Or basing my wants and needs over it." I pressed, sternly. My shoulders slumped further, as if forcing myself to muscle through the uncertainty. "We are their children, not the puppet-master of their marriage to interfere with their decisions involving that space. I want them to be happy-"

"You don't care about our family, do you?"

It was like a vicious punch to my chest as my heart fell immediately, twisting and freezing, with a vulture preying on it as though it were a carcass.

"Get out."

"Did you actually say this to them as well while I have been trying to beg them to change their mind?-"

"Get OUT." I spat, repeating my words with a glare, not paying any heed to my younger sister wincing before walking out and slamming the door behind her.

-

There was one place I could think of that Pax would go to, that was like the Aquaria to me.

She rarely went to the little fields that surrounded the skatepark.

The skatepark at the other side of the town that Pax and I used to go to when we were four and six, respectively.

Most often, I found amusement in teasing her about the stars that shone so brightly. Even among the city lights in the distance reminding her of her perception of Life as a symphony bridging the unique counterpoints, we ought to cherish.

Even through the shadow of nights, it was the rhythmic *harmony* of the importance of freedom in recognising our identity that brought forth the serene balance of *harmony* among us all.

Pax merely smacked the back of my head, if I vocalised my true opinion about it, and questioned the reason behind subjecting her to *unnecessary sappiness*.

"You haven't been here for a while." I sighed, sitting with my knees curling up slightly, beside the figure laying flat on the grass.

"I don't think I can ever face Ma, again." Pax sighed defeatedly, frowning to see through the dim lighting from the moon.

"So, are we camping here until then?" I quipped, quirking an eyebrow as Pax scoffed lightly. A soft, tired thing, like a weak little breath from a broken lung. "Gotta tell you, Pax… I think we are way too sheltered to survive till then."

"Ma finally told me about the actual reason, you changed your last name-" Pax winced, before sitting up and curling around her knees tighter. "-when I accused her of breaking our family, again…Why didn't you tell me?"

Despite hating to have Pax spend time around faces who dismissed her every time she wasn't spending time helping them catch up with their missed notes.

It was better than having her being around our grandparents who started blaming Ma immediately even using Pax's words as a weapon against Ma, as soon as the custody hearing didn't head in their favour.

As soon as they started belittling Ma again, over a lack of family and a family name, yammering on about the joke of a family she had or how adoption didn't guarantee a *real* family- I felt victorious changing my last name to Ma's, to prove the existence and continuation of her real family.

"Pax, I don't think it's a shocker that we are massively stubborn. If we didn't, then I would doubt if we shared the same genes." I stated, grinning slightly and offering a wry smile. "It never mattered what I had to say about it, until you saw the truth for yourself and accepted it."

Unfortunately, our grandparents had managed to seed the plant of notion onto Pax that I had merely changed it to choose Ma's side and was driving a wedge between Ma and Dad.

I had to urge my Parents to let it slide instead of correcting Pax, for explaining the situation would mean making her aware of the dark orthodox opinions that still existed in the world and hurting her.

Or else it would have defeated the final purpose of preventing my grandparents to find the chance to blame Pax, directly or indirectly.

"All those things I said over the years-" Pax muttered under her breath, shaking her head in despondence. "-I don't even know if I can ever forgive myself."

"Pax, you can't blame yourself for taking your time to adapt to a change-" I pressed as a matter-of-factly, placing my hand over her shoulder, carefully.

"You adapted to it, right away."

"Actually, I did not." I confessed quietly, as Pax took my hand in hers and started shaking it, shortly. "I did confuse the conventional requirements of a '*happy family*' until I actually saw Ma and Dad be happy around each other, since the longest time, ever."

Ever since their decision to separate, the changes that were meant to be subtle became jarringly obvious over the smallest things.

Whether it was Dad laughing and bickering with Ma to switch channels before settling onto to be engrossed onto the show himself and bombarding her with questions instead of their earlier preferences to watch in separate rooms.

Or asking about each other's work without ending the conversation in seconds as if they were speaking about the weather.

Or teasing each other about the produce either of them might have purchased in bulk while restocking, instead of pinning check-lists on the fridge magnets.

The checklists meant to cut down any array of conversations over the essentials had disappeared.

"Unlike me, you didn't actually hurt anyone for years, to discover that immediately." Pax said softly, looking at me in bewilderment. "I am really sor-"

"Pax, I will be there if you need me while speaking to Ma, tomorrow." I interjected, attempting to cut down her growing cloud of guilt.

"I wouldn't know where to start…"

"I think you should direct that apology to her." I offered gently, as Pax nodded her head in confirmation, slowing down the pace of swinging our arms, until it stilled.

"Do you remember when we used to be around Felicity's age…-" Pax cracked a smile, but the base heaviness didn't wear away. "-You were the only one who put up with waking up at crazy hours or the strict discipline of hers, that seem like habits to you, now." She chuckled, leaning back on her elbows. "I used to hate you for making things harder for me 'cause if you hadn't listened then we would have been together whilst sleeping through the weekend like most kids of our age."

"Back then, I hated it as well, but I just put up with it, 'cause I didn't wish to disrespect Ma." I couldn't help but sigh, shaking my head in amusement. "I hated that feeling the most and didn't want to do that to Ma…"

"Oh yeah, I remember picking up using the dictionary just to learn *'pompous'* to use that on you." Pax grinned, nodding as I hid my face in my hands.

"Those were the only times you did, when Ma used to make us use the dictionary words alphabetically in sentences to improve our vocabulary." I said quietly, before chuckling and elbowing her sides, lightly. "Admit it…It did, didn't it?"

"Like I said, *Pompous* kid." Pax repeated, rolling her eyes. "But I guess, everyone knew and could clearly see that no one respected Ma more than you..." Pax mumbled, head falling onto my shoulder, eyes closing tightly. "I realised that you didn't put up with those rigorous standards to please her, but you did it 'cause you genuinely respected her ethics."

"I did." I confirmed, flicking her forehead lightly as she stared at me, unimpressed. "I *do*..." I corrected, sternly. "She got me...got *us* to where we are today."

"I don't know how easily I took that for granted." Pax's smile disappeared like a candle being snuffed.

"Yeah, it's easy for people to undermine our feelings and moments as information 'cause it's easy for us to use information against each other."

"You are going to get through this, you know?" Pax said quietly, voice quick, as I stared at her confused. "I know, you don't like to overestimate or underestimate your skills-" It dawned on me immediately, that Pax must have seen my crossed-out list of rejected sources of fund, I failed to convince - in our room, yet chose not to press further about it directly knowing that I would have merely pretended to feign confusion over the details written on the sheet. "-but you are a damn great artist with hella powerful imagination-"

"You should know by now that flattery will definitely not get me to open up-" I broke in, nevertheless grateful that she didn't vocalise it out-loud, directly.

"How did you-"

"Hey, I observe well."

"You don't open up when I taunt you or compliment you." Pax swallowed, throat crackling painfully. "So, what should I do to get you to open up to me?" She teased, flicking my forehead in retaliation when I tried to protest. "Use a human head-size bottle opener to snap up your skull to get a look at your brain and see where your neurons are firing?"

"So, you did listen?"

"So, you pretty much cancel things you wanna say by dividing it by half, and speaking the half that's just painfully vague." Pax said quietly, voice burdened.

"It's not that I cancel, it's just that I don't find any purpose speaking about it-" I shrugged, waving a hand and staring at my knees when enough silence had passed to be uncomfortable.

"You know that you don't have to over analyse things inside your head, you can-"

"Look I am not hiding." I hesitated, dropping my head to rub at my face, tiredly.

"You are the only one who doesn't recognise that you are good at hiding, but everyone knows that you are good at hiding." Pax huffed laughing in irony, as I squinted my eyes trying to figure if she had hit her head somewhere, to enter an unknown realm of madness.

"I am just the type of person to not speak about anything inside my mind unless I couldn't resolve it or it has something to do with the person I am speaking to." I sighed, struggling to voice my thoughts coherently, before stating the basic purpose behind my reasoning. "I just don't want you to worry-"

"You are doing it again." She trailed off, voice dying and expression flickering, like someone trying to think of two things at once. "You are acting like the confused *third parent.*"

"What on earth is that now?"

"Oh, come on-" She chuckled at my confusion, eyes distant like she was whispering an obvious fact that need not be stated out loud. "-You spoil Felicity more than Ma and Dad combined, and that's saying something."

"I don't do that! I just like to uphold my bargains." I couldn't decide if she was sleepy or left her brain behind in the freezer, before walking over here. "I just have a constant streak for losing bets."

"You realise that you are acting just like Dad, right?" Pax stated with a wicked grin and furrowing her eyebrows. "It's just like him to hide anything troubles him and brood, until he fixes it by himself."

"Well, you are technically acting like Ma, cleverly jumping around the bush to get the information you want..." I retorted poignantly, as Pax burst out laughing at my half-attempted glare.

"What if Ma had never mentioned this to me and I actually ended up hating you?" Pax asked gingerly, voice dropping to something more curved around the edges. "Would you still have stayed avoidant and let our relationship get ruined?"

"I really don't know, truth to be told I was scared 'cause I couldn't find any way out of it to fix things." I assured, playing with closely-chopped grass on the ground, as the sound of swatting wings of the fireflies swarming around, was the only sound occupying the silence between our words. "In fact, I never even considered if you would find it or if you already knew or what would happen when you did find out."

"For years, since the separation, I have blamed you. Why didn't you say anything?"

"You are my younger sister." I said, coming to the realisation that why this came as a surprise to Pax: since the separation, the dynamic that had actually broken was the one between us, to the point that things that guaranteed certainty needed clarity, now. "I could not possibly take the chance to undermine your feelings, intentionally."

"We barely have two years of difference." She murmured, picking at the sides of her nails near the fingertips, until I merely wrapped my hand around her fingers. "You don't have to shelter me with this, I have always wanted you to rely on me, too."

"I wasn't trying to shelter you, but I ended up doing the exact opposite, because I don't ever want you to be hurt." I recalled, taking a deep breath, staring at the horizon, and feeling something thick settle in my throat. "During the process of the separation, I just assumed that you knew..." I sighed, dropping my head. "You saw what I did, so I assumed you weren't completely in the dark."

"I did." Pax said flatly, like she was speaking a language she didn't know the words of, but recognised. "I just shrugged it away so carelessly 'cause I was so involved in the lives of people who aren't even there for me." She added. "So much so that, I refused to see the obvious shift of genuine happiness in my family, if it weren't for my-"

"All I can tell you is that it's hard for people to be there for someone when they are in pain especially when they haven't experienced that situation-"

"Are you defending *them* now?" Pax frowned, wondering how after so long we could question this.

"I am not defending them, so hear me out." I said, firmly. There were several times I didn't miss any chance to spare them from reminding them of the clear consequences of their dismissive actions and having the nerve to show up to our home and making my sister feel guilty, if she wasn't in the right headspace to have the emotional capacity to comfort them, during their vulnerable moments… "If they haven't experienced that situation, they will try their best to *sympathise* with you instead of *empathising* with you."

But this wasn't about them - this was about my sister. The same person who left no stone unturned to read between the lines and care for the person, even when she couldn't stand them

"Yeah, but doesn't everyone?"

"Maybe they were *good people* just not *good friends* to you who believed that they had to put up with you through a phase-" I offered good-naturedly. I wasn't going to let those self-absorbed insolents change her. I wanted them to stay away from her, but I wasn't going to let them affect her. I knew that the last thing she needed right now was hearing me bad-mouth them again. I had plenty of time to do that later. "-'cause good friends would have empathised with you and believed that you would get through this at your own pace and all they had to do was to be there and support you."

"All I got were eye rolls to stop my *whining*." Pax admitted, playing with her fingers.

People are used to making the most out of someone's feelings through their selfish motives.

Affection can no longer nurture the soul, it spoils their ego.

I felt my blood boil hearing this, but it was more of a manageable level and I hid it with a forced smile.

"It's hard to have that patience unless you have complete respect and trust for that person which can take years to build." I said sternly, pinching the bridge of my nose, to control my expressions. "I guess things like these make it hard and most people want things to be breezy to escape their hardships...-" I smiled faintly as Pax returned a small smile before standing up on her feet and dusting the back of her jeans. "-so several notions of a possible good friendship get shattered during these times."

"Did you empathise and put up with my blaming, just 'cause we are family?" She asked, voice causal as if she were asking about preheating dinner.

"I never *put up* with you." I pressed firmly, before standing up on my feet. "I wanted to be there for you 'cause you are my sister, and although you don't give yourself enough credit you have always been there for me too."

"Glad it got through you. You, bonehead."

Even if it caught me by surprise, I couldn't help but chuckle at my sister bending to my height, and engulfing me in a hug before placing her chin on my shoulder. "You always notice whenever I am troubled even when I am trying to resolve it in my head." My grin got wider, when Pax huffed, taking one of my immobile hands, to pat her head, before I started repeating the action myself. "You always notice even when you yell at my face about it."

"Yeah, sorry about that."

"Don't be." I said stolidly, as Pax pulled away trying to look over my shoulders blinking her eyes to get a better vision. "It's us, and I like that."

"It's the blue-haired chic, from the hospital. Well brown-hair, now." Pax whispered with a small smile, pointing towards none other than Hope who was looking at us with dreaded concern. "I guess she finally managed to speak to you."

"What on earth are you talking about?"

"At first, when she approached me and said she really had to speak to you.-" Pax shrugged, knowing my habit of whining or investing my time conversing with anyone, besides the people I was familiarised with, already. "-I was confused if this stranger mistook you for someone else."

"Since when did she approach you?" I asked flatly, staring back at Hope who stayed frozen to the spot, while playing with her fingers.

"Probably two years ago, but the moment she refused to tell me anything to pass on the message to you and insisted on speaking to you directly-" Pax shrugged, creasing her eyebrows while trying to remember. "- 'cause it was *important*, I knew that she was someone who must have actually spoken with you. Do you know her?"

"I do."

***

It was a wonder that Pax didn't utter a single word all the way back home, despite looking at me with a wicked grin as I returned an unimpressed stare.

I was merely thankful that Pax walked into the home, without protesting, even offering to check up on Felicity before going to sleep.

Was I concerned that she gave in, way too easily?

Well, I could worry about that, after speaking to the person, still waiting outside our gates.

There was a long silence, and I kept waiting for Hope to leave or say something, but there was only the silence that was pounding at my ears loud enough to hurt.

I looked at Hope, one eyebrow lifting up as I found Hope staring with an unexplainable expression. "Are you going to tell me why you're staring, or am I supposed to guess?"

And it wasn't the harsh bitterness that I spent most of my acquaintanceship wielding, but closer to this new middle-ground they had been building- sharp and expectant, but not angry.

Not anymore.

But now, Hope only got a strange look in her eyes that I kept seeing but could never quite place in an emotional category.

Hope didn't react physically to the question, only her eyes looking a little further away, as if looking past me. (An action that would have caused me to be more puzzled, before. But it was different now.)

"Would you like to go for a walk?"

It was spoken quite… softly. A tone that was familiar to be expected only from Hope in this exact lilt.

It made me frown slightly, leaning against the gates of our home. "At this hour?"

Hope blinked, and she was looking fully at me again, her shoulders squaring. "I think we need to talk about a few things." Her tone took on a sudden air of severity. "I didn't mean to overhear you, I just wanted to ensure that you were okay. I know that I crossed your boundaries-"

"You didn't." I interjected not wanting her to rant as if she owed an explanation as if she was in tribulation. We both knew the very aspect about each other, that we never chose to indulge speaking about in regular conversations.

"All my poor attempts of finding an excuse to start a conversation with you, was to merely thank you." She explained, everything startlingly still even as I felt like the ground was shaking beneath us.

"But I did the bare minimum-"

"I don't think that you realise that you have an aura that can naturally either feel like home or a battlefield." Hope's smile was small, but more genuine as if she had known this all along. "I stopped trying because of the very same reason. I hadn't mentioned that we had known each other from earlier, mostly because I figured that you were trying your best to wipe that time period of your life from your memories."

"I have been told I have the terrible habit of speaking on a need-to-know basis." I chuckled sheepishly, as Hope nodded in confirmation. "Back then, that was the only function that reminded me to not blame myself for respecting my parents' decision while still hoping to get my sister what she wanted." We both knew about the obvious jarringly loud fights occurring in my room, that the entire floor must have been aware about, much less the person abiding in the room, next to mine. "I only managed to uphold one of them. Speaking to you, unconsciously reminded me to prioritise the former."

"I still remember the very words you had typed, when I had mocked you for being stupidly optimistic…" Hope's smile broke, with an unreadable expression reflecting across her orbs. "It was the very first time I felt the presence of accountability in one's words rather than toxic positivity, in their attempts to comfort."

The regret of failing to keep my word with the girl standing right in front of me- all those years ago, had ended up being submerged along with any incident involving that time period.

When the fights between Dad and his Parents started to become frequent- disturbing the entire ward on a regular basis, we were asked to let me recover at home. I had jumped at the chance to agree with Ma's suggestion to do the same as advised.

The regret that had ended up being buried, for leaving a day earlier, without a chance to give any explanations for not being able to show up on the day. We could finally converse face-to-face - resurfaced in ten-folds, flooding back without a warning.

-

- 'You have always been enough just the way you are.'

Fadel: *You must live your life easily, to have the audacity to say that. Not all of us have had the fortune to not have our ambitions be dismissed as nothing but foolish dreams, before we even began.'*

I felt my heart grow heavier reading each word.

I really had no right to ask what might have occurred, but I could never barge the resolute she hadn't overpassed by never asking me directly about mine.

- 'No matter how much time it takes for your ambitions to be played into unnecessary hurdles of unpredictability in this reality. The person you are today is

shaped through all those
moments you have conquered
and will continue to do for the
unpredictable future to seize your
dream.'

Fadel: *'Conquer? You really do live in your little
world, don't you? What makes you think that I even
have a future?'*

- 'Cause your present was
also once the future to
your past.'

One of the largest fears that kept consuming
me like the hail destroying the delicate, pink
blossoms into confetti, was letting the notion
of discovering that I never had adequate
natural skills to seize my dream - become a
reality.

Time was the very hailstorm that could
become my solution, all I needed to ensure
was braving that very storm by prioritising
my time to harness my skills - regardless of
the reality that if they happened to be natural
or an outcome of practice and zeal.

All that mattered was adapting to the latter
like adding the apple peel of a morning
sunrise, with a hint of jasmine breeze rippling
through the hail.

Who said storms couldn't have an
undetectable presence of wrapping around us
like light mist?

Fadel: *'Would you continue to believe in yourself even when the rest of the world stays adamant in being convinced, that it's in vain?'*

- 'I would be lying if I said if it was anything else besides my anger to grow more attached to believing in myself over our wretched reality constantly barking their opinions to shape us.'

Fadel: *'There has to be a better way than feeling this angry against it. What if my anger drives me from what I seek, instead driving me to believe in myself?'*

- 'But during all those times, there is just one thing I remembered that kept me going: the only reason they have time to spew opinions regarding someone else is because they don't prioritise themselves. So lemme prioritise myself more.'

I couldn't help but be tense about any action I took at the expense of someone else, any word that I directed towards them- for I knew I was naive to never consider, that what I considered as helpful might come across as an insulting reminder regardless of whether it was right.

I might have just patronised their own journey through their struggle.

What I wanted to offer - was my support but through that, I never sought to undermine their strength.

Fadel: *'Then why am I so affected by their dismissal? Why am I still seeking their approval?'*

All I had was the right to be aware that something was amiss, and that often resonated with the visit of an old Italian woman, yelling in the next room, with the repetition of either the words of *disgrazia* (disgrace) or *diseredazione* (disinheritance) or *disapprovare* (disapprove), roped into every single conversation.

(Granted my Italian was very rudimentary being only my second language, and I felt guilty to listen to even those few words that slipped through only when both the doors were open.)

During those days, the vagueness of the words typed by her, made me fear the existence of all my coherent thoughts, and made me self-reflect on a whole new magnitude.

> **- 'Your worth was never, and will never be, measured by people cherishing your significance. It shines regardless of their negligence.'**

Fadel: *'Who exactly determines my worth?'*

> **- 'There will be several people who will neither see nor value**

**your worth. Don't let that person
be you. It's unfair to lose yourself
to their negligence. You are the
only one that can value what's
inside of you. That will take time
to embrace…but that's okay'**

Fadel: *'I am scared of being so ignorant and self-absorbed that I end up being miserable.'*

- 'Not true and never will be.'

Fadel: *'Why does it even matter? Why would I ever matter?'*

Weeks of holding everything in.

Of all the people I had spoken with - the calmest conversations I had for days was with a stranger.

I…had made so many mistakes during a time when I really shouldn't have. At a time when it was crucial that I keep it together.

**- 'You will always be immortalised
by your words, your actions and
your consistency and this is the
beginning of you consistently
raising the pedestal.'**

Fadel: *'I want to be immortalised by my works, but I am not sure if it wouldn't end up being mere nothing, against the scale of this world.'*

**- 'We often ponder about how we
don't matter in the scale of the
entire world, but we end up being**

the world of many people, most
preciously us.'

Fadel: *What would you do to remember that?
How do you remember that good in yourself?'*

The last thing I wanted to do was type
anything, toxically pathetic and hollow. But
now…now I just felt like I was floating out
on the thunderclouds, as I stared at the
fading tips of hair falling over the misty
timber-chromed eyes, blinking harshly, across
the other side of the glass pane.

- 'I can't even recognise when I
am good at something but the
only thing that keeps me from
dwelling on that is; the chase of
— I have to give my best, doing
what matters to me.'

Fadel: *How did you overcome the former aspect to
be so unwavering in your chase?'*

- 'I can't acknowledge that
anything good could ever exist
within me, yet I believe that I
should live my life trying not to
harm anyone else and being
unforgivingly protective of my
values.'

Fadel: *'Are you trying to say that they coexist
simultaneously?'*

- 'What I am trying to say is that
the impact of those opinions will

manifest in a way that we can't control.'

Fadel: *'There has to be a way to not let that impact continue to affect us for an unpredictable amount of time…'*

I wasn't even sure whether the words were said aloud instead of just being etched across a screen, but the words resonated inside me like an echo bouncing off the curves of a cave, rebounding and reverberating until it vibrated the very air inside of me.

- **'But I also know that we prioritise our ambitions and dreams so devotedly that it's strong enough to overshadow those impacts even during our hardest times.'**

Fadel: *'I really like your name. I think I am starting to get why it fits you perfectly, Spes Clepsen.'*

-

"If it's alright to ask, why hadn't you come by to get your diary back, sooner?" I asked, clutching the wrought iron bars of our gates barely reaching the tip of my head.

"My Nonno had just passed away." Hope swallowed, voice hoarse and eyes rough. "So, I had to head back to their home, and I was supposed to come back within 15 days but Nonna didn't handle his passing well and fell into a comatose phase herself." Hope said gingerly, voice muffled by the sleeves of her jumper, before sighing with a tired laugh and pressing the heels of her palms over her closed eyes. "I was glad that Mrs. Khalili gave me an extension to stay until she got better."

"I am really sorry-"

"Don't be, my Nonna wasn't thrilled to see me at all. But after all these years, I am still that eight-year old wanting to seek her approval..." Hope shook her head slowly, scanning my distraught expression for bringing it up in the first place. "I just hoped that she would acknowledge me instead of continuing to ignore my existence like she had for the past 3 years." Hope confessed, voice pinching. "Sony and a few of her friends came by to seek the diary on my behalf." It wasn't rocket science to realise that those could have possibly been the names of those faces, that got on my nerves.

"I am truly sorry... I should have heard them out-"

"Knowing you, you would have merely asked them to scram out if you had ended up hearing their reason." Hope huffed with a small smile, as I winced sheepishly. "I am quite relieved that the diary was with you, rather than in the possession of their hands."

"But you barely knew me-"

"They were the first ones to support me after they discovered my non-existent feelings, bordering on magnetic repulsion, towards the opposite sex and attraction towards my own." Hope said without missing a beat. "Even going as far as to encourage me by offering to set up blind dates for me, but that's quite hard." She added, scoffing with a soft frown and leaning her back against the gate. "To me, that was support I could never afford, especially when this was the very reason my Nonna started hating me, claiming that not only was I tarnishing my femininity, but that of those around me, because of my *phase*."

"Whether we like to admit it or not, most people around us have a constant need for dictating our sexuality to us." I said firmly, gritting my teeth to direct my anger at the very person who clearly had a complicated dynamic with Hope - as if finally deciding.

"I didn't want to lose that, so I had to put up with them mocking my dreams or even using the diary as a plate for their snacks." Hope nodded slowly, before sighing defeatedly. "I felt that I was being unreasonable, whenever I lost my temper through their actions." She murmured, pushing her tongue against the insides of her cheeks. "I couldn't be more glad to have my diary in the hands of someone, who was afraid to leave a crease on the spine rather than on the hands of people who wouldn't have batted an eyelid if the flowers I had spent days, preserving fell off or if they spilled anything over something that was merely old and rattled to them."

-Those faces were being unceremoniously vocal about their opinions that this was nothing, but a foolish dream and people shouldn't spare their faces as canvases out of pity, to make Hope feel better about her appearance.

"The other day, you were talking about them, weren't you?" I said, trying to force down a snarl directed towards those unavoidable weeds, whose snobbish negligence never stayed uprooted no matter how many times you tried. Constantly preying upon the host through the consequences of their actions.

"Their chatter is affecting the opinions of people, who are regular customers to your studio, like a domino effect."

"I hate being angry. I am scared that I might spill things that have bothered me for so long and might end up coming off as ungrateful and drive them away." Hope sighed, throwing her head towards my side. "More than ever, I hated the silence when I did end up confronting them when the sea of the jar that I had been bottling my feelings up in, finally broke." She chuckled, as if now, the mere notion of it sounded unreasonable to her. "Watching you not compromise to put up with the disrespect that had always troubled me for ages and not hesitating to be angry, was unfamiliar to me."

"I didn't have any right to be that reactive. No matter, what I had no right directing that at you-"

"Probably not... but in a way if you hadn't, then I wouldn't have been surprised by my capability to express my anger and getting a sense of relief from the constant suffocation here." Hope shook her head slowly, before waving her hand in reassurance.

"I am truly sorry...the derisive excuse I had selfishly built,-" I grimaced apologetically with guilt. "-because I couldn't decide whether I was sick of them being disrespectful or fearing that I would do the same by interfering in how you choose to handle it."

"Spes-"

"And I ended up doing the latter-"

"Spes, it would be ridiculous to expect a constantly smooth-sailing dynamic, unless one side is hiding their true self." Hope remarked sternly, "We barely knew each other, and over time we always, authentically, talk it out."

"That wouldn't have occurred if it weren't for you." I reminded stolidly, playing with my fingers

"No, you have an odd sense of being as present as familiarity itself almost as though you had been expecting them-" Hope smiled, placing her hand over mine "-even when I ask you questions that clearly put you in a tough spot."

"Clarity doesn't come easy." I said firmly, offering a small smile in return. "It takes time and effort from both sides, and I would do anything to maintain it, especially when you have always sought it as well."

"How do you end up finding calmness in situations that lividly corner you, as if you in a trial?" Hope hummed, head dropping a little.

"I am not sure about that. Maybe it's a realm beyond extreme anger." I admitted, feeling my expression twist in uncertainty like missing a step in the dark. "It's easy to get clouded by the confinements of the flaws set by society, which prevent us from recognising the individuality in each of us."

"Do you appreciate those differences?"

"I do but-" I paused, feeling my chest swell with something unnameable, to vocalise the remaining words.

"You are scared of change." Hope said as a matter-of-factly with a note of realisation, her eyes widening by the slightest, as I nodded my head quietly. "You are scared of the other side not recognising your individuality. You don't want to risk a negative outcome."

It felt like laying on a cloud. As if nothing on this earth could touch what I sought. As if nothing were against me, like an anchor that ensured I didn't drift too far.

"In my head, in my rationality." I said hoarsely, looking down to play with my fingers. "In my heart, I know that that's just reality, a variable and not particularly negative or positive but I have lived all my life weighing the rewards over risks and I don't believe this is a risk worth taking."

"The temptations of chasing to evolve into our best selves is so alluring that we often forget to take the time to accept ourselves." Hope pressed firmly, with her smile widening to the unwavering curve that was uniquely definitive only with respect to her.

"What would you choose?"

"Do choices guarantee the manifestation of reality?" Hope scoffed, eyes shutting tight.

"No but will does-"

"Ideally yes." She said, voice helplessly weak. "In reality, anomalies like you have the drive to keep going, no matter what's thrown at you."

"Everyone does-"

"No Spes. They don't." She whispered, voice haggard and raw. "They let their fear, embedded by people's degradation that has been seeping inside of them for years, get in between. They let time get in between.

They let external decisions overpower their own control."

"Hope, what would you tell these barriers obstructing them?"

"Well, nothing," she admitted. "There's nothing special about us compared to anyone else." She pressed her lips together as I thought about all those hours, we spent killing ourselves to be perfect. "Hard work will only carry us so far," she said. "That's only half of success… the other half is pure luck." It probably wasn't what I had wanted to hear, but it was the truth. "But we have half of it covered. And the other half is completely out of our control. So, we shouldn't worry about it, right?"

"Perhaps not." I shook my head, slowly.

"I think it's better this way," Hope said quickly, filling the silence. "I would rather have something be completely out of my control. It's more comforting to know you can't influence it, isn't it? It's freeing to just be out of control like that."

"Perhaps they are like entities that seem separate yet impact each other-"

"-as if they had always been codependent. Like pain and happiness." Hope whispered, almost to herself, suddenly looking painfully wistful. "It's difficult to have comfort during pain, but when something or someone manages to, then you can't help but cherish that comfort onto irrevocable happiness."

"The things, the people, the world, the dreams that compromise our happiness are the very notions that

are capable of causing us the most excruciating pain."
I said in confirmation, sighing tiredly.

"We could have a thousand reasons that would make
it impossible to ever feel like our dream could ever
see the light of day." Hope said, expression splitting
into an unexplainable sparkle in her eyes.

"But we need one reason that started it all, the reason
that gives us the very purpose of happiness that
nothing else ever can and ever will." I remarked,
returning the small smile.

"The fascination that started it all." Hope recalled
with a noise of realisation as if it were secret, before
looking up at me with a widening grin. "It's *magnetically
incredible*."

"Hope-"

"Spes, please stay still." I barely had time to be
completely confused by those very words, before I
felt arms wrapping around my shoulders. "Just three
seconds." I merely squeezed her sides in response, as
I felt Hope's chin press further into the jugular
between neck and shoulder.

The numbness in my limbs still felt heavy
synchronising with the sleepless eyes of Pax dying to
bombard me with an endless array of questions, once
I walked back into our room after Hope headed back
home.

"Does asparagus actually have a meaning?" Pax asked
skeptically, jumping over my bed to snatch my phone
and look at the quick drawing Hope had sent over
after confirming that she had reached home, before
handing it back to me in bewilderment.

"Fascination." I said flatly, my mind continuing to stay blank, as Pax waited for an explanation.

I almost wondered if I was letting my guard down too fast, but...really what did I have to lose?

"Of course. I always look at asparagus and can barely look away." She teased in an attempt to make me laugh, her chuckle faltering as if she came to a realisation, staring at the transparent wrap tied pristinely over the German chamomile oil "The unmistakable floral fragrance. This gift is meant for her."

***

Over the next two months, the schedules became predictably tighter.

It led to staying up later some nights, and having to work a bit faster on some projects, and taking more time at lunch to study for the endless quizzes squeezing in between the CLEP papers, plaguing over us.

The stress was familiar, but I had been stressed before, to be familiarly content with a very real, supportive family that both understood and supported my need to chase any goal I sought. But that also meant that they were equally stubborn in their ways to draw me away when they knew I had crossed the line from *prepared* to *obsessive*.

It became Hope's habit to leave my favourite drink placed pristinely at the corner of my desk if I forgot to have my lunch. Despite appreciating the gesture and getting whiplashed by growing guilt, I could never shake of the suffocation to consume it, leaving it untouched, even if I really wanted to…and Hope just smiled a smile that seemed to rival the hurdles of reality from ever daring to affect its curve.

No words were spoken.

No questions were asked.

No explanations were demanded, when they were simply replaced by canned lychees or pineapples, or rice cakes, yet I always got teased in return, boisterous laughter echoing through my ears, if I returned the gesture by trying to get meat skewers or the right laksa, whenever I found her skipping lunch.

It was an unexpected adaptation that barely took time to settle in like familiarity whenever I heard the words -"*If we are buying our favourite meals for each other separately, then why aren't we spending lunch time together? Whether you like it or not, I am going to sit beside you during lunch.*"

The more I looked at the materials that might be on the exam… and it was like the teachers were trying to shove a year's worth of information into a 2-hour, 150 question time slot.

Which is probably why, week-three of the exams was basically a must cafeteria-avoidance zone under all circumstances. Most students crying on the floor, unable to even look at their work that made them want to vomit at the thought of taking the exam.

Anxiety and frustration warred like clashing elements in their blood.

So, when our exams came to a halt and Hope absently insisted on accompanying and waiting for me till my shift in the convenience store wrapped up.

I made no objections as soon as I caught up to her being unpredictably uncoordinated and pale - Whatever might have occurred, I would rather not leave her alone with her thoughts alone regardless of her choice to address whatever was clearly troubling her.

Ever since Jove started her training period, her shifts working in the convenience store have been reduced to only on weekends and Friday nights.

I found it hard to find the will to complain when Jove and Hope jumped onto a conversation shifting like a pendulum from teasing me, together. Or being enraged by the commonality of prejudices they face at work where any help they received was expected to be treated like they owed *them* their entire existence in return or be expected to be taunted that they never belonged there or ever deserved to have their position outside of pity.

I have probably never thanked Jove for this, but she was the first person I had ever come across who valued clarity almost as much as Ma.

To understand and prioritise that, despite all the misunderstandings and disagreements that came along the way, we would never compromise on speaking our mind and communicating with each other. Staying around, and learning and better understanding each other every passing day.

"I think it's a misconception that any other existence, in our lives has the capacity to make us better, because the expectation of that capacity is just toxic." Jove tsked tiredly, her voice gentle and heavy, waving her hand when Hope offered to split carrying over the packets of chips that were yet to be restocked in the aisles.

"That's true, we often sell ourselves short and fail to recognise our own efforts to be better." Hope said bluntly, making me chuckle lightly as I walked beside them to restock the grilled food aisle.

"Unfortunately, that makes it easy to confuse the people who remind us of the existence of our better selves; guilt us into the incapability of being better without their existence." Jove sighed silently, letting Hope help her stack the top shelves, while she stacked the middle ones. "Because the line between gratitude and of cherishing their presence of letting it develop into dependency is quite blurred."

"I get it. It's natural to feel - *'I couldn't have done this without your help'* as a form of appreciation towards people by your side…-" Hope murmured warmly, offering a small smile, quietly asking if she could help Jove, with anything else around the shop. "-But they are only a few who will remind us tenaciously that - *'It was all you, do not forget that. You could have easily done this without me, too. But I am glad that I could merely stay by your side while you seized what you wanted. It's all you. Never forget that'…*"

"Being around people who don't exploit those blurred lines is an alarming rarity." Jove said, voice a little more upbeat, chuckling when she caught up to me trying to give them space by trying to stuff the instant-food meals aisle, at the furthest end from the counter. "Spes, don't those very words sound like *someone,* that I know, would say?"

I could practically hear the obvious grin in her voice as I gave her an unimpressed glare before picking up the empty carton to put it in the dumpster.

"People who support us through thick and thin and pull us back to remind us to cherish-" Hope merely grinned wider at me, before chuckling at my confusion and following Jove back to the counter as the latter assured that there was nothing left to be done, for the day. "-and recognise our efforts instead of relishing in their ego boost of reigning in our belief of being incapable of acquiring our goals without their assistance."

"Well said." Jove said calmly, as Hope asked her, why I was still working instead of taking the chance to relax for the rest of my shift. "Whoa! Spes, why weren't we introduced sooner?" Jove laughed, trying to fluster me on purpose, as she assured Hope, there truly was no more work to help me around with, when the latter kept asking to do so.

"J-Jove...do you want me to reheat the instant fried rice from the shelves for your dinner?" I asked quickly, desperately wanting to shift the attention from me, giving Jove a plea look to just go along with it.

"Nope, I am all good." Jove assured me firmly, giving me a look to indicate that she was refusing to play along and help me with whatever scheme I was trying to brew, to escape. "Hope got me some snacks earlier."

"Wow, you really are like the all-knowing older sibling everyone dreams to have." Hope said quietly, eyes earnest, warm and comforting…

"Well, colour me flattered." Jove laughed gently, before looking over at me and mouthing me to get over the counter, immediately. "Because I tend to be the youngest in most bunches among my family or at work."

"I feel like you are the human incarnation of this book of all the wise soothing words in existence."

"Spes, where did you find her?" Jove chuckled, patting Hope's hand "At this rate, I might replace you with her as my personal motivator."

"Actually, I found her." Hope corrected, before laughing along with Jove

"So, you had to do all the work?" Jove asked, feigning faux surprise.

"Sadly yeah. Come on it's Spes." Hope tilted her head, her smile casting heat like a lamp. "The entire continuity will fall out of balance if she were to make the first step to interfere in someone else's world."

"Sure, continue speaking as if I don't exist" I scoffed before breaking into a chuckle as I walked over to the counter, and took the can of lychees from Hope's outstretched hand, muttering a quick '*thank you*' in return.

"It's Spes, what do you expect?" Jove snickered as I continued to frown while trying to chew, quirking an eyebrow with an unamused glare. "I call her my guardian angel and she fights me to accept that she is the righteous spawn of Satan, instead."

"Ah! So that's the origin of that analogy." Hope said, her voice tinted with an amused glee. I couldn't help but smile to myself, with the unexpected outcome of cheering up Hope with Jove, even when I threatened to walk out if they continued to tease me without sparing me to let me have my food in peace.

"Spes!" Jove laughed "Don't you dare leave!"

"You haven't even finished your lychees."

"So, do I have to get used to you two ganging up on me like this?" I huffed trying to bite back my smile.

"Pretty much." Hope teased, as Jove mouthed 'Go-out-for-a-while' to me, behind her. I quietly mouthed back if everything was alright when Hope looked away, while throwing her head back in laughter.

I had barely stepped out of sight making an excuse to throw out the garbage, before I heard Jove.

"Please don't take this as an insult and granted I have merely known you only for a few hours, it's Spes so those details don't matter much to me." Jove assured Hope, eyeing me to stay back when I made an attempt to walk back in through the glass doors at the entrance, not wanting to know where this conversation might be heading.

"Spes doesn't have a middle ground, she either doesn't trust people even if they sell her their kidneys-" Hope's back was turned towards me, but her shoulders barely flinched, not bothered by Jove's words in the slightest as my grip on the handle of the door loosened. "-or trusts people to the point where she wouldn't refuse that the earth is flat, if they told her so."

"Yeah, there is a reason that kid is sincerely adamant about consistency and is damn good at it. Please don't take it for granted." Despite the air of severity in her tone, Jove still eased into a small smile. "She is one of those rare old souls you meet - stuck in a child's body, who never says anything for granted." She chuckled, although her tone held no guarantee that it was a mere joke. "If you dare to undermine that or take advantage of that because you are still trying to grow past your fickleness in the name of easy-going, you wouldn't know when you lose the sensation in both your feet after they have been run over by these wheels."

"I will hold on to that deal."

***

CHAPTER - VIII

In my entire existence, I had never contemplated this long, the tormenting conflict of wanting to avoid someone on all accords for having done something behind their backs while still wanting to fess up about it in the open already.

It wasn't a surprise that I was breaking into cold sweat, trying to contemplate the quick turn of events, praying that the unpredictability of it would excuse my utter disrespect of making a decision, without confirming things with her beforehand.

I mean we did discuss it beforehand, but it was way too vague to be classified as clarity-

"I am trying, even when the world's first reaction is to mock me, I am trying to focus on me despite that-" Hope murmured dolefully, eyes heavy.

It was the third month, where the studio had refused to pay her in full, throwing in her face the fact - that *nobody would hire someone that looked like her*, and that she should be *utterly grateful* instead of, daring to ask why.

"-I am trying, but sometimes I can't help but fall prey to believing their opinions of wondering if I am in over my head?" She sighed heavily. If I wasn't lost in my inner-conflict of trying to find the right words to break the news to her, then I might have ended up piercing the sewing needle right into my fingers, especially through the tulle exposed sleeves of the jacket. "Then I see you, the way you are so certain of what you want, and you don't let anything faze you…"

"That's not true, my temper skyrockets immediately." I scoffed.

We sat in the courtyard, with the after-school hours nearing an end as I sewed in the last of the tobacco topstitch details of the parka peplum curves into the hybrid biker jacket for my chosen concept, to submit for the Parsons' challenge.

Since the past month, I had more clarity of the world around me outside of the worry of enrolment into any of my targeted schools of art and design, through my preferred major, after receiving the offer letter for my early acceptance into Politecnico di Milano.

I still remembered that very day, when Hope refused to pay any heed to my half-hearted protests. When she dragged me to celebrate the occasion by relaxing in the bask of the radiance and the warmth of the seemingly endless array of the calming amber lanterns lit in the Thean Hou temple.

Aimlessly speaking for hours over the koi pond etched like a lonely canvas inextricably linked to the lotus leaves floating above like a painter's palette, waiting to collide their chemistry like an inferno against the reflection of the casted by the lights of the lanterns.

"I have only seen you work harder, even when that happens, even when you doubt yourself… your first instinct is to shift into the gear of working harder." Hope remarked with a small smile, shaking her head quietly. "I have seen the contrast of those words against your actions." She offered firmly, as I looked at her in bewilderment. "And me? I wish I wouldn't stop when I get fazed by them. I wish that I gave them a piece of my mind even when I am conflicted between believing their words over mine and strive to put even more effort into my dream, just like you..."

Where was this coming from?

I wanted to call it unfair, for her to dismiss the recognition of the same within her.

"You do-"

"Do you remember asking me - what could I possibly want from you, to be glued to your vicinity?" Hope recalled with an unreadable expression, as I immediately winced in response and grimaced apologetically.

"Hope, I didn't-"

"Anchor." She said, answering her own question. "Watching you reminds me - to remember my beginning through the chaos, to protect my dream against their opinions by anchoring myself even deeper towards it,-" She stated gently, before breaking into a chuckle directed more towards to herself than anyone else, as if it were a secret meant to be hidden for eternity. "-chase it harder for even considering to take it for granted while adhering to the barks around me."

"No, that's all you." I reminded, firmly, looking up to assure that.

"Stop doing that." Hope snapped, shutting her eyes tight and sighing defeatedly.

"Doing what?" I asked, frowning slightly in confusion.

"Giving me false hope for seeing me as something that I am not." Hope protested, pressing her hands over her face. "As something that no one else does. Stop patronising-"

"I don't believe in just what I see." I corrected cutting her off mid-sentence, before deciding that it's about time that I made up my mind to just say it aloud. "I believe in what I know."

"Do enlighten me about exactly that, then."

"Do you remember telling me about the Lilies of the Valley?" I asked, calmly.

"I do, they are one of my favourites." She nodded easily.

"So, you must remember telling me about the misnomer that they don't belong to the lily family but rather the asparagus family." I reminded softly, offering half a smile remembering the fascination in her tone, while reminiscing about those very flowers.

"Are you telling me that you remember this instead of what they mean?" She sighed heavily, before settling onto a frown.

I shook my head, before choosing my words carefully, hoping that they held some sense and were coherent. "They carry the strong connotation of *'the return of happiness'*" I recalled, brows drawn down. "Happiness that is unexplainably astronomical to be limited by human constraints."

"Where are you going with this?"

"When it comes to human dynamics over the passage of time, it can head in two ways." I swallowed thickly, glancing between the fabric I was clutching in my hands, and Hope's face.

"Spes, I really don't get this-"

"The longer we know someone the easier it gets to take them for granted unintentionally just like knowing more about the genus of the flower - like the everyday food of asparagus." I promised, momentarily pausing as Hope stared at me with a lost expression as I were speaking in a foreign dialect. "Or we could choose to cherish in the happiness of the time and the company of a person cementing the guarantee like the symbolism of the flower of May."

"What would you choose to describe us?" Some of Hope's cloudy demeanour melted away into something completely unreadable. "The genus or the symbolism?"

"As someone who has always enjoyed speaking to you through the language of flower symbolism, do you think I would choose anything else besides Symbolism?" I demanded laughing softly to express my obvious choice.

"But time…" She pressed, grimacing apologetically. "You have always hated never getting enough time to know someone, when it comes to the unpredictability of the facades of people-"

"That's why I would always choose the time-" I assured firmly, as Hope broke into a smile. "-as that provides more space to consistency over that unpredictability."

"How do you do that-"

"You should quit your job here." I said firmly.

There was a short pause, as she stared at me in disbelief.

"You have never said that before." She said despondently, after taking a breath as her shoulder slumped further into herself.

"No, I haven't." I replied, easily. "Not until there was an alternative where you could walk away from people hindering your creative freedom without sacrificing the path to your dream-" I urged quickly, as her eyes widened before shaking her head in disbelief. "-or even slow things down because of the insolence of other people."

"Why are you saying it now?" She asked, carefully.

"I found an alternative."

"What do you mean?"

"Remember the time when you asked me to keep a copy of your portfolio-" I remarked, recalling back to the time- last month, where I insisted on a distraction that could work as a perfect retaliation to the Machiavellians daring to hinder her dreams. "-after we worked on designing the digital arts of the designs of the make-up brushes of your own brand?"

"Spes, I have never had to say this, before, around you, because you never beat around the bush unless you are worried about something." She threatened sharply, catching up to my squeamish aura for the entire day. "So, get to the point, you are starting to scare me."

"I crossed paths with Para Huda and her sister in one of their studios-" I informed, carefully.

Over the past three months, only one of the potential investors - that I had met up with, right around the time period of our break occurring just before the start of our second term - had been invested in wanting to meet again, to find a way to invest in our final exhibition with certainty.

Para Huda.

During my last encounter with the older Huda sister, yesterday, we were accompanied by her younger sister - Isabel Huda.

While both sisters shared similar styles, where they looked like they were seconds away from being casted in a biopic about Empresses who barely were in their mid-30's, that were determined to declare wars against lands that had committed treason.

The older one preferred stripes while the younger preferred to be adorned with sequined clothes to compliment her blown-out-wavy-raven hair framing the curved arches of her brows and pale complexion.

Isabel Huda was one of the revolutionary make-up artists in the recent years to find the right blend between effortless looks with that of the iconic elegant regal looks recognised in the 90's, who seemed ecstatic to convince her sister to stop considering anything else and invest in our exhibition already.

By the end of the conversation, I was still unclear how she had offered to invest in our exhibition as well as to fast track the process of going through the procedures that were needed to overpower the initial objections placed by the hold of the administration controlled by Mrs. Khalili.

Or agreeing to have Hope work for her, with barely controllable glee, when I proposed the offer after showing Hope's portfolio, and hearing her talk about wanting to find new aspirants to work in her recently launched pop-up stores.

"Her sister? Isabel Huda?!" Hope gasped, as if waiting for me to tell her that this was just a joke. "You actually met her? In Person? What was she like?"

It wasn't a surprise to see why Isabel Huda was Hope's idol, or why she would fit in perfectly working for the former, or the similarity in their styles while still preserving the unique individuality of their own styles - as proclaimed by the younger Huda sister herself.

"I think you can find that out by yourself, when you work with her." I confirmed with a small smile, pushing over the offer letter towards her side of the table.

"What?!" She yelped, looking over the letter.

"Well, *for* her…for now." I corrected, tilting my head… "She wants you to work as her apprentice in her Penang studio. Your first meeting with her is scheduled this Monday…" I promised, informing the details, as she stared at the letter waiting for it to suddenly burst in flames or something, blinking harshly and scrubbing her face. "It's not even an interview, she offered you the position as soon as she saw your designs-" Like the last time, I got no warning before arms engulfed me onto a tight, nearly bone-crushing hug. I tried to find my voice, to inquire the reasoning behind her actions as my limbs stayed frozen to their spot. "Hope-"

"You never say things just to be dismissive." She said taking a deep breath and fanning her cheeks, after pulling away immediately and muttering a quick 'sorry', as I waved my hand gingerly. "That's w-why all those times I asked you why you never asked me to just quit unlike the others and you never gave me a definitive answer besides that." She said simply, a bright smile fading to something unfamiliar that spread to her eyes. "I don't know what to say-"

"Just say that you will be on time on Monday as soon as you quit working at that wretched make-up studio in the mall." I teased, winking at her and smiling widely as she laughed, throwing her head back.

"Walk in with me?" She asked hesitantly, as the final bell rang to indicate that if we didn't rush out, the gates would be closed, nevertheless.

"Oh, I wouldn't miss this for the world." I assured, packing my things swiftly and checking the time to be certain that we did have time to spare before her shift at the studio began. Besides I did have unresolved issues to sort out with someone else, from that very studio. "I have been waiting for a very long time where you don't hesitate to set them straight without worrying about any consequences."

***

"Now this certainly calls for a celebration." Quinsy quipped before dropping the numerous packets of snacks that she was struggling to hold in her arms, on to the table, as we looked at her waiting for an explanation after swiftly removing our works from the table to make space.

"Is this about Spes and I submitting our portfolios for the Parsons' Challenge?" René asked, before stuffing the sewing pin she was holding, in her hair tied onto a pristine volumed-out braid and rummaging through the snacks. "Shouldn't we celebrate after we get our acceptance letters? But if you are offering to celebrate twice, then I am not gonna complain."

Things had started to ease up after submitting our portfolio for the Parson's challenge, we no longer had to work on two projects and merely focus on the exhibition after classes during the extended school hours, as the final showcase grew closer.

"I am so glad that you finally called it quits from that place and are finally working for a studio that recognises your potential." Quinsy explained as a matter-of-factly, swatting René's hand and smiling at Hope to have the first pick.

"Exactly, this was long overdue Hope." René momentarily threw a glare at Quinsy before turning towards Hope with a genuine smile, as she paused trying a new look on Destiny who had dozed off. "You got this."

"Yeah, snobby orthodox people tend to be the worst kind of orthodox air-heads." Quinsy sighed bitterly, as Hope carefully placed her brushes in her stand, before coming over to thank Quinsy and picking a snack.

"Aren't all orthodox air-heads snobby?" René frowned, as they broke into another squabble.

"I can never comprehend how the conversation somehow tends to take this turn." I sighed as Hope chuckled quietly, leaning her elbows against the sides of my chair, watching them bicker and offering me half of her rice-cake

"Come on… Admit it, it's hilarious." She said, laughing around the words, as I took the cake from her outstretched hand, to eat it in one go.

"Oh, I am certainly not disagreeing with that."

"Which reminds me, I forgot to mention do you know the lead make-up artist in-charge from my old studio, Nor?" Hope asked, clearing her throat.

"What about her?"

"She actually handed me my share of the tips and portion of the earnings, that she had refused to give me for the past months - right after I quit." She prompted quietly, voice carefully reserved.

"Really? That's good." I said flatly

"It's right." Hope corrected immediately. "She was constantly degrading my appearance and using that an excuse to take a portion of what I earned, as she wished."

"I am really loving this side of yours-" I couldn't help but grin smugly, looking up at her, beaming with a bright smile, before we were interrupted by the *ignorant faces* walking towards our table, situated within our spot in the arena.

"See, Didn't we tell you?" One of them remarked, taking a snack from the table even as her hands shook. It was clear that she was trying her best to keep a brave face, with René and Quinsy's glares following her movements. "That quitting something that's not meant for you would solve all your troubles…"

Wow, their combined IQ would have to be lower than the room temperature to classify that nonsense as logic.

"Not meant for *her*?" Quinsy demanded, in a low snarl. "I don't remember inviting you here."

"We are Hope's friends, too" She gasped. "You are being rude. Aren't you supposed to be polite as the junior prefect for the Photography department?"

"Impressive, you expect me to be incapable of thoughts other than the butterflies and rainbows or to have rudeness shoved down my throat!?" Quinsy scoffed, before rolling her eyes.

"Looks like you live in a delusional world filled with butterflies and rainbows-" She pressed, voice rising from anger to disbelief. "-…if you were truly her friend then you would know that people don't want their spots or pores covered by someone who naturally has white patches-"

"She is right, you weren't invited, Sony." Hope said firmly.

It was clear that she hadn't spared them her time to needlessly inform them about her new place of work, especially when they had no ounce of shame for yammering similar nonsense, like they are now. With nearly everyone in their communities, which had reached so far in their pettiness as to affect Hope while working in the make-up studio in the mall.

From the corner of my eyes, I saw René's fingers curling tighter into her fists. Before she could storm towards those *insolent faces*, I pulled her back, harshly, by holding her shoulders in a vice grip.

"Don't interfere for now." I urged firmly "Let them be."

"I make no such promises-" René immediately shook loose from my grip, looking at me as if I had grown an extra limb and hissing quietly, before she was interrupted by the annoying shrill noise emanating from one of those *faces*.

"You are making us sound like jerks, for asking you to compromise with false hopes-"

"We grow up in a world where it's a growing normality for many to associate compromise with sacrifice." Hope clicked her tongue sympathetically, which only made their expressions sour further.

"We are just stating the bitter reality." One of the *faces* (possibly Sony?) fought back, her voice distraught. "Aren't you being ungrateful, for our support especially through things normal people would shun-"

"You have an issue with my looks, you are more than welcome to entertain yourself with your belittling opinions." Hope broke in sharply, staring coldly. "But if you jeopardise my work by hampering my clients with those opinions, you will become the source of my entertainment in an excruciatingly unsavoury manner." She pressed firmly with a smirk, brows drawn down. "Shut your mouth so as to spare people from absorbing the stupidity you are going to spew. Unless you have an incurable case of verbal diarrhoea or that of being a dramatic bitch? "

Hope wasn't holding back, shoulders squaring, as the *faces* started huffing in disbelief and wincing in shame, before walking away.

Sue me for being endeared by it.

"Damn! You were right." René chuckled with a broad grin. "It would've been utterly useless to interfere."

It was a wonder how Destiny slept through it all.

-

Besides not wanting to get Hope in trouble indirectly, if Nor or the studio owner's daughter finally showed up, recognised me - I never wanted to pass by the studio for I didn't trust myself storming in to create unwanted spectacle of chaos by confronting the blatant money that Nor stole from the salaries of various employees including Hope's, keeping them to herself.

I really didn't want my interference to cause Hope to lose her job. But now...well-

"Do I look like someone who cares about your opinions?" Nor asked with a bored expression, raising her hands in mock surrender. "You are not even a customer here, so what's your issue?"

"Oh, I have several opinions about you, just that none can be vocalised without utterly shattering your ego... and oh look! We have such a large audience to witness it." I smirked, before gritting my teeth. "I am contemplating if I wanna put myself through that."

"So, are you gonna use the lie I fabricated in front of Hope to use against me as blackmail?" She asked with a quiet laugh, merely confirming my doubts, that she was guilt-tripping Hope. "Not everything was a lie, I wasn't lying about my sister-"

"I am not an amateur." I laughed, as she started avoiding my glare. "I would never stoop to your level and play your shots."

"Why not?" She demanded stiffly "You are just avoiding it because it can affect someone you know."

"It's cute how you think I have the time to give you assurances." I gave her a cocky smirk and tilted my head.

"You seem like a person who is more than capable of cutting down people without looking back." She hissed, fingers curling tightly around the primer brush she was washing under the basin. "So, it could be nothing but just collateral damage to you. If you know anything more about me then you wouldn't care how the consequences affect me."

"I am not a fan of collateral damage and neither do I see people as that, not that I owe you an explanation." I assured sternly.

"So, what are you going to do?"

"The thing about selective memory I can hit right where I want-" I nodded primly, her expression dropping immediately, as if I knew something worse that could clearly jeopardise things. "-without causing any disruptions. Besides what do you have to the contrary?"

"So, you expect me to just give it to you?"

"I am glad that we are finally coming to an understanding."

"Why would I ever do that?" She asked, raising her finger, trying to test if I did actually know something. I still wasn't sure if the owner was aware of the stunts Nor was pulling with respect to earnings, much less supporting and encouraging her actions.

If the latter was true, then Nor wouldn't have felt the need to guilt-trip Hope, for needing the money to support the education of her younger sister, when Hope demanded to rightfully get her share of the earnings, that she was promised to.

"If you don't, I could always go out there and let them know of a... kleptomaniac." I shrugged my shoulders nonchalantly.

"I have no idea what you are talking about-" She snapped, expression pale.

" Oh really? Then I am sure that the ripples of a rumour would not cause an earthquake of guilt in your conscience-" I said darkly, tilting my head. "-you know, the past has various ways to rise from the grave to humiliate you."

"What's that going to do?-"

"You know best what your favourite weapon is capable of-" I snapped, holding my breath harshly, remembering all the times she humiliated Hope to create a spectacle, and escape from the owner ever finding about her stealing money from Hope's earnings. "-shooting off the shoulder of that dramatic turd that you call your *boss*."

"Fine, I will admit it-"

"Do I look like I am here to be enchanted by your candour?"

"So what? You want me to quit my job, and replace Hope?-" She snapped agitatedly.

So, she has no idea that Hope was speaking to the owner in the other room, to inform the latter about quitting her work at the studio.

"I am sure we could come up with an agreement to avoid that." I offered, playing along.

"What do you want?" She demanded, taking quick and short breaths, and pinching the bridge of her nose. "Look, I can't afford to lose my job here, I will do anything-"

Even if I didn't believe her completely, I still wanted to respect Hope's faith in believing her, that Nor required the extra money to provide livelihood for her younger sibling.

"I want the money you kept taking for yourself from Hope's payment and her tips,-" I said flatly. "-in exchange for my silence."

"You are just going to let this slide even if there is a chance, I may do this to someone else?" She snapped, expression crackling in disbelief.

"Just like you, I too have selfish motives." I grit through my teeth. "Anything that doesn't affect me or anyone I care for, is immaterial."

Compromise? Well, I always found it rather *fitting* having the situation adapt according to me, rather than adapting to a situation. Life wasn't fair, and compromising to it… To let my dreams slip by and have my people get taken for granted wasn't an option.

"Fine, I will give it to you."

"Not me. It's not mine." I corrected, pointing over to the shut glass doors at the furthest corner of the studio, that granted access only to the staff. "Give it to your employee, after she heads out that door."

It was an hour later, when Quinsy had asked unexpected question to ease the atmosphere.

"Hope, if you were to predict a flower that would be Spes' favourite, what would it be?"

"Are we sure it's not something like cactus?" Rene chuckled as I glared at her, point-blank.

"Very original." I chided

"Go to hell, Zrey!" Rene laughed, throwing her head back as Quinsy threw a defeated sigh at Rene's antics.

"As the ascender to the throne in hell, I can assure you are also going to end up there for gambling!" I said, as Hope rested her head on the crook of my shoulder, laughing quietly.

"Probably. I will pick you up." Rene nodded agreeing easily as Quinsy questioned our sanities.

"Carpool?" I wasn't sure what came over me or perhaps it was just instinct. I wrapped my arm around Hope's shoulders as she leaned closer.

"Deal!" Rene said throwing a wink at both of us. "It looks like Hope agrees with me after all."

"I don't." Hope said firmly, the vibrations of her laughter still echoing around the beats of my heart.

"Then what it would be?" Quinsy asked, hitting Rene's shoulder jovially, continuing to be proud of her own joke.

"Yeah what would it be?" I teased, turning around, before leaning my forehead against Hope's and locking my eyes with her's.

"Lily of the incas." Hope said in a strained breath, gulping around nothing as the tips of ears grew alarmingly flushed.

I backed away immediately, growing concerned at the increasing warmth of her skin against mine. "Hope, are you alright?" I asked, pressing the back of my hand against Hope's forehead when she averted her eyes away.

"I think I just need some air." Hope declared, laughing forcibly and fanning her face, before leaving the courtyard.

"Do you think any of these were expired?" I asked, muttering to myself and checking the dates of the wrappers on Hope's sides, frantically.

"I don't think that was the issue, you blind bonehead." Rene grinned wickedly I looked at her waiting for her to offer an explanation for what might have been the cause, instead.

"No, we had double-checked them, before paying for them." Quinsy offered, good-naturedly. "You know just how much Rene is ridiculously iffy about them."

Quinsy started coughing loudly to cover up Rene's smirking openly and uttering nonsensical words like, "Zrey, you are an oblivious idiot."

"I'll go and check on her." I said, hardly paying attention to Rene's quips as mind drifted off to Hope.

"Maybe you aren't completely '*hope*'less, Spes. Get it?"

"That was a horrible pun, even by your standards, Fares."

***

"Everyone's individuality is designed to be extraordinary-" It was probably those very words of Mrs Bronywyn that had motivated her students for years - to not hesitate for a second and fly over from different parts of the world, for the feature-rich pop-art in the gallery displaying their individualistic styles of art.

The very same gallery in which she had worked for years as a curator before taking up her passion to teach Art History. "-What matters is the direction, that the desire of your ambition is chasing - you can decide whether to be ordinary to accommodate according to the standards set by others or be consistent in your standards to preserve '*who you are*' and flourish into '*who you are meant to be*'." The catenary arches of the gallery featured both her former and current students' works graduating by the end of this term. "Because the world is not going to be easy on you, you need to be wise about the direction of that ambition."

The moment Hope excused herself to head to the Ceramics section of the gallery and I stayed back to check the Mosaic Murals section, a familiar mop of Burnt Sienna hair that flown over from Sydney, yesterday, towered over me with a smug grin - Theus Brumoy.

"So, what's going on between you two?" Theus asked quietly, pointing his finger between me and Hope's back disappearing onto the curve of the hall farther away from where we stood, trying his best to fight the smile threatening to break over his face.

"Currently, I would say roughly a yard of distance."

"From what I have heard, you two have travelled across several yards together." He teased, side-stepping before I could elbow his sides. "So where is the next destination? Perhaps a global destination?"

"So, we are deciding travel plans, already?" I chuckled in disbelief as Theus nodded with a wicked grin.

"Based on what I have heard, you guys plan that on a quite a frequent basis." He pressed, winking cheekily. "So, where would Spes Zrey be flying off to for a break?"

"Okay. I gotta ask, where do you hear these things?"

"I have my sources." He shrugged

"What sources?" I burst into laughter "Who could possibly be interested in my travelling plans?"

"So, you do agree that they exist." He smirked, with a smug smile widening further than what was humanly possible.

"I agreed to no such thing!" I huffed, throwing my hands in the air.

"I was kidding, I just wanted to confirm my instincts." He laughed knowingly, as I glared at him for having tricked me easily.

"One of these days you might never know when your kneecaps end up getting smashed for that joke." I hissed, rolling my lips as he laughed harder, holding his sides and throwing his head back.

"Oh please, that doesn't work on me." He scoffed, quirking his eyebrow with an unimpressed expression. "We both know it would be much easier if you just heeded my phenomenal advice sooner."

"You have a peculiar definition of *advice*." I murmured gingerly.

"Answer the damn question." He asked impatiently, trying to stop his laughter, as the confused glances walking by us became more frequent.

"Hawai'i."

"Wow, although I certainly didn't mean that question,-" Theus said, voice audibly confused. "-now I am actually invested in knowing the reasoning behind this one."

"I like their grammar." I shrugged with a small smile. "No unnecessary quantifying of any so-called expected gender binary norms, existing as a prolonged casing of the colonial construct."

"That has to be one of the most unexpected reasonings I have ever heard." He chuckled lightly, before waving his hands at Destiny and Grace, who were animatedly engrossed in a conversation with René in the Ornamental section. "But it's you... so, I am not that surprised, either. I kinda figured that you wouldn't simply just pack your bags just because you were in the mood for Pina coladas or shrimp cocktails."

"That's a big delusional '*if*' not '*when*'." I clarified, pursuing my lips.

"Aesthetically is that the dream destination too?" He asked quietly, voice sombre. "Have you always known or are you still discovering your preference?"

"I am not sure, I always thought I would fit perfectly in the Harbour islands of the Bahamas." I hummed, tilting my head, glancing at the same mural.

"So, is it always a beach?" He offered carefully "Kinda explains your obsession with tropical fruits."

"I think so…-" I nodded, absently "-but I guess there is no better place that appreciates the perfect blend of the tones of pink and blue, while holding its individualistic hues, separately."

"Are you stating that it's never mattered whether you find yourself in the pink sands or the blue water?" He asked with a quiet smile "Huh…the shore does suit you."

"I am still not much of a travelling person." I sighed heavily.

"Because you are scared of time going astray from your plans?"

"I didn't say that-" I protested half-heartedly, looking up at him, in disbelief.

"You didn't have to-" Theus assured matter-of-factly, as the three walked over to us. "-you forget that I have known you for years as well."

"Spes plans to travel to Hawaii with Hope." Theus announced to them in a whisper after he and René quickly exchanged pleasantries, to introduce themselves.

"What?!" I hissed, glaring up at him in disbelief as he chuckled airily.

"I knew it!" Destiny smirked, smacking Grace on her shoulder, who huffed dejectedly. "Pay up."

"I should have stuck with my initial choice." Grace muttered quietly to herself, handing over a few bills to Destiny bitterly "So close."

My eyes widened at the exchange as we waited for either of them to give an explanation, as they sheepishly waved their hands-

"So, you are the aquarium chic?" René remarked with an air of realisation. "That makes more sense than ever."

"The *what*, now?" I asked in bewilderment

"Wait, that must mean you are the one from the camp. She was quite ecstatic about it a few month ago, screaming about them being the same person." Destiny recalled, clicking her fingers in excitement.

"I get why we are confused-" Grace pressed, looking at me sympathetically. "-but why the hell are you confused?"

"I wouldn't be, if I had the slightest idea about any of the words either of them just said." I said flatly, voice rising to slightly accusing.

"You seriously don't know about Fadel fawning over the girl she met at some camp in the woods where they conversed only via some primitive forms of writing?" René interjected matter-of-factly, chuckling lightly. "If you ask me, I was more shocked about the part of - going to a camp in the woods, with no internet for days."

"Well, I am more shocked about the fact that Spes actually went to a camp." Destiny shrugged, brows drawing down. "But the aquarium one - just screams you."

"I mean she brought it up every time I trashed the concept of *'Destiny'* around meeting the *'right'* people - to ever use that as a concept for my art." René quipped good-naturedly when my confusion failed to waver by the slightest. "So, we made a bet that if I ever ended up finding the proof behind her words then I use that as the concept for my final canvas piece for the exhibition."

"How are you even more clueless about this than all of us combined?" Destiny laughed, poking my shoulder repeatedly to highlight her amusement. "She is practically joined to you by the hip!"

"It's actually quite fun, when narrations about three different people turn out to be the same person." René hummed nodding

"Three?" I frowned, pinching the bridge of my nose.

"Well technically, the third one is not a narration but an obvious sight." Destiny clarified, narrowing her eyes and rolling her lips. "She wears that damn pin every day and *you*- well you have always been the same around us."

"Oh please, Zrey is constantly calculative over every single aspect except when it comes to Hope, and personally I am here for the '*confused cat*' state of hers." René chuckled heartily, throwing an arm over my shoulder. "It's comical and cute."

"I am glad you find amusement at the expense of my confusion, Fares." I scoffed with an unimpressed glare, expression pinching.

"I do too, Zrey." René repeated her words, cheekily as I glared daggers. "I do too."

"At this point, I can't even warn you sooner that you are digging your own grave." Destiny warned gingerly and offered a gentle pat on René's back, before pointing at Hope examining Ceramics at the farthest corner of the centric floor and back at me. "Those two won't hesitate to be on the same side in seconds, to destroy you."

"Oh please, I can take them." René protested, as Destiny scoffed in laughter before rolling her eyes.

"And that is one of the flawless representations of - what I like to define as - Delusion." Grace said firmly as Destiny and Theus muttered a quiet *'Good one'*, to her.

"Told you, we had sources." Theus who had been quietly laughing all this while, quipped as he shrugged his shoulders.

"So, basically my new team is ratting me out to my old team?" I sighed tiredly.

"Well, that's basic Friendship 101 when it comes to knocking some sense into the mind of the oblivious one." Theus chuckled good-naturedly.

I need new friends.

"I am not oblivious!" I protested firmly.

"Well, I didn't take any names- you did." Theus said, with a smirk. "If you are waiting for me to disagree with that, I can't lie."

"I am thinking of various ways to catapult you back to Sydney." I scoffed, throwing a half-hearted glare.

I could tell Theus was merely pulling up an excuse when he insisted on going back to the Modern Georgian architectural section to check the positioning of his work's display. Waving his hand at

Grace to go ahead with René and Destiny to check René's work in the postmodernism display section.

"So, what is going on between you, two?"

"I really don't know." I sighed heavily, before rolling my eyes. "Apparently everyone is well aware of this difference between us, except me."

"Forget about their opinions." He assured, practically tugging my arm towards the architectural display section, as Grace leaned back to ask if they should wait for us. "Do you feel that difference?"

"I wouldn't know...I have never been in a position to know." I said, truthfully as I gave an *okay* sign towards Grace, to assure that they could go ahead. "Would I do anything to try and help to assure that she is happy? Yeah. But I would that for every single person that I care for-"

"Does she make you happy?"

"Yeah." I said, quietly, "If that qualifies as difference, then there are several people who fit that category."

"Technically yeah, a lot of us could pass on as your foster siblings."

"That's not untrue." I chuckled, nodding in confirmation

"Well how about this, if there is any person that you would find in that beach?" He asked, quirking his eyebrows, "As much as you adore us, I doubt you would want any of us bozos on that beach." He remarked pointing towards himself and the three heading over to the postmodernism section, as I shook my head, chuckling in agreement. "Which face would make you happy? Who would belong there?"

Perhaps, the answer had been staring at me all along.

Perhaps, I did recognise the familiar sharp timbre-coloured irises looking back at me, sitting on the shore with an unwavering smile, that was willing to stay around for decades.

"I am not sure if I am even capable of acting upon that difference without coming off as disrespectful." I offered absently, trying to bite the air, to feel my teeth, my jaw, to accept that this wasn't a dream but reality.

"Being in love with your life entails you to have the emotional capacity to be in love with another person."

"I doubt she would feel the same." I pressed, matter-of-factly.

"So, I am guessing there is indeed someone on that beach." He smiled knowingly, as I nodded by the slightest. "And from what I have heard, I highly doubt that she doesn't." He continued quietly "Even if she didn't, you shouldn't be compelled to forcibly act upon it in return, just out of convenience, just because she does…"

"It's not that." I prompted in a murmur, more to myself than anyone else. "I doubt I would ever do anything, just for the sake of convenience over aspects that demand authenticity. Or because of the compulsion resulting from the implantation of opinions from anyone else."

"That's absolutely true." He nodded, tilting his head. "But it's something else, what is it?"

"I am scared of disturbing and losing what we already have, if I decide to be selfish about this…" I said, gritting my teeth.

"Have you ever hesitated to be selfish for your life?" He asked carefully "Your goals?"

"No, I would never risk my time over them, to just wait around-" I confirmed, shaking my head slowly.

"Why?"

"Why are you asking me about something, you already know the answer to?"

"Let's just say that I am forgetful, momentarily…" He shrugged.

"Regret." I answered, smiling regretfully. "I don't ever wanna let regret waste my time."

"Then don't let this slip away as regret, without facing it till the end." Theus smiled knowingly.

"Would you do the same, instead of beating yourself up and believing that no one would want to read the completed draft, that you have been carrying around?" I asked, pointing towards the thick bundle of pages peeping out of his bag, which he sheepishly pushed back in, looking around if anyone else had noticed.

"How did you know that it was completed?"

"Just did." I smirked, as he chuckled at my attempt pulling his trick back at him.

"I just don't know if people would even bat an eye at the blueprints of the concepts of an architect, who isn't even officially one yet…" He sighed in disdain. "Who has barely even graduated high school yet…"

"Shouldn't that be even more the reason why people would?" I offered, with a small smile.

"You have a funny way of looking at things, Spes."

"All I am saying is people gravitate more towards appreciating complexity built from the very beginning-" I said firmly. "-instead of targeting that complexity just for the ones classified "*officially*". After all, even we did start from the beginning, too."

"How about this, Zrey? If you decide to make time to go to your beach, then I will consider making this a reality-" He returned a knowing smile, chuckling good-naturedly. "-from the very beginning to complexity."

***

-

"I am sorry but I can't, I don't like to draw things and people that are most precious to me." I said, pushing my tongue against the inside of my cheeks, knowing that this might not be an ideal answer under any circumstances. "I can never do justice to depict the emotions I have absorbed and felt in my life with them into paper…It always feels incomplete…So I never use the portraits of people I cherish the most in my works…"

"Do you think there will ever be a time, where you find yourself drawn in, to be inspired in using them as muses to create inimitable portraits?" Jove questioned, grinning.

"It's easier to draw when I can't read and recognise their emotions well...So the only form of art I wish to capture them is by painting more of their storyboard, in the canvas of my life." I answered, admitting the reality more to myself than the interviewer, "I am not skilled enough to portray that yet and I don't know if I ever will."

It was that very answer during my very first interview, that had bonded Jove and I since our very first conversations to recognise the authenticity of things our vision treasured.

As I stared at Hope's regal caramel irises fading into pale malachite on the right, I couldn't recognise why my lack of acknowledgement or appreciation of the physical parameters of people around me started crumbling into trash.

The mapping of the concentration of the melanin diluted around the eyes as if they wanted to highlight the captivation of those demanding yet warm orbs even further, and concentrated on the arcs of the cheekbones to accentuate them endlessly...

Yet I was certain that arcs of the eyebrows mimicking the cheekbones, could only be significantly drawn in justice by her.

If I ever decided to capture that on my paper, would I ever manage to complete it?

"Do you think there will ever be a time where we might run out of the drive to channel our muses into our creations?" Hope asked, tilting her head as she finalised her drafts for her Design-class test.

"As long as we have a muse, I think we'll always have that drive." I said sagely, nodding going through the photographs of our demo-run of our outfits and joint individual paintings tying along with our umbrella concept, trying to come up for a title for that very *umbrella concept.*

With barely twenty-two days left to go, I was still drawing blanks to sketch my final painting for the final showcase of the exhibition.

"Paradoxical eternity." Hope quipped, playing with the pencil between her fingers, leaning her elbows against our usual table in the courtyard.

"That's an inimitable balance." I said earnestly, dusting my hands to remove the tiny crumbs and wiping my hands clean with the last tissue in the stand, after chewing on my last piece of sandwich. "Balance is always a good necessity." I added, before going back to scroll through the photographs that Quinsy had retouched.

"You must have missed your friends." She said with a small smile, glancing at my hands as I applied her hand-cream, as if it had always been a familiarised habit.

"Good guess."

"I am a little offended that you are underestimating my incredible observant skills to sheer luck." Hope huffed, hiding a smile

"Enlighten me on your observation then?"

"I guess that the ease with which the conversation shifted and the change in the range of decibels with Theus-" Hope offered, narrowing her eyes. "-reflects the eased solace you have around them, like you know that you can always pick it up later."

"Quite true." I nodded in confirmation. It felt like the good old days, with Grace and Theus sticking around longer, until the official opening to the Public, for the pop-art organised by Mrs. Bronywyn.

"And with Grace…you seem quite rigid on not letting the conversation head into anything irrelevant to you-" She continued, tapping the end of her pencil against the corner of the table, monotonously. "-like the loudness is just an indicator that this moment is rare, and that's the only consistency of it."

"Whoa, I really did underestimate your keen observation to sheer luck." I admitted, pursing my lips

"Oh please, you try spending time with someone who appreciates attention to detail-" She chuckled heartily "-you will adapt to this power as well."

"So, we are not going to stress on the fact that you basically reflected on my habit of speaking in a louder tone,-" I asked, leaning forward on my elbows by pushing my laptop gingerly to the side. "-by elegantly wrapping them in words of *"change of range in decibels?""* I said with air quotes.

"Who do you think, I have picked it from?"

"I don't have the slightest clue on that." I said, feigning faux surprise as she slapped my shoulder, throwing her head back in laughter.

"Shut up... This is the moment you give me praise for my keen observation skills by explaining further." Hope laughed around her words as I rolled my eyes before nodding.

"I mean you aren't wrong... I have always felt the connection of '*this person is going to exist in my life*' from them, just different vibes." I agreed, drawing my brows down. "I tend to irrevocably cherish people who radiate this aura to me. I don't intend to take that for granted."

"True. If there is anything that can overshadow the importance of consistency for you, then it has to be authenticity." Hope stated firmly, before unwrapping her lunch, to have her sandwich.

"I don't really like to handle people being inconsistent in my life with regards to any aspect." I murmured quietly "I am quite unforgiving to that."

"You should be."

"But I respect that sincerity." I prompted, tapping my fingers absently against the sides of the table. "It's the only aspect worth letting inconsistency slide by."

"Sincerity is worth being negligent over inconsistency." Hope assured, smile widening to reach her eyes. "Because inconsistency wouldn't exist in the presence of sincerity."

"Over the most valuable matters to me, the words of the conversations I have with people I care for-" I admitted sagely "-end up holding more weightage and they blindly influence my concepts heavily."

"Would you consider me at least as your friend,-" Hope asked, sheepishly. "-if I maintain your trust and always cherish your values?"

"It's a two-way street, If I always try my best to respect yours." I offered carefully "Then perhaps, I might consider the possibility of *'always'*."

"Always. That's pleasantly long." Hope smiled, closing her eyes and taking a deep breath "I like the sound of that."

I felt my stomach flip, releasing that I didn't need a reference to count Hope's eyelashes in order to draw them accurately.

I was doomed, wasn't I?

"It is." I confirmed, more than just her statement.

Even if neither of us had sent a follow-up message. That very night, I had finally replied back to Hope's sketch of lily of valley with the the flowers that promised *'Eternal devotion of mutual support'* : Lily of **the incas.**

***

I really don't know what I was thinking while drawing these portraits instead of completing my final piece.

"Remember when I was asked about the future I envisioned to acquire through the skills of my art?" I asked absently, as Ma walked into my room to remind me to have my dinner already.

"I do...capturing the portraits of people you value the most..." She nodded with a small smile, leaning against the edge of the door of my room. "I believe Jove asked that during your very first interview."

"Yeah." I chuckled tiredly, before pushing the portraits that I was hiding behind the aisle, towards her.

"Isn't this me?" She asked with a wide grin, sitting down cross-legged beside me, and etching her hands carefully over the portraits. "And this one...your sisters... Your friends... And that's our family... you finally did it! Whoa! Isn't that-"

"Hope?" I remarked sagely, taking the portrait that was the least close to being complete compared to the rest. "Yeah..."

"Aren't you gonna complete it?"

"I don't think I can." I sighed heavily. "I am just going to tear it off, it's just a rough sketch anyways-"

"No, you are not." Ma said sternly, snatching the sketches, from my grip before I could react.

"Ma, I have no idea how to complete it and it's just going to stay around-"

"That's okay, they will stay with me"

"Why?"

"I am not letting you tear up the effort and passion and have poured into this, capturing the emotions of your memories." She prompted firmly

"They are my memories... I will remember them regardless of this." I protested half-heartedly

"Then I am going to keep it." She repeated with a knowing smile "Until you are ready to take it back, to recognise the beauty in them."

"Ma, do you think I would be going astray-" I asked tapping my fingers against the edge of the aisle, to break the deafening silence "-if I live in moments that doesn't involve impacting my plan getting closer to seizing my dreams?"

"Spes, I have always been proud of you for never letting anything sway you from your goals, -" Ma grinned softly, before patting my head and running her hands through my freshly-washed hair, that was still yet to dry completely . "-and I know that you think that they are the driving force of the purpose of your life."

"There is a *but* to that statement, isn't there?"

"But it's not your entire life."

"Don't you think that you are trusting me way too easily over investing time on aspects that don't involve concentrating on my goals?" I laughed, squinting my nose "What if I end up getting distracted?"

"If you end up getting distracted or let anything or anyone distract you from your goals-" Ma offered, drawing her brows down. "-then I will know for certain you have been replaced by your clone."

"You trust me way too easily."

"Well, if you ever choose to be a mother then you would know why that trust was always granted, by being earned rightfully."

"In my defence, you particularly never doubted any of us." I smiled earnestly, recalling.

"Have you ever wondered why only you were offered the ultimatum to prove your decision of pursuing Art and design, while Pax wasn't?" She asked, ruffling my hair as I laughed absently.

"I always thought Pax was a prodigy when it came to her interest - gifted from the start, unlike me." I shrugged, trying to stop my laughter "So, I figured that must have been why her choice must have been obvious since the very beginning."

"So were you." She corrected in confirmation, before smacking my head when I scoffed. "Only you refuse to acknowledge that."

"I always thought you just agreed to my ultimatum, because you weren't completely sure of my final decision of pursuing a particular domain." I said, raising my hands in mock-surrender.

"You were the only one among my kids, to accompany me to the hospital and you had naturally been invested in medicine,-" Ma stated quietly, as I held her fingers, combing through my hair, tightly "-even if you explicitly spoke about pursuing it."

Recalling the days when Ma and I used to spend time looking at her patients' reports and going through journals, especially the ones with Melanoma or Hodgkin lymphoma or chronic myeloid leukaemia, until I stopped doing so...for the past four years.

Since then, Ma sat beside me as I worked on a piece, until she fell asleep beside me.

"You never told me that you thought I would follow your footsteps."

"Not mine, but I presumed it would be naturally logical for you to choose this domain." She quipped, shaking her head in disagreement and leaning back on her cushion near my easel. "I wasn't surprised that you chose the domain that you were not only good at, but passionate about as well."

"That's true, I did consider heading up into your domain, when I wasn't sure of what I wanted."

"I know…"

"For the longest time, I wanted to take up the logical guarantee of a path that I had witnessed from the life of the person who inspired me the most." I recalled, loosening my grip on hand, as she sandwiched my hand between hers.

"Most days, your Dad used to joke that you are like a self-cleaning oven, who planned ten steps ahead for any major decision of your life."

"That would be an insult to technology." I chuckled, before Ma went back to tussling my front hair.

"Even before we could check our financial status to afford any of your classes,-" Ma smiled gently, as I looked at her, waiting for her to give an explanation as to why she was talking about it as if it was remotely unexpected. "-you never proposed it without checking it's impact to assure that it didn't affect the funds for the goal pursuits of your sisters."

"Ma, everyone does that-"

"But that's just scared me more, where you push yourself to handle everything on your own." She pressed with a crestfallen expression reflecting across her eyes. "Keeping things to yourself, instead of asking for help because you are scared of worrying us."

"Ma, I don't have any real problems that can't be resolved by a kid-"

"Spes I hate to break this to you but you have never been a kid-"

"I was the oldest, you know how many times I was nagged about that reminder, every time we went back to Dad's hometown." I deadpanned flatly.

"I am so glad that I cut off the opportunities to give them a chance to yammer about that." She sighed with relief, irately, before handing me the varnish and wrinkling her nose in disgust at its smell.

"Thanks for cutting down our trips back there."

"The fact that you gave an ultimatum yourself to prove the certainty in your decision just because we were slightly unsure about your finality to not change your mind later-" Ma said stolidly "-is one of the very reasons why that trust seems easily granted."

"But you always supported me, even before I actually got in."

"Oh we supported you from the beginning, but we are your parents,-" She assured. "-we are always going to worry and want the best for our kids, until you took up the responsibility of your decisions on a whole new level of guarantee. To seize any goal, once you made up your mind."

"That's merely my stubbornness, Ma."

"All I am saying is, I know for a fact that you tend to gravitate towards people whose presence supports and influences you to chase your dreams even more tenaciously...-" She offered quietly. "-so the possibilities of a distraction from them would be undoubtedly impossible."

"That's a fancy way of saying I am choosy."

"Good, continue to keep your standards elevated." Ma said sternly with a proud smile "-'cause forget about being a warrior or a queen, be a damn Empress who just doesn't fight the ideals driving her world into doom, but rises and reshapes the world according to the morals of her ideals..." She continued, pursing her lips and patting my back with reassurance "Spes, you have always been an empress, all you have to do is believe in claiming your throne from this sinister reality."

"I feel like this is going to be my origin story, if I end up being an evil-tempered Monarch."

"All I am saying is I approve your gravitation around their presence." Ma said cheekily with a small smile, pointing towards Hope's unfinished portrait, as soon as my eyes widened in disbelief. "From what I have heard, Pax approves too, with quite a large magnitude of unrivalled glee."

"PAX!" I yelled, figuring out in seconds, that it was Pax who must have spoken about Hope and I, to Ma, merely hearing boisterous waves of laughter from the living room. -

Pax and her obnoxiously large mouth. I am going to have to sew it shut by myself.

***

V

"Creators of crowns lack the patience to wait for their ascent to the throne, enamoured by the prospect of making one for themselves."

CHAPTER - IX

"You are coming over to eat with us, tomorrow." Theus told me in Design on Friday. "Bring along Hope, too." Design was one of the two subjects, that wasn't offered by the GED test, and needed to be completed separately, by one of the very few arts high school offering the course.

I paused my coloured pencil, glancing over. "Come again?" I asked, lowering my head to stare at him, chiselling the ceramics on the floor.

"You are coming over to this amazing Pan-Asian restaurant, near my old place." Theus said without breaking his concentration of lines. "Destiny is coming along, too. Besides, Hope already said yes."

"Why? What are we doing?" I questioned, frowning.

Theus glanced over with an equally confused frown. "Hanging out?"

"What does that entail?"

"Food? Games? Talking?" Theus said, bewildered. "You have hung out with us before, Spes. This isn't your first time."

"No, I know," I said, waving a hand. "But why am I going, especially with barely a one-day notification?"

Theus took a full moment to stare at me like I was insane. "Because... we are friends? And I know you do not have work until tomorrow evening? And you are a hermit who needs social interaction aside from the bitches who you glare at school? What part of this is confusing to you?"

"The sudden declaration of plans."

"Anyway, it doesn't matter if you are confused," Theus said, returning to his design. "You are just following me out of class, and we will drive to my place."

"How long is this going to take?" I questioned.

"I don't know? A couple hours? A few? People will come and go as they have to." Theus told me absently. "It's a pretty quaint and casual restaurant, unlike your style."

I was still worried by the lack of information.

The last part of me was recoiling in fear. "I have studying to do," I warned him. "So, I might need to do it while I am over."

Theus stopped drawing over the layout on the ceramic, long enough to glare at me. "Do you really think that hour of studying is going to make a difference for an exam you have in a week?"

I merely narrowed my eyes. "Yes, actually, I think it will."

Theus sighed, rolling his eyes as he smiled pityingly. "Good luck trying to study. Things can get pretty wild."

"Wild how? I thought you just said that it was a 'pretty quaint and casual place'." I demanded, feeling my stomach drop. "Why did you only tell me this now? Why not give me time to prepare?"

"You don't have to prepare to hang out, Spes." Theus sighed, tsking. "But either way, we almost weren't going to - because of Destiny's dance recitals for the 'Swan Lake' performance, but it recently got postponed so we are good to go."

"Do you not hang out if everyone can't make it?" I asked, knowing that there was certainly something fishy given his hidden smiles and vague statements. "It's actually quite revolutionary that since your move to Sydney, your usual French architectural designs have become more easternised." I offered stolidly as he rechecked his work, looking for non-existent cracks, holding his breath.

"Every place comes with its own solace yet confinements." Theus said, more to himself.

"I agree." Destiny prompted, leaning against the doorway, probably walking in right after completing her recitals for the day. "It's quite unique how you have cleverly reflected the culture you have always had a keen interest about, along with the culture that is rooted into your home-country."

"The reason I believe my culture is capable of embracing the empire I envision, is because it's capable of engulfing new concepts and still remaining embedded in its roots." Theus stated, with a relaxed grin, polishing his work, once again. "I cherish the synergy of that adaptation of life."

"Which culture would you consider as your own?" Destiny asked, quirking an eyebrow. "Your interest or your home?"

"Granted, I have hated the fear of unreasonable norms shaping my society, but it doesn't mean I have ever detested the solace of home." Theus stated, pursing his lips and tilting his head to the side. "It's like the dynamic of a family. It's *joie de vivre* - the euphoric enjoyment of life."

"In a way, we don't realise when our art gets completely ingrained within ourselves to envision our life and our people, from that very prospective." Destiny smiled, matter-of-factly with a small noise of realisation.

"There is nothing else I treasure more, but because I do…even during the times I get agitated with the short-comings with my thoughts-" Theus huffed, finally willing himself to submit his work and knowing that there was nothing more he could have done. "-I still have the blinding trust to know it would still accept me."

"Maybe that trust is what defines our era." I prompted with half a grin, shrugging my shoulders lightly. "Ambition that drives our era, built from our muses and dreams."

" I have always been the type to derive my muses from the webs of concepts and perceptions around me." Theus nodded in confirmation, before heading over to recheck his work, until Destiny and I interfered, by physically pulling him back by his arms, to assure that he would end up messing it up, if he retouched it any further. "I never had to look further to derive inspiration of the complexity of human dynamics intertwining with the continuously evolving stages of the society, farther away from Asian communities."

"We do have an enriching community that's naturally instilled in our Asian roots, that never lets us give up." Destiny assured with a relaxed grin.

"Through all that idolisation revolving around STEM being the only major domain to assure stability in the unpredictable future. Our drive to *'always try till the end,'* is also rooted in those very communities." Theus confirmed, before throwing his hands in mock surrender to ensure that he wouldn't be heading anywhere near his work to retouch it again. "I take immense pride in that."

"That's true, we aren't just encouraged to attempt something only based on interest, but try everything beforehand to help recognise our interest sprouting among them." I stated, leaning my elbows on my desk and my chin against the heels of my palms. "This is rooted since the time we are enrolled into the *classic five-six zone* classes from our toddlerhood."

"Sometimes, it's actually smarter to narrow down your best choice, by reaching towards it, through rounds of striking down choices that you know for a fact aren't meant for you." Destiny added, by skipping to sit atop a desk.

"This eliminates the notion of *'what ifs'* compared to selecting one choice from the very get go, without even considering the plausibility of other choices." Theus said, laying his head on the desk, tiredly.

"Speaking of choices, don't you dare think that you are forgiven for heading back to Sydney, already." Destiny reminded, glaring at Theus.

"Gotten bored of us already, Brumoy?" I teased

"Come on, we would get to tease Destiny about being the Black Swan." Theus protested looking at both of us like a meerkat, before trying to shift the attention towards Destiny. "Or was it the white swan?"

"Nope Odette." Destiny corrected with a quiet smile, shaking her legs back and forth, absently. "So technically both, but neither as well. You know that the play is not based on the movie but rather the other way around, right?"

"I don't know why I always presumed that it was the 'Swan Song', like you would think Song would be a fitting name for the rhythms of performance arts compared to Lake." Theus quipped, brows drawn down and shaking his head monotonously. "Turns out it's just an idiom based on some folklore."

"Yeah, the fable incorporates that when the swan was captured instead of the goose, it was recognised by its song." I recalled, remembering the vague details about the fable behind the idiom. "But the idiom is actually derived from the folklore that swans never sing as beautifully in their early lives as they do right before they die."

"Their final best performance as declared by the public."

"I think that's quite tragic. Another reminder that society gets to decide and declare and dictate when we have our final best performance." Destiny remarked, scoffing lightly.

"Yeah, it is." I related, nodding flatly in realisation. "It's declaring the creative death of an artist before they get a chance to decide if they still have some drive igniting their inspirations into art."

"Because the declaration gets into our heads. Starts to chew up the remaining drive."

"We have always been the persistent doers, stubborn enough, to *redefine* even that idiom for ourselves." Theus declared with a challenging grin.

"True, if we ever manage to put a spin on it, we would never get any more ambitious than that." Destiny smirked, raising her fist for a fist pump.

The onset of a beginning always indicated the end of chaos.

All along, every step of our journey, we had to fight through the chaos predetermining our story.

All along, their determination and predicament for our final best piece, was simply the beginning for the onset of a *new Era.*

Our Era.

My Era.

"I think I finally have the title for our umbrella concept." I grinned broadly, before rushing towards my team to pitch and confirm it, immediately.

"Hey, having an epiphany doesn't give you a free pass from bailing out tomorrow, Zrey!"

***

While the restaurant was most certainly not the fanciest, I knew existed in the city. It was most definitely fancier than the chicken joint, Theus and Destiny had under-exaggerated while describing this place and conveniently bailing at the last minute by insisting to pay for our dinner instead to make-up for their disappearance.

Since when did those two join hands to gang up on me?

Hope sat silently, glancing around the tables that were covered in white tablecloths and wine glasses that I immediately requested to be removed from our table.

Most people around wore formal black suits and dresses.

It was clear from the beginning that Hope and I were the most underdressed people...but I could see Hope sigh in relief and minimally go slack from her stiff posture, when I immediately removed my suit jacket, leaving me in just slacks and my silky beige button up, and messed my hair as Hope absently played with the Aquarius pin, pinned to her faded jean jacket that synced quite well with the perfectly frayed jeans, that synergistically brought out the classic 90's make-up look that she had gone for.

I was going to kill those two...for claiming that I always looked glaringly out of place in casual outings, while warning us to throw on something as casual as possible for this restaurant.

"Spes, I am not-" Hope gestured for me to take the lead in selecting something from the menu, tugging at the frayed edges of her jeans. "I am -I am not dressed for a restaurant like this, no matter how casual...I am in jeans."

The waitress was nice, even if she eyed the two of us slowly as if she were hoping that we had walked in here by mistake. I ordered for the both of us, glancing at Hope after each statement, which Hope just nodded along with.

I am going to get back at those two for pretending to be sneaky with their obvious intentions and bailing at the last minute.

We were brought a little basket of bread and butter, small plates to eat off of, and were assured our food would be right out.

When Hope took a roll, gesturing for me to do the same, glancing up when I didn't move to take any food, slowly placing her bread down, as her expression sobered.

"I am really sorry about those two." I winced gingerly, before glancing up calmly. "I think you look perfectly lovely." I said as a matter-of-fact as Hope looked at me if she wasn't aware that this was obvious.

"You do know that, you blend in perfectly here, right?" Hope assured, chuckling with a relaxed smile, slowly lifting the weights from her eyes into something more genuine as I tousled up my hair to make it messy. "Even when you do that."

"Oh please!"

"So… this is probably a super rude question," Hope said, tapping the corners of the table, gingerly. "I wanted to know what Spes Zrey would be like, if this were a blind date that she had decided to go on, to give a chance to someone who is crushing on her?"

"I wouldn't know." I said flatly, shrugging my shoulders as Hope stared at me in disbelief. "I have never met these people, neither do I believe in crushes being concretely real."

"You are kidding, right?"

"Do you want my expected generalised perception of it or my personal opinion?" I asked quietly

"Is there a difference between the two?" I could tell that Hope still felt a little queasy as she nodded.

"Yeah, there are certain aspects of the latter that are important to me...-" I nodded easily, pushing away my plate and setting my elbows on the table, leaning on my hands. "-well more specifically biased to me, because they are shaped specifically according to my perspective and I can't force that on anyone else."

"You never fail to surprise me." Hope huffed with a small smile, as she leaned forward as well.

"I fail to understand the reasoning behind your amusement." I shrugged, squinting my eyebrows in confusion, as her smile grew wider.

"Not amusement, just a pleasant reminder those words are so *you*." Hope told me, still laughing quietly, demurely.

"So, I am being used as an '*adjective*' now?"

"Yeah, because I don't think any other word would do justice." Hope said quickly, leaning further in.

"So, which one is it?"

"Oh! The latter." Hope said as she straightened, smiling gently.

"If I were to be completely honest, there would be several blank spaces regarding it-" I shrugged, as

Hope's eyes continued to widen quite comically. "-because I have rarely ever had the consistency with someone, to venture further into the burning dumpster fire of developing feelings for them."

"Never? Not even any fleeting crushes here and there." She murmured, suddenly aware of how quiet the restaurant was. Hope tried not to be loud as she placed her fork down on the table, listening to the little *clink* that she couldn't stop from sounding in the near silence of the restaurant, no matter how careful she was.

"You are uncomfortable…"

Hope stopped glancing around at the surrounding tables, eyes snapping back to me quickly, as I stared at her with quiet, concerned severity.

"What? No!" she replied quickly, picking up her bread and tearing it to pieces for no reason. "We've only been here ten minutes, why would I be uncomfortable?"

I could tell by now that she wasn't defensive. She was just a bit… awkward.

Not uncomfortable. Awkward.

I was silent for a few moments, waiting as Hope looked almost afraid to look back up at me, staring resolutely at her empty glass of water that she had swiftly chugged down in one go.

"We can leave, if you would like…" I offered firmly, genuinely apologetic and open to leaving the restaurant, without issue.

Hope did look up at that, with the somber tension around her eyes and mouth fading, leaving just a smooth, quiet concern with a gentle frown and jaw tightening slightly as she stared at me, with an unreadable expression, but setting her glass down slowly.

"I am… I am sorry, I'm getting a little whiplashed," she sighed, rubbing at her eyes.

I lowered my fork, setting it on the table with a gentle expression aimed at Hope. "Come on," I said quietly, standing and setting my napkin aside. "We will talk… somewhere else."

"We don't have to-" Hope stood as I did, shaking her head. "I was the one who insisted you to head out for dinner, without a concrete purpose of discovering the muse for your next work, when you have already completed your portfolio for the Parsons challenge-"

"This isn't really the place for conversation," I said, lips quirking up stolidly as I gestured Hope towards the door. "Hope, we can spend time without worrying about assuring that it has to centralise around work in some form or other."

"But you hate-"

"I like spending time with you, regardless of the purpose anymore." I pressed firmly, as Hope finally broke in a small smile, once again, before settling onto a frown once again remembering something.

"What about the bill-"

"It will be taken care of." I assured her as we both exited through the doors without looking back. "There are some food stalls further down the street,"

I noted, a warm hand suddenly wrapping around mine. "We will talk on the way."

I could feel the unwavering gaze of Hope's eyes, glancing at me to search for any signs of annoyance, exasperation, or any sort of negative emotion.

I couldn't help but feel amused- a quiet amusement that mingled with something like lingering apologeticism.

"I am sorry," Hope repeated quietly as we began to walk down the sidewalk that was dark and empty at this time of night. "I didn't mean-"

"Is it wrong to want to go somewhere more comfortable?" I asked plainly, as Hope shook her head.

"So, not even a single one?" She asked, continuing the conversation from the restaurant, as we passed apartments and walked through streetlights.

"No, that's quite a foreign concept to me." I chuckled, shaking my head good-naturedly, as we shared an order of rice cakes and meat skewers. Sitting at the little plastic table under a tent with only a streetlamp and the stalls' lights to see by, besides the luminance of the half-moon engulfing the entire night sky, tonight.

"Never not even a few fleeting random crushes during the start of your puberty, perhaps?" Hope asked, placing her hand over her slacked lower jaw.

"Oh no definitely not. If anything, I started being more sure of what makes me - me, when I started going through my puberty phase." I nodded, lips twitching at the memory of fawning over Barry Allen and Alex Danvers, while fighting with Pax if she dared to switch channels. "It's not that I have not had a few negligent sappy childhood crushes fleeting in confusion here and there-"

"Oh, picturing that, gives me such joy. Tiny you - brooding yet being all soft for the person who catches your eye." Hope chuckled, shaking her head and chewing the end of her chopsticks for a moment, staring off.

"*And* I'm done." I announced, with an unamused glare.

"No no no, please tell me." Hope insisted, trying her best to stop her laughter, before taking a sudden shift to warn me with a teasing glint to her words. "I'll purposely make the effort of buying out all the coconut drinks from all the local stores in a 5-mile radius, if you don't continue."

"Going after my drinks is uncalled for." I said flatly, as Hope shrugged before waving her hand to clarify that her threat held no true malice. "But yeah, I have always wanted to be sure of my feelings, my actions and my words…because if I wasn't sure then they wouldn't matter, and that notion always bothered me."

Over the past months, I had learnt to stop insisting Hope that sitting beside me while I work on the outfits might be boring. She started to warn me about going through the trouble of buying out my favourite beverage, available in my vicinity if I ever brought it up while she sat beside me to wait until I completed mine.

She stayed, despite having completed her own sketches for Design class, merely saying - "*You work in a rhythm while you sew, it sounds like sea waves and that reminder calms me.*"

"You haven't changed much since then." Hope said simply, her smile never wavering by the slightest.

"As I started shedding my childhood, I think it came with feeling the need to be more concrete of all that mattered to me." I mused, pushing my tongue against the inside of my cheeks, "I just haven't met someone, where my feelings for them, beyond platonic, surely mattered to me. So those childish silly confusions of mine during my fetus ages never fleeted by, after I started out-growing it."

Cars roared down the road, loud in the silence as we ate our food as Hope talked about her first project as the official make-up artist for her first photoshoot in a magazine, which was astronomically huge for her career.

"So…am I allowed to throw back the same question to you." I asked as we stopped at a light.

She glanced at me to search my reaction, lips twitching as we continued walking at a much slower pace. "Yes, I suppose you could, but unlike you I might have several quite embarrassing tales that are better left unsaid. As far as I believe, I am just going to continue to pretend that they are non-existent."

I laughed, shoulders shaking as Hope's cheeks visibly started to get more flushed every passing second, expression scrunching as I grinned, "Now I can definitively sense the amusement in this."

"Why are you keep laughing at me?" Hope demanded, her own defensive laugh stuck in her chest, spreading her arms. "I am making conversation!"

I shook my head quickly, waving an apologetic hand, though I was still laughing. "No, but it has just been a long time since I have laughed over something... so-so...-"

"Silly?" Hope offered, smirking as she crossed her arms pointedly.

"Unrelated to concepts, commissions, schedules or goals." I said, over-enunciating and smiling at Hope. "Most often these questions often lead to me losing our bets, when I fail to choose between equally disastrous choices."

"So, it's funny that I have dug my own grave this time?"

"Yes."

"I'm beginning to think you're not as nice as I thought," Hope said, leaning back on her heels and staring at me in shock. She laughed breathlessly. "I mean, you, with your fancy words and your- your stupid hair- "

"My hair isn't stupid," I gasped in disbelief, glancing at Hope to see if she was serious. "It's normal! You're the one who looks like your hair got dumped by the insides of a mauve pinata."

"I spent 120 Ringgits on this dye!" Hope snapped back, aghast as she pressed a hand to her chest. "It turned out great, for doing it myself!" She glanced over at me and ran her hands through her mauve hair-strands that had been freshly dyed since she started working at Huda's Make-Up Studio. "Holy shit, you're mean!"

"You insulted my hair first!" I laughed in disbelief, glancing at Hope while keeping my eyes on the road.

Hope rolled her eyes. "It's stupid because it looks perfect and nice and soft, there are you happy? Ms. I-probably-didn't-even-style-it-this-morning."

I opened my mouth, looking ready to retort, before I snapped it shut. "Okay, I didn't style it this morning-"

"See!"

"But why does that make it stupid? That doesn't even make sense!" I demanded helplessly. "I'm being attacked, and I don't understand why!"

Hope sighed, rubbing at her face. "You need to hang out with me more," she sighed. "Calling someone's hair stupid is like... the highest compliment you can give." She gestured vaguely, chuckling to herself at the ridiculousness of it all.

There was a long moment of silence as we walked up beside Hope's place.

I stared at the gates pointedly for a moment, trying something new. "Your hair," I murmured, not looking at Hope. "It's stupid."

Hope blinked in surprise, and then it cleared into waves of laughter as if it were about to break out of her chest... and then it faded in embarrassment as her face flushed pink. "Your face is stupid-"

"Is that a compliment, too?"

Hope whipped back around, pointing a threatening finger at me, as I tried to prevent myself from breaking down into laughter any moment.

Her eyes were light, with a smile on her face.

In the dim light of the streetlights, it made them sparkle a little.

Hope swallowed thickly. "I will kiss you," she threatened seriously, as my chest tightened and I blinked and then smiled slowly.

"Is that a threat or a promise?" I asked quietly, glancing Hope up and down.

"I promise I am threatening you."

I chuckled, leaning on the gates leisurely. "Keep talking like that and I might have to threaten to let you."

Hope looked like she was either going to combust from embarrassment or just die.

She clenched her fists as my smile turned into more of a stupid, pretty smirk, continuing the banter.

"Oh, for the love of-" Hope grabbed me by the lapels of my jacket as she surged forward, pressing a light kiss to the very corner of my mouth. "Shit, I am really sorry-" and suddenly backing away, looking at me as if I had lethally electrocuted her and rushing into her place before I could say anything. Or even react.

"Hope wait-"

What the hell just happened?

***

Before I had the chance to ask Hope that we should talk out the events of last night, the chances of the Huda sisters investing their funds in our showcase had hit another roadblock.

So, when Hope nervously proposed if I would like to accompany her to her Nonna's Bar Mitzvah, I was too occupied about the possibility of not having a showcase at all and having all our works be reduced to nothing, all our efforts being in vain, I found myself absently nodding along.

To the surprise of us both, that night was a party night, with Hope gingerly recalling how her Nonna called it while announcing she wanted her closest people and their closest ones to gather up for dinner…except her, forcing her to attend out of compulsion. Compulsion, that I couldn't possibly pry about.

I couldn't decide if I wanted to leave the catering tents as soon as the lighting ceremony wrapped up or if Hope wanted to storm out before she could grind her teeth to dust, as the whispers and scoffs directed towards us got louder, while picking up their drinks.

"How long do you want me to be here, Mom?" Hope closed her eyes, sighing in disdain as a woman in her late-40s with nearly ghostly-pale complexion, short dark blonde hair and gradually greying roots, with the same defined arc of cheekbones and similarly high arc of the nasal bridge lying between her eyes like that of her daughter. She sympathetically asks Hope to bear through the night, before glancing over at me and patting her daughter's shoulder.

"You must be Space, I really like your jacket, is that ivory? Am I recognising it right, Hope?" She asked with a polite smile, carefully brushing the contrast of the ivory wrapped bow peplum and lapels of my jacket and looking up and down at her daughter's ivory trench frock coat fitted over her fuchsia-rose deconstructed skirt. "My daughter has developed quite a habit of gushing about-"

"It's *Spes*, Mamma." Hope corrected irately, through her gritted teeth before either of us could react.

"That's what I said, didn't I?" She asked, smiling with a grimace, gripping her daughter's arm in a vice grip as if to ask her why she was irritated in a party, glaring back at people who were whispering and jeering behind our backs. "What's the big deal? It was just a mispronunciation, can't you just let it slide?"

"That's what you do, Mamma. You let everything *slide*, you walk past it and expect me to silently *tolerate-*"

"You are making a *scene*." Hope scoffed, as her mother whispered with a small smile, picking up a drink of the over sweetened punch, herself and turning towards me, "I am sorry, my daughter doesn't like parties, you have to excuse her sour-"

"With all due respect, Mrs. Fadel, neither do I-" I said with a forced smile, through my closely shut jaws.

"Hope, why have you covered your entire face with make-up. You don't need to camouflage your spots." She asked, trying to smudge the make-up off Hope's face in an attempt to remove it, before Hope swatted her hand. "You don't have to hide your face among your family, they are not talking about that-"

"I don't care what the hell *they* might be talking about, Mamma." Hope snapped, grinding her jaws together, "I told you I didn't even want to be here, the least you could do is not be ignorant over remembering the name of the person, helping me to be sane among *these* people!"

"What is your problem, dear?"

"Can I ever have any? If I do, all I am doing is not having the *strength* to not let it slide, right?" Hope scoffed back in a whisper. "Why don't you continue doing that for the both of us?"

"Hope, it's just for an hour…please calm down."

"Don't worry, I will *fix* that." Hope scoffed, turning her head away, when her mom tried to pat her head.

"She will come around… You have to give her more time to get used to what's relatively new for her…and them." Hope's mother smiled regretfully "You just have to tolerate it, until then-"

"I know." Hope declared with finality, before her mother sighed tiredly and walked up to her husband towering over her and stopping him from rushing over towards Hope as he looked at his daughter with deep concern - the same timber-coloured eyes inherited by his daughter, with dark-olive skin, thick eyebrows and wide forehead.

"I am really sorry for dragging you here-"

"I am going to propose something. You would have done the same for me if I were in your shoes." I offered, stolidly, interjecting her immediately. "Hold my hand, when anyone of them decides to yammer again."

"If you propose that, then I might never let go of your hand." Hope snickered cheekily, with half a smile "We are surrounded by several who don't have the slightest clue on how to mind their own business."

"Don't worry, Hope." I promised, returning the smile, as we walked past the gifts table. "I don't offer proposals without planning for all its accountability."

"I could use that." Hope nodded, holding my hand as the jeerings continued behind us. "If I have to live through this night, without punching one of them muttering '*hiding her abnormality*' like a chipmunk chewing its preserved food."

"Well, perhaps we could pity their poor sight, together." I quipped, raising my eyebrows, as I felt fingers intertwined with mine.

"Why? Because I look normal to you, now?" She teased, despite her words holding no joke in her tone... eyes narrowing more towards people over my shoulder and biting the air with her lower lip trembling.

"You are Hope Vale, you will always look regally stunning to me." I said firmly, tugging the hand holding mine until their eyes were looking right back at mine.

"At this point, I don't think you are even trying to look like a Designer." Hope said with a lazy grin blinking away her tears before they fall down her cheeks, tousling my hair as I laughed

"Is that so?" I asked, trying to fight back a smile, closing my eyes as my hair fell over them. "Did I ever?"

"No, you have always had that aura."

"And I am guessing that's good?" I teased, as Hope went back to the lazy routine of fixing my hair before tousling it once again.

"Guess better next time, because good is an understatement. If you look kinda like a young Audrey Tautou, tonight." She chuckled as I placed the back of my free hand over my closed eyes, laughing, when I felt my cheeks flush, before her voice took an air of severity. "You don't think I am hiding?"

"Hope, you are *magnetically* radiant and are *one-hell-of-a* make-up artist, it's an unrivalled fact that you are an absolute force of elemental creativity, to be reckoned with." I smiled, squeezing the hand tightly wrapped around mine. "You can choose to continue feeling beautiful in the comfort of your skin."

"This never bothered me…" Hope muttered more to herself, to fill the silence settling between us, poking her cheek lightly before shrugging. "-and my family used to remind me of the feeling of embracing my own skin all the time…that it never mattered what *they* had to say or mock or degrade me, especially my Nonna-" Despite everything, Hope had an absent smile, across her lips. "-but that changed soon after she found out…she gave me an ultimatum."

"An *ultimatum*?"

"An *ultimatum,* to get over my '*phase*' of comfortability of attraction exclusively towards people of my gender, that has no *future-*" Hope swallowed thickly, as her knuckles whitened around the plate. "-or undergo skin-grafting to be *normal* at least through one aspect."

"That's when we first met." I realised carefully, recalling back to the time, we interacted, with a wall separating our hospital rooms. Hope nodded, expression tense.

"It tore my world apart, and everything felt like a lie. All this time they felt the same about me as the rest of those people out there...someone *abnormal.*" Hope dropped her eyes to stare at her white knuckles. "I had to choose between living within one of those lies. So, I chose the latter. I was constantly reminded that I wasn't someone who deserved love until I made a choice or be forced to accept the choice decided for me. I would have been forced to undergo it if my parents hadn't called it off at the last minute..." Hope placed her plate beside the array of food laid out for the guests, before her hand formed a fist at her side. "I really don't know what actually qualifies as being *deserving* enough of someone's love."

"You don't '*deserve*' love," I whispered, frowning at Hope who had frozen right beside me. "It's not something that has anything to do with your end. You simply exist... and then people give it to you, Hope. You shouldn't have to do a single thing to get it. You will never have to do a single thing to receive love. Just stay as you are."

"I-"

"Hope, you should walk out of here-"

"Trust me, there is nothing I would like to do more." Hope sighed quietly, expression innocent, before breaking into a hopeful smile. "So, I am going to do the only thing that helps me lose track of time. Eat spicy food with you from the buffet, and make fun of you for struggling to eat it."

"I *do not* struggle-"

"You have to be one of the only Malaysians with the lowest tolerance for spices." She noted with a snicker

"It's not on me that your tolerance levels can handle lethal spices that are practically poison!" I protested half-heartedly

"My dad's side is from Penang, and they have lowered the spice levels to suit the Italian tastes of my Mom's side-" Hope remarked absently, before taking the ladle to place a spoonful of jasmine-scented rice on her plate. "-and Nonna, well she eats fresh whipped meringue like breath mints."

"I hate *meringues*." I snapped petulantly, glaring.

"I don't think you are capable of not liking any dessert." Hope reminded quietly with a knowing smile, following her gaze onto my glare towards the old Italian woman laughing boisterously, sitting atop a classic oakwood chair raised by several people, spinning around, chanting a folk song. "What you are trying to say is that you dislike something or rather someone else…"

"I don't like it-" I repeated, jaw clenched. "-I don't like it at all."

"I can't believe you are *actually* parading *this*." A face jeered, pointing his finger at us, with his nose nearly occupying over half the volume of his face. "I thought you would get to your senses, after I had the decency to tell the truth to your family, first, ever since this *phase* began…I thought you would be more grateful."

More disgusting jeerings continued behind him.

"Right, excuse me if I don't feel grateful about talking about an *important* aspect about *me* as if it was ever *your* story to tell." Hope hissed through gritted teeth, sighing heavily before placing her plate carefully on the table. "Just buzz off, Neil."

"Come on, Hope…you are my favourite cousin." He protested, feigning faux concern. "You were like my younger sister, we were practically inseparable…we can get back to the old days, after you come back to your senses-"

"I mean this in the nicest way possible, when I say this-" Hope muttered lowly, through gritted teeth "-Get the *hell* out of *my* sight, or I am going to *punch* your enlarged nose."

"Why are *you* glaring at *me*?" His expression changing from shock to genuine apprehension, shifting his gaze towards me.

"Why on earth are you spewing your over-inflated vapid narcissism?" I snapped taking a step forward, as Hope held my hand tighter with a small smile, pulling me back as my empty fist curled by my side

"Is *she* the reason, you are acting so *cheap,* Hope? So *mannerless*?" He scoffed, rolling his eyes. From the corner of my eyes, I could see Hope's father gritting his teeth, shoulders squaring, as her mother practically used her entire force to hold him back.

"Say another word, I dare you…" Hope said, through her clenched jaw, lips curling in visible disgust. "I am going to give you ten seconds to apologise, because I am respectful."

"You aren't even acting like a woman of our family-" He barked a loud laugh, arms crossing over his chest, before his expression lost its amusement and he crumpled with a scream when Hope punched him straight at his bloated-nose.

Looking more like walrus' snout than a human's nose at this point.

I couldn't help but start laughing in sheer amazement.

"I warned you." Hope said calmly, staring at the guy clutching his broken nose in pain, coldly. "I don't even want to be associated with *scum* like you." She merely glared at the others as they stayed frozen in shock, as his screams became muffled when Hope's grandmother finally yelled 'ENOUGH'

Hope didn't spare them a glance, taking deep breaths before silently asking me with a wide grin - If we could walk out of here, at once.

I couldn't nod any sooner, in confirmation.

***

We walked to the empty lands, further away from those tents lit by different chrome of lights, until we moved to the wooden benches that surrounded a nice table, probably made of white clean stone, a full moon above us and it was all happening in a circle.

"Can I ask you something?" Hope asked, before resting her hands on the table, as the breeze enveloping us started getting immensely colder.

"Since when had we gone back to asking permission to do that?" I sat down beside Hope, before she moved slightly closer towards my side, so close that our shoulders were slightly touching.

"This is important, and it may cross boundaries, so I have to ask and I really don't want to disregard-" Hope pressed, carefully

"It's alright." I assured. "Go ahead."

"You are going to gamble the accountability of the impact, my question might hold?" Hope asked and tilted her head aside, giving a light squeeze to my hand for reassurance.

"I am not gambling anything. It's you…" I confirmed, with a small grin. "It's us."

"If you say things like this, I am actually going to forget what I wanted to ask you." Hope laughed lightly, as if she was expecting me to reconsider my mind to back away.

"Go ahead, ask me."

"I don't know if you do this… just with me, and I can't tell if it's a subconscious habit where you always wait and tend to ask if something is troubling me first-" Hope said impassively, sighing in concern. "-before even considering to talk about something that's been troubling you for days where you just need someone there by your side."

"Hope-"

"Spes, if that's your way of checking if I have the emotional capacity to listen to you, during that moment, you can just ask me…" She urged gently, looking at me while waiting for a reaction. "I don't want you to wait like you are walking on eggshells to rely on me…"

"It's not like that." I sighed with a chuckle "It's more of an adaptation to the frequency of the coincidences of bad-timings."

"I am guessing you might hate hearing, '*You can talk to me whenever you need someone by your side. I will be there for you*'?" She asked, swallowing thickly. "Even if I actually mean it?"

"Not always." I prompted, shaking my head slowly in denial. "It's not along the lines of *hate*, but rather more along the lines of feeling '*nothingness*'." I continued, absently kicking my legs in the air, in a slow randomised rhythm. "I am so used to always having the people going through so much more gigantic in their lives, when I need them the most, that I know they really don't have the emotional capacity to even bother accommodating my petty issues on top of theirs-"

"They are not petty-" Hope snapped, gritting her teeth, turning towards me to shake me by my shoulders.

"During those moments, all I knew was that I would be the most selfish person if I was inconsiderate enough to dump my issues, especially when they were struggling to navigate through theirs." I murmured quietly, holding her hands over my shoulders and slowly prying them away, as she lightly slumped her forehead atop my shoulder. "During the times I tend to prioritise my feelings, during those sensitive moments, I can't help but feel even more helpless and hurt." I carefully started patting her back, she merely shifted, placing her hand over my shoulder and pressing her chin atop it. "But then I remember... that...They are not accountable to listen to my venting by compromising their boundaries and neither would I consciously put them in such a position."

"Do you believe the promises of people being there for you, when you need them?"

"Yeah, because they stay accountable to be there for me when they listen, instead of being there half-heartedly." I said matter-of-factly, in a monotonous tone. "I value that more...I just don't like hearing those promises, especially only after I stay by their side. Conveniently, those are the times when people tend to say those very words, the most."

"But it feels more like they are saying it as if they owe you, even when you know that they aren't." She said in realisation, though her tone held the air of a question raised, instead.

"I am used to never starting a conversation especially with the intention of needing someone's support during the suffocating moments." I nodded lazily in confirmation. "It tends to be more of an unconscious comfortability to speak about it ages later, if they have the capacity to hear mine, only after having the space to be vulnerable, themselves."

"Vulnerability encourages vulnerability." She reminded, recalling my words as I chuckled, nodding again. "I just want you to know that I don't need a reason to value the feelings you have vocalised." She promised.

"Why?" I teased, trying to buy time to unfreeze my limbs that had frozen in reaction to her words. "Are you just that unreal or just that good of a smooth-talker who knows just the right words to throw around?"

"We have time to let you figure that out by yourself, don't we?"

"We do."

"Spes? Why did you never accept those coconut beverages from me? Did I perhaps get the wrong brand?" She asked carefully breaking the silence between us, as I felt her tremble in my arms. I shook my head sharply, before she asked the question that I dreaded the most. "Why did you push yourself to overdose on those sleeping pills, back then ?"

"I really don't know why I feel the alarming need to force myself to calm down more in the sense of danger." I swallowed thickly, feeling my throat dry up, immediately, as Hope's grip over my shoulder tightened in sync. "Maybe it always felt like... if I panicked, I would lose consciousness sooner and run out of my adrenaline-driven panic to make any reformed decision without thinking straight." I really didn't know why I was still talking. "I don't think any of my family knows about the reason behind my sleeping disorder."

"You are indeed very good at brushing over and hiding things well, whenever you want to." Hope muttered, trying to keep her voice as stable as possible.

"I have been told that several times by my family, especially Pax and Ma." I laughed regretfully, feeling my jaws clench unconsciously.

"Does anyone have the slightest idea?"

"I think Pax does."

"She is the only one, you told this to?"

"No, she was notified of the family emergency when I was in the ER of the clinic-" I corrected, flatly. "-but thankfully she missed the call-"

"Can we go back to the part where you talk about being in the ER as if you were vacationing in Hawai'i?" She gritted through her teeth, flinching and cupping my face in her hands instead, carefully as I avoided her gaze. "Were you with your mother during her shift or something?"

"No, she wasn't in town." I admitted, placing my hands over hers, as she tried to turn my head to hold her gaze. "Neither of my parents were."

"Then why were you in the ER?"

"Because I ended up drinking an energy drink that had been mixed with one of those art supplies liquid glue, meant as an accomplishment to cement someone's bravado." I snapped, dropping my head in a slump.

"Y-you what?!" She asked, looking at me in utter disbelief. "How on earth did you hide this from everyone around you?!"

There was no denying that I was aware that I wasn't a '*nice*' person, and I certainly had no intention in being one.

"One of those *careless bastards* of his friends had mixed the glue in the bottle." I always had the biggest reminder of that, whenever I had to bite down my tongue from speaking my actual mind, while coming across people who accomplished pursuing interests carelessly, spoke about it equivalently to relate to the interests I pursued ambitiously through all my will. I clearly didn't understand speaking regarding the pursuit of relating with the matters of dreams and interests, when there was an obvious difference of the frequency of ambition and dedication to the respective interest. "I already knew that they had been manipulating him to accomplish humiliating tasks, disguised as testing his bravery to fit into their team."

"Wait, did one of them involve daring him to play this prank on you?"

So, it was no brainer that I was at my end at being supportive for his dream, which constantly kept changing because of the lack of chase of the said dream over the excuse of fleeting time frame. "Yeah, I discovered it quite later, when he fessed up during his apology, that they thought - '*he feared me, and was afraid to lead our team instead*'. To prove that he wasn't, he was dared to play a practical prank on me. To prove that he should be the only one, up there, receiving the award if we won the art-mural contest."

Did I assume mindlessly from my own standards that the spoken interest could be his dream or were my intuitions all along and was at its expiration date of subsided?

Was I being shallow-minded? There are millions who spend years exploring, before finding their choice.

But even when we are exploring the fitting choice made for us, don't we pursue what we love ambitiously, forgetting the constraints of time while getting lost in them?

Were they just empty or half-hearted words or was I the worst for not recognising the drive behind their dreams?

"How is that whining?" She protested, as if she were contemplating whether she wanted to knock some sense into head or shake my shoulders vigorously to reconsider. "If you are troubled by something, it's still your choice to speak about it, and not force yourself to accommodate it for their sakes even if it's with the presence of someone you trust."

"People change, people are variables and I realised that more concretely for misplacing my trust due to my first misconception of a '*best friend*'." I spat, bitterly more towards myself than anyone else, shoulders slumping further into myself "People can always take that trust for granted, even unintentionally, and they view it as nothing but putting up with the person out of familiarity."

"Spes…"

"Instead of having the decency to just throw it away…" I grit through my teeth, trying to stabilise my stuttering words. "All I know is, after drowning down that juice… I was glad to be walking down the buildings nearest to the infirmary."

All I knew is that I needed to stop getting invested in them, before my irritation surfaces at its bay and I end up saying words that could clearly hurt him, and despite everything…the memories spent together, were precious to me, to respect the boundaries and try my best to not hurt them by voicing out my opinions regarding their drive.

"And they didn't raise any alarms?" She asked softly as I continued avoiding her gaze.

"The entire school was occupied with the event, I doubt that they had time to go around raising alarms-" I scoffed, shortly. "-and scaring the guest schools away instead of just getting me the quick fix for cough."

"Something tells me you are heavily undermining the usage of *heavily* in your context."

"The resulting outcome is I felt better!" I said, trying to convince myself, as I felt her hand wipe the tears that I hadn't realised, were beginning to streak down my cheeks.

"You have a very twisted understanding of the definition of '*better*'-" She said, quietly as I shook my head sharply, blinking my tears away. "-if you felt all better, how did you land up in the ER?"

"I usually walked home alone. By the time I started getting unusually dizzy, I had collapsed. I was already inside the ER of the nearest clinic on my way back home." Besides I figured coughing up blood wasn't going to be easy to hide or ignore. It certainly wasn't easier to clean either, when it ended up seeping through that wretched cobalt-blue shirt.

I had already informed Pax and Felicity that I may arrive late if things got delayed during the event, and if Felicity hadn't noticed my shirt in the laundry, Pax wouldn't have started doubting anything at all.

Looking back, I really should have worn a black shirt inside my black jumper, instead of letting that stupid shirt act as a sponge. I really wouldn't have had to go through the trouble of sneakily cleaning it spotless, for days.

"Spes…"

"Throughout the entire walk back, all I could think about was remembering how stupid it was, to grant him that trust…" I whispered defeatedly, wondering why my belief in one's dreams developed into blinding trust towards that person, irrevocably… Even when they no longer had any ambition to pursue theirs and their proclaimed dream had just been a common interest stated to elicit a conversation out of boredom, from their side. "*Why*? Because of time measured by years?"

Why had I failed to recognise attachment that no longer encouraged reciprocation, merely facilitated manipulation, instead?

"Why haven't you told your family, it's not like you don't trust them? I have seen you with them, you-"

"Telling them would have just caused them more worry, my mother didn't take it well when I gave the excuse of scrapping my knees because I fell on the concrete due to a misstep, I just skipped the part of what caused the misstep.-" I sighed tiredly. "-I don't like seeing them in pain or worry because of me especially over something that had already occurred."

"Spes… it's been years, were you ever considering-"

"No. That's not a circumstance I was ever going to consider…at least, not for now." I snapped sternly, taking deep breaths to even them to calmness. "I still can't believe I am talking about it with you."

"Why did Pax start doubting more?"

"Probably because, I struggled to drink any kind of beverage from any bottle." For over a year, I struggled with the paranoia of wanting to throw the water in my water bottles that may have been accidentally touched by anyone even by my own sisters, and I did. "I felt irritated and weak from letting that accident control something basic, so I started developing a habit for never consuming water for hours and then drinking over litres of water from my bottles at once, just to end up throwing up.

"Is that why you used to refuse to drink the coconut drink from me, during lunch?" Hope asked, more as an admittance, instead of a question, as I nodded in default. "Because it was in a bottle and not in a tetra-pack? There is no way you would deny to actively skip out on anything based on lychees or coconut." She added, trying to lighten the mood.

"It's not that I don't trust you, because I do…" I confirmed, honestly, surprising even myself with my words in resonance to her shock. "It's just I haven't gotten rid of that accident controlling me completely."

"And you never felt the slightest hint of anger at his petty ego and inferiority, that could have prevented this entire accident?"

"No, I didn't. I felt angry at myself, but him?-" I admitted firmly "-No."

"Why?"

"There is no point being angry or telling him about something that is gonna bring forward secondary guilt." I said quietly, finding the will to lock my gaze with hers.

Several people offer empty words, so I could easily be saving my sanity by offering empty words in response to pursuit of their goals, that lack the drive to be fulfilled by all means or at least until their drive started to exist with staggering stability... But I never could.

Man, I really wasn't a people person.

"Wait, hold on so you never told them about the aftermath of the pain resulting from the absolute disaster they sprung forth on you?"

"No, I haven't." I remarked, shortly

"Why not?" She yelled, agitated. "How are you so calm about this?!"

"It's not that I actively hid it, I just had no reason to speak about it with him. I don't see the point of talking about it when he ended up apologising about it." I prompted, stolidly. "What else can I do about it when he has already done me a favour by walking out of my life since then?"

"Did you end up finding out about your Parents' separation after that?" She asked carefully.

"No, I already knew. I made the mistake of talking about it with one person. With him, right before the competition and all he told me was that - it was all in my head and I might be hearing things that weren't going to happen." I sighed defeatedly. "Over-exaggerating things, to find something tragic to fuel my inspiration for art."

"I am going to hunt him down and punch him." She threatened, coldly

"I did." I smiled quietly, raising my eyebrow as Hope smirked with a smug grin. "In retrospect, that might have pushed him to get back at me."

"I hate that I ended up being one of those people that needed a gruesome reason-" She grimaced apologetically, as I shook my head in disagreement "-to understand the weightage of your words and values, that you never compromise with."

"I wouldn't have told you, if I didn't believe that you wouldn't understand the weightage of my opinions even when you didn't know the reasons fuelling them." I confessed, truthfully "You don't have to pity me."

"I would never pity you." Hope said, sternly. "Even now I am rather shocked than anything else, because all I can think about is the truth behind your sister's words about you." She added, dropping her head with a light chuckle.

"Which one was it? Pax or Felicity?" I winced, as she waved her hand.

"You are indeed paradoxical." She recalled, with a broadening grin, as I huffed in recognition, as Hope recalled the words Pax had stated to her - '*If there was a single word to describe my sister then it would be Paradoxical.*

The persona in front is completely different than the one inside, but neither ones are just an upfront and both co-exist in sync, that's who she is…She is one of the most stubborn pricks you will come across, who would always keep their words whether it's promised to herself or to others.'

"So, it was Pax." I huffed, pressing my hands over my face as Hope nodded, wincing before breaking into a smile.

"Spes?""

"Hmmm?"

"Just know that you can ask for my help without having to explain the situation to me, if you can't speak about it." Hope said with an unreadable expression, as if she knew something but didn't want to press further until I admitted it myself. "Promise me that you will consider that, even if it's for the very thing that was troubling you this morning, that made you accidentally say yes for tagging along with me to this." She mouthed '*I figured*' with a quiet shrug as I stared at her in disbelief. "I am here for you just as equally as you are there for me."

She basically worked with Isabel Huda, who was one of our two primary investors, where they, currently, had an equal 50/50 chance of completing the process of funding our exhibition or failing to do so, through the obstructions held by the administration controlling the trust-fund of the school.

Did she know?

"I promise."

"You know what I have always wondered?" She asked, to break the silence starting to settle between us once again. "For someone who claims to have a very short temper, you never throw around vulgar profanities through your language."

"I mean I can express my anger while still maintaining the eloquence of my vocabulary." I shrugged, with a small smirk "I am angry at the circumstances or the actions of the person not the language, I am not going to disrespect that."

"That's still not someone who has a short-temper, Spes." Hope corrected, snickering.

"Wait, you don't think I have a short temper? Have you met me?" I huffed, chuckling in return.

"I have, that's why I have grown to observe that you are one of the most patient people I have ever come across in my life-" She said, smiling warmly "-whether it's the way you listen sincerely till the end, or persistently keep going no matter how many hurdles block your path or are naturally attentive to the smallest things that matter to one's time and boundary but most of all…"

"Hope, you are someone who always sees the best in people, even if it may not exist-" I fought back in faux protest, trying to change the subject as I felt my cheeks warm up.

"I think it's your growing desire to constantly improve the way you express your respect for the people you care for, no matter how long you have known them…" Hope continued, her smile never wavering by the slightest. "-You always wish to treasure the very thing that often gets taken for granted over time."

"Are you mistaking me for someone else?"

"Hard to, when no one else fits that description in my life." She shook her head slowly, pursuing her lips before grinning and tilting her head. "Granted, you reasonably shove away the bullshit that you refuse to put up with, through your apathetic exterior towards random people... but you are also the same person who tenaciously supports the dreams of anyone you meet, as long as they are unapologetically devoted to their dream."

"Yeah, that misconception... my belief in their dream, blinds me from recognising the person that I had trusted, ceased existing for a long time..." I quipped, looking down at our hands, wondering how long I had been running my thumb over her knuckles, in absent circles.

"I really don't know how you see through that, but you always do, and once you do... your belief in them is as strong as your ambition towards your dreams-" Hope said, squeezing her eyes shut, momentarily, before absently trying to brush the non-existent creases over my ivory lapels as my eyes zeroed in towards the Aquarius pin pinned to her trench coat. "-and that's saying something knowing your *magnetic* dedication to your dreams - even when they doubt their dreams during various moments of struggle."

"You are something else."

"I know, that's why we have always connected and always will." Hope beamed easily, before taking a pause, and looking lost as if she were looking for words, to rightfully describe something. "You... are an enigma."

"And why is that?" I asked, returning the grin

"You are earnestly honest that I can't constantly help but fear that you are unreal. So, breathtakingly unreal, that every reason I can conjure up fades in comparison." Hope murmured with the same unreadable expression, reflecting across her eyes, that I never recognised. "Truthfully, all I know is- It's you, how can you not be?"

"You say that as if it is self-explanatory?" I chuckled, before carefully placing the small, wrapped gift from my pocket of my box-pleat lapels and placing it in her hands. "I don't care, if it's not your bar-mitzvah, but this was long overdue for the one, that was denied to you, six years ago." I explained, as she stared at me in bewilderment before carefully unwrapping it.

"The German-chamomile essential oil, I had been saving for…that ran out of stocks for months…"

"I know that it's nothing, but-"

"Don't do this to me…if it falls like an illusion then it's going to be excruciatingly cruel…"

"What?"

"I admit… it was perhaps ambitious to take that admiration I held for you and try to turn it romantic." Hope sighed, before pulling her hands away and standing up. "That was unfair of me, and looking back, rather presumptuous-"

"It was never presumptuous." I corrected sternly, stopping her in her tracks, finally getting a chance to speak about last night's events that I had been wanting to discuss, since this morning. "You just never gave me a chance to clarify that certainty."

"You don't actively hide your words, yet excruciatingly break down the authenticity of a person to open up completely." Hope said, turning back towards me, and holding out her hand gingerly as her fingertips shook by the slightest, waiting, before I intertwined her fingers with mine... as if it had been a habit, all along. "I mean I can't imagine what you must have felt hearing all the suggestions when you calmly state that you can't sleep or your tethering grasp on consistency." Hope murmured, as I felt her trace my face before settling on my eyes.

"Fortunately, I have had people in my life, who never crossed the sheer audacity to whine about getting me to change, if they couldn't respect my opinions. They motivate me to believe in humanity." Her hand felt warm as she cupped my cheek, so gentle it was like a butterfly landing against my cheek, hand shaking a little as our foreheads touched gently.

"Do you have a thing for people who are passionate for art?" Hope teased, wrinkling her nose as the tip of her nose brushed against mine. "Or is it ambition?"

"I have a thing for you." I hummed matter-of-factly, watching Hope's cheeks heat up even more. "I thought you were avoiding me because you might have regretted what happened last night."

"How can you be this oblivious, you idiot?" Hope asked, a laugh caught in her throat that didn't leave, despite knowing the answer to that already.

I couldn't help but wrap my arms around her, silently trying to make up for the lost time, wordlessly.

"Even if they might not be aware of the impact of their actions, they remind me to be unapologetically sincere to who I am. Whether it's my family, or even Jove, or Grace, Theus or Destiny, Quinsy or René, or you." I felt my voice waver dangerously as Hope merely brushed her lips against mine, as if it were an action that had always been habitual between us. "What was that for?"

"I hope that you can see yourself for the person that you are."

"And who would that be?"

"What do you want for yourself?" She asked, nodding quietly. My thumb swiped Hope's cheek gently.

For myself.

I had only ever wanted one thing, mingled among all the other dreams that were unrecognisable to control over.

"I want to be happy."

Hope's eyes smiled, curling up as something like a broken laugh echoed in her chest. "Of course." She whispered, voice wavering, eyes bright, the golden tendril drawn in pristinely atop her eyelashes, from the edge of her eyes, shining brighter. "But, what would make you happy?"

Home. Art. Clarity. Authenticity.

Authenticity, that Ma explained was like - *'There are few things in this world more powerful than the devotion of an artist, Spes'*

I was happy. When I was with my family, when I was with my friends, when they were laughing. When I was with Hope, when she smiled genuinely that encased around rarity. When Hope could fall carelessly next to me and ask what I was doing or drag me to venture around the town to rediscover our muses, as if we couldn't be anyone else in the world but ourselves.

What would make me happy?

Hope closed the miniscule distance between us.

Her eyes closed, pressing but slow as I wound a hand around her waist as best she could, and she was...

Hope...

I smiled against Hope's mouth, small and private, but it somehow buried in my chest like a knife as I drew Hope closer, and it was different from the last time. It tasted different, it said something different-

It was Hope extending a branch for me to grab.

And I grabbed it...But this time, I grabbed it because I wanted it. Not because I thought it felt right or because it was instinctual to do so or be surprised to barely have time to react.

For once in my life, I didn't feel the need to be calculative over time.

And Hope encased me in her arms, like placing walls between them and the world, blocking out the cold and responsibilities so that all I could see was the thing I wanted.

Hope and I had been a different kind of support to each other.

But shivers unrelated to the cold ran down my spine as Hope stroked a hand down my side, maybe to warm me up, maybe just because she wanted to.

And the fire kindling in my chest was a lot like what it felt like the last time I felt it.

We parted, breathing each other's air as Hope opened her eyes and I...

I had never had much use for sunrises or sunsets.

Hope's eyes were bursting with things that I had never seen anywhere else. Emotions and shimmers and colours that fell onto Hope in the form of little droplets that made her face twitch with each that hit her cold skin.

Hope forced her head back up, eyes wide as I stared at her, expression twisting with something that made my heart tear.

"Why?" I breathed, everything startlingly still even as I felt like the ground was shaking beneath them. "Why are you-"

The words died in her throat as Hope dropped her head, resting against my shoulder as I felt tears soak through into my skin.

Hope's fingers twisting in my shirt as she shook.

"Hope..." My hand came automatically to her back, rubbing small circles there. "Why..."

"I promise, Spes." she said, voice thick around tears that kept forcing their way out, "I'm happy, I'm so... so magnetically happy."

Her hands shook, and Hope guided her head to lift up again, tears smeared across her cheek, but her eyes...

They were twisted, but it wasn't pain. Wasn't what I knew the tears of agony and fear looked like. Her eyes were brighter. Hidden by the cloud of tears, but it was there.

I kissed her again, tasting salt against my lips, and I felt Hope lean into me automatically, fingers strong where they gripped my shoulders. My hand ran along Hope's spine reciprocating the comforting gesture, the other still resting against the curve of her cheek, wiping away the wetness there as best I could.

I thought it would be more earth shattering when I next saw Hope cry.

But it just settled on my chest like a weight, a reminder. Something I could carry with me. Something I shouldn't forget.

It was languid, almost lazy, just tasting and existing and no clear goal in mind. I could hear my blood thrumming in the background slow, powerful pumps that raced through my veins like white-noise.

Hope pulled away, resting her face in the curve of my neck.

"You..." Her voice was thick and unwavering. "You have always meant so much to me, Spes." she breathed, lips brushing against the skin of my neck, making me shiver. "Ever since the beginning, you have been... I feel...-"

"Thank you." I whispered, pressing a gentle kiss to the line of her throat.

"What-" Hope looked at me in confusion before asking what I was thanking her for. But she already knew. Perhaps I had always known as well, but I never wanted to think it was enough. I had always wanted to give more, be more... even if Hope didn't need it.

"Time. Guarantee of time, would make me happy." I whispered, heart expanding like a balloon that threatened to pop. "Hope Vale, you *anchor* my time."

Hope hugged me. Tight and crushing, and I could only squeeze Hope's side in response, both of us with our faces buried in the other, wrapped around as best we could manage.

"Good." she croaked, sounding like she was almost near tears again. "I quite like the sound of looking forward to that."

***

CHAPTER - X

By the time, we had rushed out of our foreign-language examinations for our finals and rushed in towards Mrs. Khalili's board room, to let us leave the school early and head to the Huda Studios - so, that at least one of us could be there to sign the confirmation of getting our funds from the Huda sisters - it didn't even take a fraction of a second for her to impassively deny either of us the access to head out, having no regards for either of our pleading urges to protest that we didn't have any more tests or classes.

"It's done, we have lost it. The only investors who wanted to go through their bullshit, to invest in our final showcase... Gone." René sighed defeatedly, slamming the door behind her and slumping down the stairs outside the board-room. "Gone, because neither of us could show up to finalise the final straw, to sign and that damn fund. She knew...that's why she stopped us ...people give the crappiest excuses to skip classes...and she lets them off the hook."

"We have to break it to them... We don't have a choice." I said flatly, gingerly sitting down beside René and absently patting her back as I thought about my vapid selfishness of hiding the ugly truth that had rendered all our works, all the time spent working for the exhibition...- *Useless.*

"How are we supposed to tell them that all their efforts for their exhibition was in vain, that we should have told them to have chosen another team-" René snapped, slamming the side of her right fist right against the railing. Before I could glare at her in alarm to examine her hand for any signs of injury, her phone started ringing immediately "Hello-".

The shift in her tones were numerous, despite the repentance of one single word in reply.

"Are you okay?" I asked carefully, as soon as the call came to an end. "Is everything alright?" I prompted, as her lower stayed slack open, eyes staring ahead, absently. "René, what was that call about?"

"We got it." She quipped, simply, looking at me in disbelief.

"What?"

"We got the fundings." She clarified, slowly breaking into a huge grin.

"What?- How?-"

"Someone from our team was there to sign to confirm the fundings for our team." She smiled, holding her temple with her hands before drawing back her hand, wincing in pain, as I clapped her chin in a scolding way. "I am not even mad that you told Vale about this, because if it weren't for that gorgeous human-being, we would have lost this…"

"I never told her." I broke out in a smile with sheer joy.

"You didn't tell her-" She asked, before I warned her to not move her hand any further. "Then how-"

"She works for one of our investors." I realised, slowly with a smile.

"She was right, it's destiny...meeting the right people at the right time." René broke in, smirking triumphantly.

"We couldn't have asked for a better timing."

"We are off by a day, but we have enough fundings to design our set for the backdrop..." René said, stolidly "-and if we join in the sophomores from the architectural department assigned to our team, we can pull off the second design instead of settling with the first."

"So, you changed your mind about the Spinning Carousel, instead of the swan's wings?" I asked, with a knowing smile.

"After seeing the list of journalists, we are bound to be stuck with, I say we could use a bold statement." René scoffed, before bursting into laughter. "Quinsy is gonna lose her mind, if any of the lenses get damaged by accident."

"We could also incorporate the wings."

"Talk me through it."

"In the orchestra hall, we would no longer be sidelined to be denied a musical backdrop for the show-" I offered, contemplating Mey's offer that we perfectly went on to our showcase, now. "-and one of my friends had genuinely loved the concept and repeatedly offered to compose the musical backdrop, so..."

"So that means, we would be able to incorporate a sculpture, that would generally be moved onto the bowels of the hall, onto our set." René added, as a matter-of-factly. The orchestra hall was situated right in the centre of the campus, with the buildings of the Performing Arts Department surrounding the hall.

"Now, that we have the corner with the stairs, we could incorporate them onto our set,-" I stated firmly, as we walked into the infirmary. "-and finally use both the mimicry of transforming them into Piano keys acting as the stairs in Stairway to Heaven, to fit the common setting of the galaxy backdrop of the hall's glass ceiling."

"So, your friend from the musical Department is playing the Piano?" René asked with a small smile, waving a hand to quietly ask me to leave, as the nurse refused to let me in.

"Do you know where she is?" I asked, as René snickered and merely mouthed '*Courtyard*'.

I recognised her, from the familiar backpack thrown over her left shoulder, running over towards her as Hope merely turned her head to grin widely as I gently pulled her towards me, by pulling on the buckle of the bag to loosen the strap and throw the strap over us before hugging her, from the back.

"You knew." I murmured, finding it impossible to bit back the smile threatening to break free.

"No, I started to pick up on it, after noticing how the resources and supplies for our team were exclusively provided by Mrs. Bronywyn." Hope admitted, tightening her hold over my arms draping around her shoulders. "When one of the students from the other teams did the same…she stated about the rules about every team having an assigned fund and it's their responsibility to keep their expenditure in check and even if they run out of their resources…they won't be restocked by the teachers."

"You aren't going to ask… why I never told you about it?" I quipped in confusion.

"We had the least amount of resources compared to the other teams,-" She continued, quietly tapping my hands to loosen my hold, as she turned to wrap her arms around my waist. "-only you and René ever picked up the resources for the entire team, and never once did you go to pick them up from the storage room set up for the exhibition."

"I thought perhaps Isabel Huda, herself, might have discussed it with you, whenever she comes over to check up on her stores." I said, offering my own reasoning.

"Isabel didn't know that only you and René knew about the withdrawal of the funds from our team, when she told me about why you met her in the first place, to present my portfolio to her…before she offered to hire me to work for her." Hope explained, "So, she called me too, when neither you nor René could get out of your tests sooner, to confirm the papers for the funds of our team."

"You are *magnetically incredible*, you know that, right?" I smiled, cupping her cheeks

"So, I have been told… by a certain *Spes Zrey*." She nodded with a wide grin contentedly, spreading to the corners of her eyes.

"Perhaps it's like the very same reason, neither of us admitted to our intuitions that we knew over time, that it had to be the other, in the aquaria."

"Have you met yourself? No one talks the way you do." She teased, as I looked at her in disbelief, tickling her sides in protest, not paying any heed to half-hearted words of '*Stop, I was just teasing*' surrounding her laughter. "Trust me, that fanciness is uniquely *you.*"

"That was so uncalled for." I fought back, innocently before letting her go.

"I really meant it when I said you can rely on me without feeling the need to explain-" Hope promised, as her lips quietly turned upwards. "-and I will be there for you."

***

For the past four days, I finally managed to get through to Quinsy, trying my best not to corner her when she looked at the lenses being hung from the carousel, as if she were looking at them for the last time instead of her usual look of trying to protect them from any accidental damage.

"Spes, I think I may quit pursuing photography as a profession…" She admitted, sighing in relief, as I stared at her disbelief before rearranging my emotions immediately releasing how it might cause her more panic, especially when she was finally talking about it out loud, with me. "I know it sounds like I am being a quitter, but I am not, and I know it's pretty late to change my mind but I don't think it's the one for me…"

"Quinsy, it's never too late." I said, truthfully.

"It's not like I am not going to quit it completely. I like it. I am still going to pursue it as a hobby…" She continued in a single breath, before stopping in her tracks. "Wait, you are not mad?"

"Why would I be mad?" I asked with a quiet smile, eyeing her to move away from the waiting line in front of the cafeteria, so that we could speak clearly instead of whispering, and drawing unnecessary attention for whispering in a noisy crowd, as if we were discussing illegal mafia trade.

"But you hate people who give up their dream halfway?-" Quinsy murmured defeatedly "-And I am basically throwing one to follow one so late…"

"There is a difference between not trying hard enough and quitting when you know with certainty that something isn't right for you…" I shook my head, explaining calmly. "It takes courage to let go of that familiarity. You never threw your dream away, for years you have respected this interest to pursue it sincerely."

"I am scared."

"That's alright and it's human to be scared." I confirmed, firmly.

"What if I end up wasting up time chasing something that I might possibly not be good at, by throwing away something that I actually am good at?" She asked, voicing shaking by the slightest at the end.

"What if it doesn't work out? What if I lose interest in it?"

"The only aspect I believe that wastes time besides not giving your all is - *regret*. When you started out with photography, you couldn't have possibly imagined the magnitude of your skills over all these years." I stated, carefully, trying to be honest with my words, as much I possibly could. "You did it, steadily. So, give this an equal chance. The start is always scary."

"Do you think it would be unfair to fall back into photography, if this doesn't work out?"

"Absolutely not." I assured. "Knowing you I am undoubtedly sure that you would have given it your all before taking the decision to pursue photography as a profession once again. Consider it as your safety-net."

"What if my time away fails to guarantee me any offer to pursue my safety-net?" She sighed, taking deep breaths to even them out.

"I am not certain if it may hold any assurance, but I give you my word-" I offered, stolidly "-that you would have the same position with us, as an offer to pursue that very safety net."

"I still can't believe René actually drafted a proposal for the contract for you guys to start your brand together, already." Quinsy remarked with a laugh. I nodded in confirmation, thinking back to our first deal if either of us didn't get into Parsons New York then we would compromise, by René pursuing Parsons in Paris while I studied in Politecnico di Milano…and only if I got into Parsons New York, then René would head to SAIC.

"When you are certain, why wait?" I shrugged

"Here, I wanted to complete this exhibition before jump-starting onto pursuing law." Quinsy said half a smile, before dragging me onto our set in the orchestra hall, finally revealing her photographs that had recently been framed

The Lanterns lighting up during the Chinese New Year in Thean Hou temple, glowing radiantly like the molten metals right before they were moulded.

Or the photograph capturing the lotus leaves floating on the koi pond mimicking the shape of that of a painter's palette.

They were just magnificent as the shot encapsulating the fireworks sparkling atop the cables of Seri-Saujana Bridge, reminiscing the times of a perfect night for firefly hunting in the cities of Malaysia.

But the picture that had stolen the beauty of everyday-life in a single shot, was that of a hand swirling a pair of chopsticks in a laksa bowl, as the reflection of a grand clock reflected upon the soup... with the hands of the clock aligning in sync with that of the chopsticks.

"When did you-" I stuttered in disbelief. "How did you-"

"I had to give it my all. After all, I couldn't let the efforts of your travels with Hope, to rediscover the symbolism in the absorption of muses around us, go in vain." She said, easily. "Plus, Theus' words got to me, while I went through these travel notes of yours, to capture these shots."

"Indeed." I nodded, mouthing *'Thank You'*, as she waved her hand, before raising her fist for a fist bump.

"I think we actually do have a perfect shot of winning this, once again." She declared, before rechecking if we could have our lunch later after working on finishing the set, for today. "Even if it's not our era-"

"Then we will make it our's." I nodded, tilting my head.

***

The hall wasn't frightening, but the sight of it created a huge mess inside of my head. It was captivating how the lights surrounding us, was like a fantasy world under a shimmering array of pigmented cocktails painting the night sky.

Flashes of cameras and microphones were being adjusted every minute, as the crowd took their seats, while the teams took turns travelling under the bowels of the building, before going upstage for the showcase of their exhibition.

The marble sculpture was redesigned with the adornment of a Ballerina's outfit over it, with glowing translucent wings attached, forming to replace the black wings piercing through the backbone of the sculpture.

One golden ballet-shoe to represent the credentials awarded for the best performance, while the other battered foot to represent ongoing journey.

The perfect grand piano being played by Mey, in an oyster ruffle dress with a high neck and scalloped back in washed dip-dyed honeysuckle flower chromed print.

With the stairs painted as fallen translucent keys to mimic the stairs in stairway to heaven to fit the backdrop of the Orchestra hall's ceiling revealing the endless promise of the galaxy.

The sculpture was mounted atop the larger-than-life spinning carousel and the ballet shoe strings wrapped around the hands of the clocks to stop time, or wrapped around camera lenses to block the media defining the artist's last best performance.

When it was finally our turn...

There was one giant aspect of the set that I hadn't anticipated...I hadn't seen...

It is always easy to get swayed by the void that swallowed me from appreciating anything except chase the beauty of the final legacy of the bigger picture. The hypocrisy didn't have to stumble far from finding its home in me.

I had ended up valuing the very stage of outcome, that I hated being determined by.

All along, it wasn't their pedestal of the idolising the '*swan song*' of a person's limitless creativity that held me back, it was my own ambitious obsession of cherishing the final outcome above everything else that had blind-sided the joy of breathing in my dreams.

Instead of my twelfth painting, I found myself looking at all the framed unfinished portraits of mine, hung over the spinning carousel, that I never wanted to face the light of the day, I recognised the feeling of being freely happy for the very first time.

"This is our era. This is merely the beginning of our story. They can determine the '*swan songs*' of our works as much as they would want to, but I don't want you to constantly chase the final storyboard." Hope explained, before I could utter a word, to express my disbelief, and shook me out of my thoughts. "The portraits are inimitably beautiful, every single one of them." Hope said quietly, intertwining our fingers together, and giving my hand a reassuring squeeze as she explained about making the last change, by getting the portraits from Pax. "Just live in this moment with me. We are going to redefine the '*swan songs of our era*' by making it our beginning." I couldn't help the smile that broke across, as I nodded in reassurance for now, unable to form any coherent words to describe just how thankful I was for the last-minute change, that I would have been too scared for them to ever face the light of day.

***

We split into two teams, to handle the interviewers as they made the final decision to decide which team had the best showcase. Recognising the interviewer, who had interviewed me for '*Savoire Faire*', and the disappointment in her face was so palpable that I couldn't but smirk at Destiny to pull the oldest trick in our books, as soon as we discovered she would be stuck interviewing us for *Round-2*.

It was better than ever saying - '*Why do you assume that my arrogance is a method of acting out due to the separation? Are you going to sympathise with my actions with the necessity of a hurtful origin story? Huh? Well then as far as origin stories go, I had been beaming with arrogance ever since the bane of my existence in this damned world!*', the moment she asked, impassively - "Did your passion in art begin after the separation? Did it begin as a method of acting, to cope up with your arrogance? It's almost poetic how your team has driven tragic origin stories into inspiration for art."

"Life is all about morphing our dreams into our reality. We are creating *our everything* out of nothing." I shrugged, knowing that it wasn't worth correcting and explaining the concept to her. "So, it's guaranteed that sometimes it's going to slip away, sometimes it's easier remaining in our heads as fragments of our imagination, it's going to be hard."

"It was never meant to be easy, but the promise of what adulthood beholds for us is merely a suffocating prison cell." Destiny stated with a chagrined look towards the Interviewer, as the latter questioned her about her uptake on the outfits she was modelling for our exhibition.

"What?" The raven-haired woman asked in confusion, as we danced around her questions. Not sparing her any straight answers that she could use for her interview. "Well, why are you charting onto an uncharted art scene? Is it a new marketing concept to elevate your roots into the art scene?"

"Well, it wouldn't be too far-fetched to claim that the orthodox society often determines the predictability of our dreams,-" I remarked, trying my best not to roll my eyes, directly at her. "-it barely has any chances of survival in our future, kinda acting like Cell-guards guarding that Prison."

"Spes, don't use *fancy* words to call out adults undermining our dreams, just 'cause our dreams involve the creative route." Destiny tried to hide her smirk, before gritting her teeth. "I really can't stand people sugarcoating the taunt of how they think my future is doomed, just 'cause it doesn't involve a cubicle space with a fixed life-schedule just dragging on without a purpose."

"This is how marketing works. You can never build your image if you stay this stubborn." She scoffed, looking at us pitifully. "This is a relatively unknown field, people don't care, you are relatively no different from the guy hired to put up the wallpapers in my apartment."

"It's mostly adults who associate security and stability by following everyone's plan, the society's standards of status and worth." I forced a smile, trying my best to not snap at her.

"Does that worth even have a value when it's not their worth?" The interviewer asked, laughing in mockery, quirking an eyebrow. "How can one possess worth when they have no individuality?"

"People forget that sense and stability can only exist when we are certain of desiring to authentically chase our passion." Destiny clarified, pursing her lips and narrowing her eyes.

"Your talent won't get you anywhere, even if you keep hunting by switching your interests in Art or Design." She snapped, after switching her microphone off and aggressively brushing back the strands of hair falling on her face. "That strong arrogant complex you are putting up is going to get you nowhere, and just crash the entire fashion empire if you stay involved in it and ruin their status."

"So, people find it absurd when we have no desire in their so-called plan of the '*standard status*' and take every blow possible to destroy that difference, but you know what?" Destiny asked in a quiet snarl, before breaking into a smug grin. "I am damn proud to be that difference."

" 'Cause that difference is us living our lives, fulfilling the standards of our lives at our own pace,-" I continued, returning the triumphant smile as the interviewer groaned in disdain. "-to define our status through the stories of our individuality."

"*Individuality*? You get to say that because you choose to continue to be selfish-" The slender-built interviewer spat as she started going against her own words. "-And that selfishness will stop you from growing up to be an adult, no matter how many fancy concepts you base your works on."

"Knowing what *I want* and seeking that through *my time* is my happiness." Destiny declared, glaring back straight at the interviewer, before turning towards me to get back at her by refusing to acknowledge her, directly. "So, I don't want to hear the notion to '*grow up and be an adult*', 'cause they think it's foolish to believe in my dreams."

"I don't wanna live a life without the thrill of passion-" I grit through my teeth, merely staring back at Destiny, playing along. "-and give up on my dreams due to the struggles that will always loom across my entire journey."

"The promise of adulthood for this *youth* is *doomed*." She burst out laughing, as if her mind finally snapped, any sign of sanity locked in her orthodox pea-sized brain, finally wafting away. "They want to coddle themselves forever in this *phase. Pathetic.*"

"Spes, if this is what adulthood promises, then I don't want to let go of youth where I find it foolish to believe in myself and lose my sense of purpose in life." Destiny quipped, grinding her teeth and rolling her eyes as the interviewer stomped her feet like a toddler, agitated. "I don't want to grow up."

"Youth is the fire that drives the passion and that will extinguish the flames of doubts to ignite the catalyst making our dreams exist in our reality." I said, pressing my tongue against the inside of my cheeks, watching the interviewer visibly clinch her jaws, tighter, every passing second. "Our youth isn't just a period of time, or any definitive age. Youth is not just a *phase*. Youth is an *era*."

***

Looking back, I can't remember why the cheerings echoing through the hall after we won the first exhibition, felt more real than the utter magnitude of the chaotic noise ramming through my head, as I

checked the final updates of my application to
Parsons, in the empty arena.

Empty, except the person that quietly placed a
bouquet of red salvia and bluebells. Instead of the
habitual drawings of the flowers, I had gotten used to,
it was a bouquet.

"I got in." I said, simply. "Hope, I got in." I repeated,
as I felt Hope's lips press against mine, as if we both
existed in a bubble that never worried about
something as trivial as the weather.

"That position had always been yours..." Hope
breathed, chest rising and falling against mine.
"Undoubtedly yours..."

"I still can't believe it..."

"Believe it." Hope assured firmly "You have worked
for this ambitiously, for years."

"Yeah, I don't know why it still feels so unreal..."

"I kinda feel guilty that you are not finding this out
with your family." She prompted, quietly before
standing up and outstretching her hand, waiting for
me, to hold her hand. "But this has to be one of the
happiest moments of my life. I am so happy for
you...I have never seen you be so earnestly happy."

"I enjoyed your flowers." I said casually as we walked,
after I stood up grabbing on to her hand, gently.

I could practically feel the way Hope brightened. "Did
you?"

I nodded. "I almost cried."

"Ha! I knew you would, you big baby," she said, pressing her face into my arm teasingly.

"*You* gave me flowers that basically said you would be mine forever." I teased, chuckling

"Yeah! That's a roundabout way of saying it!" She gasped, hitting my shoulder when I made no attempts to stop my laughter. "I also gave you bluebells along with the red salvia." Hope immediately raced on. "You just say it, and it's cheesy and plants a lot of delusions-"

"No, they are bold and elegant...always have been."

"Have you never had the urge to change that?"

"No..." I said, sternly "Would you?"

"Never." She promised, genuine and warm and... earnest. "And *later*, would it change *later*?"

"Nothing changes." I clarified wondering why there might be a question about it, glancing around before settling back on Hope. "Why would anything change?"

"It's just that I am scared of what you might say regarding the '*later*' I propose, because I know you, too." She rasped, quietly.

"Why?" I hesitated, my heart practically shrivelling in my chest.

"Would you ask me to go to New York with you, and find work there?"

"What?"

"For that '*later*' to exist, I am not bonkers to even consider asking you to throw your dreams, to ask you to abandon what makes '*you*' and stay here." She wet her lips, nervously, voice shaking slightly. "So would you ask me to go to New York?"

"NO, I wouldn't-" I swore, desperately, stopping in my tracks.

"Even if I considered risking it?"

"Hope, where is this coming from?" I asked, blinking in concern.

"Answer me."

"No, I can't. I never would. Because what makes you - '*you*' - are your dreams, too." I rushed out, fingers curling tightly around hers. "I would never dare to even consider the possibility of uprooting everything and starting in the doubts and risks in a larger chaos, when you already have your beginning, right here." I whispered, expression pinching. "You already have two professional regular clients here and from the 21st of next month, you are officially beginning your work as the leading make-up artist for your first Cosmopolitan photoshoot-"

"Then I don't think that that '*later*' will exist for us, now."

"What? You are throwing this away because I don't want you to throw away the start of the dream, that you have always struggled to get to-" I said without stopping, fearing that I might hesitate if I let myself stop.

"No, it's not that. In fact, one of the reasons we understand each other is because we know how much our dreams matter to us and how we would never compromise on them." Hope's hand trembled like a leaf, looking torn between warmth and sadness. "I don't think I can ever leave here until Asia's beauty standards start adapting the notion of abandoning whitening products."

"Then what is it? Do you not trust me?-" I broke in, swallowing.

"I would be blind not to." Hope muttered, looking practically near tears, as the corners of her eyes reddened.

"Then why are we throwing this away, now?" I finally managed, softly curling my fingers around the back of her neck, to press her forehead against mine, staring into galaxies that shimmer with tears but exploded with sunlight

"It's not you, whom I don't trust, because you are the type of person to believe in me even when I get lost and spontaneously decide to foolishly uproot everything I have dreamed and start from the rags of nothing in New York." Hope assured, sharply... blinking away her tears as her lower lip started trembling. "You are the type of person to go out of your way to even find time to make it '*your*' responsibility to not stop until you help me find the same *start* there." Hope slowly buried her face in my shoulder, embracing me tightly, crying into my shirt, as her arms shook. "Although I won't ever dare to do that to you ever again. I know it as a fact, it's just the type of person you are..."

"Then why-"

"I don't trust the strains of reality and time, to not affect me." She admitted, voice hoarse. "I also know you well enough, to not bear putting you through the hurt you will bite down, when someone doesn't keep their words to you." She urged, eyes closing tight as more tears streaked down her cheeks, smudging the ends of her eyes. "How can I give you my word, when I am not certain of it, myself?"

"I don't know what to say." I couldn't do anything besides, rub her back in absent circles, and practically feel her heartbeat against mine.

Hope had always been someone completely different. Friend or more - Hope stood in her own circle, none of her Venn diagram touching a single other person's.

"I don't think I ever dreamed of a moment where I would ever hear you say that...I am really sorry-"

"Why are you apologising?"

"I am really sorry... I don't know why it's so unbearable to hear you say that." She expressed that defeatedly, with a broken expression. "You are always so sure and prepared when it comes to your words. I am really sorry for not being certain of conquering through that *later.*"

"Then I am glad that you told me so." I assured, speaking to Hope with a voice that was reserved for her, trying to understand Hope in every way I possibly could- "I understand...even if I take some time to adjust my own feelings over the acceptance of this."

"I am really sorry...This is not how I ever imagined our *'later'* to head out to be, for the upcoming years, . because it's *'us'*, it has always fit..." She murmured weakly, clutching my shoulders in vice grip, as I tried to pull away to look directly at her. "Don't go! Please don't go…Don't leave me now, please stay, just for this moment."

"Hey, I am not going anywhere, I am just going to get water, in case you feel dizzy later. I am not going anywhere." I promised, cupping her cheeks, before she carefully wiped the corners of my eyes, with the edges of her knuckles. I hadn't even realised, when my tears had started cascading down my cheeks of the fact that I was crying, too. "I will stay in this moment, as long as you want me to. I am here."

"Spes…"

"Hmmm?"

"Please don't ask me to move past this and pretend as if this moment never existed, as if our feelings weren't real." She asked, with more fear in her eyes than I have seen, as if I would have ever considered to propose to forget everything. "I don't think I can handle that especially for not having the courage to put up with the strains of the reality through the mediums of distance-"

"I won't."

"Spes, what happens to us, from now?" Hope winced, shoulders slumping further in defeat, visibly paling.

I don't know, even if I know the inevitable answer to it, I didn't wish to consider it. But I knew, she was right. Respecting time, before I started contemplating to do the same.

I knew that both of us would be needing all the time we have, to ensure that our dreams start becoming a reality against all the hurdles that were going to pose a stronger obstacle.

It was merely the beginning...and we were bound to not have any time to spare, to find the balance between work and life.

"Let's just live in this moment and in the certainty of this moment." I offered quietly, a bit closer than before, even if it wasn't physically possible to get any closer. "Is that alright?"

"No, it's not...none of this is supposed to be, we aren't supposed to settle with this, but stay." She practically choked out, clenching her fists, eyes soft and devastated, that did nothing to stop the inimitable pain slowly piercing through my heart. "Don't leave me... Just stay...until New York, just exist beside me."

"I am not going anywhere. I am here." I repeated, tongue feeling heavy, as Hope's hand tightened on mine, warm and firm and comforting. "Existing here, until you want me to."

That light was still in her eyes.

That Light shone through a thousand times brighter than ever before, stealing my breath faster than any kiss ever had, my eyes widening- still so shocked at the way Hope could look at me-

Even after everything.

"I don't even want to think about the timeline of that." Hope swallowed a breath that came dangerously close to a sob, wiping her eyes roughly. "Of all the people, who were robbed by time, I never expected us to succumb to the excuse of being overrun by it."

Hope's eyes swam as she stared at me taking several shaking breaths, both of us so much closer.

The curvature of the crescent moon looked like, it was starving to bite down the temperature.

To make it drop its degree even further, every passing second... with the luminescence of the stars dimming like the petals of a flower, nearly stilling its movement in the absence of a strong breeze.

"I am here. No interruptions of any timelines disturbing the promises of that." I held my breath, resolutely, before moving my hand down to her jaw as I kissed her stolidly, afraid to hold her any tighter. I felt her arms wrap around my neck, holding on a bit tighter, like she was scared that I would slip away-"I am here."

That's when I realised what those Bluebells meant today; a promise of *constancy*.

"If either of us, find the balance of time, after we establish the groundwork of our dreams. Time, where we can equally contribute to us like now, and work." Hope whispered quietly, hand caressing my cheek. Her eyes flickered over mine, searching for my answer and smiling through her tears, hopefully. "Would you promise to tell me, if things still haven't changed for you?"

It was almost intoxicating, how easy it was to love Hope.

"I promise." I assured earnestly. "We have time."

***

Five Years Later

"Speaking of articles, that you have asked our Media-team to bury." René announced, through the bowels of the building, as we monitored the last collection of the set, for our show, tonight. *"Designer Spes Zrey sells paintings at auction for $11,000... All proceeds going to the designer's charity of choice, dedicated to scholarships for children in low-income families in various countries..."* She remarked, volumising her hair, one last time as the show neared to an end. "Why do you want this to be buried?"

"I don't mind it acting as good press, for us or the *charity of my choice,* that's what the auctions are for." I said absently, barely tearing my eyes from the monitor, checking if the outfits being walked down the runaway, were still maintaining the right order. "But when it's the kind of press that barges on their lives and disturbs them, then I would like to get back at that kind of *Press.*"

"Done, I don't want those kinds affecting our brand, by the slightest." She prompted, leaning against one of the numerous clothing racks, piled around. "I thought you were going to take vacation, before this show, so what was the auction for?...Not that I am complaining."

"I decided to postpone my break, I just didn't find a purpose to take a break, for now."

"For the last time, you don't need a purpose to take a break." She sighed, exasperatedly, flicking my forehead. "The purpose of taking a break is pretty-much self-explanatory, you *luxurious hermit*!"

"I am not a *luxurious hermit*!"

"When was the last time, you took a break, even when we had plenty of time to start embracing the work-life balance?" She asked knowingly, quirking an eyebrow, as we walked up towards the backstage. Before carefully eyeing me to choose between the untouched glass placed beside the 8-ounces bottles of water, silently asking if my progress after finding the *right fit*, had been coming along well for the past few months.

"I went to Hamburg to attend Pax's concert-" I recalled, before picking up one of the water bottles and watching René smile quietly from the corner of my eyes. "That's a purpose for the right break, and it's not on me that my family comes over to visit me or else I could use a break to visit them instead."

"How about you stop sending them tickets to travel? And get a ticket to travel back home, *yourself*, instead?" She asked, as I threw her an unamused glare.

"Hey! My parents have always wanted to travel around the world."

"So, travelling around the world is a good purpose for a break"

"I do-"

"Not for work." She clarified, before retouching her perfume. "Fine, but because I am a good friend stuck with you, I am going to give a purpose even if I am not sure if it's going to be worrisome." She quipped gingerly, before handing over an invitation to the launch of '*Ancorare* Cosmetics'

"Why would you be worried about it?"

"Because you never spoke a word about her, even during the times I mentioned her name in College?" She asked in confusion.

"I don't like to speak about people who are important to me, as mere stories with random people." I smiled stolidly, tracing my hands over the name of the owner, *Hope Vale*

"But you never said anything, when I spoke about her or when I gave her updates about you, during my rare calls with her…to keep in touch." René stated, voice still in residual shock. "So, I assumed you two were trying hard to pretend that the other didn't exist."

"The last time, I had a conversation with Hope." I recalled, fondly. "The last time we spent alone, before we left for New York…Hope gave me a painting of red azaleas."

"Those red flowers on your lock screen." René laughed earnestly. "Those are azaleas?"

"They are." I nodded, quietly

"What do they mean?" She asked with a warm smile, before rolling her eyes at my silence. "Come on, it's you two…you pretty much used the language of flower symbolism as a secret language, so what do they mean?"

"Take care of yourself for me."

"Then…Were the white flowers that she gave you in the airport…like an amicable break-up goodbye?" She asked, expression pinching further in confusion, trying to connect the dots.

"White Clovers." I explained, chuckling "They mean that the person giving the flowers is always going to be thinking of you."

"All those years in Parsons, you never spoke about her, not because you were hurt by a break-up, but because it was so much more..." She chuckled, with a noise of realisation.

"Yeah, that was the furthest from that truth." I confirmed, tilting my head. "I never spoke about it, because she was... *she is* extremely precious to me, and I treasure her."

"Kinda explains that silent smile, you always had whenever I mentioned her." She grinned widely, after making fake gagging noises to tease me. "Why didn't you say anything?"

"You never asked." I snickered at her antics, as she winked cheekily.

"You are very sly, Zrey. I will give you that."

"We didn't wish to test the turmoil of time, and pursue things half-hearted especially when we knew we would need all the time in our hands to lay the groundwork of our dreams-" I continued, before explaining further. "-Which has just started taking its shape...in the past few months, for the both of us."

Had we not received the Council of Fashion Designers Of America's Perry Ellis award for New Fashion Talent, then we would have to wait for a few years more to pursue our own independent design plan. In fact, if it hadn't been for the Scholarship

Program offered by the same, I would be still paying up my debt for my tuition and educational expenses.

"I would have given this to you sooner if I had known this. I thought I was protecting your feelings, by not giving this to you." She smiled regretfully

"But we had promised that if either of us knew, and felt the certainty of the balance of time for the other, then we wouldn't hesitate to guarantee that." I waved my hand, before assuring her sternly that she had nothing to worry about.

"This came for you, two months before I got one too…but you also got flowers that kinda dried up in my apartment…" She prompted, pointing towards the card.

"Your dog ate them up, didn't he?"

"Not actively! But I remember the flowers she sent." She protested, as I burst out laughing, throwing her hands in the air. "They were Violets. But rather than a vibrant blue, they were white. They mean anything to you?"

"White violets…*Let's take a chance on happiness.*" I recognised, making no attempts to hide my grin. "Looks like I have plans, after the runaway show."

"Spes? What happens if those red azaleas no longer hold a meaning or hold a meaning towards someone else?" René asked sheepishly, before correcting herself as my brows drew down. "And that's a big *if*, cause from the looks of your stupid sappy grin and the big gesturing flowers…that '*if*' seems quite impossible to exist."

"Fares, I don't care if either of those *'what ifs'* are true…-" I confessed, truthfully "-I don't think I would care about anything but being happy to see her after five long years, the *'what ifs'* don't matter."

"I really admire that certainty, even after five long years…that's rare."

"Someone wise once told me - *'Being in love with your life entails you to cherish the emotional capacity to be in love with another person, but you just gotta respect the time'*…" I declared, as René shook her head in laughter, muttering - *'Only Brumoy can say such random poetic words that make sense.'*

"Sounds like someone who designed the set of this show's backdrop would say-" René teased before scoffing her face in disgust towards the mere referral of Panda Express. "-and happens to always order Panda Express when he comes to visit us."

Theus had redesigned the biggest dockside warehouse in Bali, onto to a vast concert hall atop it, staging the city's new Opera house - *'Harmoni-Seni'*

"It's wise advice-" I laughed, clutching my sides and throwing my head back. "-almost like a wise *Guru.*"

"A Guru who eats Panda Express! Unacceptable, Brumoy!" She exclaimed in disdain, before one of the stylists reminded us, to finish the show before meeting up with the Press. "So, you are going…"

"I am."

"Guess, it's unfair that I missed the chance to threaten you,-" She murmured with a quiet smile, before mouthing *'remember to not get blinded by the flashes'*, before walking down the runaway. "-had you protested against going for the launch."

Yet, it wasn't the flashes of the array of the cameras, that blinded me, but the familiar unwavering, radiant smile and sharp timber-chromed orbs, standing at the foot of the runaway, that blinded my sight. The same Aquarius pin attached to the lapels of the Cerulean-blue twill trench coat with an open neckline, as she gently waved the bouquet of Honeysuckles and Bluebells, at me before tapping at the note attached to it that read - *'If you are still anchoring on to our promise as I am, do you have time for me?'*

"For a person who doesn't believe in coincidences created by movie magic, your script just writes its own flow." René smirked, pushing her tongue against the inside of her cheeks and waving a small hand at Hope. I had to physically summon all my will to not roll my eyes at René, before looking back at the person who was elegantly holding flowers that meant - *'Unchanging bonds of love'*, and mouthing…

"I have time."

~Fin~

BONUS READ - I (Hope's POV)

"Why does she owe you or do you possibly like her?…" Pax asked with a stoic expression, slightly tilting her head, before her face broke into a smug smile, the longer Hope delayed to confirm the latter. "You like her!"

Hope choked at the statement, scratching the back of her neck, sheepishly, not expecting the younger to bite the bullet from the start, almost as if she could sense Hope's admiration.

Spes didn't recognise her name, at all and any sane person might have concluded that the former was just a smooth talker who had a way with words.

But Hope Vale could never come anywhere close to that conclusion even if she ended up losing her *sanity*.

"Your sister is not seeing someone else, right?" She asked, chewing the insides of her cheeks as the younger looked at her as if Hope had willingly traded away her brain, to even consider this question.

Even if Hope had recognised Spes by the way she spoke, the same hardened unmistakable words that always held back their complete weightage, she could clearly recognise the face of her younger sister, who stayed outside the older's ward longer than anyone else in their family.

Spes' actions matched her speech pattern- poetic, careful, calculated, and completely unique to her.

"As if, the times she gets her head out of her canvases she probably glares at anything that meets her sight…" The younger scoffed, dismissing with a wave of her head. The nerves and apprehension melted from Hope's face slightly, after the confirmation.

"She is in love with her passion for art, I don't think there is anything more authentic than that." Hope defended, swallowing thickly when the pianist quirked her eyebrow in confusion. "And it's not blinding to see the way, she looks at her people like they are her world." Pax smirked in amusement, noticing the hint of envy in the former's words.

Unlike the Fine-arts department, the music department accepted students nearly two years earlier compared to the other and the younger was of the finest pianists of their school so neither of the two sisters could keep the low profile that they desperately sought. It was practically impossible, when bitter envy followed the sisters as they seamlessly excelled in their respective departments, without a care for their monthly ranks.

Monthly ranks that expelled the students who ranked at the bottom, for at most seven consecutive months.

"You are pretty as a muse." Pax interrupted abruptly, barely noticing Hope's cheeks heating up at the unexpected compliment. "And unlike my sister, you have really good bedside manners-"

"That's not true! Your sister does too!" Hope chuckled, brokenly. "Even when she is working, she doesn't hesitate to give her best materials when you ask her for spares."

Hope knew that very well.

It was an embarrassing remainder of her pathetic attempts to start a conversation with the other. But Spes barely even acknowledged her, not shifting her glance from the canvas leaning on her easel while handing her anything that she had asked for.

She didn't remember…

It was like reality was bitterly mocking her as soon as Hope rejoiced that they had gotten acceptance to the same school, by giving her another opportunity to be closer to her yet farther than before.

"If you have spoken to her in class, why do you need my help?" Pax demanded, blankly

"I mean yes, I have tried speaking but your sister isn't much of a talker." Hope admitted, shifting and gently nudging her to side-step to a quiet corner so that they don't get pushed around during the rush hour in the Cafeteria.

> The sisters faced relentless jabs on a frequent routine because of their family's status. By the third remark of mockery from another parade of jerks, regarding her parents' divorce, Hope hadn't expected Spes to ask the jerk about what brand of pencil he used. Nobody did.
>
> Even if the rat-head was taken aback by the piercing gaze that kept glaring at his arm resting on her desk as if it were a slob of arm that was yet to be butchered, he scoffed before answering, and handing over his pencil to taunt her, further.
>
> "I use the same brand."

There wasn't a single soul who wouldn't have been shaken to the core, when Spes snatched the pencil from his grasp and slammed it right between the space of his fingers and his thumb. As the graphite shattered against the desk, her expression never wavered in the slightest as the jerk shook like a rotten leaf when she handed over a new pencil from her bag. "Rant about a story that isn't yours to tell, you may never know what might get punctured, *permanently*."

Hope barely had time to realise that she was smiling unconsciously at Spes who was formidable in a way that was different, before realising that the piercing gaze wasn't cold neither did they hold anger.

As her heart sank further, as she realised Spes's emotionless expression merely held a void.

The piercing gaze easily gave away the impression that they were either plotting one's murder or staring into one's soul, were merely in a daze, instead. They didn't care.

"If you want me to talk about you and act as your wingwoman, you are barking up the wrong tree. She would just zone out." Pax whined, before rolling her eyes and hitting her own head with the roll of music sheets as if the mere idea of it was draining.

"No, no, I don't want you to do any of that. We were actually next-room neighbours, during the time-"

"You are the chic from the hospital!" Pax laughed, face brightening as her eyes widened in recognition. "No wonder, you looked familiar."

"We had promised each other that we would meet when we got out, and I was hoping that you could tell me when your sister might be free after school so that-"

"No." Hope couldn't tell why the younger snapped, jaws clenched as the colours drained from her face.

There was no glint of amusement in her eyes but rather something along the lines of guilt and anger.

"I just wanted to apologise, you have no idea how much she meant to me during my worst times there." Hope explained, trying to reason with her watching the younger's breath get even more uneven. "I couldn't show up because my Nonna took me back me home by force, when I made my choice-"

Hope had to walk out of there from the moment Nonna figured about Spes within a single visit, seen through her growing feelings as if they were covered by a transparent glass.

Hope constantly felt like a field mouse desperately trying to hide from a hawk that had already long since caught sight of it, under her fury... Warning her to get out of her *phase* before she disappointed her, any longer.

The person who had always seen through Hope was seethingly revolted by her existence... Spes had been through enough, she didn't need Hope's grandmother demeaning her especially when there wasn't a sliver of possibility that she could possibly like Hope.

It was easier denying the reality of a home that no longer felt like a home. *Home* that chided her to not be ungrateful and make the effort to be worthy of her family.

Something much worse than fear.

Inevitability. Acceptance. Realisation.

"I don't care if you want to ask Spes out on a date." Pax clarified with an exasperated sigh, debating if she should even be talking about this with a stranger, much less a stranger who already knew way too much to create wildfire involving her sister. "But you can't talk about this unless she figures out her memories with you, on her own. After you left, things got worse for her before they got better and she clearly remembers the trial, chances are she might have forced herself to forget you, when you did not keep your word."

"What do you mean?" She pressed carefully, getting even more confused with the new information.

"She has a habit of being very inflexible with them, everything is like a verbal agreement to her." The younger huffed, defeatedly, speaking more to herself than Hope at this point. "She waited for you, on the day the custody settlement was finalised and she locked us out to speak to our grandparents when they gave her some papers, because she was the oldest."

Once, Hope's Nonna told her a story about a bird that was locked up in a cage for years, watching the sky from behind the bars. It longed for freedom so much that was the only thing the bird ever dreamed of. When the birds managed to run away someday, finally to the arms of the sky, it couldn't fly. It fell and fell, until broken wings hit onto a puddle and laid dead on the surface. When Hope asked her why the bird couldn't fly, her Nonna told her that '*If you kept something locked away for too long, you forgot them.*' The bird's dreams were all about freedom but it forgot how to fly. How freedom felt. Wings couldn't carry the bird, only dropping it somewhere so faraway from the sky. Almost reaching the stars yet falling before touching them.

Hope felt the same way. Her wings were broken, feathers plucked, it was bleeding from where they sheared off.

The violets, lavenders, sunflowers that bloomed in their balcony were thrown away to prove a point. She would make a bouquet of them for her Nonna and give it to her whenever she felt down. Her favourite were the daffodils but she used to accept everything with the same joy when her dear grandchild tried to make her happy. The beautiful smile on her face was alight, giving life to each flower so they would never fade. It would give Hope a reason to live as well, sometimes she would curl up in the corner of her smile and sleep there. Safe and cozy, feeling of being loved embracing her whole body.

Now the flowers didn't smell, they didn't look pretty, they were wilted with the absence of the brightest sun, the essence of life. She had broken their cage and separated their bond and it was what drove Hope crazy.

"What happened?" Hope asked, swallowing the thorn in her throat.

Why did she care?

What could she possibly do, even if she knew?

Why was she looking for yet another human being to disappoint? Hope barely knew her, yet the other treated her with unbiased kindness without any ounce of pity or disgust. But that trivial gesture was a comfort that a rare few offered to spare.

"I don't know, that idiot never told me and neither did my parents. Whatever she said to them, they pretty much haven't spoken to us since then." Pax threw her hands in the air, the anger and frustration clearly evident in her snarl and clenched fists. "All I know is, after she collapsed we found out that she doesn't remember that day so chances are she won't remember waiting for you. So, you don't owe any explanations."

"Is she alright?" Her voice shook. It was weak. Barely a whisper. "Just tell me that she is alright."

"This has happened before, so we don't speak about it unless she remembers it on her own." Pax said, voice helplessly weak.

"What does this mean?"

"Look, my sister has a habit of manipulating her mind into forgetting the worst moments of her life, to find some bizzare peace with isolating herself into her art." The word came out as a breathy hiss that made Pax cough, an ugly hacking sound that made her chest burn, her eyes were tight with something darker. She blinked, slow and painful. "She finds solace in knowing she is not losing out on time, by manipulating herself into remembering only fragments of those memories to move on... I really don't know how much she remembers of it and I can't have you talking to her about things, she might have forced herself to forget."

It wasn't quite guilt, but it hurt, whatever it was burrowing in the younger's chest. Maybe it was responsibility.

They were hurting.

Hope never felt this helpless, knowing that nothing she said would make things better when it might be the first time Pax was talking about it with anyone.

And perhaps, all the younger wanted to do was to get a chance to talk about it instead being ignorantly told to do something about it.

So, Hope quietly chose to change the subject.

"What if she does remember me?" She trailed off, voice dying and expression flickering, like someone trying to think of two things at once.

"If she does, then talk to her about it only around the fragments she does tell you about, from her own accord." Pax warned in dull panic, and the older waved a hand frantically to assure that she wouldn't dare to be careless about it.

"And if she doesn't?"

"You seem like a nice person. So, I am only going to say this once. Don't wait around, you don't deserve that." Pax snapped, anger replacing the fear. Whether it was genuine, or just a way to try and hide the tremor of her words, Hope didn't know. "She might be a pompous brooding jerk but she is deadly loyal to people she cares about, and ignores the existence of people she doesn't know. You are going to hurt if she doesn't remember you and your efforts might go in vain." Her jaw tightened, looking stricken. "So, stay away from her unless she speaks to you first. For your sake."

"Can I ask you something?"

"You are a very curious person." Pax bemused simply, eyes sparking a bit with amusement.

There was a silence that even Hope could feel the weight of pressing against her lungs, a longing question hanging without a single word.

"What's your sister's type?" Hope broke in firmly, though her own voice echoed oddly in her head, surprising herself with her bluntness. "Why don't you have an issue with me liking her?"

Hope averted her eyes, almost like bracing herself, fists clenched at her side as she swallowed thickly, jaw clenched as if waiting for a blow.

But nothing could prepare her to expect the younger to howl in laughter.

Hope felt a mixture of warmth and nervousness settle in her stomach, a little unsure of what to do.

"Spes doesn't have a type, and if this is your way of asking about her sexual orientation. Then I can't give you a concrete answer, but I can guarantee that she certainly won't have any issues with you liking her." The younger assured, shrugging her shoulders with a warm smile as if she could sense Hope's insecurity. "As far as I know, she hasn't expressed any interest towards anyone, because of their physical appearance." Her lips curling slightly, her expression quiet, voice matching Hope's instinct. "To her, there are just *ratios and parameters* that she needs to use to model her designs on. Unless she starts viewing them as a human or else-"

Hope's eyes searched the pianist's face frantically, as if looking for anger or a lie.

She had left all remnants of fear and nervousness behind, showing only shock as she stared at Pax, like rapidly deciphering whatever language she was speaking.

"They are just *faces* to her. I know. I have heard her speak." Hope laughed quietly, eyes scrunched up as she smiled softly. "Don't tell her about this, I think I would like to follow your advice and speak to her, without any remainders of the past."

"I can already feel like you are way too nice for her brooding ass." Pax scoffed, as if she swallowed the complete extent of the sarcasm that threatened to come out with it.

Hope found herself growing fond of the younger's antics, baffling and hilarious.

"Thank you, you didn't have to entertain me about this but you still took the time to do that." Hope confessed, sincerely watching the other offer a small smile in return, waving her hand. "I really appreciate that. She is getting paler, just continue to take care of her."

"As if she would let anyone do that." Pax huffed, looking annoyed but the older clearly saw through the concern that was brimming across her eyes, for her sister. "She thinks that she is the one who has the audacity to take care of us because she is older than us, and never the other way around."

"You are a good sister, just continue to be there for her. There is a thing that she told me - *Don't stay alone with your thoughts, during your darkest times.*" Hope muttered, rubbing at her cheek absently, knowing that she probably had no place to say this. "Even if it leads to silly disagreements, just be there for her."

Pax snickered, patting Hope's shoulders if she were secretly rooting for her.

BONUS READ - II (Hope's POV)

Spes' eyes shimmered like a mirage in the sand. "You are something else." She said, too soft, too fond.

"I know, that's why we have always connected and always will." Hope grinned under the light rainfall clouding the night sky, bright and warm as Spes tucked a slightly-damp piece of long hair behind her ear before rechecking her knuckles for bruises, silently asking her if this was okay as Hope nodded with an enamoured chuckle. "You... are an enigma."

That's just another beautiful thing about Spes, she's always cautious.

She doesn't want to ever overstep boundaries or step out of her lane. Hope appreciates the extra mindfulness, always. That's a charm about Spes she doesn't find in a lot of other people, the need to know that her people were comfortable around her at all times.

During times like this, Hope couldn't help but smile about how selective Spes was to her surroundings. She would zone out of her environment unless she heard the mere mention of her friends or family in a negative light.

Even when she glared daggers or threw threatening snide remarks threading in cold anger, at anyone who dared to scoff at Hope even by the slightest, whether they knew her or were just random strangers walking by the street... She would still apologise profusely to ensure that she wasn't trying to disrespect Hope's strength by letting her anger interfere and smile smugly whenever Hope chose to get back at those people who looked at her as if she was nothing more than contagious filth.

Despite assuring that she didn't have to apologise for standing up for her, reminding Spes that she appreciated her support, she would still check with a silent glance.

Hope doesn't think Spes knows about just how much damage she does to her heart with a mere few words, and she wonders if she has a similar effect on Spes.

If it was any other person she wouldn't have hesitated to know that they reciprocated her feelings.

"And why is that?" Spes asked, returning the grin, something heartbreaking and elating in the way she smiled with such abandon.

Even when Spes held boundaries between them and refused to spend time with her outside school, unless it involved work for the joint-exhibition, she ensured to save Hope's favourite snacks from their cafeteria incase they run out of them while Hope finalised the make-up for the outfits that either Spes or Rene by finalising the looks on Quinsy.

Hope had been in the same Art History class as Spes since the start, to know that she didn't acknowledge anyone or anything besides her sketches, having inhumane levels of ignorance and concentration to block out everything.

It's not like Hope hadn't heard about Spes' indifference bothering people massively to tarnish her image, which only aggravated when she could hardly be bothered by it.

It was amusing to watch them have the guts to only whisper about her behind her back, fearing that that would end up with the same fate as the jerk who had dared to mock Theus. He clearly had it coming when Spes kicked the desk, merely smirking, when the edge of the desk ended up nearly impaling him in the region where the Sun never shone.

So, it came as a surprise when Spes didn't hesitate to stop working to give her undivided attention to Hope even if she extended the conversation by talking about their similar artistic muses.

Hope doesn't think it's merely because she remembers that one time she told Spes that one of her pet peeves was when people didn't listen to her when she was talking.

But she could never tell.

"You are earnestly honest that I can't constantly help but fear that you are unreal. So, breathtakingly unreal, that every reason I can conjure up fades in comparison." Hope said, laying all her emotions vulnerable through her eyes, blood a little warm in her face. "Truthfully, all I know is- It's you, how can you not be?"

Hope liked to believe that she was a person who didn't resort to anger easily but she couldn't stand it as soon as she heard people spreading the wildfire that Spes was threatening and using the *charity case,* losing her temper on those bastards in a split second.

The latter being as oblivious as expected. Hope was thankful that she was still clueless about that degrading name, knowing that Spes would set out on a rampage once she found out.

"You say that as if it is self-explanatory?" Spes asked, voice and terse before carefully placing the small, wrapped gift from the pocket of her box-pleat lapels and placing it in her hands. "I don't care, if it's not your bar-mitzvah, but this was long overdue for the one, that was denied to you, six years ago." She explained, as Hope's eyes widened in bewilderment before carefully unwrapping it.

"The German-chamomile essential oil, I had been saving for...that ran out of stocks for months..."

"I know that it's nothing, but-" She hesitated, still peering at her curiously, breathing a little uneven... cheeks flushed.

"Don't do this to me...if it falls like an illusion then it's going to be excruciatingly cruel..." Hope made a negative noise in the back of her throat, opening and closing her fist once, forcing her heart rate to calm down.

She wanted to hope that Spes might reciprocate her feelings, more than just a friend.

She wanted to hope that Spes didn't offer false hope by studying in the secluded corner of the Huda's Studio and waited for Hope until she completed her shift.

It felt like home, when she would smile as if Hope was the only person in the world, while comforting Hope by sending her sketches of her favourite flowers in return or use their symbolism to venture into their muses.

"What?"

"I admit… it was perhaps ambitious to take that admiration I held for you and try to turn it romantic." Hope's throat closed up, surprisingly, as she watched Spes' face- softened and gentle, instead. "That was unfair of me, and looking back, rather presumptuous-"

She swallowed, feeling like a needle was stuck in her throat.

She couldn't have made a bigger fool of herself by ruining what they had. She could clearly tell Spes wanted to talk to Hope desperately, about last night's events, despite running almost everywhere after her classes.

Hope couldn't help but chicken out and invite her to the Bar-Mitzvah, instead, not expecting Spes to agree immediately realising how much she must have wanted to talk about it and possibly turn Hope down as sternly as she could.

Hope *really* shouldn't have believed the words of Destiny and her friend from Sydney, when they insisted that Spes was *painfully* oblivious, even when Hope sent her sketch of lily of the valley that basically screamed '*You are the irreplaceable happiness in my life.*'

They had been nothing but incredibly nice by staging their first real date and it was easy to believe their words when Spes didn't hesitate to send her drawings of the lily of the incas, despite knowing the meaning that it held.

'*Eternal devotion of mutual support*'

Hope had to try to convince herself that even if Spes didn't reciprocate her feelings, it would be enough. Even if it was a lie she would force herself to believe, it had to be enough because she didn't wish to lose Spes... Not when she treated Hope as a priority without a second thought.

But she had to go and care for Hope's dream as if it were her own. Look at her as if Hope getting her dream-job was like winning the lottery to Parsons.

Say things like - she simply had to exist as the person she was, to be loved. Breaking everyone's perception of love, when they took every shot at Hope to warn her that she wasn't worthy of love if she didn't fit according to their moulds.

She couldn't tell if Spes was just patient or rather enamoured by listening to Hope talk about testing out new fragrances to go along with her shadow palettes, for hours even if the former had no prior interest regarding this form of art.

It was during times like these where Hope could witness Spes act her age, her almond eyes widening like a curious child as she asked Hope about her choice of contours and their densities, without a care for time.

Time that Spes was always stingy about, when it came to being kind to herself.

It made no sense for a person who was as guarded as Spes, who barely had any faith of humanity in herself to never expect anything back from her.

She wore her heart on her sleeve unapologetically around Hope, as if they had known each other for eternity. Hope, selfishly wanted that eternity with her.

Resolutely.

"It was never presumptuous." Spes' eyes bore into her, as she spoke, choked off and genuine. "You just never gave me a chance to clarify that certainty."

She searched Spes' eyes, only filled with fierce decisiveness.

Spes' eyes were as open as Hope could ever remember seeing, genuine and hooded and gentle- She simply glanced at Hope, eyes a cool sort of peaceful- like ripples in a still lake.

Falling for Spes was like falling for art.

Humans always adorned different facades to mask their personas but make-up was a form of art that brought out the same raw persona of the person in different forms, stripped off any facades.

Strange how the very thing that helped her hide her insecurity of being vulnerable of her spots that alienated her from everyone, helped her to embrace them.

Strange how the very person, who pushed her buttons to vent out all the anger she had bottled up for years, stayed by her side more concretely than anyone else despite being at the opposite end of facing that anger.

"You don't actively hide your words, yet excruciatingly break down the authenticity of a person to open up completely." Hope hummed, eyes falling closed, when Spes held her hand as she tried to pull against the grip to check if reality wasn't playing a cruel joke to her. "I mean I can't imagine what you must have felt hearing all the suggestions when you calmly state that you can't sleep or your tethering grasp on consistency."

Spes, to her vague relief, laughed a little breathlessly.

"Fortunately, I have had people in my life, who never crossed the sheer audacity to whine about getting me to change, if they couldn't respect my opinions. They motivate me to believe in humanity." Spes... honestly looked like she wasn't sure if she was versed enough to have this conversation, but she didn't flinch by the slightest, when Hope placed her hands along the angles of Spes' cheeks gently.

Her eyes opened for only a moment, glancing at the gesture, before falling closed again, unbothered by it.

"Do you have a thing for people who are passionate for art?" Hope swallowed a chuckle, trying to give a getaway to let Spes laugh at her face and scream that she was just pulling a miserable joke with Hope's feelings. "Or is it ambition?"

"I have a thing for you." Spes hummed warmly, as she watched Hope's cheeks heat up even more. "I thought you were avoiding me because you might have regretted what happened last night."

Yeah, Spes Zrey was *unbelievably* oblivious.

There's something about Spes' eyes, even if her face is impassive, and without emotion - Hope has learned that just by looking at her eyes she can know what Spes is feeling, her eyes betray her every time.

"How can you be this oblivious, you idiot?" Hope asked, a laugh caught in her throat that didn't leave, despite knowing the answer to that already. She saw the corner of Spes' lip twitch, sheepishly, bronze skin lighting up as they continued being enveloped by the dense fog.

And Hope didn't know if it was instinct or habit or a conscious choice, but Spes' arms encircled around her carefully...wrapping around Hope, surrounding them like a castle wall intending to keep out even the most violent of attacks... Standing there as Hope pressed against her, waiting for the moment she pushed too hard and Spes would pull away, but she never did, she just continued speaking her thoughts, with a small smile-

Spes pulled away, their foreheads pressed firmly together, her eyes a stained glass of emotion.

"Even if you might not be aware of the impact of your actions, you remind me to be unapologetically sincere to who I am. Whether it's my family, or even Jove, or Grace, Theus or Destiny, Quinsy or René, or you." Hope grabbed that fierce, stupidly oblivious artist by the front of her jacket, dragging her down to Hope's height, their noses brushed and their lips tingling with the presence of the other so close. Her heart expanded to dangerous levels, pulling Spes down against her lips. Spes made a subdued noise in the back of her throat as her grip on Hope's hip tightened the smallest amount- a bare reaction, but enough of one that made Hope grin against her lips. "What was that for?"

"I hope that you can see yourself for the person that you are."

And somewhere, since the very beginning, that unforgiving ambition and guarded loyalty had remained infuriating but was tinged with something inside of Hope that never wanted to watch that fire die.

Hope wanted to keep guarding that spark. That flame. She wanted to ensure that nothing ever threatened it.

Why did a person who fought tooth and nail for her own dreams, feel so detached from her own life?

"And who would that be?" Spes' lips quirked, but it almost seemed like she barely heard Hope, eyes tracing slowly over her face, memorising and committing to memory.

"What do you want for yourself, Spes ?"

"I want to be happy." Spes answered, looking gently starstruck.

Hope could never get used to watching Spes' smile, her smile so pure and contagious that ached Hope's heart in remainder about why this smile was jarringly rare.

But when Spes would smile at her... when she would let Hope take her hand absentmindedly while speaking to her... when she would gravitate towards Hope, more as a reflex now, instead of always asking if the minimal space between them disrupted Hope's boundaries.

Hope's vision blurred slightly as she sucked in a sharp breath, something almost like a laugh in her chest.

"Of course." Hope felt free. Light, as if she was floating away, but tethered to the ground by Spes' hand on the small of her back pulling her forward. "But, what would make you happy?"

She held her breath sharply when Spes' arm snaked around her waist, pulling her flush against her, her head resting on her shoulder, and the lines of their bodies melding together.

Hope was only shocked for a moment before relaxing automatically.

This was home.

Hope looked at her again, but this time, Spes was looking at her, eyes a soft sort of gaze that made Hope feel like all her barriers had just been stripped away. She felt like her pulse stopped. Started. And she wet her lips.

She shifted a little closer, until she was more comfortable, Spes' arm around her waist and resting at her hip. Hope could hear Spes' heartbeat, and that was infinitely more comforting than Hope could ever imagine it being.

Spes held her by her hips, something simmering low in her veins as she kissed her and Hope kissed her back, rushing like boiling water through her body.

Spes pressed careful, purposeful kisses down Hope's throat, a gentle hand threading fingers through the back of her hair gently.

Hope swallowed thickly, the skin tingling where she left a trail, very carefully avoiding the curve of her neck.

Individually, Spes had distinctly soft features with her a softer arch of eyebrows and full lips but the sharper ends of her almond eyes and large pecan-brown irises, that made her profile more defined to make uneven hair easily elegant, instead.

Perhaps, that's what caught Hope's sight when she first saw Spes, her long fingers squeezing her slender wrists, absent-mindedly. A habit that the latter had developed to ease the pain of the frequent cramps in her hands, while writing, eating, drawing, stitching or cutting.

In the simplest moments like these, Hope wanted to knock some sense onto Spes' beautiful mind that was *ridiculously* stubborn, complaining about sleeping *too much* and not getting enough time to harness her skills to make up for her belief that she *wasn't* talented because she didn't want to admit that she still clearly suffered from sleep paralysis. Hope just felt helpless, realising how she continued to self-sabotage herself even if she didn't overdose on sleeping pills like she had, leading to their first encounter.

Spes wasn't angry with the world as much as she was angry with herself. She blamed herself.

She felt torn that the memories of the first cherished encounter held such bitter undertone that just refused to fade, and Hope could do nothing to erase that soon.

Just until winter. It felt like ice slowly digging into her heart.

She hadn't met anyone who had such god-tier levels of expectations for themselves and pushed themselves, even harder to seize them. The mere thought of this ugly truth, reflecting transparently in Hope's crestfallen expression, desperately wanting to yell at Spes that she indeed was *ridiculously* talented, until she started to believe in it herself.

Hope didn't look up immediately, clenching a fist to keep from either punching Spes in the stomach or kissing her until neither of them could breathe.

But when Spes' hand touched her cheek, trailing over the skin slowly, just feeling and tracing. Hope couldn't tell why she was tearing up, still finding it hard to believe that this wasn't a dream.

And all of Spes' gentleness... never once made Hope feel fragile. It made her feel treasured. Like knowing something wouldn't break, but treating it carefully just out of... respect.

"Why?" Spes' panicked inquiry cut off as she realised what happened, eyes scanning Hope frantically, looking so confused as if she feared for Hope to run off. "Why are you-"

Spes' arms were around her carefully, Hope's face burying in her collar as Spes embraced her oh so carefully, her head falling to hit Spes' shoulder, her arms falling from her face to lay pressed between the two of them.

Hope's hand lowered from her neck, brushing down her side as she sought out the hand resting at her waist. Their fingers laced tightly, Hope's eyes dropping down to stare at their intertwined hands. She brought their hands up, resting her lips against their knuckles.

Hope twisted in the jacket around her fingers, heat burning out of her eyes and tracing down her cheeks. "Spes-"

"Hope..." Spes coaxed, quiet and a little hoarse, voice like the lavender fields that Hope dreamed to sleep in, as a comforting hand ran down her spine, synchronising with the rhythm of her breath, until it steadily evened down. "Why..."

"I promise, Spes." Hope breathed, barely audible, but not trusting her voice to go any louder without breaking horrifically. "I'm happy, I'm so... so magnetically happy."

Because this is Spes Zrey.

Someone with an abundance of patience and tenacity, someone who was stupidly oblivious about how easily she pulled Hope's heartstrings, snatching every chance to remind Hope of her worth even if she held doubts about it as a joke.

It was the same piercing gaze that easily locked anyone in their sight, softened by the slightest as if they were staring into Hope's soul.

It was a beautiful feeling, being with Spes.

The only thing stilling her tongue was the distant fear of losing all of it.

Hope pulled on the hand she held. And she was surprised by how easily Spes fell forward, lips crashing together, not fighting the movement as Hope tasted the salt of her own tears.

Because in no universe was Hope strong enough not to melt when Spes kissed her, her shoulders falling as her warm lips covered Hope's gently-

Spes kissed her, sweet and soft and not hard or desperate, pulling away mere seconds later, foreheads resting.

Minutes passed until the cold got too much and their breath ran too low, leaving them leaning against each other, breathing heavily and skin pressing firmly against each other. Their eyes were closed against the world, trying to hold down the walls to their little world that crumbled with the cold breeze, as Spes wordlessly wiped the tears cascading down the slope of Hope's cheeks with the end of her sleeves as if the mere sight of tears brimming across Hope's eyes caused her excruciating agony.

"You…" she admitted in a breath, feeling like a boulder was slowly being lifted off of her chest. Hope was losing her voice to it, the syllables weakening, and she paused, taking a moment to breathe, and when she spoke again, it was calmer. More level. "You have always meant so much to me, Spes." she smiled, feeling the skin brushing against her lips, shiver. "Ever since the beginning, you have been… I feel…-"

-like we belonged.

Spes freezes for a moment, it's almost funny with the way her eyes blank for a while before flooding with the same warmth and love there's always been in them. The warmth and love that Spes believed that she was incapable of.

Something that felt like laying beside Spes and surviving everything, against all odds.

Not forgetting it. Never forgetting. But surviving. Getting through in one piece and coming out the other end. Stronger. Better.

Together.

It felt like finally, finally gaining solid footing after running through shifting gravel for so long, just desperate for a smoother patch. Like grabbing onto Spes' hand and both of them making it to the top where they stood, clinging together and trying not to fall off.

"Thank you." Spes whispered into the molecules between them, accentuating each confession a gentle kiss to the line of her throat.

This was the first time Hope had watched Spes let herself be vulnerable around anyone, knowing that the latter strongly believed that she didn't have the time to let herself be affected by '*mundane*' issues that didn't matter.

Issues that were undermined by adults who abused their powers to belittle a child who refused to bend to their will. It broke Hope's heart to realise that Spes had truly convinced herself that her problems weren't worthy being a problem for they were nothing more than a whining bother.

"What-" Hope asked, realising that Spes' words held a bigger promise than she led on.

Hope stared at the eyes of the girl who just held the pain of a child who wanted to help but had grown up in a world that had forced her to believe it didn't matter unless that fit into the moulds of stereotypical 'boxes'. Humans loved confining everything into boxes.

"Time. Guarantee of time would make me happy." Spes' eyes danced a captivating song that Hope couldn't look away from, even as Spes nodded firmly. "Hope Vale, you *anchor* my time."

Hope wanted to know why Spes had taken so fiercely to all this. But... the how didn't matter, because Hope was pretty sure the why was the same as her.

It was a reason she was afraid to voice so quickly, so she kept it tucked away, ready to wield at a moment's notice, but knowing that now was not the time.

Spes pulled away, looking up at Hope, their noses brushing at their proximity, and Spes' eyes were still soft, still gentle, still staring as if she had no intention of ever looking away, and Hope's stomach was twisting violently at the thought that Spes really had promised to stay with her for as long as Hope wanted.

The home that she wanted.

Wishing they could just fall into snowflakes and just land on the ground, melt when the sun came back up and just... just be encapsulated in this bubble.

Seeing another person who had been with you through so much... and stayed regardless. Someone who promised you so much, someone who just made you feel like everything inside of you was trying to force its way into your heart-

Hope wrapped her arms around her neck, smiling uncontrollably as Spes' hands landed at her waist, holding on a bit tighter, like she was scared Hope might slip away-

"Good." she confessed, words tumbling over each other, like snow rolling over itself in an avalanche that couldn't be held back any longer. "I quite like the sound of looking forward to that."

Hope laughed again, feeling breathless, like getting off of a rollercoaster and giggling off of pure adrenaline-

Also Available In
US Edition:

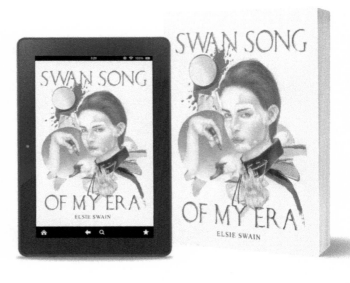

Milton Keynes UK
Ingram Content Group UK Ltd.
UKHW010937280823
427620UK00001B/10